~ THE ~

# DISAGREEMENT

A NOVEL

## Nick Taylor

**Simon & Schuster**

NEW YORK   LONDON   TORONTO   SYDNEY

Simon & Schuster
1230 Avenue of the Americas
New York, NY 10020

This book is a work of fiction. Names, characters, places, and incidents either are products
of the author's imagination or are used fictitiously. Any resemblance to actual events
or locales or persons, living or dead, is entirely coincidental.

Copyright © 2008 by Nick Taylor

First Simon & Schuster hardcover edition April 2008

SIMON & SCHUSTER and colophon are registered trademarks
of Simon & Schuster, Inc.

Designed by Paul Dippolito

Manufactured in the United States of America

1   3   5   7   9   10   8   6   4   2

For information about special discounts for bulk purchases,
please contact Simon & Schuster Special Sales at 1-800-456-6798
or business@simonandschuster.com.

Library of Congress Cataloging-in-Publication Data

Taylor, Nick, 1976–
The disagreement : a novel / Nick Taylor—1st Simon & Schuster hardcover ed.
p.   cm.
ISBN-13: 978-1-4165-5065-5
ISBN-10:      1-4165-5065-8
1. Medical students—Fiction. 2. Virginia—Fiction. 3. United States—
History—Civil War, 1861–1865—Fiction. I. Title.
PS3620.A95945D57            2008
813'.6—dc22
2007017427

*For Jessica*

For the entertainment of my children and grandchildren, the tutelage of the next generation of Southern physicians, and the simple gratification of the curious, I have set down here an account of my life. In so doing I find that I have dwelt chiefly on my student years at the University of Virginia in Charlottesville during our late war. Though it has become the fashion in recent times for professional men to sketch their lives for public consumption, it remains uncommon to elaborate upon one's school years. Rather, the focus is laid (naturally) on the details of a man's profession. I should argue that my case is unique. *For me the pedagogic and professional experiences existed simultaneously.* Thus I aim to describe both together, herein.

JOHN A. MURO, M.D.
LYNCHBURG, VIRGINIA
SEPTEMBER 1, 1895

# Part One

# 1

ON APRIL 17TH, 1861, I enjoyed the sensation of one whose birthday falls on Christmas. I woke unusually early, along with everyone in the Commonwealth of Virginia. That day our legislature was to vote on secession—a crisis that had begun as a whisper among gossipmongers not a year prior but had grown with the frenzy of a revival into a statewide obsession. The newspapers had for weeks detailed the debate in Richmond, from the rhetorical thrusts and parries at the statehouse to the curt and somber replies of Mr. Lincoln, whose anointment the previous autumn so inflamed the passions of our men.

As a youth of fifteen, I had not been involved substantially in the secession crisis, but I enjoyed the high drama of the proceedings, and I followed them with a greedy eye. Earlier that spring my father had hosted a meal for our delegate and a dozen men of business. The ostensible purpose of the gathering had been to gauge local support for secession, but these being men of practical appetites, the talk soon turned to the prospect of war and the demands this might place on our local mills and factories. "If there is any fighting," the pompous delegate announced, "it shan't continue long enough to bring any lucre hereabouts, fellows. The Yanks know our purpose, and they know our differences, and they will respect our intention sooner or later. The thought in Richmond, I must tell you, is that they will be too blanched to fight." The men laughed and clapped one another on the back. This I observed from the sanctuary of our kitchen, where I had finished helping Mother and Peg with the service and was eating my share at the kitchen table.

The delegate—his name was Coggin—was distinguished by a pair of unruly snow white eyebrows that sprung from his face like owl feathers. He was a consummate politician—which is to say he was given to expedient speech and lacked even a vestigial spine.

The telegraph from Mr. Coggin, who was in Richmond for the vote, arrived at the Lynchburg post office just after one o'clock. I had spent the morning in the square, pitching horse- shoes with some other boys from school. Though it was a Wednesday we had not shown our faces at school, feeling assured that a Special Circumstance excused us from truancy.

The taverns along the square were packed with a rare noonday crowd. Like me, these citizens could not bear to wait any longer for the news than was absolutely necessary. However, decorum mandated that these men not be seen loitering with boys in the street, so they made pretenses at business and meal taking. The tavern doors could almost be seen to bulge with the swell.

At the doors of the town stable, across the square from the post office, a circle of five or six Negroes gathered in idle chatter. As Wednesday was seldom a slave's day at liberty, I assumed that these had been sent by their masters to await the news and carry it back post- haste. Indeed, the animals in the first stalls were ready in saddle, with reins tied quickly to the rail.

Just after the one o'clock bell the post office door swung open and the postmaster—a wasted but well- meaning old man by the name of Tad Keithly—strode out onto the top step. Those of us near enough saw his smile ablaze, and we could guess the news. In truth, though, no one ever questioned what the news would be. "I have word from Mr. Coggin!" the postmaster shouted generally—the taverns having emptied into the square, so that his audience numbered well into the hundreds. "The votes are in, and they are eighty- eight in favor, fifty-five opposed." He paused and let that little bit of silence grow like the drop of melt at the tip of an icicle. "Gentlemen, we have it! God bless the unencumbered Commonwealth of Virginia!" And then Keithly's eyes began to water. Indeed, all around me grown men began to weep and embrace one another. I saw that it was not regret in their tears but rather the opposite. With unbridled joy men commenced to cheer and whoop and fire their pistols into the air. I hollered from a place deep between my lungs, but the crack of gunfire obscured my voice. I did not know if I was creating any sound at all.

The air reeked with the acrid tang of powder. My nose filled up with dust from the street as horses thundered out of the stable. I ran to the door of the nearest tavern to avoid being trampled. A few men remained inside the tavern, and I recognized several as business acquaintances of my father, men who had been present at our dinner with Mr. Coggin. The eldest of these, a man whose mustache puffed out over his lip like a squirrel's tail, stood up to begin a toast. I could not hear his words, but several times he brought laughter from the group and had to pause. At last he raised a bottle of whiskey above his head. As the others cheered, the old man put the bottle to his lips and drank a ten count. When he pulled off, a runnel of brown liquor leaked from the side of his mouth and he wiped it with his starched white cuff.

Taking heed not to fall into the path of a messenger's horse, I picked my way to the other side of the square, beyond which I would hasten home. On Wednesdays the street that led most directly from the square to our neighborhood was filled out with grocers' stalls, and it was in front of one of these that I was stopped by a flat hand in my chest. A white farmer obscured my path. His beard was shot through with petals from the spring lungwort. After a moment's consideration of my face, he lowered his hand and plunged it into a sack hanging at his side, from which he removed a yellow rose. "God bless," he said, and he handed me the flower.

# 2

OUR HOME WAS IN THE Federal Hill district of Lynchburg, a neighborhood popular among the professional men of our small city. My father was in the textile trade. His mill, the Bedford Woolery, had been established some fifteen years prior, through a deal struck with a fellow in the War Department in Washington City. This acquaintance from my father's college days in New Jersey awarded a contract to sew uniforms for soldiers in the Mexican War. My father had no mill at that time, nor any expertise in manufacturing. In fact, he was a physician, but he was unhappy in that vocation. Keeping a roster of patients (whom he saw two mornings a week) only to pay the coal bill, he assembled men and machinery for the mill, trading our family's good name for credit with the bank. As you may recall, that particular war did not last long. But the Bedford Woolery gained its footing, and other contracts followed—though it has never been clear to me whether my father's continuing fortunes came from his own enterprise or from the same hidden source.

In time, the mill proved profitable, and Father was able to quit his medical practice. He purchased property in West Street, on Federal Hill, and hired men to build a modern house fit for a man of industry.

It was a grand structure of three floors and a basement, encased by a wood veranda and buttressed with turrets. The family's elevated circumstances afforded our house servants—the beloved old Peg and her man, Heathcliff—their own quarters in the backyard. Their cabin steamed day and night from the generous supply of coal my father provided them (over no small share of whispers from the neighbors.)

Though my sister and I strutted the great wooden halls like Piedmont pashas, the new house proved a disappointment to our parents. "A great wooden curse," my mother called it, for once she was installed there, the Lord did not see to bless her with any more children. Thus Parthenia and I occupied the entire third story—eight rooms—while our dear parents spread themselves about the *piano nobile* below. Mother endeavored to fill the empty bedrooms with cousins from the counties. Nearly all our relations still farmed the family acres—hers in Appomattox County, my father's in Botetourt, on the other side of the Blue Ridge. Visits to town amused them as pleasant diversions. However, all returned sooner or later to the land.

Neither did the mill business pour a bottomless cup. By the end of the decade—1859 or thereabouts—my father was forced to roll back production to one shift five days a week. This was down from two shifts every day except Sunday. The decreased fortunes registered clearly on my father's countenance: the green eyes, so bright since he had quit doctoring, faded once again, and the creases on the forehead no longer disappeared when he relaxed.

It was then that I began to loathe the vagaries of commerce. I decided, privately, that my father had been a fool to desert an honest profession for a life of gambling. What could one expect, after all, from an enterprise forged in conspiracy? Much of this was just youthful foolishness, but I held the central charge as truth, and I resolved to make my living as my father had in the first instance, not the second. I resolved to become a doctor.

Moreover, I resolved to better my father by attending the most prestigious medical school that anyone had ever heard of—the renowned Jefferson Medical College of Philadelphia. My father had always assumed—and he had told me as much—that I would follow him to Princeton, that venerable institute which had schooled so many sons of Virginia. He had made the mistake, however, of speaking ill of the medical faculty at Princeton on many occasions during the course of his practice. The outbreaks were rare, but the young ear is like a trap for such things, and I remembered his words well. "The medical men of that school have not a practical brain in their heads!" he'd exhort when he realized after a complex procedure that his training had come up short once again. "They ought to call it the Faculty of Guesses! Or the Faculty of Filthy Lies!" In the same sermons he praised the Philadelphia medical colleges, which were then producing, in his words, "a crop of sane- witted men of science, not sorcery. Clearheaded practical men—just what is needed in this field."

I was at that time enrolled at the boys' preparatory school in Lynchburg, in the penultimate form, where I studied Latin, Greek, and the mathematical precepts of Euclid, Descartes, Newton, &c. I expected to complete the course of study there in a year's time. Thus my tenure in Lynchburg was on the wane, no matter how the idea upset my mother.


"Mother! Father!" I cried as I swung open the door. "The vote was yes!" I heard no reply, so I raced to the kitchen, where I found our Peg putting up the dishes from the noon meal. I still clutched the yellow rose in my right hand. Without thinking, I thrust it under her nose. Peg was a dignified house girl, but one could see that my gift of the rose confused her. "I do thank you, Marse John Alan," she said. She took a vase down and stuck the rose stem in it, adding some water from the pitcher on the counter and a pinch of sugar from the bowl. "A fine birthday for you, I imagine."

"Where is Father?" I asked.

"Ain't seen your father since dinner."

I bounded up the back stairs, taking two with each stride, and raced down the second- floor hall to the door of my father's study. Putting my ear to the cool wood, I heard the distinctive creak of his chair. I knocked softly. "Father," I said, "I have the news."

He gave a grunt, and I opened the door. The room smelled of sweet tobacco smoke; his pipe lay smoldering on the side table. He was a slight man, not more than five and a half feet, even in the riding boots he wore indoors for their lifting effect. "Sir, the tally has come from Richmond—a large majority for secession."

Father took up the pipe and puffed until the weed glowed in the bowl. He gave no reaction to the news.

"Sir? Did you hear? I said—"

My father snapped the pipe from his mouth. "I heard your news," he said.

"The square is bedlam, Father. It was like a thunderclap when the message came, with the hollering and the pistols and what- all." I searched his face for a hint of what I felt, so that we might share it together, as father and son. His cool worried me. I wondered if it was wrong to feel as I did.

"Let us hope there is much to celebrate," he said. "I will hold my applause, however."

I was perplexed. "If I may speak frankly, sir," I said, "you must be joyed at least for the benefit of the mill."

"Ah, that." My father returned the pipe to his mouth. "There is that." The idea of war profits did not seem to bring him much comfort—though he must have known that without a fresh line of business, the mill would surely have suffered from the cancelation of his contracts with Washington City.

"Do you mean to say that you side with Coggin?" I said. "Do you really believe there will be no fight?"

"Are there sides to be taken?"

"Sir, I didn't mean to suggest that."

"You are only trying to sort out what you've heard, which is no small task for a boy your age."

"It is my birthday today, sir. I am sixteen now."

My father lifted his brow. "So you are." He took his pipe up, puffed it again to a bright smolder, and handed it over. "Happy birthday, son." It was the first time my father had ever passed me his pipe—and the first time I had ever smoked in his presence. The rich fog filled my mouth with a sensation of nuts and old wood. I feigned discomfort.

"You are not long with us, then," he said.

"Sir?"

"You will be off to college in what—a year?" He chuckled at this.

"I have been meaning to speak with you about college, sir," I said. I had not prepared my argument as well as I might have, but I doubted there would be a better time for the discussion. "Regarding Princeton, sir—"

"Ho! You should hope indeed that the fight is prompt! I don't imagine you will be allowed in New Jersey under the present circumstance."

Would you believe the thought had not occurred to me? And yet it was so obvious that I chastised myself for not foreseeing it. In my elation that afternoon I had not understood that I was cheering the demise of my ambition!

"I am as disappointed as you are," my father continued. "You must have sensed these years that I hoped for a legacy at the college."

My sails hung slack. There was no point in mentioning Philadelphia. I would easier attend the school of Athens.

Suddenly pleased with himself, Father waxed poetical: "Our freedom comes at the price of sacrifice, son. Heed that I have not lost all of my medical training; I still have a keen sense of the unknown—and of the unknowable, which is a wholly different thing. The vote today is certainly the latter, and thus we will wait and see what God brings."

"Yes sir."

"Now go and get your sister. It is not safe for her to be out in this—what did you say it was?"

"Bedlam."

"Yes. No place for a girl." He hooked his thumbs into the waistband of his trousers and leaned back in the chair, which swiveled on a neat ball bearing as well as a hinge. As he bounced gently in the chair, the squeaking of the hinge marked what seemed to be a hundred minutes of silence between us, though it couldn't have been more than thirty seconds.

"Son," he said eventually, "do you have something more to say?"

"No sir," I said. "I will go right away."

"Perhaps Coggin is right," he said. "Who can say? Perhaps you will make New Jersey on time after all."

"I would like that very much, sir."

"Don't worry. This will pass, one way or another."

# 3

I FOUND HEATHCLIFF IN the stable shop, which is where the old fellow spent most of his time in those days. Cliff had once been a strong worker—in fact he had served with the strength of three or four men during the construction of our house—but he had been crippled in an accident at the public stable. Another slave had been tending to his master's exhausted team—the gentleman was a day visitor from one of the counties—when the boy lost control of one of the animals, and it tore through the corridor. The horse ran over poor Cliff, who was down on one knee scraping mud from the hoof of my father's mare Sun Flower.

Father hadn't the heart to give Cliff's place in our household to a fresh body, though my mother urged him by various means to do so. First, she drew up a list of the tasks Cliff would no longer be able to perform—everything from wood portage to clearing the roof gutters of leaves in spring. Father demurred, claiming that he and I would pick up what chores Cliff could not complete. As it happened, Father hired a neighbor's boy to do those things—a fact I am sure my mother noted in the invisible ledger she kept on all my father's shortcomings. On the issue of replacing Cliff, she next attempted flattery, asserting that it was my father's right as a successful businessman to expand his holdings with another slave. Father dismissed this straightaway, pointing out, correctly, that none of our neighbors were adding slaves to their homes. "That is because their niggers breed!" Mother countered. "That is God's business, Regina," my father said. Undaunted, Mother next tried guilt: "You know that old nigger is not going to quit his tasks—he's liable to run himself into the ground on account of your negligence!" Cool as always, Father did not rise to the bait. He said he would have a talk with Heathcliff, wherein he would lay out what he expected. Finally Mother resorted to outright bribery. Donning her most flattering dress—one she'd had Peg sew after a plate in Godey's Lady's—she set an elaborate supper in the front parlor. Parthenia and I were ordered to eat in the kitchen that night. We heard Mother's entreaties through the pocket door. "I would be very pleased," she crooned to our father, "if you would grant me this favor. You see, another boy would make my work so much easier—and dear, I could make it very easy for you as well . . ." For Father, the question of replacing Heathcliff was not about economy, convenience, or extracting favors from his wife. Nor was it a question of Moral Right. Rather it was the reticence one feels about taking on a puppy before an old bitch passes away—the sense of dignity owed a faithful servant.

So Heathcliff remained, and like a tomato plant pruned to spread, he sprouted new talents. He took to leatherwork, tinkering in his leisure time with our horse tack using improvised tools. When Father saw the improvements he managed—a set of new, double- reinforced stirrups for our training saddle, for instance—he went straight to the smith's and purchased a set of proper punches and several sturdy needles, explaining proudly to Mother that Heathcliff would save us a mint in saddler's fees. Though I doubt Cliff ever earned out that bold prognostication, I noticed on several occasions hence that our saddles, and other tack, had never been in such good repair.

Heathcliff rose up from his workbench when he saw me at the door. A pair of my sister's boots lay dissected on the bench. She was just two years younger than I, but her feet were still those of a small child. Heathcliff leaned on his cane and bowed his head, scratching at his beard with his free hand. "Afternoon, Marse."

"Hello, Cliff," I said. "How goes the work today?"

"Not too bad, suh. Little miss's ridin' boots giving me considerable trouble with they soles."

"I'm sure you will set them right."

"I aim to. And I do appreciate you sayin' so."

"Father's asked me to fetch Parthenia from Miss Pelham's on account of the celebrations." I paused, sure that Heathcliff had not heard the news. "Everyone is celebrating, you know. Virginia has left the Union."

"That so?"

"It's good news, I think."

Heathcliff twisted his cane. "Yessuh, I reckon it is."

I wished I had prepared something to say on the subject, something to show him that he and Peg would be protected no matter what came of us. I knew that black folks, more than whites, tended to be scared of uncertainty, and one ought to be careful not to upset them unduly.

"Was you planning to take the surrey, Marse?" He lurched forward, using his cane as a fulcrum.

"Actually, I was going to ride. Is the surrey fixed?" Our two- seat carriage had been laid up with a broken axle. Need I mention that the resourceful Cliff was also an amateur wheelwright?

"It's ready, suh. Been a week now."

"A week?"

Cliff nodded and I crossed to the stable. The carriage was there under its familiar beige tarpaulin. There was even a fresh coat of lacquer.

# 4

IT WAS NOW MIDAFTERNOON, and clouds grayed the sky. En route to Daniel's Hill, I took the carriage back toward the center of town. The square sparkled with glass ground up under horseshoes and carriage wheels. The celebration had apparently moved elsewhere; in the distance I heard hoots and hollers but saw no revelers—only a pair of slave women fussing over an overturned cart of lettuces. I continued down the incline to the crossing of Blackwater Creek on Church Street. As the crow flies, the trip to Miss Pelham's was not more than two miles—but Lynchburg well merits the sobriquet "City of Seven Hills." Indeed, if its streets were laid flat, I imagine they would fill the better part of Richmond.

The spinster Miss Margaret Pelham held a girls' school in the ground- floor parlor of her home on D Street. The house was neither as large nor as tastefully appointed as our own, but Miss Pelham kept it well—as needs she must, for housekeeping was an important part of her curriculum. Parthenia joined a class of a dozen other girls at Miss Pelham's on Mondays, Wednesdays, and Fridays outside of Lent to learn the things a woman should—but that, according to Miss Pelham, were difficult to teach informally.

I tied Sun Flower to Miss Pelham's post, which was oddly placed around the rear of the house, as if to convey the message that this home did not accept casual callers. I always rather enjoyed the detour, however, because Miss Pelham's was the last house on D Street and it overlooked the James River, which crept along at the foot of the palisade.

I went around the porch to the front door and engaged the brass knocker. Miss Pelham's girl Ida opened it and stepped aside to let me in. Setting foot inside Miss Pelham's home evoked fresh horror, as I imagined my presence served as an object lesson in the High Court of Manners. *"See the young man, dears, and the work we have ahead of us!"* I had learned never to move beyond the entry hall without thoroughly scouring my boot soles for traces of mud, wet leaves, &c. Ida furnished a sturdy wire brush and a stool for this task, which I accepted, and I set down in a corner of the hall to begin the work.

Ida was unlike any house girl I had ever encountered. Round and sweet- smelling like our Peg, she featured an uncommon hauteur that I attributed to her marmish mistress. A good majority of slaves would not look a white person in the eye — not even a child—when this Ida took my coat she not only looked but verily *glared*, as if searching me for weakness.

Soles scrubbed, I walked to the parlor door, where Ida rang a handbell and announced me. The girls were seated around the handsome upholstered furniture, each with the same staid look of composure upon her face. Aside from the tint of the hair and the various fabrics in their dresses, the girls were virtually indistinguishable. I assumed this was Miss Pelham's intent.

To my eye, however, Parthenia leapt from the group. The pallor of her skin suggested a negative space, as in a photographic plate. Under Miss Pelham's tutelage, the natural glow of her fair cheeks had been discouraged with corn- starch powder and her lips rouged a hue only a blind man would have found subtle.

Parthenia acknowledged me with a cool nod. She had always been a shy girl, but Miss Pelham had hardened her natural inclination into a discipline.

I doffed my cap. "Afternoon, all." Then directly to Parthenia, I said, "Father asked that I fetch you on account of the reveling downtown—"

"I say, John," Miss Pelham crowed from her perch on a high stool next to the window. Her long, sharp nose swung around like a weather vane. "Did you say there was news? Perhaps it would be considerate to give your remarks generally."

"Of course, ma'am," I said. I had developed over the months Parthenia had been attending the school a supercilious manner that I rolled out as a defense against Miss Pelham's attacks. "My apologies for not telling you at once. How rude of me to hoard the news." I addressed this to Miss Pelham directly, for it was obvious that her inquiry was intended only to satisfy her own curiosity about the vote, and not to give the girls any lesson in demeanor. "The vote in favor," I said, "was eighty- eight. With fifty- five against."

A smile crept onto the powdered sheet she called a face. I wondered what meaning secession could have for her—she was not, to my knowledge, the least bit interested in anything bearing on politics.

"You may go, Parthenia," Miss Pelham said.

"Yes, ma'am," Parthenia said gingerly. She rose from her tuffet and gave a short bow.

"Many thanks," I said, taking my sister by the arm. I nodded to the others, making sure not to grimace, and we retreated to the entry hall, where Ida delivered us our coats. Parthenia had lately taken to wearing rubber galoshes over her shoes—another of Miss Pelham's imperatives. I bent down to help her into them. My sister raised her foot like a disinterested horse.

"Take care if it rains, dear," Ida said.

# THE DISAGREEMENT

I had the devil's time with those galoshes. Parthie's foot flopped like a rag doll's under pressure. Exaggerating my exertion with little grunts and sighs, I squinted up to see if my sister was observing my struggle. I found her instead staring blankly at the chair rail. It was as if she were in the process of calcification, from the head down: her feet in my hands still bore the suppleness of life, but her face seemed already hardened to stone.

# 5

IT RAINED AS IDA PREDICTED, a steady pelting of tiny, stinging drops like needles. I pulled the hood of the surrey over our heads, but the light canvas soaked through almost immediately and the water dribbled down the back of the seat. The mare, Sun Flower, was good in the mud, and she delivered us home from Daniel's Hill with no more tarry than I had taken—on dry roads—in the going there.

Unsurprisingly, Parthenia said nothing as we went, maintaining the same staid focus (or was it lack of focus?) she had displayed at Miss Pelham's. I wondered if she wasn't ill. "Are you well?" I asked.

"I certainly am," she said. "Are you?" Her expression indicated that she did not want me to answer the question; she would have preferred that I let her petulance hang in the air.

"I am quite well," I said. "Thank you very much for asking." For the record, I was not then, nor was I ever, willing to let silence serve my sister's purposes. I resumed the interrogation. "Is there something the matter at school?"

"John! Please do not pester me. It ought to be clear to you that I do not wish to discuss this."

"To discuss what?"

"Oh, never mind you!" And here she snapped shut again, tight as a river mussel. The color that had briefly flowed to her cheeks ebbed away.

"*Oh* yourself, Parthenia," I said. We were just then crossing the market square, and I noticed my sister's head turn at each window as if cataloging the occupants. She was preoccupied, but I was determined to draw her out. I had one more line—a last, crude weapon to use against her impenetrable shell. "You know it's my birthday," I said.

Her head snapped around. "Oh John! Why, of course it is! Heaven—how could I have forgotten? Shame on me! It is just that with all of this—" She indicated the lighted window nearest our carriage. "I know it is hardly an excuse. Oh, I feel terrible."

She clutched my arm as I drove. I felt guilty.

"Forget it," I said. "I will have fifty more birthdays, but there will be only one day like this. We will remember this date like July, Fourth, I think—but for you and me it will be easy because April 17 is a date we mark already."

"But I forgot it!"

"Maybe now you won't ."

# 6

WE ARRIVED HOME TO FIND our mother entertaining a guest whose appearance made clear several things. First, it explained Mother's curious absence that afternoon when I arrived home with the news. Second, it solved the riddle over Parthenia's odd mood.

The guest was our cousin Samuel Brightwood, the son of my mother's eldest brother, the Reverend James Brightwood. The Brightwoods lived in Appomattox County on a farm whose fields they leased to white tenants. When young Sam followed his father in the study of the Scripture at the Baptist seminary in Lynchburg, I always suspected that my own parents paid his tuition—not only because it was so unlikely that the Reverend Brightwood could afford it, but because the boy, Sam, had always been so close to my mother's heart. Mother was crestfallen when Sam refused her invitation to stay with us, in order to board with a pastor whose church sat nearer the campus.

This is not to say that he never called. In fact, he ate supper with us often—once a fortnight, I would estimate—and so Parthenia and I had seen much of him during the three years he'd been at seminary. He had grown into a handsome chap, with a broad, strong chest and a full beard. Parthenia had carried a torch for Sam since she was old enough to pronounce his name. The timing of this visit, however, allowed her no opportunity for preparation at her vanity. As we drew near the house, she began licking her palms like a cat and pasting back her hair.

Mother stood when we entered the parlor. "Thank heavens, children. Your father should never have sent you out alone on a night like this! Don't you agree, Samuel?"

"But Aunt Regina, there has never been a night like this! The greatest risk tonight, as I see it, is a death by too much joy! How about it, John Alan—have you heard the news?"

"And on my birthday to boot!"

"Well, it is a singular day, then! Shame on you, Auntie, neglecting to mention that it was the young man's birthday."

The secret of Sam's magnetism was the way he suggested to his audience that they were worth a little more than they assumed. I was not "the boy," you see, but "the young man." Naturally, Sam nudged my mother's age in the opposite direction.

"Why yes, how silly of me—our John is sixteen today." She said this without joy, but only as a matter of fact.

"Sixteen," Sam pondered. "Well, that's close, but I'm afraid you'll miss the cut this time around. It's too bad, really—it's going to be a hoot."

About a month prior—that is, at the height of the debate on secession—cousin Samuel Brightwood had, quite abruptly and with no advance notice whatsoever, quit his studies at the seminary and joined the militia. His father had reportedly been furious—I say *reportedly* because all this was relayed to me through Mother—and had accused cousin Sam of "wasting the finest opportunity he was ever likely to receive." Sam, of course, saw it differently. He told Mother that the finer opportunity was the one he had taken, because in his lifetime there was unlikely to be another chance for a man to see battle firsthand. As a seminarian, he said, he had a solemn duty to learn what he could about the true nature of man in order best to do Christ's work among the people.

In our parlor that evening, Sam wore the regalia of the Lynchburg Guard, where he had been commissioned second lieutenant. When he rose to greet Parthenia and me, the tassels on his epaulettes swayed and the lamplight shone in the brass jacket buttons. Need I say I was envious?

"The Federals are gathering at Washington City right now. I have heard it for a fact. They are hungry to pay us back for Fort Sumter. No one is predicting a long fight," Sam said with a long face, "but if it were prolonged another six months—well, then you might pass yourself off as eighteen."

This was too much for Mother. "He will do nothing of the sort! He is a boy, and besides that he has no intention of becoming a soldier."

"How about it, John Alan? Tell it straight: do you wish to remain as you are—or is there something else burning in your breast?"

Mother turned away from Sam and faced me, hands on hips. "Well? Tell us your intentions loud and clear so that we can stop this drumming- in."

After a long pause, I said, "I wish to continue in school, ma'am. And I wish to become a doctor."

"There you have it," Mother said to Sam. "The boy does not intend to be a soldier. Rather, he—" Then it occurred to her exactly what I had said. "Did you mean to say that you wished to become . . . *a doctor?*"

"No, ma'am. Is that what you heard? In fact I said that I wished to remain in school, and then...and then I—"

"You said doctor, John Alan." Ah, Parthenia, my darling sister. Ever the seeker of truth. "I heard it plain as day," she said. "You said you wished to remain in school and become a doctor. Isn't that right, Sam?"

"Dismally, yes."

"Oh!" Mother said. "This is precious . . . Your father will split his side. I trust you have not told him this?"

"No, ma'am."

"Of course not. He would laugh you out of the room! Have you not learned a thing from your father's successes?"

I meant no disrespect to my father; she must have understood this.

"Parthenia, dear—go upstairs and fetch your father. Oh, this is *rich*!" Mother cast a conspiratorial glance at cousin Sam, clearly relishing the opportunity to humiliate me before a man she knew I admired.

Father came downstairs with his smiling daughter on one arm, and I took a measure of relief from his demeanor, which was uncommonly pleasant, and even cheerful. "Why, Samuel! How good of you to visit."

"Not at all, sir."

Father made no mention of Sam's uniform—nor the greater news of the day. Instead, he turned to me. "What of your news then, son? Parthenia tells me you have some item to share."

Mother answered for me. "He wishes to study doctoring."

"Is that so?"

"It is, sir." I felt much older, as if the heat of interrogation had caused my age to expand like a balloon filled with heated gas.

"I certainly understand your urge," he said.

"But John!" Mother exclaimed.

"How could I not? I once had the same ambition. But it is a different profession today, I'm afraid."

"Yes sir."

"It is full of precepts and procedures we never learned. Which is to say, we would have learned them, if any one had thought them up yet—but you catch my meaning. All these methods and literature and whatnot. It baffles me."

"John!" Mother again. "Talk sense."

Father rose up. "I will make myself known, Regina! Hear me, John Alan. Look around you. Right here, in this room. Or any room in this house. This is not a doctor's home. These oaken floors, these wide halls are the product of another type of work entirely, as you well know."

"Yes sir."

"Well, then."

"Sir, I mean no disrespect, but—"

"Why, for heaven's sake, John!" Mother cried out. "Tell it plain! Tell him what you believe—that doctoring is the work of paupers and fools!"

"Is that what I believe? Do you now purport to know my mind?"

Mother dropped her hands and rushed off by the side passage. Her exit disturbed Father, as her tantrums always did, and he began tapping his left foot compulsively. "Son," he said, now hurrying his words, "you shall not study to be a doctor. It is as your mother says. Do you understand me?"

I was astonished. How had he given way so easily? What of his understanding of this urge?

"Did you hear me, son?"

"Yes sir."

"Now, I applaud your ambition, however much I disagree with its direction. Therefore I am prepared to begin your training at the mill. As of Monday, you will spend your afternoons under the supervision of my foreman. Is that clear?"

I nodded. There was a tapping in the passage, and Father's head twisted over his shoulder. It was only the cat padding along. I looked to Sam and Parthenia for sympathy, but neither would hold my eyes.

# 7

AS I ASSUME OUR READER will be familiar with the events of our late and tragic war, I will not recount them in any great detail here except where they affect my story directly. I should remind, however, that the Disagreement, as it was still called in that summer of 1861, did not unfold at all as cousin Sam Brightwood (or, in truth, any of the people whose province it was to know such things) predicted it would. The chief error among them all was their underestimation of Lincoln's desire to keep us. You will recall that Mr. Coggin assured us that the Yanks did not care enough to fight. That may have been true among the rank and file, but the government in Washington City surprised every one with a strange and steady resolve.

"It don't make sense. It just don't ." Mr. Calvin Stokes, Father's foreman at the Woolery, could be counted on to give the sentiment of the average Lynchburger in fewer words than one should think possible: "I will tell you this, though: the Yanks themselves don't give a damn if we go. Abe's sore, is all. Won't last." Before joining the mill, Stokes had been a pilot on the James, ferrying cargo the hundred miles between Lynchburg and Richmond in a flat- bottomed barge known as a "batteau."

Perhaps because he feared the demands that war would place on our mill—and especially on his own service there—Stokes held fast to his opinion that there would be no battle. "I cain't see it, John Alan—not with the cash'ties both sides liable to take. This ain't the year seventeen and seventy- six, you know. Our boys got cannons now liable to disinnagrate a Clydesdale right where he's standin'. Just— boof! Rider too, natch'ly."

One of my plays for Stokes's affection had been to lower my speech to a level that I thought less pretentious and therefore more likely to demonstrate that I was worthy of real work.

"Whoa there, Mr. Stokes," I drawled. "You don't reckon the Yanks is haulin' the same artill'ry we got?"

"But that's just *exactly* my point!" Stokes exploded, his face glowing red as a French radish. "The fightin's bound to be too *dear*, is my point."

"Ahhh," I said, pretending to have just then caught his meaning. "That is a fine point, right there."

As usual, my strategy succeeded—which is to say that it stood me in the worst possible stead. Pleased by my flattery, Stokes dispatched me on another cream- puff chore, to the saddler's to fetch a mended bridle. Reaching into his billfold to take out a five- dollar note—one of the new, blue- tinted Confederate bills—he said, "Don't you worry none about the change, John Alan."

Then he went off to the toil he'd been so kind to spare me.

# 8

AMONG ALL THE STRANGE and wonderful truths I discovered during my medical training, I was perhaps most impressed by the caprice of heredity. The blood of mother and father mix according to no predetermined formula—even if siblings resemble one another in countenance, they may not match in character. Such was the case between Parthenia and myself. In the outward aspect, we were twins, sharing the same chestnut- tinted hair, stiff as the bristles on a husk broom. Our eyes were so identical in color and contour that if we were to obscure ourselves by cloak and slotted veil (in the manner of the Musselman harem), you could not tell us each from the other.

Thus it was with surprise, but also a sparkle of recognition, that I witnessed Parthenia's uncharacteristic behavior upon the departure of our cousin Sam. It was June, and the Lynchburg Guard was about to be amalgamated with a cavalry regiment from Lexington, under the command of a bright general by the name of Thomas Jackson. My cousin's ebullience at describing the man made clear that he was unique among field commanders.

Parthenia, of course, cared not a whit.

"But you can't be ready to go," she stated in a sort of plea. "Why, certainly you and your fellows haven't had enough practice!"

Sam threw back his shoulders and chuckled. "Ah, Miss Parthie, the fight won't wait for practice. The fight is the practice. We might drill another five months and never reach the readiness you mean."

It was Sunday evening, and we were seated around the parlor—Father, Parthie, Sam, and me. Mother was in the kitchen fetching a tea service (Sunday being Peg's day at liberty).

"But there must be something else!" Parthie bore a countenance I would later associate with war widows, a sort of pallor caused by tired blood. "There must be something you can do!" she pleaded to Father.

Father put the onus directly on Sam: "Why, I believe that even if I could do, as you say, something to keep Sam here, I doubt he would want it. Isn't that correct, Sam?"

"Indeed, sir. This is my strongest desire."

"But Father! What if Sam is harmed, what will you say then? How will you feel then, if you could have done something?"

Father crossed his arms over his chest. "That is the Lord's business, Parthenia. If our cause is just, then He will deliver our men unharmed."

"If the Lord was just," said Parthenia, "then He would keep Sam home."

Father began to answer, but Sam stood up. "I shan't expect you to understand me, Parthenia. I am willing to accept it as the due ignorance of your age. But your pouting protests are something else entirely: an indignity I simply cannot endure. Particularly not when in twelve hours time I will be afield in your defense!"

I expected this would cow Parthenia—unaccustomed as she was to passionate argument—but in fact she rose from her seat on the couch and confronted our cousin. "Samuel, you astound me," she said. "If this were not my father's house I would ask that we be left alone so that I could tell you exactly what I think of your righteous blatherings. No, don't speak—you will let me finish or I will tell them everything."

She paused and smiled impishly, as if realizing for the first time her special power over us all. "Or perhaps I will tell them anyway. You shan't prevent my telling. You will be away, which is your preference. So be it. But you must not think that I will wait for you indefinitely."

From the passage came my mother's voice. "Oh, you fresh girl!"

Parthenia turned and rushed past her, spilling the tea tray onto the floor with a horrible crash. Mother followed, and loud cries echoed from the kitchen.

Cousin Sam was mortified. He stood in front of his chair with his hands at his sides and his mouth clenched shut. Father exhaled loudly to break the silence and shifted position on his wing chair. Several times he parted his lips to speak, but each time he closed them again before any sound issued forth.

I did not know what to make of the scene. On the one hand I had no reason to disbelieve my sister, but on the other I could not imagine that Sam had dishonored her in any way. Parthenia seemed to be suggesting such gross improprieties, such unspeakable trespasses, that I could hardly believe that our cousin had the gall, guilty or not, to remain in our parlor!

At last Father said, "We will sort this out, son."

"Sir, I assure you—," Sam said hurriedly.

"Go," my father said. "God protect you."

# 9

IN THE MIDDLE OF JUNE the Bedford Woolery received an order to produce ten thousand sack coats for the Confederate States government, which Father negotiated through an agent in Richmond. It was Father's richest move—worth more than the receipts of the previous five years combined.

The coats were to be delivered to the Richmond Arsenal in lots of one thousand, due the first of each month. The first lot was expected August 1, which gave Father scarcely six weeks to cut the patterns, arrange the line, contract for transport, &c. The largest obstacle, of course, was labor; at the time, the Bedford Woolery ran a crew of just twelve. Beside the foreman, Mr. Stokes, this included an elderly clerk who kept the books; two mechanics, father and son, who kept the sewing machines in order; and eight Negro slaves, who worked the floor.

I realize that I may have misspoken previously when I said that my family owned only two slaves. Naturally I omitted the factory hands, who numbered anywhere from just a few to as many as ten or twelve. We were raised to view these as inputs for production—as commodities, the same as wool, coal, or lye. Father never spoke of them except to complain (for example) that the line was slow "on account of half the niggers being ill."

The new contract, then, presented a new challenge, but there was never any question how to meet the need for more labor. Concurrent with his negotiations with the government, Father arranged to purchase an additional ten slaves from a dealer in Richmond. The price for the lot was $12,500 Confederate, which Father borrowed from the bank. Although he owed other debts—the mortgage on the Woolery premises, for instance—he resolved to retire this new one with the first proceeds from the coat contract.

"It is simply bad practice," he lectured Stokes during the noon meal in the Woolery's upstairs office, "to hold chattel one does not own outright."

The food that day was cold ham- steak and corn bread, the former left over from the previous evening and the latter baked fresh that morning by our Peg. Father next took up the subject of a draper in Danville with whom he had been bargaining for a quantity of raw-wool cloth.

"A hard driver he is, to be sure," Father said. "Mister Muro, he tells me, I do 'pologize, sir, but I cain't accept nothing less than sixty a hundred- length."

Stokes chuckled. "He do 'pologize! Oh, my..."

"Aye, but I gave it to him."

"You did what?"

"For the first hundred, I did. You see, I had seventy- five in coin, so I convinced him to take it all for the first hundred, so long as he sold the next three for fifty apiece."

"And he shook on that?"

"Ha! I sent for the notary and he swore it all on paper!" Father clapped his hands together, projecting a bit of butter from his fingertip to the far wall. He wiped his hands on a dining towel and began

rifling through a stack of papers on the desktop. have the orders here,"
he said, holding three wrinkled sheets aloft. Each bore a round seal
pressed into the paper

"Hee- hoo." Stokes whistled. "Wager he'd've signed away his
daughter, if you'd asked."

"I reckon so. The smell of coin makes a man do crazy things."

"Sure it do," Stokes said. "Sure it do."

Father paid Stokes a fixed salary that neither rose nor fell with the
tide of business, but the foreman nonetheless reveled in all the successes of the enterprise. It was a source of pride and disappointment
for him, as if he owned the shop himself. "When's the delivery?" he
asked Father.

"First hundred arrives tomorrow, another on Monday next, and so
on like that."

"And the slaves?"

"Soon's we have the cabins up. I've been holding off the agent, but
I doubt he'll abide much longer."

"Ain't going to be much longer, now we got young master on it,"
Stokes said. He draped a thick arm across my shoulder. "What do
you say, young man?"

I swallowed a mouthful of corn bread. "Yes sir," I said. "Cabins
are going right up."

Father stood up and brushed the crumbs off the desk. "You take
care in that sun, John Alan. Don't work too hard now. Your mother
will have my jewels."

"But I want to work," I said.

Father caught his foreman's eye and the two shared a chuckle at my
expense. "Of course you do," Father said, tapping my head lightly as
you would a toddling child. It appeared that my plan to convince him
of my business acumen was failing miserably. Still, I was disinclined

to loafing, if on no other account than the restlessness of youth. I took up my straw hat and cinched the thong tight under my chin.

The slaves sang as they worked—a phenomenon I had heard about from my country cousins but never witnessed firsthand. Their song took its measure from the slap of boards and the sound of exertion as the men struggled for purchase under the load. Father had purchased the crudest grade of lumber, of varying length, which was mildewed in places and ground to powder by dry rot in others. To make the most of the knotty boards, they were laid simply one atop another, the chinks filled in with red clay, which was brought from a pit in a wheelbarrow.

I continued my sawing, making sure to keep a few boards ahead of the stackers so as not to err in haste. By four o'clock the men had laid ten courses. The one called Adam came to me and asked that I reserve the longest boards for roof beams. "Then chop up the rest of those'n for joists." He explained that these were the short lengths that ran between the beams. "Like a skeleton," he said.

At once we were distracted by the whistle of an incoming train. A line of box cars stretched across the James River bridge. A number of the giant doors on the cars were held open by soldiers waving flags and firing their rifles in the air. The rail road was at most a hundred yards from our mill, and on closer inspection I saw other soldiers bending over pallets on the floors of the cars. As the roaring engine passed out of earshot, the whoops and cries of the exultant soldiers came to us more clearly, and I was able to glean the news. It was just a single word, over and over:

*Manassas!*

# 10

THE TRAIN STOPPED BRIEFLY at our depot—long enough to uncouple three cars of wounded, who were carried by cart to our small infirmary. The throng of the curious swelled around the building like hogs at a trough. After gathering the general sense of the news—there had been a battle at a railroad junction some thirty- five miles west of Washington City—the crowd asked after our boys, the Lynchburg Guard. The soldiers on the train were from an Alabama unit and had been engaged on a different flank from the Virginia men. The Alabamans had heard, however, that General Thomas Jackson's regiment had stopped several Union charges and had, in many observers' opinions, won the day for our side. When I mentioned this fact to Mr. Stokes, who had rushed with me from the mill to the depot, the foreman immediately stepped up on a low wall and began bellowing the word that it was our boys who had won the day.

There were other rumors in the air. I heard that the Union Army had not bothered to load their artillery pieces, so confident were they that our men would run scared at the sight of them. And that Abe Lincoln had come down from Washington City with his wife and a picnic lunch at the promise of a show of running rebels. Or, alternatively, that Lincoln watched the battle from atop a viewing stand, like a European potentate. Most people who had spoken with soldiers reported that the Yankees had been forced to retreat the thirty miles back to Washington City on foot, many wet from having waded through a creek over which our guns had demolished the only bridge. Some of these reports proved false, but at that moment, as in all frenzies, every wild claim was taken as truth until proved otherwise.

As more trains passed through town on their way to more southerly hospitals, one fact was established beyond a reasonable doubt: we had won a decisive victory at Manassas Junction. There was talk of electing General "Stone Wall" Jackson president of the Confederate States (for "Stone Wall" was the general's new name, brought to us by the same trainloads of soldiers). No one knew much about the first Confederate president except that he was from Mississippi, and since the capital was Richmond, shouldn't the president be a Virginian? This is only one example of the kind of thinking that pervaded Lynchburg after Manassas. I am sure it was the same in other cities. No one knew that the battle (however glorious—and I do not mean to diminish its glory in the slightest) would come to be called "First" Manassas, in order to set it apart from a reprise transpiring at the same location (and with the same outcome) two years later. Naturally, we did not think Manassas would be the "first" of anything. Rather, at that point, it was the entire war—and we had won! We had our freedom from the North—and wasn't it grand?

Of course, not everyone shared in jubilating at the news. After a few hours milling about in the crowd at the depot—during which time I lost Stokes, found him again, and then lost him for good—I walked home to take stock of the incredible lightness I felt, which was completely unlike any sensation I had ever known. It was well past dark—I had lost count of the hour at nine chimes of the courthouse bell—and I had not eaten a morsel since noon. Strangely, I was not hungry in the slightest.

I found the house dark except for a lamp in the back stockroom, a small cell off the kitchen that served as our slaves' day chamber. From early childhood, my sister often retreated there to hide, preferring it, in fact, to her own bedroom. I pushed the door gently, to reveal Parthenia sitting on a short wooden bench. Her head was buried in her hands.

My appearance startled her. She quit her sobs right away. "John Alan!"

"Are you ill?"

"What time is it? Do you have news of him? You do! I can see it on your face, John Alan. Don't tell it to me; I don't wish to know."

I felt an immediate crush of pity. "Come here," I said, gathering her up from the bench. "There is no news from Sam, but that is to be expected. His unit was engaged, I know that for fact, but it will be days before we receive word from him. I have been down at the depot, and some men there—men who know these things—say that our army will remain in the northern counties several weeks to ensure that the Yanks do not attempt another encroachment. So, then—even if we had a letter from Sam, we may not see him for some time yet."

"I haven't time for this war talk, all those tactics and all the rest of it. Men are so cold." Here she clutched her thin breast. "I have a sensation, do you hear? Sam is not well, and I know this as clear as your facts from the depot."

"Parthenia, please—"

"Hear me, brother. You would not know it, of course, but this is the way of lovers, to send the news through the air. And yes, you might as well know it—we are lovers, Sam and I."

I nodded, careful to mask the terror I felt at the revelation. I had suspected after Sam's farewell, after Parthie's curious display of ire, that my cousin may have allowed her the wrong impression of his affections—but now an entirely new avenue of interpretation came to me, wherein my sister was not, as we had assumed, making love with the flutters of a girl's heart, but rather with another region of her corpus.

"He has promised to marry me," she said.

"But you are not yet fifteen years old!"

"He will wait."

I was flabbergasted. The possibility seemed unlikely to me still. "Where did this transpire? Was it here, in our parents' home? Surely I would have noticed!"

"You are not quick with that sort of thing, brother," Parthie said, in the flat manner of a schoolmarm answering the most remedial query. "I often think that you would not notice if I were replaced one day by a changeling."

I deeply resented her belittlements, which I considered utterly baseless, and yet when I tried to refute her, my tongue failed. "I notice . . . *certain things.*"

"Yes, you do," she said. "To the exclusion of all else, I'm afraid. This rowdy- dow over secession, for example—you followed all that much more closely than I ever could. And your silly notion of doctoring, for what it's worth, consumes its due thought. But did you ever notice, brother, when your little girl became a woman?"

I felt a stinging heat on my cheeks, and I must have turned a shade of crimson that would make a she- cardinal sing. In retrospect, I believe my shame derived not from the exact subject of Parthie's *adulthood* but out of plain fear of ignorance. I knew nothing about the female sex—neither in body nor in heart—and I had only the vaguest notion of what it meant to become, as she said, a *woman.* If I was to believe Parthenia, the answers were plain for me to see if I would only look, but I doubted that. The mysteries of womanhood were so great that they explained both the width and the hue of the dark crinoline-stuffed skirts then in fashion, as I was certain they were hidden under there.

"In two years I will finish Miss Pelham's," she said. "I will be grown, and you will have no choice but to acknowledge me as such. Mother and Father also. Sam and I have a dream, John Alan, and it is quite specific. We desire a house in the hill country west of here, where Sam will work amongst the ignorant and I will raise our children. I see you blush, brother—did you not imagine that your sister would some day have children?"

"You are not—*pregnant*?"

"Psh. Of course not. Your cousin is an honest man. In fact he is noble." Her gaze left the room as she followed this fantasy in her mind. "He should sit at the Round Table, Sam should, with Lancelop and Galahack and all of those fellows." She paused. "I don't know where you'd be—in the viewing gallery, perhaps?"

"What is that supposed to mean?"

"I don't know—I see what I see."

"I am not old enough for the army, if that's your suggestion."

"It's no matter," Parthie said. "Sam said this won't last, and your depot men agree. I only hope that he hasn't been too badly hurt."

I thought to say, "Why, he hasn't been hurt at all!" but I swallowed it. She had embarrassed me. Let her think him hurt, I thought. Let her suffer a bit.

# 11

THE SLAVES CAME UP FROM the hold in two lines—separated by sex—and they were joined one to the next by leg cuffs and chains. They were six adult males, two females, and two children. All wore filthy tunics of cheap broadcloth cinched at the waist with twine. Two of them—the largest males—wore a kind of paper slippers upon their feet. The rest were unshod.

The sight struck a pang in my gut, for I had never witnessed slaves thus constrained, though I had heard of the practice, and indeed had seen drawings of slave auctions in periodicals. (We had no permanent auction in Lynchburg, and whenever itinerant slavers came to the square, Father forbade me from attending.) The further knowledge that although Father had not clamped the cuffs on the ankles himself, his order had forced it, gave me reason to regret the purchase. I knew, of course, that there was no other way Father might fill the sack- coat contract—but the actual presence of these pathetic souls chastened me greatly.

Father signed the necessary papers, gave the agent his payment, and the batteau pushed off. The six existing mill hands showed their new counterparts to the living quarters. The sixteen would be crowded into the two finished cabins—another one was in the works, though only the foundation piles had been laid so far. As the batteau drifted out of sight, Father returned to the office to sort out the county filings and registrations of the new property.

On the question of an overseer, Stokes had told my father, "Save your money. Give me a whip and I'll manage." Like Father, Stokes had no direct experience overseeing slaves, but he had spent a few years in his youth—as a hired man at a tobacco warehouse in Pittsylvania County. "I seen plenty overseers there, coming in with the deliveries. No smilin', never. That's the key."

Father was unswayed by Stokes's assertions of competence at a job he'd never tried. "I reckon there's more to driving niggers than a prod and a hard expression," he said. But ultimately Father heeded the advice of his pocketbook and agreed to give Stokes a turn as overseer. Stokes already lived on the premises, in an apartment over the dye house, and though he had never been considered overseer of the six slaves who lived at the mill, he had been their de facto master during the hours Father was home with us.

Stokes took his time walking to the cabins, strutting in a most unusual, high- stepping manner, like a show horse. He trailed his whip like a tail from the back loop of his dungarees. As he neared the cabin, loud voices issued from within. Stokes rushed inside. I secreted myself behind an abandoned mangle in the drainage field.

The foreman's voice rose over the rest. "That's enough!" I heard him say. There was the noise of scratching, and of grunts, and the *thump- thump* of bodies scuffling in the dirt. "You there—hold him down. No, over there. And you—hey!" More bellows from the Negro men, and then the report of Stokes's whip. "One of y'all best tell me right now what is doin' here—or else I gon' burn down this fine new cabin."

There was silence, followed by mumbling.

Then Stokes: "One them new niggers looked at yo' woman—that's what you telling me?" (A grunted "yes suh.") "And this mamie here—this yo' woman?" ("Yes suh, thas her.") "Which'n did it?" ("Thas him yonder, suh.") *Crack!* "That one there?" (Shaky now: "Yes suh.") "What you say?" ("I says yes suh.") *Crack!* "Teach you not to be scrappin' when you should be workin', hear?" (No answer.) "Well then, I come over here to lay out the reg'lations this here mill..."

# 12

WE HAD WORD FROM SAM Brightwood the next week—that being the first of August 1861. Father read the letter first. Parthenia and I waited breathlessly as he refolded the paper and passed it without expression to his wife.

"Hurry, Mother!" Parthie cried. "Oh Father—what does he say?" Since Parthenia's demonstration at Sam's farewell, Father had thought it best not to mention our cousin at all in her company. Father scarcely spoke of the war when there was a chance it might drift to Parthie's ears. This was, of course, nearly impossible to do. The war was all anyone spoke of by then, and this was especially true of Father, whose every working hour was devoted to the support (that is, the *profitable* support) of our men in arms.

As Mother read the letter, her eyebrows, those fastidiously plucked indicators of her innermost toil, fell from Gothic arches to Roman. Always a slow reader, she took a full minute to get through the two-paragraph missive.

Parthenia snatched it up as soon as Mother's eyes broke from the page. She raced to the far wall of the parlor. Like Father, she read the dispatch without expression. "As I expected," she announced.

"He has told me all this—and other things which he has not included here." She sat down on the piano bench and read the letter again. "It is two weeks old," she said. Mother and Father exchanged looks— apparently neither had noticed this detail.

I decided then that I had waited long enough. I stepped over and took the paper from Parthie's weak grip.

"Dear Uncle," it began.

> *Doubtless you have heard the News of our triumph at Manassas. I will not spend more Ink to recount the Glories of that day, but instead wish to call out a Specific Fact resulting from it, that being the slight Injury I sustained there. Though it is hardly a Scratch, the Army has seen fit to discharge me from duty forthwith (with all earned decorations).*
>
> *I am told that I will be returned to Lynchburg within several weeks' time. If it is not much trouble, Uncle, would you mind sending your boy, or perhaps young John Alan, to fetch me at the Depot? I will write with the Specific Time when I know it.*
>
> *Sincerely, I am*
> *Your grateful Nephew,*
> *Samuel Carr Brightwood*

# 13

"LOOK FOR THE TRAIN AFTER eight o'clock," Father instructed as he saddled Sun Flower for the ride to work. "Perhaps don't bring him by the house right away. Look him over with a mind on your sister's feelings." I helped him up to the saddle. "Use your good judgment, son."

The neighborhood of the depot was isolated in the narrow bottom between two hills. The dense fog accumulating there did not bother the train engineers, nor did it faze the district's other residents, the brothel keepers and tavern owners, whose business relied precious little on eyesight. The fog did, however, make travel by carriage exceptionally difficult, and my horse gave a whinnying protest at what amounted to walking into a cloud. Somehow I managed to shush the animal, and we made the depot by seven- thirty.

"Pardon me," I said to the stationmaster. "Is there any word on the army train this morning?"

The clerk looked up from his work. "The army train, you say? There was a transport through here earlier this morning. Before I arrived, even." He jerked his thumb toward the line of windows facing the platform. A man sat on a bench with his back to us. "Fellow there was present when I got here. Didn't care to come inside—said he's waitin' for someone. Could be your man, I reckon."

I rushed out to the quay. It was Sam, all right—his beard had grown thicker, and he sported the bushy side- whiskers so popular among soldiers. He had in his hand a broadside on a biblical theme, wrinkled from wear, which he read to the exclusion of all distractions—including my footsteps on the wooden decking.

"Hello, Sam!" I cried.

My cousin lifted his head and acknowledged me.

I held out my hand, but it fell again to my side when Sam reached under the bench to produce . . . a pair of crutches! With great effort he lifted himself from the bench. The right leg of his britches hung as slack and empty as a stocking on a clothesline.

"I gather that your father did not tell you," Sam said. This seemed to please him, as if a bit of faith had been validated by my father's silence.

"No," I said. "Pardon me. I—I did not know." Now I remembered Father's warning and realized that there must have been a second letter. I was struck by the same fear that must have gripped Father when he read it: *Parthenia must not see him this way!*

Sam was not yet adept with the crutches, and he stumbled as he freed a hand to shake. I pressed his palm.

"The train was early," he said. "I've been sitting here too long already." He looked to the street, where the gelding was tied up alongside the surrey. "I suppose we shall go home now?" There was a note of fear in this question, as if the trip to our home—and thus to my sister's dismay—was an ordeal of Herculean proportions, the necessity of which he resisted with every sinew in his body.

"We needn't rush home," I said. "What if we were to stop for a drink? You must be thirsty."

Sam caught my meaning. "I suppose that would be smart. Do you know a place?" But how would I know an establishment that would serve us at eight o'clock in the morning—let alone *any* drinking establishment? I was sixteen years old—and very newly that! Sam craned his neck to observe the doors opposite the depot. "There," he said, peeling one finger off the crutch handle for pointing. He indicated the one storefront that gave any sign of life: a small dram house where a man—his figure blurred by the soaping on the window—could be seen pushing a broom across the floor.

I went to the bench and took up Sam's belongings. Then I offered him my arm, but he shrugged it off. He refused all assistance, pushing forward alone at tremendous expense in effort. At last we reached the tavern, and I asked the keeper if we might sit for a draft. Evidently he had watched our approach and anticipated the request, as he had already laid a table with cloth and two pints of cider. "Take a load off, soldier," he said, pulling out the chair for Sam to sit.

Sam eased his person down onto the stiff chair and laid his crutches against the grubby wainscot. He shifted his weight on the seat and then, confident in the position, reached for the pint. "Sure it's not too early now?" he asked the keeper, who had laid up his broom. He hovered behind Sam's chair like a wraith.

"You go ahead. Plenty more where that came from, too. Drink up."

Sam raised his pint. I eyed the other, waiting for the tavern keeper to step in and claim it for himself. (This was my fear, that the man had observed me from a distance and mistaken my age, by which time the pint was already poured, &c., &c.) When a moment passed with no motion from the man toward the glass, I grabbed it. I did my best to sip casually, but I was not in the habit of drinking much alcohol, nor even any cider. Father gave us wine with Sunday dinner, but Mother cut it with water—which adulteration led directly, I believe, to my long- standing distaste for that beverage.

The cider, however, was quite good. More important, it had a loosening effect on Sam, and by the second pint my cousin was recounting the tale of Manassas for the keeper, who had relented his eerie watch and pulled up a chair.

"Around two o'clock in the afternoon—or was it three yet?—the Yanks gave another try at our position. We were on the high ground, above this little crick they were trying to cross. If you can picture it, there a was a church yonder..."

With drink, Sam's voice dropped to a low register I had never heard from him, a smooth and drowsy drawl that immediately impressed me for its attractive, rough- hewn aspect. In conjunction with the side-whiskers—and no doubt also with the cider in my belly—he seemed foreign to me. Here was my cousin, the same Samuel Brightwood I had known all my days. And yet I hardly knew him.

# 14

AT NOON I HOISTED SAM into the surrey—he was by that point more amenable to assistance—and we made the trip home. Cliff met us in the carriage house and held the horse while I lifted Sam down. He stared at Sam's slack trouser leg but did not call it out.

"Happy returns, Marse Sam," he said with customary deference. I imagine that on account of his own hobbling, Cliff might have enjoyed a special empathy with Sam. And then again, perhaps not. Too often we excise the unpleasant emotions from our assessments of colored folk; they are as given to cruel intention as any of us, and why not?

The women heard our carriage in the drive, but evidently had not taken a clear view of our cousin. I knew this because they poured forth from the front door like butterflies released from a net: brimming with the exuberance of reunion. But as they noticed the crutches and the tied- off trouser- leg, the two women collapsed to the ground like wet rags. Mother even tripped on the hem of her skirt, a miscue I had never witnessed from her, and she tumbled to her knees in grass. For a long while (a count of twenty, perhaps) she made no sound, but instead held her mouth open in a soundless grimace like that of a child more scared than injured.

In due course, Mother did wail, but by then the horrible screaming of Parthenia had begun. That is all I heard. As I have mentioned, my sister was a slight creature, like me in countenance but at most half my poundage. Her voice, however, exceeded mine in range and volume. At the sight of Sam, little Parthenia parted her lips and let loose a wail like Satan's own rooster. It was a cry of despair, encompassing fear as well as grief. The tiny girl rushed to the soldier and pressed herself against him, wrapping her thin arms as far around his girth (made thicker by the crutches) as she could manage. Her cheek stood against the gray wool of Sam's cavalry jacket, occupying hardly more space than the vertical distance between two buttons.

Sam lost control of his crutches. He was light- headed still from the cider—as conquering hero he had guzzled far more than I—but it was not intoxication that caused him to lose his grip. With Parthenia hanging off him, screaming at the top of her range, Sam fell to one knee—the only knee he had left—and swiped at the ground, struggling for purchase on the gravel walk. In frustration, he flung the wretched poles away and embraced my sister with both arms. The two of them fell to the earth sidelong.

It was a public display of affection such as I had never seen—and that I hope never to see again. But alas. The thought of a man and his girl holding each other in that manner, in plain view of the neighbors, would have been an unforgivable offense even one month before. But the war changed many things—or *all things,* as it seems now—and I tell this incident specifically because it occurred in a special window between the old and the new, when the thrill of consequence was fresh and real sorrow was still possible in our unknowing hearts.

# 15

"UNCLE, IT IS NOT AS they say—mark my words, this war will cripple both sides. I saw it in their eyes: they will fight. I am confident in our men, naturally, but I am afraid we have miscalculated as regards the Yankee."

"Maybe so . . ."

I hunched outside the door of my father's study. It was the second day of Sam's convalescence—Mother insisted that he lie in bed most of the day on account of a fever she alone could detect. After supper, Father had taken Sam behind closed doors. I assumed so that he might learn the "real sense of the war" from a man who had seen it firsthand.

"They will not abate until we are punished, Uncle. Not just defeated, but punished. I spoke with a Yankee in the sick ward at Manassas— he was in the cot nearest mine. A regular fellow, I must say, from the west of Maryland. He explained that most ordinary folks take personal umbrage at our secession."

"Bah!" Father snorted.

"He said it."

"He was yanking your chain, son."

"I don't think so; he volunteered the same as I did, with the same good intentions."

"You say he's a Cumberlander? That's poor country. Federal army pays well."

"You can believe what you want, sir. As for me, I'm happy to escape with this—" I heard the dull whack of Sam's hand on his empty trouser leg. "What's more, a general muster is a sure bet," he said. "I heard this from good sources. If I were you, sir, I would do everything I could to protect John Alan. He is sixteen, now, but . . . well, I would not be surprised if the fighting carried on another year. By which point the muster would catch him up, sure as daylight."

Here Sam paused, and there was a scratch on the floor as if he were pulling his chair close to Father's. "Listen," he said, "the price of a commutation will be five hundred, according to my source. Five hundred! Surely you would pay that much to spare your son?"

"I will do no such thing!"

"Well, that is your decision."

Someone rose inside the study—a shadow broke the light under the door. I hurried down the hall, careful to dampen my footfall on the rug. A moment later I was upstairs in my bedroom, curled on the mattress with a head full of facts I did not know how to digest.

Yet I could not ease my mind, which should not surprise anyone who has ever been a boy of sixteen. I lay on my stomach for several minutes watching the dappled moonlight on the floor. Outside my window there was an old hickory whose branches yielded generously to even the slightest breeze. I would often sit and watch them nod to-and- fro, as some men watch hearth fires. On this occasion, however, the sight brought me no peace. I rolled onto my back and pulled at the buttons on my trousers. A quaking hickory is a lovely sight, but there is really only one way to calm the sixteen- year- old mind.

# 16

REGARDING MYSELF AND the army, Father's hand was forced when the government enacted the draft, just as Sam had foretold. In a hideous coincidence, the Conscription Act was passed just one day shy of the first anniversary of our state's secession—that date being, of course, also my birthday. I turned seventeen on April 17, 1862—just a year shy of the low end of the conscription. Thus I was not yet in line, but Father suspected that the eighteen- year minimum age would not stand over a prolonged conflictindeed a year later it was lowered by one year to seventeen.

Several odd practices came about as a result of the Conscription Act, which I will list here because I am certain they must have tempted my father. The practice of substitution, whereby a man hired someone to take his stead in the ranks, was more widespread than is commonly acknowledged—at least in the early days of the war, before all the spare men were used up. There was also the outright commutation—which, in fulfillment of Sam's prediction, was set at $500 Confederate. On his profit from the sack- coat contract, Father had plenty enough money to fund either of these dodges, but he knew that to do so would effectively end his worthiness as a military contractor. This was a sacrifice he could not, for the sake of our family's livelihood, undertake, and neither sub-stitution nor commutation was ever addressed around our dinner table, least of all upon the occasion of my birthday.

As was her custom when there was an occasion to mark, Mother had prepared a tray of sweets to enjoy after supper. Mother took tre-mendous pride in her baking, and it was the only kitchen chore she performed regularly. Dessert was also the only course she insisted on serving herself—this so that she could relish our delight as we unwrapped the little tarts and puddings and cakes.

But on this evening she sent Peg out with the sweets. As usual, we attacked like a pack of greedy vultures. Sam bit first into a petit four containing an abundance of raspberry preserves, which spilled over his lower lip like a second tongue. We all laughed, Father included. A moment passed in silence as we stuffed our mouths, and then Mother entered by the rear passage, dabbing her eyes with a handkerchief.

Sam wiped his mouth. He held aloft the remains of the petit four. "Auntie!" he cried. "This little one is an absolute triumph!"

Ordinarily, Mother dismissed flattery as one commonly does, showing the usual appreciation for the flatterer's intention, but this night it was plain that she was in no mood for it. She dusted off Sam's compliment like so much dander off the shoulders of his coat. "Remember to clean your teeth," she said.

Father had by that point indulged in one of the lemon tarts he favored, and which she baked especially for him, the others of us pre-ferring the sweet to the bitter. "The boy is right, Regina," he said. "A fine showing."

I looked at my cousin, propped on his crutch (he had reduced the number of crutches necessary to one), and doubted, suddenly, whether it was appropriate to call this hobbled soldier a boy any lon-ger. "Father, I wonder what I would be, then, if cousin Sam is yet a boy—an infant, perhaps?"

This tickled Father. "Aye, that's it," he said. "But alas, it is your birthday today. Shall we instruct Peg to begin your training at the privy? Lord knows you will need that skill where you are going."

Mother began to cry. Though a lady in all senses, she was never so squeamish that Father's occasional toilet jokes made her weep. I could not account for her tears.

Father ignored his wife's display and downed another tart. Satisfied with his usual ration, he retreated to an armchair and waited for the rest of us to finish. I nibbled an iced strawberry cake, but my appetite was gone; I could think of nothing but Mother's strange tears. Call it the solipsism of the birthday boy, but I was absolutely certain she was crying over me.

"Now then," Father announced when Mother, Parthie, Sam, and I had all taken seats in the parlor, "I have an unusual gift for you this year, John Alan." He rang the handbell, and Peg emerged from the kitchen with a cardboard box approximately one foot cubed, topped with a gleaming red ribbon.

Parthenia came alive then as she always did in the presence of gifts, and she encouraged me to open it immediately. "Why, it is so large!" she cried. "Father, I should like something so large for my birthday."

Father snorted. "This gift is for your brother only. It shall not be repeated."

I pulled the ribbon and opened the box. Inside were two things that, though meaningless in themselves, carried in them the entire course of my life—from that very moment to the day of this writing.

The first was familiar at once: a small satchel of pebbled black leather, with wooden handles that had also once been black, but that under years of wear had been burnished to a natural shine as if the raw grain had been rubbed with oil. The two halves of the bag were married by a brass clasp—recently polished, it seemed—and the sturdy bottom extruded four nubs of the same metal, which elevated the satchel a finger's width above the tabletop and which produced a certain *click- click* like marbles colliding when I placed it there. I did not open the satchel, for I knew its contents as well as I knew the wishes in my own heart.

Nestled against the leather of the satchel was a small picture frame, of the correct dimensions to hold a lover's *carte de visite*. But this frame held no tintype; rather, it contained a print of a city scene, with tiny persons rushing this way and that across a busy square. My heart seized as I realized the significance of the gifts, taken together. This was the fulfillment of my greatest desire! The scene on the card was surely the City of Brotherly Love, and considering the doctor's bag, I must have been—I was!—on my way to study medicine there!

Somehow, my father had found a way to breach the walls—so many of them, military and political—that stood between me and Philadelphia. My mind was free of logistical concerns, and I imagined that I would pass unmolested across the Potomac, the Susquehanna, and all the other natural boundaries until I arrived safe and sound, satchel in hand, to take my place among the incoming class of doctors at the Jefferson Medical College.

All this came in a flash; in a single breath. As I exhaled, then, my eyes continued down to read the title of the engraving, printed in a scroll across the bottom: *University of Virginia, Charlottesville.*

As soon as my heart had leapt with joy, it clenched with anger. A moment earlier, I had been bound neither for medical college nor Philadelphia, yet I now felt entitled to both.

Mother was bent over in tears, with Parthenia wrapped around her shoulders like a shawl. "Here, Mother," my sister said. "It is best. I am sure it is best."

Cousin Sam took the picture frame, looked it over once, and began peppering my father with queries. "Will he be going soon, then?"

"The first of July," Father said. His replies had the quick, high tenor of recital, as if the lines had been rehearsed.

"This is a clever picture," Sam said, turning the frame in his hand. "Is it a recent view?"

"No, actually," Father said, and here he appeared to move off his script. "I have kept that a long time. Twenty years perhaps."

My father had never been fond of Jefferson; he favored Patrick Henry among the first generation of Virginia patriots. Around quite a few dinner tables he had inveighed against the legacy of Jefferson's so-called progressive ideas, including the nascent University of Virginia, which he derided as "Jeff's Folly."

Sam, who knew my father's feelings on this topic, said, "Forgive me, Uncle, but it seems a strange memento for you. I would have expected you to keep a card of Princeton. Was this perhaps a wager against the school's success?"

Father forced a smile. "Perhaps it was. I don't know."

But suddenly it was all clear to me: the young John Muro, my father, purchasing a likeness of the new university—the university of his home state—only to find, when the time came for his education, that the place did not measure well against the old college up north where Muro men had always been schooled. It was widely known that the early sessions at Charlottesville had been marked by lawlessness and vice, and surely my grandfather would not have agreed to fund a residency at such a place. Thus a hope of my father's—a hope I had not previously known, but that I could not but see in him now—was dashed by the foolishness of those early, lucky few.

The thought brought me peace, and my anger subsided. In the weeks following, as arrangements were made for my departure, I retained some disappointment, but gradually I came to peace with what was in truth a rare opportunity in a time of privation. My send-ing- off was in fact the last instance in many years when I felt the luxe of good birth. In a year's time even the richest among us would be strained, and even this greatest gift would feel like an ox's yoke.

# Part Two

# 17

THE GREETING STATION WAS called Hotel A—one of four such houses staked about the perimeter of the university like fence posts. The scene in the ground- floor receiving room was chaotic, reminding me a bit of the fracas at the depot in Lynchburg when the first train arrived from Manassas. This gathering, however, was governed by that forced politeness gentlemen employ when they are strangers to one another but know they will be intimates before long.

A man in a starched dickey and a well- tailored frock coat stood at a table, rifling through a file box for a document pertaining to the gentleman before him. At intervals he gave orders with quick flicks of his chin to the men flanking him on either side. These two attendants—white men of middle age, dressed similarly—nodded obsequiously to each command and in turn dispatched someone else to satisfy the request. A half dozen slaves in maids' attire waited against the back wall. Whenever one of the subalterns snapped his fingers, the next girl in line stepped forward to receive the command. It was an efficient system, and I stood in the queue not five minutes before I was served.

The frock- coated man did not look up from the file box as he addressed me. "Name?"

"Muro."

The man's fingers walked across the top edge of the papers before plunging down to retrieve a slim packet. "Muro..." His lips moved as he read in silence. "Your dormitory is on the East Lawn. Room fifty-two." He mumbled instructions to the man on his right, who passed it on as I've described.

I understood from the way Frock Coat glanced anxiously over my shoulder to the next fellow that our conversation was done, and that I was to step aside. I walked to the far edge of the table, where a tandem of porters stood with their gloved hands crossed, awaiting instructions with disinterest.

I followed my luggage along a brick arcade. My sense of the university's plan was not yet firm, but from my father's engraving, I knew that the buildings were arranged in two horseshoes, one inside the other. Service buildings such as Hotel A sat on the outer row. The grand Rotunda, which served as the library, fit like the keystone in the top of both rows.

The service road ended at the rear of a dormitory building—I saw through the window a gentleman arranging his books on a shelf—and we jogged left to ascend a narrow flight of steps. At the top of these, my heart seized: this was the centerpiece of my father's engraving— the "town square" across which I had seen Philadelphia merchants running their errands. The vast Lawn was divided into terraces, each separated from the next by a path of bricks. Like opened arms, the colonnades stretched south, marking the distance with the black doors of dormitories, and bejeweled now and again with the broad porticoes of professors' homes.

We crossed the Lawn on the southernmost path. My dormitory was the last door on the east colonnade, adjacent to the final pavilion. Though there was a keyhole under the knob, the door was not locked. The stouter of the two porters entered first. He went directly to the window and flung aside the curtains, causing a beam of orange twilight to fall upon the floor.

The chamber was modest: a small brick hearth occupied one wall, two stained- pine bedsteads lay against the other. Against the far wall—under the window—was a writing table and a light button-backed chair. I thought it oddly asymmetric that there should be only one desk. The extra bed frame told me I was to have a roommate. I supposed we would have to arrange a scheme to share the desk. Even having yet to meet the fellow, I had no doubt this could be simply done, so carried away was I by a sense of well- being. Indeed, the satisfaction of finally arriving at college burned away my traveling ague as the sun does morning fog, and I felt refreshed without so much as a cracker or a cup of tea.

The servants stacked my luggage at the hearth and hastened back to their frock- coated master. I took a notebook and a pencil from my traveling bag and began a list of all the items I would need to furnish the room. A strong mattress would be essential, as would an armoire or a sturdy chest of drawers for clothing and personal effects. I was excited to see a door in the far corner of the room, hoping that it concealed a clothes closet, but it turned out to contain only a short porcelain basin such as one might use to cleanse the face before bed. The brick privies were in the garden behind—I had seen a gentleman emerge from one of these during the walk from the greeting house. Besides the wooden furniture, I would require also a set of bed linens and a pillow, and also some metal tacks or hooks for fastening pictures to the wall. As yet I had only my father's engraving to hang up—and that seemed a bit strange, seeing that the university itself was just outside the door.

After an hour's elapse I had a list occupying three pages in my book. Many of the items were too vague to be acted upon but seemed important to put down as notes to myself: *Graphing paper for math-*

*ematics ? Chemical glassware, all types. Will need gaseous ether (yes or no?).* When I finally put down my pencil to rest my aching hand, I was surprised to detect the faint stirrings of hunger in my gut. I had not eaten since breakfast. Mother had packed a basket of biscuits and ham for the journey, but I had been too nervous to eat. Now I realized that in my haste I had left the basket in the coach.

It is remarkable that in my state of bliss, buoyed by a confidence that told me I might hold the very moon in my hands, I should be humbled—almost brought to the knees—by a thought so pedestrian as not knowing where to find my next meal. But so it was.

I went outside. The sky had dimmed, and there was a smattering of pink clouds above the Rotunda. A pair of young men walked past my door. From their amiable chatter, I assumed they were acquainted— and thus further along in the process of accommodation to this place than I was. I followed them down the graveled alley behind the dormitories, hoping that they would lead me to food.

Thus it was the complaining of my stomach that brought me to Hotel F that first night, and not the echoes of a lonely heart or some other such rubbish. It is among my goals for this narrative that it be a refutation of those sentimental beliefs that, though widely held among members of society even today, are nothing more than the fancies of children. One of these is the notion that love comes of purpose, with a determination superceding the intentions of either party. In my experience this is false: nothing breeds love like proximity, and perhaps nothing *but.*

The great room of Hotel F was much darker than Hotel A. Fresh tapers burned in pewter cups on each of the tables. Mind—this was a luxury even at that early stage of the war. An assortment of tasteful pictures hung on the walls, and the window treatments had the look of recent laundering.

Half a dozen diners were arrayed at the various tables, forking avidly at their plates with what looked to be real silver. The dish was macaroni adorned with a type of mustard- colored cream sauce. The patrons sipped mugs of a hot, rusty drink that I fancied to be coffee, even though there was little chance of it—those beans being the first foreign commodity to dry up in Lynchburg.

I sat right down at the closest empty table. A few minutes passed with only the noise of the other gents chewing their food. I did not engage anyone in conversation. In my defense, none of the them approached me, either. Nonchalance seemed to be the etiquette of the place, and I affected it with relief.

After a time the kitchen door swung open and a man with a chubby face and just a fringe of greasy black hair upon his head peered out. He did not look long, but retreated immediately back behind the door. I had hoped he would see me and that I would be served without having to petition. But I had not seen his eyes in the brief moment he was out. I would have to get up.

As I struggled to my feet—I was by this time dizzy with hunger—the kitchen door opened again. This time it opened all the way, and a girl strode out. She resembled the bald man in no wise—fortunate for her—and I surmised that if they were kin, there was surely but a drop of the father's blood in her veins. Her hair was thick and smooth, a lustrous auburn like polished mahogany. As she proceeded to my table, her eyes rested calmly on my face, never diverting to her feet, which negotiated the tables and chairs like the agile hooves of a doe. Her carriage was immediately recognizable to me as that of a finished lady—such as my sister was to become at Miss Pelham's. Yet this girl had somehow retained a vital essence that my sister had lost already. Her skin gave a healthy glow, and her cheeks swelled over the bones in that tender proportion one sees in young children. She was not a child, however, but altogether grown, with a woman's full hips and bosom. I guessed she was my age—if not a year or two my senior.

"Good evening," she said, giving a shallow curtsy to put me at ease. Her voice was a surprise—a throaty rasp like a stiff brush on canvas.

I struggled to respond, so charmed was I by her manner. After several preparatory gulps I managed, "Evening, ma'am. I thank you kindly for having me in." I readied my hand to take hers in greeting— as I had been trained to do upon the acquaintance of a lady—but the hand did not come forth. The omission—which was in fact not an omission at all, but rather the perfect etiquette of a table servant—was like a pin piercing an inflated balloon: I wondered if I had not overes- timated the girl's standing, and surmised that she might very well be a simple servant.

And yet, her soft, sloping shoulders were unmistakably ladylike. Even the style of her hair—plaited doubly, wound, and pinned atop the crown—was of a fashion sufficiently modern that it could not pos- sibly have come of coarse taste. When she turned her head at a noise from the kitchen, I caught view of the many delicate combs of bone, or tortoiseshell, holding her plaits in order. These reinforced my suspi- cion that she came from good standing, if not from actual privilege.

"Will you be dining with us tonight?" she asked, returning her full attention to me. "We are serving *maccheroni e formaggio*—very popu- lar with the gentlemen, as you can see—and a bit of greens with oil and vinegar." At the reference to the "gentlemen," the girl swept her delicate hand through the air. The fluid quality of this gesture struck me as a perfect cadence to the menu recitation, which possessed simul- taneously an air of spontaneity and the flawless polish of rehearsal.

"I should like very much to dine here," I said. "Have I found the right house? My name is Muro."

She did not react to the mention of my name—which mentioning, I must add, I thought particularly clever. I expected her to come forth with her own introduction, as was called for by etiquette, but as with the handshake, she did not. "Very well," she said. "I shall bring your plate out right away."

She danced back to the kitchen, lifting along the way—with no visible effort—the abandoned dishes from a vacant table. At the kitchen door, she spun around and pushed it open with her backside. Her head and then her skirts vanished within.

The rest of the meal passed uneventfully; I was too timid to engage the girl in further conversation, and she brought my food without any elaboration of her own. The dish fulfilled neither the promise of its appearance nor the touting of the girl, proving bland and tasteless in actual fact. I was so wracked with hunger, though, that I did not notice any shortcoming whatever until the last few bites, by which time my stomach had already begun to cramp.

The coffee, however, proved genuine, and I drank three cups of it. This served to accelerate my thoughts, and I remembered that I had forgotten to write Mother—a task I had promised to execute immediately on my arrival in Charlottesville, so as to get the letter into that evening's post.

I hauled myself back to the dormitory and sat down at the writing desk. But when I spread a fresh page out in front of me, I found that I had nothing to compose. The coffee had affected me to a greater extent than I thought possible, on account of my long, forced hiatus from it. My mind thus scrambled, I could manage only the following lines.

*June the 26th, 1862*

*Dearest Mother,*

> *I have arrived safe in Charlottesville. The coach-ride was Tolerable if a bit rough, but I am well. I have been assigned dormitory number 52, and all correspon-*

*dence can be sent to me at that Address. I miss you*
*and Father much already, though the Stewards here*
*have been hospitable. The Food is decent—*

(Here, in my haste, I actually scribbled "The *Girl* is decent," which I
quickly blacked out and replaced with the correct sentiment.)

*—but I much prefer Peg's cooking (and yours). I will*
*write again when lectures begin, as that is the true rea-*
*son I am here, and I trust you will be interested to hear*
*of my Studies.*

*Respectfully yours,*

*John Alan*

I sealed the letter and left it on the desk. It was too late to make
the post that day. Then I settled myself on the floor of the dormitory. From my traveling case I took a light cotton blanket that Mother
had insisted I include among my belongings "as a precaution." She'd
meant a precaution against the elements in the event that the stagecoach was stranded en route—but it would serve just as well this way.
It was close in the room, and no other linens were necessary.

Lying there on the mat of coats, I dwelt on what I had seen of
the university so far. It seemed as though the bustle of a small city
existed within these brick walls, what with the stewards and slaves and
cooks and students and all else. There hardly seemed time or place
for study. I imagined the lectures, teeming with hungry men, and the
vivid debates that would follow. In short, I let my mind run like a colt
at new pasture. Only, this horse of mine was possessed by the stupor
of coffee—real coffee!—and he would not heel when the sun was set.
The crickets began their song in the magnolia outside the window,

and it seemed that an hour passed with a single breath, so dense was each moment, and so still the June air.

And then—nothing. Like a kerosene lamp that burns brighter than any candle but snuffs out at once when its fuel is spent, I collapsed as soon as the last drop of coffee passed from my blood. I would sleep that night without dreaming—the warm, black torpor of exhaustion.

# 18

NEXT DAY I WOKE TO the sound of horse feet. A glance out the window showed a partial darkness, and I guessed that it was no later than six.

There was the thud of a man jumping down from the saddle. I searched the room, nervous that I had forgotten perhaps to perform some important task of orientation the previous evening. Then I noticed something curious. There was a mail slot in the door, the metal flap of which now appeared to be moving of its own accord. There was a brief flash of light as the flap was lifted open, and then two eyes appeared there. The eyes and I regarded each other silently for a moment, neither willing to acknowledge the other. Then the flap snapped shut and a loud cry came from behind the door: "Yip! Yip! Yeeeeee- aaaayyyye!"

I opened the door forthwith and found a fellow standing in the colonnade. He was my own age or thereabouts, with soft creamy skin visible above the well- groomed contours of his beard. This he wore in the distinctive style of General "Stone Wall" Jackson, cut square like a cow's tongue and twisted into points on the end. The resemblance to Jackson was really quite arresting. He had the same pale eyes, the blade of a scalpel for a nose, thin mannish lips, and straight teeth. He might even have struck a resemblance without the beard—but subtlety, I'd learn, was not his way.

He was dressed in the most current fashion—a tailored waistcoat and full- length trousers, his shirt topped with a collar so fresh and white it must not have been affixed but a moment before his arrival. His boots were new—imported from abroad, I supposed, as I had never seen a pair like them. They had been polished to the shine of a looking glass; indeed, the sky's pinking just then was reflected on the tips of his feet.

He thrust his hand out at me. "I am Braxton Baucom—the third of the same, if you'll believe it—but you should call me B.B. The fellow down at the greeting house said your name is Muro. Well, Muro—let me say it is a pleasure. We shall be great confidants."

I would learn later that B.B. had been at a boarding school in the North when the war began. His speech betrayed the slightly English flavor that was then the fashion of the Northern gentry.

"A pleasure," I repeated, and I shook his hand. His grip was firm, but the palm was as soft as kid's leather. "John Muro."

"May I call you Jack?"

"Muro is fine."

"Then Muro it is! Ho ho!" He looked me up and down quickly, noticing my hastily assembled suit of clothes. I had donned the first items I could reach. "We shan't keep you long," he said, and at that point I saw the entourage waiting just down the Lawn from our room. Strange indeed that I hadn't noticed an assemblage of three wagons, loaded to the sky with all manner of furniture—drawn by teams of the finest- looking horses I had ever seen and driven by well- attired Negroes in matching uniforms.

"I only mean to leave off a few things here, if that is acceptable. I've acquired a house in town for the rest." Here he jerked a thumb over one shoulder, indicating the wagon train, and he smiled knowingly, as if to make sure I understood that all of his freight would not be made to fit in our little dormitory. "I fully intend to see you later, once all this is properly disposed. We shall have a drink. Are you free this afternoon?"

At this point, one of the Negroes jumped down from the tailgate of the rearmost wagon and proceeded to lift upon his shoulders an enormous mahogany armoire. As if it were a bread box, the man heaved it effortlessly up the grassy incline, threaded between two columns, and passed into our room. Only when he set the item down inside did I hear any exertion on his part—a loud, satisfied hiss as he exhaled. The Negro returned to the truck, climbed up, and called back to B.B. "Marse Brax'n—"

B.B. touched my arm, manually preserving our conversation while he dealt with this business. "Is there a problem, Aristotle?"

"How many these here matt'ses you want in there?"

B.B. looked at me. "Have you bought a mattress yet?"

"I mean to do it today," I said.

"Ah! Then we have saved the trip!" He turned back to the servant. "Bring two, Aristotle! And two pillows, two sets of linen—do you understand?"

"Yessuh."

In a flash, B.B.'s Negro had the mattresses in our room and was tucking the linens in on all sides.

"So, this afternoon, then? I shall call here."

"Come whenever," I said. "I will be . . . here."

Tell me—what else could I say?

# 19

I SPENT THE MORNING tending to the remaining chores on my list—those trips that my solicitous roommate had not "saved" me. First thing, I posted the letter home. The post office struck me as quite abustle for so small a community, and I surmised this was because of the Charlottesville General Hospital, which shared the university's property and had in fact spilled over into many school buildings. On the east side of the university, a forest of canvas and oilcloth tents had been erected to house ill soldiers. A vast corps of nurses hustled in and around the tents, carrying trays of food and drink from the steaming kitchens.

There was a small commercial district across the main road from the university, and I purchased what I needed there. Returning later to the university grounds, I busied myself with a tour of the walled gardens behind the pavilions. There were ten of these gardens, one behind each of the professors' homes. I had observed students relaxing on the various stone benches and mellow knolls inside these cloisters during my walking to and from the dining hall the night before, and thus deduced that the gardens were a public space and could be explored freely. I began my tour with the first garden on the east side—that is, the one most proximate to the Rotunda—and was immediately impressed with the variety of flowering bushes and fruit trees therein: a dwarfed- apple tree dangled green fruit already the size of a child's fist; a wiry plum hung drupes as tender as the same child's cheeks; the fruit of the tallest tree among them, a pear, showed red dapples on the lowest- hanging set. I made a note to revisit this place within the month, when the first of these would be ready to consume.

This garden was divided into terraces, with low brick walls between each. I unlatched the gate to ascend, but upon reaching the top step I froze in my tracks. There, in a wide wrought- iron chair, reading with her back to me, was the girl from the dining hall! She was wearing a striking yellow calico dress that bunched at the sleeves. Again, I noticed the fine shoulders, but from my vantage on the lower terrace, I fixed on something else: she was not wearing socks or stockings of any kind, and her naked ankles were crossed delicately beneath the chair.

Struck timid, I backed silently down the terrace, concealing my self inside a flowering- quince bush. Over the wall I heard the occasional rustle of paper as the girl turned over the pages in her book. My heart beat so loud in my ears that I felt sure it would give me away. I worried furthermore that this was a dangerous precedent, to be cowering in a way that might be construed as, well, *perverted.* If I ever wished to strike up a meaningful conversation, this was surely not the way to do it.

At last, a voice: "That is a quince, I believe."

Shamed, I looked up and found the girl leaning over the brick wall.

"I don't believe it will bear this year. Perhaps next—we shall see. Though it may be a barren variety." She spoke with a casual air, as if we had been conversing all the morning on this very subject.

Not knowing how to extricate myself gracefully from the situation, I merely sprung from the bush and wiped the fallen leaves off my coat.

"Indeed," I said, "I was just wondering if this quince were barren. Is there anything sadder than a barren quince?"

It was as if another man were speaking this blather, and I was beside him looking on. But I pressed forward.

"We have not been properly introduced," I said. "I am John Muro."

The girl, still poised at the wall above me, bowed slightly. She said, "It is a pleasure, Mr. Muro." But still she did not give her name. The sun had by then risen full into the sky, the tender morning birds retreated to the shade. The hardier midday cast replaced them in the trees: the mockingbird, the jay, and the cardinal. A crew of pigeons swept in and lighted on the brick steps at the break in the wall.

To my astonishment, the girl did not appear anxious to break off the conversation. She raised a foot idly behind her and proceeded to pick a pebble from the sole of her sandal. I did my best not to stare. Naturally, I failed. She caught me watching but did not seem to mind.

"Are you a student?" she said.

"As of yesterday," I said. I pointed to the pavilion. "Is this your home?"

"Oh, no—I am here only while my father is in the field. Dr. Cabell is my uncle." She paused, as if bored by the subject of her provenance. "Say—you are not by chance of the Richmond Muros, are you?" Her eyes shone at this possibility, and I wished desperately that I could reply in the affirmative.

"I come from Lynchburg," I said. Scrambling to keep her attention, I added, "But I suppose we are all relations."

"Do you know that is precisely my sense as well? A name is so much more than is commonly acknowledged, wouldn't you agree?"

"Indeed," I said. "Let us take your name, for example . . ."

"But I have not given it."

"Of course. Forgive me, I don't wish to be rude, but I do not know how to address you."

"Mr. Muro, if you wish to know my name, you shall ask for it. Did they not teach you that in Lynchburg?"

I felt a warmth on my face as if someone had opened a stove door. I found it strange that a young woman should be so formal regarding her name, but the game of it excited me in an equal proportion. "Madam, if you would please tell me—"

"I shall tell you this evening," she said.

It was a fair play. But can I say that I have never wanted to know anything more in my life? I considered knocking a brick against my skull, so that I might be rendered unconscious for the rest of the day and the supper hour should come that much sooner.

"You can wait until supper, can't you, Mr. Muro?"

And with that she folded the book under her arm and ran away, disappearing into her uncle's home.

# 20

I TOOK THE NOON MEAL at Hotel F—a decent ham and grits—
but the service was provided this time not by the girl but by a portly
woman who neither spoke nor smiled, only heaving the platters onto
the table with a muffled grunt before returning to the kitchen to
smoke.

The girl's play at manners had further convinced me of her breed-
ing, but there remained the mystery of her employment in the dining
hall. I wondered who her father was that he should feel comfortable
sending his daughter to a place such as this university—and with a
soldiers' hospital adjacent! It seemed hardly a suitable home for a
young lady.

I returned to the dormitory after lunch to await my roommate's
call, busying myself by taking the dimensions of the corner where I
wished to install a chest of drawers. After a time I grew restless and
decided to peek inside B.B.'s grand armoire, which stood out among
the cheap university furnishings—the bedsteads and the desk—like
an oak amongst jack pines. The finish over the mahogany wood was
recent, and the sweet odor of varnish wafted off the doors as I swung
them wide. Given the display of the morning—all the wagons and

slaves, &c.—I should have been prepared for the show of wealth inside the armoire, but what I found went so far beyond any previous assortment of clothing I had ever seen that I was truly struck dumb: no less than three woolen topcoats, thick as rugs and without a single blemish or moth hole, hung on the left end of the bar. Next to these was a collection of waistcoats, jackets, and light frock coats—"dusters," as they are called—in such profusion that I surmised B.B. might wear a different one each day of a fortnight! He had trousers in the same colors and patterns to match, and enough starched blouses to last a man a month or more. A box of new French collars sat on the shelf above, with silk socks, undergarments, and many brightly colored cravats. On the floor of the armoire lay a row of shoes and boots, all of commensurate quality to the pair I had admired that morning.

Atop the giant chest was a stack of hatboxes. I borrowed the chair from the desk and stood on it, pulling down the topmost one.

"Consider it yours," came a voice behind me. I nearly toppled off the chair, wrenching my neck around to find my roommate all agrin, his arms folded across his chest in satisfaction at the discovery.

"But—you must excuse me. I meant only to arrange your boxes. You see, the one was about to fall, so I stepped up to catch it . . ."

"Many thanks for that," B.B. replied. He was clearly amused at my squirming. "I should have hated to see a hatbox fall on the floor."

I was utterly mortified, and I am sure my face flushed as crimson as a cockscomb. I also felt strangely indignant—not at B.B., for it was his room as well as mine and he was free to come and go from it as he pleased—but rather at fate generally. I came of a good home, and I had never wanted for any thing. Yet this display of opulence was so far beyond my experience that I felt reduced by it somehow. I had no intention to borrow any of my roommate's attire—much less to pilfer it—and still a strange curiosity had impelled me to pull up the chair. Thus I was guilty of the trespass, but I felt as though there were (if I may borrow here from the legal phraseology) *mitigating circumstances.*

My roommate, though, had no desire to charge me with any crime. On the contrary, he seemed to delight at my interest in his furnishings. "Do you like that hat?" he said. "It is English silk. You are welcome to it anytime. No need to ask. The same goes for any of it." Here he tapped the side of the armoire with his knuckles, and the giant case gave a weak *plink* as if it were a block of marble. "If we are to do this right," B.B. said, "you must know that what is mine is yours. I mean this honestly."

"Thank you, but I have my own clothing," I said.

"Well." B.B. took up the chair and replaced it under the desk. He looked me up and down, taking a measure of my attire. "Keep it in mind, is all."

As it was by that point in the afternoon quite warm, B.B. had shed his costume down to shirtsleeves. His hair was damp at the temples, but his collar showed an incongruous lack of perspiration. I puzzled on this for a moment before I realized that he had changed it since the morning.

"Are you ready to go?" he asked. "If you need time to finish your affairs here"—in jest he gestured up to the stack of hatboxes—"I will wait, of course, but I do recommend that we commence the frolic as soon as possible."

"The frolic?"

"Indeed. I have planned quite a thing this afternoon. My boy secured the name of a man we ought to know if we are to have any diversion at all around here." He took a pewter flask from his rear pocket and shook it before me. No sound came. "I have a thirst in me, Muro. A mighty thirst."

"I see."

"Are you a Baptist?" he asked.

"No."

"Well then."

Another strange fact of the university, which I learned first just then, is that in the preponderance of idle hours, the burden of justification for one's actions is so light that the challenge is often to think of a reason not to do a thing rather than a solid cause for it. The strictures of sound logic, given freely in the lecture halls, enjoy no jurisdiction in the dormitories. Nor should they, for while the college man hasn't the nine lives of a cat, he surely hoards an extra two or three. B.B., it turns out, had more than that—and they were now mine to borrow.

# 21

AT THE TAVERN—if you might call it that; it was in fact just the back parlor of a man's home—B.B. came to the glass as the hungry farmer comes to dinner. He tapped his fingers on the table as the barman poured measures of a crude corn whiskey he called bumbler." B.B.'s eyes grew wide with a type of prurient anticipation. The man, who gave his name as Garth (though he didn't say whether that was his family name or his Christian one) chuckled a bit when he saw B.B.'s reaction at the sight of the bottle, and he chided him, "Now, now, baby boy. Bottle's on the way."

B.B. snatched up his tumbler and took a long pull. The ensuing transformation was instructive for me from a medical perspective: at the moment the liquor touched his tongue, B.B.'s crazed countenance relaxed. The lids of his eyes fluttered a bit, as with extreme fatigue, and the lines fell out of his brow. Coincident with the draining of the glass—that is, as the liquor progressed down his throat—other symptoms of mania abated. The crushing grip of his fist on the tumbler, the compulsive finger tapping, the twitching of his nose—all of these ceased upon the application of the drink. One of the principal advancements in modern medicine is the evolution of our pharmacopoeia, which, in tandem with the careful standardization and dosing of reactive compounds, purports to render the human body into a musical instrument, with predictable results to be enjoyed if the practitioner follows the score faithfully.

But that notion is dubious at best, as it leaves out the fact of human variation, which must always be considered in dosing substances for beneficial effect. Consider the variance in individuals' tolerance of similar doses of the same medication. Observe, in a moment, my own reaction to "the bumbler."

Although from the first taste I disliked the beverage—it tasted like the squeezings of a dish towel—I stomached three glasses, so desperate was I to make a good impression with B.B. His gaiety, which grew with each glass, was catching—and as the alcohol took hold of me, I clung to the faith that Father's Sunday- dinner wine regimen would prevent any embarrassments on my part. B.B. solicited the barman for food, which he brought, in the form of a bowl of peanuts and a plate of desiccated biscuits. B.B. gobbled these straightaway and asked for more.

"Come now, Muro, you haven't had a bite! Do we need another go- round?" He waved at the man, who replenished the bowl with more of the same.

I had downed two glasses on a perfectly empty stomach, and though I was hungry and could have used some solid material to soak up the liquor, I remembered my obligation to dine at Hotel F that evening. "You know, B.B.," I said, making the best effort to keep my speech clear and sober, "I ought to be getting home."

"Bah! We have only just begun to frolic."

"I'll have to beg your pardon, then."

"Well, you shall at least take one for the road."

This is how I drank the third, damning, glass of "the bumbler." B.B. called for another setup, and when the glasses were full, he raised one in each fist, clinked them together, and handed me mine. "To our studies!" he said. I thought it a curious benediction, but as I was eager to depart, I repeated: "To our studies—here, here." The last glass might have been water for all my tongue could discern at that point. The lining of my throat was so numb that the only notice I took of the last dram of fluid passing into my gut was a painful stitch in my side when I rose. "Shall we?" I said.

"I believe I shall stay awhile longer. But there is no reason you should tarry on my account. Take the horse."

"But where shall I leave him?"

"I'll send my boy to the dormitory. Just tie him up somewhere."

There was at that time an "honor code" among University men, but with so many others about the Grounds—the slaves of the hotel keepers, &c.—no one much trusted the code for protection against thievery. Still, I was beginning to see that *property* had a different meaning for B.B. than it did for me.

And so that is how I ended up soused atop the most magnificent full- bred bay horse I had ever seen. B.B.'s stock was far and away better than anything I had encountered in Lynchburg, and that included the white mares of the bishop's team, which had been my previous exemplars of equine pefection. Naturally, the riding tack was also of the finest quality, and the fresh leather squeaked and popped as I rode. It is said that a good horse will carry you home dead, and indeed, I scarcely touched the reins before the horse was climbing the terraces of the Lawn.

I drunkenly lashed the animal to one of the plastered columns outside our dormitory and rushed in to look at myself in the mirror. I was a mess—my eyes were shot through with capillaries, and my hair was in desperate need of attention. I dipped a comb in the basin and fixed up as best I could. I noticed then that my collar was stained with perspiration—the sickly- sweet variety that comes of drinking too

much. Having not yet purchased a chest of drawers for my belongings—having chosen, instead, to spend the afternoon getting drunk in
some fellow's back parlor—I was forced to root around in my luggage
for a fresh collar. I could not recall, though, which of the four suitcases
held the collars. I checked my pocket watch: the supper service ended
in ten minutes.

Frantic, I went to B.B.'s armoire and swung open the heavy door.
There was the box of collars on the top shelf. The haberdasher's ribbon was still tight over the lid. With my penknife I cut the ribbon and
removed the topmost collar from the packing. It was a bit wide for my
neck, but it fit well enough.

When I entered the dining room the girl was folding towels at a
rear table. Her face brightened, I noticed, when she saw me. I thanked
God that I'd hurried home. She wore a rose- and- cream- patterned
dress, with a light bonnet over her auburn plaits. The same generous
lace edged both dress and bonnet.

Putting aside her folding, she rose from the table to greet me. "We
were sure you had taken your supper elsewhere," she said.

"No, no," I demurred. "I was—well, I was *reading*, you see, and I
lost track of the hour. Will you pardon me?"

She came around the table. I noticed once more her incredible
grace of carriage and wondered if she were not a student of the ballet.
A woman's skirts normally swayed to and fro as she walked, rocking
gently as handbells. Yet when this girl sauntered past it was quite different; her skirts scarcely moved at all. She appeared to glide across
the floor, skirt motionless, as if she were on skates!

"Do you favor chicken *parmigiana?* It is a most wondrous dish—
the keeper's specialty, in fact. Mr. Di Bruglio recommends that it be
sliced just after frying, which is why I was concerned when you tarried
so long."

Here she paused. She was close enough to smell my breath. "Sir?"

she said. "Have you really been reading all this time?" Her tone, which had been warm and generous since my arrival, turned sour. "Well, then. I suppose I am the one to beg pardon. I thought you were someone else."

I did not catch her meaning at first—evidence, of course, of the very problem at hand—and I puzzled over her sudden chilliness. "Miss? Have I erred in another matter of etiquette?" I thought it was a clever allusion to our previous exchange on that topic, and I could not understand why my wit brought no smile.

I must have exhaled forcefully then, because she turned her head away. This I understood perfectly well, and I scrambled to lodge a protest. "You must understand! I am not that sort!"

"Is that so?"

"No! I mean—yes! It is so!" I reached out to put my hand on her arm, a gesture I meant to demonstrate my gentle essence, but which only irritated her further. She shrugged off my touch and retreated into the manner of the officious table servant.

"As I said, you shall have fowl. I trust you will take potatoes also." She stomped to the kitchen without waiting for an answer.

"The bumbler" still swirled in my head. The sensation, which had been lightness before, was now just lethargy. I collapsed into the chair. A place had been set there, and at the center of the table a lone taper was burning its final inch. A few minutes passed, and then the kitchen door swung open. Instead of the darling face I hoped for, the meal was delivered by the man with the greasy scalp. He walked up sideways and with his free hand removed the empty plate sitting before me. In a flash he swiveled round and deposited the steaming dish of chicken in its place. He grunted as the dish hit the tabletop, and then returned to the kitchen without further comment.

As I say, I was still well intoxicated, but I believed that in the instant between the taking of the empty plate and the deposit of the full one, I had seen something on the table—some scrap of paper, or perhaps the label from a bottle of wine. When the man was safely inside the kitchen, I lifted the plate.

It was a *carte de visite*, with writing on one side and a tintype picture on the reverse. I put the candle close and examined the card. The girl stared out from the card with a sad expression that had more in common with the last I had seen of her that evening than the first. She wore a dark gown, a tall hat, and she leaned slightly upon a parasol. I knew something of picture making, as I had been with Mother when she sat for one, and I recalled that the proprietor of the photograph studio in Lynchburg kept a variety of properties inside a trunk for his clients' use in costuming themselves . The parasol had the look of these: it was old- fashioned and overly fussy for this girl. Having her likeness in my hand gave a double sensation of excitement and shame: the former for the obvious reason, and the latter because I doubted, in view of my shameful behavior, if she meant for me to have it still.

I was so taken with the guilt of having stumbled upon her gift that I nearly forgot to read the inscription. Turning my back to the kitchen door, I held the card to the light and read: *Lorrie Wigfall, March 1862.* Then, across the bottom: *Mr. Muro—You have my name— AT LAST!*

I walked slowly through the mellowing evening, weaving back to my dormitory by a circuitous route that I hoped would cross the girl's path home. In the garden behind her uncle's pavilion, the fruit trees were but vague shapes against the sky, and the birds and bugs who had witnessed our exchange that morning lay abed in their nests for the night. How fast was this university life! How exhausting, that a man's heart should be lifted to such heights only to be dropped again within a single day!

Of course, at that point I had no right to complain of exhaustion. My course of study had not yet begun. There remained the hours upon hours stooping over the workbench, poking into the minutest crevices of the human corpse. The endless, punishing mathematical proofs. The rote memorization of so many chemical formulas I might have written a textbook by means of impressing my forehead on the page. Why—I had not even set foot inside the hospital! Exhaustion? I knew nothing of that yet!

# 22

"GOOD MORNING, GENTLEMEN. I am Dr. Cabell. The name rhymes with *rabble*. Now there shall be no reason for you to mispronounce it, ever." His voice was surprisingly shrill for a lecturer of such renown. I hardly expected such high- pitched emissions from so wide a gentleman. Indeed, it seemed as if a smaller, younger man was trapped within, and it was that tiny fellow who spoke when Dr. Cabell opened his mouth.

"The subject of this lecture is Physiology, encompassing all the current scientific knowledge available on that subject, along with my own professional observations thereunto. No time shall be wasted here on tangential diversions, as the base precepts are material enough for three terms on the subject, and we have no time to spare besides. I shall present my topics in the classical manner, as a series of queries, which I shall answer in full by the conclusion of each session. It will behoove you, gentlemen, to transcribe both queries and answers for private review, as this material will be obscure to you on first hearing."

With that understatement—I assure you it was understatement—Dr. Cabell began a barrage of information that would not cease for many months, and would never slacken in intensity; rather, my own capacity for absorbing knowledge would by turns increase, albeit more slowly than I should have liked, to match the rigor of the instruction.

"Now then, here is the first query: What is Science? Define the term and list the branches relevant to our pursuit." As he spoke, he puffed out his chest and clasped his hands behind his back. This did nothing to deepen the timbre of his voice but rather gave the impression of a cock pigeon strutting about the pit, clucking determinedly.

"Science is all attainable knowledge of natural bodies and phenomena," he recited. "For our purposes, we must make a distinction between that knowledge pertaining principally to the physical body and that of the mental state."

In the first minutes of lecture I filled five sheets in my notebook, front and back. My left forearm ached as if a hatchet had been brought to bear. I stole a glance around the gallery and discovered that some of my colleagues had scribbled their notes in a type of shorthand. I resolved to learn their system forthwith, as I knew that I could not persist in copying out such voluminous lectures verbatim.

As promised, Dr. Cabell proceeded immediately to the meat, as it were, of the lesson. In thirty minutes' time he had defined all the major systems of the body and was setting about making subdivisions therein.

"Now then, there are three types of fibrous tissue. The first of these is the white fibrous tissue, which connects those parts of the body where it is desirable to have extension or linear displacement. It is therefore some times called the connective tissue."

He presented his material without benefit of visual aids, but his descriptions of the various parts of the human organism—"The Economy," as he called it—were so detailed and precise that one took from his words a vivid picture of the subject. That is, one took from *subsequent and prolonged examination of one's lecture notes* the picture he intended. Cabell was right to implore his pupils to note his words, but he might have been more forceful. He did not in my opinion emphasize the absolute *necessity* of it. I took precisely nothing from that first session except for a half notebookful of scribblings, and I would spend the next several evenings in the careful transcription of these into something legible.

Basement membranes, mucous membranes, the lachrymal apparatus, medula oblongata, pons Varolii—this is the fever song of the humbled student of medicine. It is remarkable not so much for the many parts as for the whole—the endless spiraling litany of terms and appellations, of systems and illnesses, of pox and bowel disorders, of dosages and standard preparations, of surgical implements and curious procedures, of quinine and quarantine and a thousand other words that one is expected to retain within the ill- equipped gray folds of one brain. It is possible, of course. So are many other impossible feats: fifty- mile marches over frost- ridden hills; recitation from memory of Shakespeare's long and florid speeches; the childbirth of twins. There are many, many others. But the greatest triumphs come from unbearable pain and exertion, of which I had experienced neither in my short and comfortable youth. I thus was adrift in the most terrifying of new worlds, that of essential discomfort, and I feared that I hadn't the heart to stand it.

And that was only the first course! Also that day I attended the lecture on chemistry, taught by Professor Socrates Maupin, and that on the *Materia medica*, delivered by Dr. John Staige Davis. This latter I found quite pleasant by comparison with the other two, owing to the youthful air of the professor, who leavened his lectures with sprinklings of humor, if not plain good cheer.

In the University of Virginia, I had been prepared for a gentleman's finishing school, and I should admit that I was a bit disappointed to find it otherwise. If I were meant to study this much, I reasoned, it should at least be pursuant to a diploma from a first-rate college! Here, I had neither the diversion of a city like Philadelphia nor the catchet of a Northern education. Thus every hardship endured—every excruciating hour spent perplexed over some matter of biologic arcana, thumbing hopelessly through a dog- eared copy of Dunglison's *Medical Dictionary*—each of these tasks required, in a sense, twice the resolve they might have required of me had I been enrolled at a Northern medical school, assured by a long line of esteemed alumni of the value of my toil. Why, Dunglison himself, who had been lured to this very university by a wide- eyed American president who promised an "Academical Village" to rival Oxford and Cambridge—even that young scholar had stayed only the briefest term in Charlottesville before departing for Philadelphia, which is where he made his name.

Of course, times were different then. Pennsylvania and Virginia were two organs of the same being; Dunglison's transit would have been limited only by the schedule of coaches between them. Me, I could not have traveled to Philadelphia even with a signed letter of appointment from Dr. Samuel Gross.

# 23

AS WAS MY ROUTINE—and that of every college man, whether he admits it or not—I went to the post office several times a day. The postmaster's boy delivered mail directly to our dormitories each noon, but as that meant waiting nearly twenty- four hours to receive the produce of the previous evening's post, I made it a habit to stop by the post office before breakfast and to read my mail on the steps of the Rotunda.

On this morning, my lap was speckled with my mother's lilac sealing wax. Her letter began with the usual trivia: gossip from church, the status of her late- summer garden, &c. Then came a curious passage:

> *There has been also a changing of the guard, so to*
> *speak, at the Woolery. Your father's foreman, Mr.*
> *Stokes (whom you know), has given notice that he*
> *shall vacate within the week, thereupon to take up with*
> *our Navy, a move he claims to have been considering*
> *for some time. As you might imagine, this news pleased*
> *me considerably, as I have never favored Mr. Stokes.*
> *However, your father is quite upset, considering*
> *Stokes's late successes with the new Negroes, whom*

*he has fashioned into a formidable labor force much to everyone's surprise.*

*Your father being the resourceful fellow he is, I am not concerned in the least over the continuity of production at the Mill. In fact, he has confided in me that he intends to ask your Cousin Sam to take over the responsibilities of foreman and overseer in Mr. Stokes's absence. Sam has lately been fitted with a false leg of remarkable artifice and his mobility is vastly improved just in the weeks since you left us!*

I could not have been more pleased by this news—notwithstanding the loss of Mr. Stokes, whom I had admired. I recognized that the timing could not have been better for my cousin. He was in need of some occupation to keep his mind from the miserable thoughts he was prone to dwell upon. And with Father's tutelage, I had no doubt that he would become a fine foreman. Military training, after all, was supposed to be an excellent education for a career in business.

Allowing my mind to wander, I envisioned Sam leading the Bedford Woolery to new heights. And when the time was right, I assumed he and Parthenia would be married. Thus the void I had created would be filled, and I would be free to follow my studies wherever they might lead me. Perhaps the North—perhaps even overseas.

The Lawn at that hour belonged to the crows, who were arrayed across the grassy terraces like tottering soldiers, in platoons of six or eight, nipping at the ground after grubs. From my vantage on the Rotunda's top step, I admired the view of the university's grounds, noting how the first soft rays of day seemed to burrow under the morning fog, lifting it off the ground as if by force. On my right, a hundred yards off, the clerestory windows of the Anatomical Theatre reflected the morning sun.

I was pulled from this reverie by the thundering of hooves. Two riders exploded through the brick portal at the northwest corner of the Lawn. They were military men, riding under a weathered Southern Cross. When they reached the centermost grass terrace, one man whistled and the two horses reared back. The other man drew a bugle from his saddlebag and blew a coarse reveille.

"Gentlemen!" the first soldier cried. "Hear, hear! General Lee has struck a victory for our side! Yesterday, in Maryland! Wake up, gents! There has been a great victory at Sharpsburg!"

And so on he went, giving the news in snatches. General Lee—or "Uncle Robert," as the soldier called him—had faced up a Yankee force of far greater number and inflicted carnage such as the cowardly Yanks had never seen! A nearby creek, the Antietam, ran red with the blood of Yankees! Our boys would march on Washington next! Long live the Confederate States! Long live our Commonwealth!

One by one, the black doors of the dormitories opened up, and sleepy students appeared there rubbing their eyes. Some rushed back to their rooms, upon realizing the news, to retrieve pistols for firing into the air. Soon the whole Grounds was alive with gunfire and shouting—this even before the sun had cleared the trees—and a rumor began to circulate that all lectures that day had been canceled in celebration.

This last proved false, as the esteemed Dr. Maupin, chair of the faculty senate, stood at the balcony of his pavilion, looking no less pleased at the news than his milling charges below, only to announce, "What better reason to work our minds than a glorious victory for our cause?" Then, in a more subdued tone: "Lectures will proceed as scheduled. Good day."

I returned to the dormitory late that afternoon. There I made the surprising discovery that my truant roommate, Braxton Baucom, had been along, leaving me a message of sorts. He had chosen a suit of clothes from his collection—a pair of charcoal wool trousers and a matching waistcoat alongside a blouse of soft cotton linen. He had also laid out a number of accessories, including the tall silk hat I had so admired. At the head of the clothing—which was arranged in the shape of a man along the length of the mattress—there was a note, which read thus: *Only a suggestion! (Do come by the house tonight, as we are hosting an Exclusive Group.) Your friend, B.B.*

# 24

"MR. MURO? WHY, I hardly recognized you!"

In the excitement of dressing for B.B.'s party, I had neglected to prepare for an encounter with Miss Lorrie Wigfall. I had neither seen nor heard from her since embarrassing myself, and as I stepped into the Hotel, it occurred to me that I should not even rightly know her name, as I had come across her *carte* only surreptitiously.

She wore the usual white apron and her hair was pulled back to a tight chignon, which cleared her face to accept the gentle evening light from the window. The thought of her hair made me remember my own. During my dressing proceedings, I had applied an unwise dose of B.B.'s citrus pomade and had spent the better part of an hour trying to wipe it out with a hand towel. Ultimately I heeded B.B.'s suggestion and wore the hat.

I pulled my hand down from the brim of the hat, where it had snapped up by rote, in preparation to bow. "It is the same fellow," I said, unsure whether to omit mention of my appearance or to play it for a laugh. I chose the former, with knowledge that I might fall back on the latter if the conversation should become uncomfortable.

As it turned out, Miss Lorrie wasted no words on pleasantries, nor held her tongue. "The change suits you well, I think." Her voice betrayed no hint of irony, and she meant none. She led me to a table opposite a young gentleman whose lips—whether due to a scoliotic posture or an unusually short stature, I do not know —hovered so close to his meal that he might have siphoned the soup from the bowl without help of any utensils whatsoever. Miss Lorrie held out her hand to the man and introduced us. "Mr. Gerald Hankins," she said, "do you know Mr. Muro?"

The man raised his head—or rather, *swiveled it,* like a globe in a stand—and said, "I do not believe we've met. A pleasure, sir." He returned to his soup.

"As you can see, we have an onion soup this evening. We had also a quantity of fresh rye bread, but all that is gone now. You should really come earlier to supper, Mr. Muro."

"I aim to do that precisely," I said. "But you see, miss—I am quite busy in my studies, and I often find myself distracted in heavy concentration."

"Oh," she said. "Tell me, what are you studying?"

"That is a fine question. You see, I am studying a number of subjects. There is Chemistry, of course, with Professor Maupin. I'm told he is a fine man, though I hardly know him yet. There are other courses as well."

Miss Lorrie propped her hand on one hip. "Yes, such as?"

"Such as Physiology, for one. Ah—of course! You must know that subject. Dr. Cabell is your uncle, if I am not mistaken. Did you not say it the other day in the garden?"

"You shall be a doctor, then."

"That's right."

"It has served my uncle well, that profession, though of course I have my private doubts."

"Naturally," I said. "And you rightly should. But if you'll pardon my effusion, I should say that I stand in awe of your uncle. He is a paragon for young men such as myself."

Miss Lorrie was unmoved by my praise. "Indeed—or so goes the line on him."

"Do you disagree?"

"To be honest, sir, I know nothing of my uncle's professional reputation, nor do I care a whiff to have it relayed to me by young men in his thrall. If you'll excuse me—" And she dashed off, disappearing between the swinging doors of the kitchen.

I sat down in my place. The gentleman opposite, Mr. Hankins, had by this point drained his bowl of soup and was busily wiping it clean with a crust of the fabled rye bread.

"She's a live cap, that girl," he said, with a look of genial amazement that belied no prurient interest in her, but only the fawning regard one gives a precocious brother or sister.

My own interest in Miss Lorrie was less innocent, although I was no less amused by her spirit. Long moments after her exit through the swinging doors, my arteries pumped with residual excitement. To be honest, this worried me. How was I expected to comport myself with good manners if I lost all sense of comportment in her presence?

It was, in short, thrilling.

Miss Lorrie returned with my soup and a half loaf of bread, which she held aloft as she set down the bowl. "You are in luck, Mr. Muro," she said, setting the loaf next to the spoon. "The cook found it for you, in the back of the oven or something like that." She gave a knowing smile.

"Tell me," I said, "have you any plans this evening? After your work here is through?"

She might have been surprised at the query, which was plainly an invitation—though to what she must not have known—but she did not betray it in the least. Instead, she said, in the way she might have answered the question of how she favored her tea, "I do, in fact. It is most considerate of you to ask, but here is a word of advice: in the future, you might do well to request my company in further advance of the occasion."

"You'll forgive me, but you see it only just occurred to me—"

"That is the problem precisely."

"I know it! That is—you see, I am not much experienced at this sort of thing."

"Which is why I'm offering you this advice."

"And I thank you for it."

"You are most welcome."

There was a bit of silence then, during which I was utterly baffled as to how to proceed. Miss Lorrie held my gaze as if she expected something more—but I did not have the faintest idea what that might be. She had already turned down my invitation for the evening. Perhaps she anticipated another invitation? I was in no position to extend such a thing just then. I would have to consult a calendar, find a suitable event, make the necessary arrangements for transportation, &c, &c.

"Well—I suppose I shall eat now?"

Miss Lorrie lowered her gaze. "Very well. Is that all, sir?"

She meant, ostensibly, the food.

"I shall make a plan," I said. "And I will contact you at a proper interval next time."

Her eyes opened wide. "Ah—very well!" Her poise, that curious mode of separation between us, immediately dropped away, and I saw for the first time the young girl underneath. Almost as quickly, she regained herself and went on, soberly, "I shall look forward to your bid."

# 25

THE TOWN OF CHARLOTTESVILLE is just a scant mile east of the University, at the opposite end of Main Street. On the way to B.B.'s town house, I passed a number of buildings on both sides of the road. The largest among these was a two- story structure surrounded by a low, thick, mud- plastered wall. There were infirm soldiers milling about on the front steps, propped up on an assortment of canes and crutches, taking profit from the clear evening air.

A portly gentleman walked out the front door and descended the steps to his horse. Though it was dark, I recognized the side- whiskers right away: it was Dr. Cabell. He stopped when he saw me and nodded a hesitant hello—not because he knew me, for we had not been introduced, but on account of my fancy dress. "Evening, sir," I said.

Cabell did not respond, but instead ascended the horse with the assistance of a Negro servant. Once he was in the saddle, the doctor's left side was plain to the gibbous moon, and I saw upon his trousers a quantity of blood and other smeared viscera.

I fought the urge to retch. I knew that I had to get comfortable with the sight of gore, for the bloody smock would be my uniform soon enough. Of what use is a doctor, I considered, who recoils at the sight of entrails? I resolved to harden my senses. Without that I would fail, and all my good intentions would be exposed as youthful bluster.

Cabell slapped the reins and the horse turned around. He did not speak to me as he passed, but I thought I detected a smile at the corner of his mouth. I might have imagined it, but I have reason to believe not, as you will see later. I have never felt so small, nor so cowed as by the task of purposefully dulling my natural impulses. I made excuses for myself as I continued down the muddy street: What was so lovely about blood, anyhow? And why hadn't Dr. Cabell changed his trousers before going out in public? Did he not owe it to the community to shield such ugliness?

I knew the answers. Or rather, I knew there were none. There was nothing *lovely*, or even *tolerable*, about spending eight hours on one's feet sewing up the hasty work of harried field surgeons. Dr. Cabell had been on the job continuously, with only brief snatches of sleep, since the trains had started rolling in from Maryland. He would be back, in fact, before the sun rose again. That he would think of clothes at a time like this was preposterous.

And then along I strolled, all shiny and silky. How could he not have been amused?

# 26

B.B.'S HOUSE GLOWED like a Chinese lantern on the otherwise dark, somber street. I crept into the front parlor unnoticed until a fellow in a fashionable coat, buttoned almost to his chin, put out his hand to me and called for a fresh glass. "Sir!" he cried. "I don't believe we're acquainted. I'm Knight." His voice was mellow, in the manner of the far- Southern states, lacking the odd, pinched vowels of the Virginia dialect. He reached up and plucked the hat off my head, addressing the group of young gentlemen gathered around a bowl of fizzing red punch. "Say, fellows, what do you think of that?"

Here the chatter in the parlor ceased, and the attentions of all present turned on me. My scalp itched from the pomade.

This Knight walked a circle around me, keeping my hat under his arm. "The suit, I must say, is top- notch . . . Can we agree on that, fellows?"

Two or three of the observers grunted assent.

"No question there. Excellent taste in clothes. It's the *hair* that gives me pause."

From the doorway a voice chided, "Return the hat. Or I shall force you."

B.B. pushed his way through to the front and stood before the fellow. Not two inches of air floated between their breasts.

"I suppose you mean this hat?" Knight said.

"That very one."

"Well, this is your house. I must oblige." And suddenly Knight tossed the hat (with a quick flip of the wrist as if playing quoits) into the punch bowl. The beautiful silk sank gently into the red fizz.

Before Knight had even recoiled from the toss, B.B. was upon him. He landed a blow upon the face and another to the gut. The room had not yet erupted into noise, and B.B.'s fists were heard to give a dead *thump* upon impact. Knight staggered but quickly regained himself. He was a heavy man, well over two hundred pounds, and he lowered his shoulder into my roommate's chest.

By this point, of course, the gentlemen in the room had cleared space for the pugilists and stood on the circumference barking encouragements to either or both. B.B. showed the skills of a trained wrestler, compensating for his disadvantage in weight by clever holds that used leverage to bring excruciating pain with very little force exerted. Within a minute, he had his knee on Knight's throat. Knight opened and closed his mouth, making a choking noise to indicate that he could not breathe.

"You are a bastard!" B.B. yelled to him. "You are a fool. Say it!" He eased off Knight's throat so that he could reply.

"Yes, you're right," Knight stammered, coughing and turning his head to spit out a tooth, which skittered along the hardwood floor among the onlookers' boot soles. "I am everything you say." He made to get up, but B.B. slugged him again, this time square on the nose. This caused a profusion of shining blood to erupt from one nostril.

"And what else?" B.B. prompted, pressing his knee into Knight's chest to keep him down.

Knight choked out the words, "You . . . are . . . a *god among men*."

B.B. stood up. "Much better," he said.

The gentlemen in the room chuckled. Knight pulled himself together and B.B. helped him to his feet. They shook in reconciliation, and though they did not smile, each clasped the other's elbow with his free hand.

Several women had appeared at the entrance of the room, presumably following the noise of the scuffle. I recognized a face among them, and it took me a moment to realize that it belonged to Miss Lorrie Wigfall. Her dress featured an unusually high collar, so that her head sat atop it like a globe on a pedestal. She was diked furthermore in a fanciful hat with a peacock plume. Her face was powdered as white as a porcelain doll's.

Our glances met, and I went to her, picking my way carefully through the throng.

"Mr. Muro!" Lorrie chirped. "I had not expected to see you here!"

"I should say the same for you."

"Do you know Miss Harriette Willson?" She turned to the girl at her side.

"I'm afraid not," I said. Miss Harriette was a homely girl with an abundance of cheek flesh that gave her the look of a portly catfish. "Delighted," I said, taking her hand.

"Mr. Muro is a student at the University," Lorrie explained. "A doctor, in fact."

"Oh—how lovely!" crooned Miss Harriette. "How wonderfully *useful* you must be!"

"I've only just begun at it. It will be some time before I am of any use, I'm afraid."

"Oh, no. I'm sure you are quite clever already." She turned to Miss Lorrie, as if the latter might confirm it, and thus lay the matter to rest.

"We know each other from the dining hall," Lorrie said.

Miss Harriette screwed up her face. "Oh, that *dreadful* place! For truth, Lorrie, I cannot *fathom* why you go there."

Miss Lorrie replied quite plainly, "I have explained it to you."

"Yes, but that is a silly notion . . ." Miss Harriette turned in appeal to me. "Surely you agree, sir, that it is unwise for a lady to work? And to work as she does, especially!"

I nodded instinctively, but the question was a delicate one, and felt that I should consider my reply before speaking. Indeed, I had been puzzled from the start by the sight of Miss Lorrie in that place, but since I had become accustomed to it, I no longer thought it odd. Of course, in a year's time hardly anyone in Virginia would look askance at a lady working in a public kitchen. On the contrary, it would be so regular that the opposite posture, the lady of leisure, would seem an anomaly.

"I can't speak for the other fellows," I said, "but I rather enjoy her company there."

"Company? It's hardly *company* when she's wearing an apron."

There was at that time a school of thought called psychogenesis, which stated that temperament follows directly from countenance. Thus a beautiful girl would be necessarily sweet, a homely one sour, and so on. I never cared much for the theory, as the evidence purporting to support it was largely circumstantial. Nevertheless, it is hard to refute cases such as that of Miss Harriette Willson. How such a dog-faced girl could behave so appallingly, when she should have been doing every thing in her power to appear pleasant, was beyond my comprehension. It wanted, truly, for a scientific explanation.

Ignoring her friend's abuse, Lorrie turned to me and said, "I appreciate your company, sir, as well." We shared a glance then, which gave me reason to believe that she had not only forgiven my drunken episode but perhaps even forgotten it. Her eyes showed a warmth in their batting that I interpreted as real interest.

The moment was interrupted, of course, by Miss Harriette: "But, you are acting as scullery maid! I should like to hear you defend that choice. And if, as you say, you have done so already, I should like to hear it again."

"Very well," said Miss Lorrie. "But you must promise to drop all talk of this afterward."

"Fine."

"As you know, my father is in the field with his regiment." Then, to me in particular, as if the fact meant more to me than it should to her girlfriend, she added, "He is with General Hood, you see, in the Texas Brigade. Owing to his rank he was given the opportunity to carry his family with him, but naturally he refused. He is a gentle man, my father. You will see."

The notion of a day when I might meet this lovely girl's father made my heart beat faster.

"Nonetheless my mother refused to let him come to Virginia without us, and so we made the trip together. We are from Galveston, you see. Have I told you we are from Galveston?"

In fact, she had not yet told me her name—not properly, anyway.

"At any rate, Mother is lodged near him, though not in the encampment itself. Those were Father's terms. And I am staying with Auntie and Uncle, as you know."

Miss Harriette interrupted, again: "You might do all of that without so much as *touching* a soiled dish, my dear."

"Indeed I might. And I might be locked up in a windowless room, even. So much the more ladylike, am I correct?"

"You will do as you please."

"Obviously."

"And far be it from me to criticize your service to our cause, et cetera, et cetera . . ."

"Indeed—so now you see."

"Ach!" Miss Harriette wrinkled her mouth into a pout that, if her normal countenance resembled a catfish, can only be described as a *lamprey*. Fortunately, she took the opportunity to leave us, scurrying off to the join the ladies in the other room.

"So," I said, "she is a friend of yours?"

Miss Lorrie thought about it for a moment, then said, "For lack of a better word, yes: we are friends. In truth, her mother is a friend of my aunt's."

I had all the while been conceiving, in my head, a plan for the outing I had promised her. It would begin with a carriage ride through the pass the stagecoach had traversed on the way into Charlottesville, where the shimmering rooftops of the town had so captured my fancy. Thereupon I would set a picnic. The provenance of the carriage and the food for the picnic remained to be worked out, but I had no doubt that it would be possible. As long as I had her interest, anything seemed possible.

"I have been thinking," I began to say, "about our topic last time— that is, if you'll remember. Well, what I mean to say—"

Her face bore a gentle smile. "You mean to say what, exactly?"

"Are you free next weekend? Perhaps, on Saturday afternoon?"

Just as she opened her mouth to respond—in the affirmative, oh God, how I hoped it would be that—I felt a weight across my shoulders from an arm draped there. I turned to see my roommate, his bloodied face wiped clean, but not so clean that one might miss the evidence of his toil. He held out two fresh glasses of punch.

"Bully for you, Muro, starting that mess with Knight. A right good time we had, I'd say. Did you happen to catch any of it, Miss Wigfall?"

"Fortunately, Mr. Baucom, I did not."

"Ah, that's too bad. Muro saw it—tell her."

I was stunned. "I did not realize you were acquainted."

"Ha! She and I go way back. What is it now, a week? Two?"

"We met at church," Lorrie said. And then, with eyes narrowing to slits, "I have not seen you there recently."

"I haven't been."

"And why is that, sir?"

"Why, I got what I went for!"

"And what was that?" Lorrie used a strange tone with him that I could not figure out. It was disapproving, to be sure, but there was something else. A bit of teasing, perhaps. From what I knew of B.B., I would not have expected her to tolerate him. But there they were, talking.

B.B. feigned embarrassment. "I should rightly admit, Miss Wigfall, that I went to church to make the acquaintance of young ladies like yourself, thereby to make the right mix at a party such as this. You'll forgive me if I have offended your sensibility."

Miss Lorrie affected a stiff hauteur but did not blush as one might have expected. She simply looked down her fine nose at B.B. and waited for him to say more.

"Hey- o, then," said B.B., never missing a beat. "John Muro, meet Lorrie Wigfall."

"We met at the dining hall," I said.

"Ah, yes, now I remember. In church, you said you worked in a kitchen."

"It is not the kitchen, properly," I interjected, amazed by how defensive it sounded.

"No matter," said BB, "we must sacrifice, you know. Without bitterest resolve, we shan't hope to triumph, at least not easily." This he relayed not exactly to Lorrie and me, but to the room, which had emptied considerably since the conclusion of the fight. A lone gentleman lingered at the punch bowl; all others had gone to join the ladies in the drawing room.

# THE DISAGREEMENT

"I hope you have enjoyed yourselves thus far," said our host, stepping down from his soapbox. "We aim for enjoyment here, first and foremost. I say pleasure first—and all other things after it! Though I must say the trials of the state have risen considerably as a lively topic around here. But enough of that for one evening, eh? On with it!"

# 27

THE MORNING AFTER B.B.'S house party—a Saturday morning—I took my seat in the Anatomical Theatre at half past seven, alone but for the presence of the medical school's janitor and custodian, a certain Negro called Roddick. He was a freeman, though I doubted he was any happier in his freedom than his forebears had been in bondage. He had a coal black complexion that lightened only under his eyes, where the soft skin had loosened with age and lost some of its pigment. He was forever sweeping the rows in the viewing gallery, or stretching atop a ladder to reach the high windows, or in the basement laboratory boiling the remnants of dissection. This last duty, as I understood it, had previously been carried out by the Professor of Anatomy himself, but with hospital duty taking every spare minute of Dr. Cabell's time, he had delegated it to the custodian.

On this morning I heard Roddick's dull, thudding footfalls on the rear staircase, which was the main thoroughfare between the viewing gallery and the basement. The aforementioned laboratories were located just under the sloped gallery seats, so that their ceilings were slanted on the diagonal from one wall to the other. At the shorter wall, only the most diminutive students might crouch at their work, so that area was generally given over to storage.

Roddick's footsteps followed slowly one upon the next as he climbed the stairs. It was precisely the tempo, it struck me, of a man's heartbeat at rest. Eventually Roddick reached the landing behind the topmost row of seats. He was shouldering a burden, wrapped in gray cloth, about the size of a large sack of rice. Roddick saw me then, and called out, "Be much obliged if you could help me, sir." His breath came with great effort, and he seemed to shudder under the weight. Though I never thought twice about helping him, I was surprised by the request; he had never spoken more than two words to me, and then just in salutation.

"I'll be right there." I folded up my notebook and raced up the stairs, gaining the landing in just a few bounds.

"'Preciate it," he said. "How 'bout you take that right there?" With his eyes he indicated the bottom end of the sack. They were a sight, his eyes—the whites so long shot with drink as to be tinted permanently brown. Indeed, the odor of rye hung around him like a fog.

I bent down to the floor to seize my end of the burden, but as I reached to grab it, the cloth fell to the side, and I saw before me a naked human foot. The skin was the same smoky black as Roddick's, and for a moment I was deceived in thinking that the janitor's foot had somehow slipped out of its boot and presented itself.

Mr. Roddick noted my surprise and said, "You knowed him, did you?" Again he changed his grip, this time allowing the burden—the *body*, rather—to slip downward so that the exposed foot touched the oak planks of the landing. The black ankle did not pivot upon touching down as it would have in life, but instead held the foot at full extension, the gnarled and callused toes pointing straight as a ballet dancer's.

"Nah, I reckon you ain't knowed him. You from Richmond way?"

He narrowed his eyes as if trying to place me. "I'm Roddick, by the way."

"John Muro," I said. "From Lynchburg."

"Fine, fine. So you ain't knowed this fella." He heaved the shrouded body onto his chest, leaning back for balance. Roddick's physique was not exceptional, but he had the hard, knotted muscles of a laborer. "This here gent'man come to us from the potter's field in Richmond. Don't got no fillings left in his teeth or nothing like that. No shoes, nothing. But y'all don't need none of that anyhow, right?" He chuckled again—a smarmy, self- congratulatory laugh that made me resent him because it suggested that he, Roddick, knew what went on in the Anatomical Theatre, and it was nothing a man should feel proud of.

I didn't answer, but rather bent down again to lift the foot end of the body. I expected it to be unwieldy, to crumple like a sack of rice, but the cadaver tilted up like a board. I wrapped the ankles with the sheet.

"Easy now," Roddick warned as I tapped my foot behind me in search of the aisle staircase. I found it and took an uneasy step backward. "Ten dollars Doc Cabell paid for this fella," Roddick said. "Now, I know y'all's got standards and so forth, such and such an age when died and so forth, but I know at least a dozen niggers'd be mighty glad to get that much for they sorry old selves. Ha- ha- ha!"

The progress down the aisle was slow, and though it couldn't have been more than twenty steps altogether, Roddick insisted on resting halfway. "I told Doc Cabell, I said, 'Doc, I know my old lady want to have me buried in the churchyard when I pass, but I tell you, nobody at the church going to pay her ten dollars for these old bones. You got my word,' I said, 'this body is yours.'"

We reached the pit, where an examination table had already been wheeled out. On the count of three, we hoisted the body onto the table, where it settled with a thump like a saddle slapped upon a horse's back.

"What did he say?" I said. "Dr. Cabell—did he accept your offer?"

"He said, 'Mis' Roddick, we'd be mighty glad to have you.'"

"Not precisely," said a voice behind me. Dr. Cabell stood on the stage, bearing a case of surgical tools under his right arm. He looked much the same as he had the night before, though he had of course changed the bloodied trousers. The continued deprivation of sleep had changed the flesh underneath his eyes to horrid purple welts, and his swollen midsection, straining the buttons on his waistcoat, suggested that the old doctor was compensating for the lack of one creature comfort with another. His snowy side- whiskers caught the light from the high windows as he tipped his head back to sneeze. "What I told Mr. Roddick," he said, wiping his nose with a pocket handkerchief, "is that we have appreciated his service very much over the years, but that we must decline his generous offer on the grounds that I should not prefer to go against the wishes of his family." Cabell folded the handkerchief and stowed it away in his vest pocket. After a moment's pause, he turned to me. "Mr. Muro, is it?"

"Yes sir," I said, surprised that he knew my name. Other than the brief encounter outside the hospital, we had met but once, during second week of lectures, when at the end of one session I stood in line to hand him my answers to an impromptu examination he had administered on the lymphatic system.

"I have been meaning to see you, Muro, but of course we've been so busy at the hospital of late."

"I understand, sir."

"But you couldn't possibly."

"I only meant that I saw the trains arriving—"

"Yes, the trains. Well. I have a proposition for you, and I want you to listen closely. We have an urgent need at the hospital for a type of clerk, someone who can transcribe statements from myself and Dr. Davis and post them to Richmond. It would require that you be present at each of our rounds, morning and evening, and that your work be accurate beyond any standard you may have followed hitherto."

It was too good to be true. I struggled to contain my joy! "Sir," I queried, "may I ask whether this offer follows from the results of the recent examination? Have I scored at the top?"

"On the contrary," he said. "You scored last in the class."

I did not know what to say.

"Let me explain something, son. All of the students in our curriculum must serve in some capacity at the hospital—the situation simply demands it—but I felt that you, amongst every one, had better get started right away. This clerking duty should provide an opportunity for you to acquaint yourself with the medical vocabulary in a clinical setting, which as I say all students will have to learn eventually, but which may require extra effort in your case." He paused and stroked his chin. "I wish I had thought of this sooner, as it might have helped previous stragglers. But then again, I've not previously had such a *severe* case . . . From whence do you come to us, Mr. Muro?"

The knot in my throat was such that I could not speak. Luckily Roddick piped up, "Round Lynchburg way, Doc."

Cabell looked to the janitor and said, "Have you filled the basins yet, Roddick?"

"No suh," he said, and thumped back up the aisle stairs. There were other students in the gallery seats by then, it being nearly the appointed hour for the lecture. I felt embarrassed to be standing with Dr. Cabell in view of these others, even though they had no idea of our topic.

"Do you know the Delevan Building, on Main Street?" It was clear that Cabell sought to end our exchange, as he was already busy arranging his instruments upon the foldout wing of the examination table. "It is the one with the mud wall surrounding—why, I saw you walking there just last night. It was you, was it not?"

I thought I detected a twinkle in his eye.

"Yes sir."

"Very well. I shall see you there on Monday morning. Six sharp." He waved me off, and I returned to my seat in the gallery. I made busy with my notes, but the words on the page were meaningless, the scribblings of an alien hand.

# 28

"TAKE THIS DOWN verbatim, Muro," Cabell said while continuing to walk briskly down the hall. We had already traversed what I had assumed to be the entirety of the building, eight wards of fifty beds apiece—a total of four hundred men in all stages and varieties of illness, from measles to syphilis. I was surprised at the low proportion of soldiers presenting battle wounds, relative to the ones sick of other illnesses, but as we moved from wards housing longer- term patients to the ones full of recent arrivals, it became clear that proportion of wounded was rising. It appeared that the victory at Sharpsburg—so roundly celebrated by us—had been less of a rout than was previously thought by our partisans, and perhaps a Pyrrhic victory at best.

Cabell cleared his throat and began the dictation. "Dispatch from Charlottesville General Hospital, nine September. My dear Dr. Moore . . ."

Dr. S. P. Moore was the Surgeon- General of the Confederate States and a figure of some controversy in our hospital, first because what meager funds the Richmond government saw fit to appropriate us were disbursed through him; but also because Dr. Moore had been Dr. Cabell's chief academic rival in the years before secession, and it was rumored that Cabell himself had expressed interest in the post of Surgeon- General before it became clear that President Jefferson Davis favored the milder and less controversial Dr. Moore.

In the manner common among professional men at odds, Dr. Cabell filled his correspondence with the most effusive praise for his rival. "Many thanks for your foresight, sir, in sending your deputy, the useful Dr. Twittering, to our facility the tenth of last month. His suggestions for improving the efficiency of our cleaning and dietary operations were surely your own, as they evidenced the logic of a superior intellect . . ."

Every day I posted this dispatch to the Surgeon- General's office in Richmond, containing the daily accounting of admittances, discharges, and so on required by regulations.

"Now then, begin afresh. Put this down: 'My Dearest Surgeon- General, et cetera. In your dispatch to the directors of the various general hospitals you stated that you should like to be apprised of any shortages in our pharmacy not just after but rather in due time before any such shortages occur. Thus I shall take this opportunity to account for you the quantities of various preparations of which we are in short supply . . .'"

Here the doctor paused his walk and turned. "Are you with me, Muro?"

"Yes sir," I said, pressing my notebook against the wall to make a correction. I read back, ". . . various preparations of which we are in short supply."

"Very well. 'I have consulted this morning with the steward, and we have at present sixteen ounces magnesia, two corked bottles iodinum—those being the six- ounce bottles sent most recently, not the more useful one- ounce vials, which you understand haven't the economy of the larger bottles, but which are more easily dispensed and circumvent, through their small capacity, the increased risk of spillage inherent in the tall bottles . . .'"

I scribbled furiously, straining to transcribe the unfamiliar words and phrases. "Excuse me, sir," I said. "Could you repeat the name of the last preparation?"

"Iodinum."

Just then a nurse approached and informed Dr. Cabell that a patient in the southwest ward on the first story was breathing irregularly and had disgorged an unusual quantity of brown phlegm from his throat. Cabell calmly replied that he would attend in a moment. He urged the nurse to wait for him below, then turned to me.

"How is your Latin, son?"

"Not bad, sir." In fact, languages had always been my weakest subject. I had hoped to avoid them by studying science.

"Excellent. You will have no trouble, then, with this chore. Go to the dispensary and ask the steward to list you the current quantities of all *materia* for which our present quantity falls short of the standard supply. Copy these out, apply an appropriate salutation, and affix my seal. Do you understand?"

"Certainly, sir. If you might point me toward the dispensary, though—" But Cabell was turned already and ambling rather rapidly down the hall. Dr. Cabell's habit of vagueness, or as a generous man would call it, *incomplete instruction*, would come to annoy me in my tenure at the hospital, but at that early date I had no reason to believe the omission was anything but a consequence of his harried state, and certainly not a general trait of his character.

I set about to find the nearest nurse to ask directions to the dispensary. There was no one in the hall at present, so I ducked into the nearest ward room, the last I had visited with Dr. Cabell on his rounds, and the most pleasant of the eight. The ward was perhaps ten yards deep and five wide, and it sat on the corner of the hospital building. As it was still warm outside—September is often the hottest of the twelve months in our section of Virginia—each window was propped wide for circulation.

Despite this, the air in the ward was rank beyond all scales of measure—worse than an ordinary gentleman is likely to encounter anywhere in his daily life except by the garbage heap on the steamiest day of summer. My first breath in the room annoyed my nostrils as if a solution of sulfur had been applied with a clyster syringe. I questioned my earlier assessment of the ward and realized that my relative favor of it should be taken as a dire indemnification of the seven others! I resolved to be short in my quest.

"Excuse me," I called to a woman bent over the nearest cot (these were laid out in two rows, against the walls, with a narrow aisle down the center). The woman, one of the scores of Negroes who attended patients at the Delevan, took a sponge from under an emaciated soldier's arm and wrung it into a tin bowl between her feet.

"Sir?" she said. She held the sponge under the water for moment and then withdrew it, dripping.

"I was hoping you might direct me to the dispensary. Dr. Cabell has dispatched me there on an errand, you see, but then he was called away."

"You a student?"

"Of three weeks now," I said.

The woman's eyes widened and she gave a soundless laugh. "Be seeing you around, then."

"I suppose you will," I said, though I saw nothing funny about it.

The woman returned the sponge to the patient's flank. The soldier, who from the sparseness of his beard looked to be my age or even younger, did not react in any way, but simply stared into the nurse's face, as he had done throughout my exchange with her. "Dispensary is down in the basement, Doc," she said, now fully returned to her work.

I brightened at the title, for this was the first time anyone had applied it to me. It is curious—the appellations given to professional gentlemen (*Doctor, Reverend, Esquire*, and so forth) are meant, as best I can tell, to call out a useful fellow from among the general population, for instance if a lady faints at the opera, and her companions might seek to summon Dr. Such- and- Such, who is seated with his wife two rows back. Just as often, however, they serve as marks of scorn, and engender distrust among those we purport to serve.

As I leapt down the stairs. I had a warmth within me such as I had experienced only one other time in my life—at my grandparents' farm in Appomattox, upon drinking cream from a bucket still hot from the cow. It would be many years before my title would bring me anything close to the special satisfaction I enjoyed that day. With knowledge, you see, comes disappointment, and I had yet but the briefest taste of either.

# 29

THE HOSPITAL'S STEWARD was a long-faced white man named Clarkson, who inhabited a tiny laboratory in the basement of the Delevan. The room was not larger than a broom closet, but it was well lighted from a high casement window. As steward, Clarkson was responsible for preparing any concoctions prescribed by the hospital's doctors, and for the good maintenance of the stocks of raw ingredients used to make up the same. He sat on a stool behind the lower half of a Dutch door, alone with his thoughts between requests.

I walked up to the window and introduced myself. "I've come on an errand from Dr. Cabell," I said.

This news did not faze Mr. Clarkson in the least. I remember that he had the uncanny ability to roll his eyes independently so that when his attention turned he ventured at first only one eyeball—that being the most conservative use of energy—and only if the subject was sufficiently compelling would he roll over the other. Even the most lurid and fascinating happening would have required several seconds for his two eyes to line up. It was like conversing with a flounder.

"What can I do for you, Mr. Muro?" he drawled.

I referred to my notes. "Dr. Cabell requires an accounting of all potions."

"Potions, sir?"

"The compounds you keep here. Powders and decoctions and such."

He rolled away the left eye. "Mr. Muro," he said slowly, "the ingredients you see behind me are hardly *potions*, if by that you mean they bear some magical property."

"Forgive me, sir. I did not know the proper name."

"We ought not speak of magic, out of respect for the plants whose life energy went into the creation of these compounds. No sir, what you see here is *life*. Be it powdered or whole, in aqua or alcohol, this is the very stuff." Despite the appearance of indolence, Clarkson was an astute chemist, and he rightly earned the praise of every physician who ordered his preparations.

"Might you tell me, then, which are running low?" I queried. "That is, which ingredients are below the standard supply level?"

Clarkson's left eye snapped back. "Below the standard supply, you say? That would be all of them."

I chose that moment to make a rough estimation of the number of jars on the shelves. There might have been two hundred.

"If Dr. Cabell means for me to read you the entire supply table," Clarkson said, "I would be happy to do so. However, we might more profitably employ the time on some other thing." I paused to consider what other *thing* he had in mind. Sleep, perhaps—or just staring off into the ether?

But Cabell must have known the supplies were uniformly low. And then it occurred to me what he was trying to do. It was a favor—a pedagogic master stroke.

"Please, go ahead," I said. I took up my pencil and turned over a fresh sheet in my notebook. The chemist sighed and lumbered off his stool. He set a pair of spectacles on his long nose and peered at the top shelf.

"Very well. *Acaciae pulvis*, ten ounce; *Acidum aceticum*, sixteen fluidounce; *Acidum citricum*, eighty- four fluidounce; *Acidum muriaticum*, nil; *Acidum nitricum*, eight ounce, less a dram; *Acidum phosphoricum dilutum*, six fluidounce . . ." He paused a moment. "Shall I slow down, son?"

My hand was already cramped, but I demurred. "No," I said. "Please carry on."

# 30

I SENT THE DISPATCH to Richmond per Dr. Cabell's orders, arriving at the post office just as the gentleman was closing his window for lunch.

"Excuse me, sir," I said. "Before you go—are there any letters for Muro?"

"Doubt it," the little man grunted peevishly. He went around back anyway, and returned with a thin envelope. I recognized my mother's lilac seal. "You ought to be prompt next time," the man said as he lowered the shutter. A latch clicked behind.

*September 20, 1862*

*My Dear John Alan,*

*I write with unpleasant News. Your father took ill this Wednesday evening with a complaint of the Lung, and he has not had Strength to venture out since. He refuses my demand that he summon the Doctor, which I respect as his Right, tho' I do wish he would give him-*

self some measure of Comfort besides. If you could hear him moaning in the Night! I try to console myself in the knowledge that he was once a Doctor himself, and that he should know when it is appropriate to call for professional Assistance. Oh, I so wish you were here! Not only would you give him aid—how are your Studies, by the way? Going well, I should assume, since you have not written in quite a while—but you should also console your dear Mother, who is I assure you just as Sick with Worry as your father is with Disease.

Of course, the implications of a prolonged Convalescence on your father's part are nothing short of Horror. I have surreptitiously attempted to contact Mr. Stokes, but have had no word from the Navy on his whereabouts. With the fight shaping up as it has, I doubt he would come even if I reached him. Your Cousin Sam runs the Mill.

On a happier note, our Parthenia is well, if a bit restless at Miss Pelham's. I would never tell her this, but I recall feeling the same anxiety during my own final year at that place! I suppose it is my legacy—or perhaps that witch Miss Pelham? At any rate, it seems perfectly natural to me that she should chafe at the reins a bit, and I am not overly upset over her complaining. She will come out the better for a little Suffering.

I must go now; Peg is sick too (a grippe only), but I am determined that this household shall not suffer for her absence! Take good care, my son.

Your Loving Mother

I felt at once a lump in my throat. The first paragraph of the letter reinforced my deepest fears about leaving home—chiefly, that I had abandoned my family at the worst possible time—and then redoubled them with the misfortune of Father's illness. I began calculating right away how soon I might be back in Lynchburg. Folding the paper into my jacket pocket, I set off for the depot to make inquiries of the schedule for passenger trains southward.

I walked up and over the short hill that carried the Rotunda. At the base of the hill, abutting a stone wall, was a small rectangular field, on which some gentlemen of the university were playing at baseball. This was a new game then, but already quite popular. It was said to have been invented in the North a few years prior, which made it—along with smoking, cardplaying, and the pursuit of female flesh—one of the few subjects of certain agreement between men of the warring halves. As I passed along the wall, the man at bat cracked the little leather ball in my general direction, and I quickened my pace to avoid collision with the fellow chasing after it. The ball rebounded off the wall and was promptly retrieved and hurled back by the gentleman. We exchanged a courteous nod and together followed the arching path of the ball as it soared back to the pitcher. A group of spectating ladies were gathered at the far end of the field, past the home base, and one of these, whose gaze must have followed the struck ball, was now waving her arms to me. It was Miss Lorrie.

"Oh! Mr. Muro!" she cried, her voice softened by the fifty- yard distance.

I walked over without hesitation, sliding my family trouble, as it were, into the proper pigeonhole. "Afternoon, Miss Lorrie," I said, making a short bow to her, along with nods to her acquaintances. Miss Lorrie looked fresh and lovely in a yellow gingham dress, her hair poised atop her head in two high buns. She stood out from the other girls both in countenance and in poise, with her delicate, sloping shoulders calling the eye directly. The dread Miss Harriette Willson was also present, but she was so engrossed in the game that she scarcely acknowledged my arrival.

"This is such a happy coincidence," Miss Lorrie said. "I called on you at the dormitory this morning."

"Oh?"

"Yes, but you were away. I hope all is well."

"I was at the hospital," I said, "with your uncle." I took pride in linking myself, however tenuously, with Dr. Cabell.

"Now that you mention it, he did say something to that effect. It went well for you, then?"

I wondered what else the generous Dr. Cabell had volunteered to his niece—and even more important, what she had volunteered to him!

"It was tolerable," I said, keeping my cards close. "Dr. Cabell was called away before I had a chance to thank him."

"To thank him! I would not go near that place if he paid me. In fact, that is why I took up at the dining hall. When I arrived here, Auntie told me, 'You will do something.' I just knew I couldn't bear it at the hospital. I don't think I could stand the sadness."

"I didn't find it particularly sad." In truth, I hadn't had time to find it any way at all. Perhaps it was sad. Malodorous for certain, but perhaps also sad. I would report at six o'clock regardless, so what was the use of judging the mood of the place?

Lorrie lingered on her aunt's words: "She said, 'No daughter of mine shall sit idle at such a time!' She meant the war, of course. 'But I'm not your daughter!' I said, which was quite true, but she just erupted when I said it. I admit the remark was a tad ill- considered, given that she'd taken me in of her own accord, but still . . . 'I thank Heaven every night for it!' she said. Can you believe that? Auntie has never been so frank. I don't think I like it."

We had been afforded some privacy from the other ladies in the circle, who had joined Miss Harriette nearer the action of the game. As we spoke, these hitherto meek and demure young girls called out encouragements and chastisements to the players with full- throated resolve. "What are you waiting for, you lout? Go, you old sack!" This from a girl festooned like a doll with a silver bonnet tied daintily under her chin—the younger sister, I guessed, of one of Lorrie's friends.

"Auntie has never been without her people, you see. She met Uncle very young and went straight from her parents' home to his. And now this—" Lorrie gazed up the hill, where her uncle's pavilion home stood in the shadow of the Rotunda. Its great rear gable, furnished with a semicircular window composed of glass wedges, towered over the hemlocks in the garden like the round face of an owl. "Have you found it sad to be away from your family, Mr. Muro?"

My mind went to the depot, and thence down the southern line to Lynchburg. Stopping on Federal Hill, I saw my family's home, a light burning on the second floor. My father was inside under a heap of quilts, the mill's giant ledgers opened across his lap, he squinting to read them, making corrections with the nub of a pencil.

"It was right of me to go," I said.

"Certainly," said Lorrie. "I only wondered after your experience here. You know, I often fancy that I should like this place much better if I had chosen it. It is not so bad, after all. Quite pretty, in its way."

The baseball players converged suddenly on the home base, and a dispute erupted. The cheering ladies, who had been so engrossed, now went mum and closed their little circle as if compelled to do so by a primitive reflex of self- protection. The fracas soon quieted, and the players separated. A gentleman I recognized from the dining hall—a tall fellow who, with a weak chin poorly hidden by his threadbare beard, bore an unfortunate resemblance to Abe Lincoln—held a handkerchief to his nose. The rag filled quickly with blood and the fellow looked around him for an idea of what to do. Finding noth-ing—what could he have hoped to find, after all?—he wrung the bloody cloth dry and returned it to his nose.

Throughout all this, Lorrie said not a word, but neither did she leave my side to rejoin her friends. I was silent as well, preoccupied with thoughts of home—for Miss Lorrie had put me in mind once again of my decision to leave Lynchburg, and once again I doubted my resolve to stay away from it.

Finally, Lorrie spoke. "Look here," she said, "I am glad to have met you, John Muro. I find you an honest gentleman, with many fine qualities to commend you, but I have something to say. I hope you do not take it the wrong way. It is simply this: I ought not be kept waiting any longer. How many weeks have we been acquainted? And how many times have we stood and spoken essentially the same words back and forth to one another, ending always on your pledge to take me out to a picnic? But nothing has come of it! What must I do? I left you my *carte de visite*. I discovered your whereabouts last Friday night and arranged to be present at that *horrid* affair at Braxton Baucom's house. I even took up your case with my uncle, in the hopes it might put us into more frequent contact . . ."

This last revelation struck me cold: had she called me out to Dr. Cabell? It explained why the old doctor, who did not know me from a stranger when we met on the street outside the Delevan, was so famil-iar all of a sudden.

Lorrie waited for my reply. Alas, even with that I was not quick enough. "Well?" she said. "What do you have to say about all this?"

"Is it fair to say that I am astonished?"

"You may say that, but I don't see how it helps your cause."

"My cause?"

"With me."

I was frustrated with the turn of the conversation. I felt suddenly as though she were preying on me. Even if I had been deliberately resisting her advances—which I had not—her chosen approach would hardly persuade me to change my mind.

"Excuse me—but what *cause* do I have with you?" I said this loudly, so that the ladies all turned. Miss Lorrie waited a moment for an apology. When one did not come forth, the blood rushed to her cheeks, and she went to her friends.

In my defense, I should say that I did not realize the full error of what I had said until it was too late. But is that not always the case? It is no defense. I knew this perfectly well, and I did not expect that Lorrie Wigfall should ever speak another word to me. I had ruined my last chance.

As surely as I had made up my mind to remain in Charlottesville, then, I changed it back again. I did not care if I had to walk to Lynchburg; I would wait for no more signs from God. My college days were done.

# 31

EACH SLOGGING STEP along the mud- choked Main Street brought me closer to the depot, and thus nearer to deliverance from an experience that I now perceived as an unqualified failure. The Delevan Hospital, where I was now remedially employed, lay directly between the university and the train depot, and as I passed the building, I traced with outstretched fingers the low mud wall separating it from the road. Inside the wall, in the narrow yard, a lone Negro woman washed linens at a basin. The sound of her humming was the only noise except my footsteps on the road.

Then, all at once, the front door of the hospital burst open, and a frantic nurse—the same nurse, in fact, whom I had approached that morning for directions to the dispensary—hurled herself down the stairs toward me. "Hey! Doc!" she cried. I turned around to look behind me. The street was empty.

The nurse hobbled side to side, moving down the front steps on her teetering hams. "Doc! There ain't no time to spare. Come on, now." Before I had a chance to correct her, she had propelled me to the last ward on the left hall.

Down the back row of cots lay a sweating, raving soldier. He had propped himself upright on one elbow and was scraping his other arm against the iron frame of his cot. I took a moment's relief in the sight, for I knew enough of fevers—*What is pyrexia?* being the first query in Dr. Cabell's curriculum on pathology—to be confident that a simple dose of quinine would relieve the man's symptoms until Dr. Cabell or one of his colleagues might be found.

As I reached the bedside, however, I saw that the man's condition was not as simple as it seemed. Another nurse had been kneeling beside the cot when we arrived, partially obscuring my view of the man's arm.

"I got the doctor, now get on," my escort called to her colleague. The kneeling nurse stood aside.

The delusional soldier noticed our arrival and paused in his tantrum. I met his eyes—wet, dilated pupils ringed with gray—but saw no sparkle of intelligence behind them. It was the crazed and unconscious gaze of run- down prey. The man held his left arm aloft in front of his chest. When his eyes rolled down to inspect it, mine followed. I nearly gagged at the sight: a bloody and beaten stump, ending at the approximate natural terminus of the *ulna* and *radius*—that is, at the wrist—but the flesh on the end had not mended sufficiently to cover the bones, which remained exposed to the air but for a thin mantle of scar tissue. The bifurcation and the dark color put me in mind of a pig's foot. The trauma of grating the limb against the hard cot had caused considerable inflammation, and as he paused, blood rose in the capillaries. Drops of it rolled off his elbow.

I had learned that the itching coincident with certain kinds of healing could be maddening, but I had no idea of the degree. As quickly as the man had stopped the thrashing, he began it again. The noise was made more sickening by its familiarity: it was almost precisely the sound of cabbage on a grating board.

With each successive stroke, a fresh spray of blood spread out in the air. My shirt was riddled with it. The nurses stood back some yards, forearms raised to shield their faces.

"Sir!" I called to the man. "You must stop this at once!"

The man paid me no mind, pausing only to pick a shred of filthy tissue from the ragged end of the bone.

I had noticed that Dr. Cabell often employed military etiquette with his patients, calling them by their rank if he knew it. There was no standard garb for patients at our hospital, and the men often remained in their uniforms, which were stripped away only as necessary for proper treatment of their injuries. This man wore his filthy sack coat and a pair of stained wool trousers. Both were so saturated with blood and grime that they appeared black. The coat was missing its buttons, and it hung open like a peddler's vest. The left sleeve, of course, was also absent. Over the man's right shoulder I saw the faded stripes of what must have been at one time gold braid.

"Lieutenant!" I called to him. "Can you hear me, Lieutenant?" At this, the man paused. This time he held my stare. I spoke slowly, afraid of spooking him back into stupor. "I understand that you are in pain," I said. "I will send for morphine. But I must insist that you cease this behavior at once."

The man replied—he had great difficulty forming the words, but the sentiment expressed betrayed surprisingly cogent thought—"It's the itching that I mind, Doctor. I said as much to your nurse. The pain I can handle. Save me the itch, though, and I will be forever in your debt." He had a low, mellow voice, with a pleasant tone in spite of his anguish. His was not a local accent, but that was hardly surprising; while accompanying Dr. Cabell on his rounds, I had witnessed men from nearly every state in the Confederacy, and those voices I heard varied from the familiar to the almostforeign, from the lazy French- inflected patois of Louisiana to the chopped speech of the Carolina Smokies. This man's tongue fell somewhere in between those—a moderate pace, with short vowels—but I drew no conclusions on his origin, as the trauma was surely distorting his true pattern of speech.

I wished that he would speak more, but he only gave the same faraway stare. Then, for no apparent reason, he knelt down on the end of the cot and twisted the stump of his arm like a corkscrew upon the corner joint of the bed frame. He bore down on the arm with all his weight.

I could not bear to watch any longer.

"Nurse!" I called. "Bring morphine."

The big nurse brought the medicine right away. I had witnessed Dr. Cabell giving pills that morning, and I knew the basic action. With two nurses holding the soldier against the bed frame, and another constraining his head so that he could not thrash about, I hooked my thumb into the man's mouth. He fought against the pressure, but I succeeded in prying open the jaw and forcing a pill onto his tongue. Then I withdrew my thumb, and the jaw snapped shut. I wiped my hands on my shirttail. The nurse restraining the lieutenant's head released her grip and backed away. I ordered her back.

The nurse regarded me suspiciously. She gently clutched her throat and tugged at the skin as if she were scratching a midge bite.

Another nurse was more bold. "Doctor—don't you think you had better help him?"

The patient, realizing that his restrainers had been called off, began to eye the bed frame once again. His mouth hung open, and I spotted the tiny gray pill on his tongue, where it had adhered like a nettle on wool.

I stepped quickly to the bed. In one motion, just as I had seen Cabell do it, I grasped the hair on the back of the man's skull with one hand and rubbed his Adam's apple with the other. The patient looked surprised, and also slightly annoyed, but before he could protest, his Adam's apple plunged and he swallowed.

The nurses now swarmed around the bed, tucking the man's mangy blanket under the mattress on all sides to discourage anything but surrender. More rushed in, bearing freshly dampened cloths, &c. "Thank you," I whispered to one of them. She raised one eyebrow.

Casually, I corked the bottle of pills, holding it to the light to take its measure —this was all patent mimicry of Cabell—when I caught a glimpse, in a gap between the nurses' hips, of the soldier's face. His eyes were narrowed already, and the bloody left arm slack at his side.

# 32

"MR. MURO, COME IN. Take a seat. I'm afraid I have business with you."

It was Monday morning. Dr. Cabell had taken the unusual step of asking me into his office before departing on the rounds. Three days had passed since my treatment of the lieutenant, and though I had spoken with Dr. Cabell on several occasions since, he had made no mention of the incident. I assumed he had not been apprised. I had decided not to report it myself, for fear he would think I were boasting. So I kept mum, hoping all the while that he would find out by some other source.

As I took my seat opposite his desk, I thought of phrases I might employ to describe the current state of the patient. I had made a special trip to the hospital over the weekend, even though I was not scheduled to work, just to check on the man. A fresh dressing had been applied to his wound and the blood washed from his face. The floor under the cot was mopped and shined. For a moment, I doubted whether the incident had occurred at all, or if it had been a dream.

Dr. Cabell paged through the massive clothbound ledger where the comings and goings of all the patients was put down. He paused on one of the leaves—wide, almost, as a tablecloth—and ran his finger to spot near the bottom.

"I see that you examined Lieutenant . . . what is that now? Lieutenant Stone. It says that you administered Lieutenant Stone a dose of *morphia* over the weekend?" He paused and looked up. My face grew hot as I waited for his praise to begin. I wondered, had I now moved from the bottom of my class to the top? It stood to reckon.

"It is rather an unusual treatment, is *morphia*, for inflammation. From a strict therapeutical perspective, that is. I might have applied a poultice. But I suppose you had good reason."

He stopped there. My pride sank like a lead weight.

After a moment's pause, during which I swallowed more than a healthy dose of bile, I began, "You see, sir, I was taken by surprise. And the fellow was thrashing in such a manner that I thought . . ."

"You thought what, Mr. Muro?"

"I understand that morphia is not . . . well, that it is not the favored course, necessarily, for inflammation. But I thought he might be best served by the relief of his pain. Of course he himself said that pain was not the issue, per se—"

"So you contradicted the patient?"

"I only tried to serve his interest, sir, in the best way I knew. You must understand that he was desperate. I have never seen such a thing, dashing the arm against the cot—"

The professor raised a hand to his cheek and burrowed a finger in his side-whiskers. He set his chin on his hand. "I have seen it," he said. "And worse."

"But sir—it was an exceptional circumstance!"

"Perhaps it was. I shan't know; I was not present. Ultimately it is the province of the attending physician to assess the situation. Thus

I cannot fault you for your conclusion. You were right, Mr. Muro, to act decisively. That is encouraging news, and I was pleased when the attending nurse told it to me."

I allowed myself a smile.

"That said," Cabell drew on, "I have grave concerns about the substance of your decision, and that is why I have called you here. I thought the exercise at the dispensary would have given you a better understanding of the situation we find ourselves in at present. But apparently that is not the case."

Cabell withdrew his finger from his beard, examined it, and brushed it against the lapel of his coat.

"I thought the transcription might emphasize to you the scarcity of these products better than a bald statement to that effect, but no matter—you must have the lesson both ways, as it turns out. That is fine; I blame myself completely. However, you do understand that our store of morphia is rather lower than we'd prefer? To put it mildly."

"Yes sir," I said. My undershirt clung to the skin, damp all over.

"We must endeavor to conserve that preparation—and the laudanum, and all the other analgesics—for those rare cases when no other indication will suffice. Your training hardly provides you the knowledge to recognize these cases as of yet, so for now let us assume that you are not to administer these preparations except on my orders. Is that clear?"

Desperate to recover whatever portion of Dr. Cabell's esteem I could salvage, I said, "I suppose I should have given cinchona first." Professor Davis had made much of this substance in his first lecture on the *materia medica:* "The bark of a certain tree found in the valleys of tropical Peru . . . also known as Jesuit's bark . . . cinchona is the origin of that most valuable antipyrexic, quinine . . ."

Dr. Cabell went cross at the suggestion. "I would prefer you did not give that, either."

Now I was confused. Dr. Davis had spoken as if the history of medicine were cloven into two parts: before the discovery of cinchona, and after it. Fevers of all kinds, but especially the tropical ones such as malaria, were eased almost instantly by its timely application. Granted, I was yet a stranger to the pharmacopoeia, but my limited knowledge suggested that it would be folly to deny relief of such fevers when the remedy was at hand.

"But, Dr. Cabell," I countered, "don't you think that with proper instruction, sir, I might acquire the expertise required to give these drugs?"

"Mr. Muro—" He paused, as if weighing the continuation of a thought. "I'll be honest with you: I'm not convinced I can teach what you lack."

"But I can certainly learn to recognize the symptoms! Surely through repetition—and I promise that I will devote every waking hour to this—I can train myself to see the differences—"

"It is not a matter of training, Mr. Muro. You saw the blue coat, did you not? It hardly requires advanced instruction to realize that we should prefer not to waste our stores on our enemy."

The revelation rolled over me like a runaway carriage. "You mean . . . But surely not *here*, in our hospital? Why would he be here? Pardon me, sir, but it makes no sense."

"We treat both sides, Mr. Muro. And we are charged to treat them the same. You will find, unfortunately, that not everyone adheres to it, and that's a shame. I myself attempt to give the same attention to both, but my time is a different thing from the stores in the dispensary. I can always find more time, you see, but what you saw is all the drugs we are likely to get."

Here Cabell reached into his desk drawer and handed me a telegraph sheet. It was the reply from Richmond to my first dispatch, the one in which I'd transcribed our pharmacy:

TO: DRS. CABELL, DAVIS, ET AL., CHARLOTTESVILLE
GENERAL HOSPITAL
1ST OCT. 1862

(DICTATION FOLLOWS.)
MY DEAR SIRS,

HAVE RECEIVED CATALOGUE OF PHARMA, 25 SEPT.
SITUATION HOLDS HERE REGARDING PROVENANCE
OF ADD'L QUANTITIES OF ANY AND ALL INDICA-
TIONS. CERTAIN STOCKS SEIZED, AD HOC, NOTHING
COMPREHENSIVE. WAITING ON NEWS FROM MISSPPI,
RUMORS OF 2 BOATS FROM S. AMERICA, MAY PROVE
FALSE. WILL NOTIFY IF SITUATION CHANGES. PLS.
CONTINUE POSTING HEAD- COUNTS.

GRATEFUL,
S. P. MOORE, SURGEON GENERAL, C.S.A.


I gave the sheet back to Cabell, who stuffed it into the desk. "So you see," he said. "I have little choice but to discriminate. Do you understand, Mr. Muro?"

# 33

NOTICE THAT I NEVER made it to the depot that afternoon, and thus abandoned the idea to leave school and return home to Lynchburg. In the ensuing weeks, two factors reinforced this decision, and even served to vindicate the strange role of fate in my decision.

First, I recovered quickly from Dr. Cabell's chastisement, as I realized that what he perceived as failure had more to do with the exigencies of privation than with my own practical shortcomings. Taking care to refrain from unauthorized administration of precious indications, I assumed more and greater responsibilities at the hospital, gradually convincing Cabell to allow me certain duties beyond the clerkship he had originally planned. For instance, it became my province to canvass the wards every noontime for new cases of the various camp fevers in order to furnish the hospital steward with a current list of prospects for quarantine. I thus became a frequent visitor in the wards, and I developed rapport with several of the more affable patients. This is how I came to know Lieutenant Stone—to know him, that is, in his normal state. I shall tell more on that shortly.

The other reason for my brightened spirit was the news that Father's condition was improved:

*He roams the house freely now—a ghastly sight, to*
*be sure, as he remains gaunt from the illness, but a*
*welcome vision nonetheless. I have been successful so*
*far in keeping him from the Mill, but you must know*
*it is his foremost wish to resume his work there. Your*
*Cousin returns with good news almost every evening—*
*another gross of Sack- Coats shipped or some other*
*such thing . . .*

This was wonderful news, as it allowed me to plow full into my hospital work without the added weight of guilt. I did, however, make a promise to visit my family, if only for a few days' stay, at the earliest possible occasion. I gave no date and hoped that this pledge would go unnoticed, for I was by that point well entrenched at school and beginning to feel a bit of autonomy.

But of course Mother pounced on my offer and began peppering her correspondence with mentions of mince pies, fig pudding, and other fare she gambled would whet my longing for home. *We are so looking forward to your return home for Christmas!* she wrote in late October. I had not mentioned any such visit, and in fact had suggested in at least two letters that my status as Cabell's clerk (the lowest man on the Delevan staff, and thus last in line for furloughs) might preclude a trip home for the holiday. I reiterated this in my next letter, but Mother was undeterred. She suggested a compromise—that we meet at her brother's farm in Appomattox, which she claimed would serve the double purpose of being a shorter distance for me to travel as well as an opportunity for cousin Sam to visit his parents. In truth the farm, located in the northern part of Appomattox County, almost astride the border with Nelson County, was only marginally closer to Charlottesville than Lynchburg itself—six hours' ride instead of eight, and perhaps no different at all on account of poor roads in the area. But she was insistent, sending one letter each day for a stretch of several weeks. I soon realized that resisting her entreaties would take more effort than simply persuading Dr. Cabell to grant me liberty for that one day. I wrote that I would make the trip to Appomattox. Smug in victory, Mother immediately scaled back her correspondence to the customary once- weekly note.

And so, convinced of security both in school and in family affairs, I set about trying to make amends with Miss Lorrie. I had, of course, not meant to offend her with my importune comments at the ball game, and I saw no reason why we should not be reconciled once I offered a suitable apology.

But gaining an audience with the girl proved more difficult than I expected. First of all, she was no longer working at the dining hall. When I asked after her, the proprietor—that chubby, greasy ogre— could only reply, "Oh, no, she leave me." Though I repeated the question several times, and in a variety of phrasings, each time he replied the same: "No, no—she leave me. She leave me, she leave me . . ."

The first week in November, I arrived at the Anatomical Theatre to find this note on the door: *Dr. Cabell ill, class canceled, Nov. 5th 1862.* As I returned to my dormitory, I realized that I had an opportunity. In taking a gift of lemon tea or some other thing to Dr. Cabell's house, I would gain not only the favor of my ailing professor but also possibly a moment to speak with Miss Lorrie. If that meeting went well, we might even spend the afternoon together, as I might easily dodge that day's hospital work with Dr. Cabell laid up sick.

I went to Hotel F in search of some treat to take over. The proprietor was out, but his wife, on hearing that Dr. Cabell was ill, gave me two small nut cakes and a pot of berry preserves. I took these directly to Pavilion II—the Cabell residence.

The maid led me to the front parlor, where I was to wait for

Mrs. Cabell. The ground floor of the house was raised several yards above the walk, in the manner of an English row house. The front parlor was a shallow room that in its elevation and small size gave the impression of a well- appointed train compartment. The Cabells had decorated the room with furniture carved of rich, dark wood, and upholstered in a blue floral material. Two portraits hung above the shallow mantel. One was of Jefferson. The other man I did not recognize, but from his likeness to Dr. Cabell I took him to be an ancestor of some repute.

"Why, Mr. Muro, what a pleasure!" Mrs. Cabell took her time upon entering the parlor, holding her hands out in greeting while baby- stepping around the divan, a toothy smile fixed upon her face. "My husband speaks very highly of you."

I bowed my head. "With all respect, ma'am, I doubt that."

"No! You are his best student. Why would my husband lie?" Her full, throaty laugh evinced the same Texas lilt I found so enchanting in her niece. Mrs. Cabell must have been around fifty years old, but her hair was dyed a lovely dark ocher and her figure had retained its shape through the waist.

I made up the distance between us with a few short steps, and Mrs. Cabell clutched my hands. "How fortunate that we should finally meet."

"I do regret the occasion, ma'am."

She puzzled. "Oh?"

I held out the cakes. "For Dr. Cabell," I said. "We are all praying that he makes a speedy recovery."

"Of course. I will have these sent up right away."

The maidservant came, and Mrs. Cabell instructed her to take the cakes upstairs to the patient. "Oh—and do see if Lorrie is available, would you?" She apologized for the interruption, sighed weakly, and sat. I took the seat opposite, in the matching upholstered armchair.

Mrs. Cabell's face turned stern. "Now, Mr. Muro—my Lorrie hasn't mentioned you lately, dear. I hope all is well between you two?"

"I fear not, ma'am," I said, "though I wish to set it right as soon as possible."

She crossed her hands in her lap. "I have told her the odds are not good, what with all the gentlemen away at the fighting. 'Dear,' I said, 'you should be lucky to find a suitable man in the first place, never mind a doctor!' I know she has her silly concerns about doctors and doctoring and so forth, but never mind that, Mr. Muro. As I told her, look at me! Look at this home! All this from doctoring!"

"To be fair, ma'am, your husband is not just any doctor. It would be foolish to measure myself against his example."

She purred and shook her head. "Oh, Mr. Muro . . ."

"I should hope for half your husband's renown—or even a quarter."

I noticed Miss Lorrie had appeared at the passage door. Her face was drawn, as if it caused her physical pain to be present. She bowed to her aunt. "Ma'am."

"I say, Lorrie—look who has come to visit! Mr. Muro was concerned for your uncle's health, and he brought us some lovely cakes. Did you choose them yourself, Mr. Muro?"

"No, ma'am. They were chosen for me."

Lorrie let out a little hiss, like gas escaping a balloon.

"Have you been well?" I asked her. I felt bolstered by Mrs. Cabell's presence. At least, it would compel Lorrie to remain until I finished.

"I have been well," Lorrie said, just a degree shy of petulant.

"And how have *you* been, Mr. Muro?" her aunt prodded.

"Auntie, would you excuse us for a moment?"

The woman cowed visibly at the baring of her niece's will. "Why—

yes. Excuse us. Or excuse me, rather." She lent me her hand and then hurried into the passage.

"Have you come to apologize?" Lorrie said.

I gestured toward the divan, but Lorrie did not budge. It was clear she did not intend for either of us to be comfortable.

"It's been a month," she said. "More than that. Were you waiting for my uncle to take ill?"

"You have left the dining hall."

"It doesn't suit me there," she said. "Harriette was right."

"But I thought your aunt demanded you work."

"I've joined a group," she said. There were at that time all manner of ladies' societies for war relief and social service. In Lynchburg, for instance, my mother belonged not only to our church's auxiliary, which organized knitting circles and the like, but also to the Lynchburg Lady Rangers—a group that rolled paper cartridges for the infantry—and to the Ladies' Home Guard, a so- called vigilance society, which purported to protect the community from hoodlums and interlopers in the absence of regular police.

"Good for you," I said. I did not mean it ironically.

"Oh? Is it good for me?" She was struggling quite visibly against decorum. The facility with which she reached this level of agitation suggested that she had been like a pot at a simmer, waiting for a slightest stoke to reach full boil.

Like Mrs. Cabell, I was daunted by the display, but I should confess that I found it exhilarating at the same time. It was unusual for a girl of Lorrie's age and position to be so forthright with her opinion on anything, least of all a gentleman's attention. Strangely, it spurred me forward.

"I hope that you will forgive me," I said. "I have served you ill, and I apologize for it. Regardless of my intentions—which I assure you were not foul in the slightest—it was wrong for me to speak as I did, and in earshot of your companions no less, and you must believe that my words were not supported by any great conviction on my part, but rather the fears of . . . well, of a *child*."

"I beg your pardon?" Lorrie was transfixed. The slackness in her face—mouth open just slightly, eyes shining like wet eggs—suggested that she had not expected these words, nor perhaps anything like them.

There was a change just then in the electric charge of the air. It was discernible only in the pit of my stomach, but there was no mistaking it for anything but a reversal of control, as if the reins of our carriage, which had been for so long in Miss Lorrie's gloved grasp, suddenly appeared in my own.

"I do not mean to say that I am a child. Rather, there are aspects of childhood which remain in a man's consciousness."

"And—I have acted that way as well. Oh, John, will you forgive me?" At this, she lunged forward, curling her head against my breast, and there she began to weep.

I was baffled. I confess that in years of scientific experimenting since that day, through countless unexpected discoveries, I have never felt such a sense of wonder! A new fold creased my brain to hold the knowledge of womankind! What a strange and unknowable creature—and yet how easy she is to guide about if one gives her the proper heart food!

I stroked the slippery cheek with my thumb. "You needn't ," I said. "You needn't apologize for anything."

It was a true statement—she had not trespassed against me, nor spoken ill of me, nor committed any other such offense. And yet at that moment the words felt appropriate. In fact I repeated the sentiment once more. "You needn't cry," I said. "Don't cry, love."

Love? When had I ever spoken that word to anyone? I carried on, speaking what found itself on my tongue. Each phrase seemed more perfect than the last, and each drove the girl closer to me.

"Of course I forgive you," I said. "Though, in truth, I should be the one to weep. Am I to believe you accept my apology?"

Lorrie's eyes gleamed with tears, which she blotted with the edge of her palm. "Oh, John. Don't speak another word." A strand of hair had fallen from her chignon and clung by tears to her cheek. Without moving her gaze from mine, she took up my hand and held it to her face, where she employed my fingers—thick like a giant's in her fragile clutch—to push the hair back behind her ear. She kept my hand raised like that and closed her eyes. I bowed my head, for there was a difference of nearly a foot between our statures, and kissed her gently upon the mouth. Her eyes sprung open, and for a brief moment I feared that I had trespassed; perhaps she had expected some other thing? Surely not more words. Her eyes fluttered closed as she returned the kiss.

Our embrace must not have exceeded half a minute all told, but it seemed composed of as many distinct movements as a symphony. After the delicate meanderings, the explorations of each other's terrain, as it were, I commenced to pull back every so often, in order to better observe her response. Her breath, exuding both from her mouth (between couplings) and her nose (during them), was warm and sweet, like the steam that rises from a kettle of fruit preserves on the stove. Though she kept her eyes shut throughout, the shudders of the wide brown lashes betrayed the wanderings beneath.

Her affect, surprisingly, was like that of a patient suffering from one of the tropical fevers. She was neither awake nor asleep, but confined to a restless purgatory. It has always been my suspicion that the delusions accompanying such fevers might be seen as favorable by certain sufferers—like a drunken revel, perhaps—and if it were not for the rest of it (the vomiting, diarrhea, and so forth) we might have more adventurous souls wishing those afflictions upon themselves. It occurs to me now that my first observations both of a woman in passion and of a patient in fever occurred over the same period of my life, and that I should not perhaps confuse the real similarity of these two phenomena for simple proximity in my memory.

At any rate, our kiss broke off at the sound of footsteps in the passage. We were reluctant, of course, to draw apart, and we delayed doing so until the last possible moment. Thus when Mrs. Cabell appeared in the doorway, our ruffled deportment—strands of Lorrie's hair fallen about her shoulders, her crimson complexion, and no doubt also my own continued *excitement*—left no question what had been interrupted. To my great relief, a smile crept to the woman's lips.

"Dr. Cabell extends his warmest gratitude for your concern," she said, reciting the message she had returned to deliver. "He regrets his absence, of course, and requests that you spread word to that effect amongst your colleagues." Her eyes danced between Lorrie and me. "Well, children?"

Lorrie made busy with the sleeves of her dress, avoiding her aunt's eye. "Mr. Muro was just leaving," she said. "There was some concern, I think, about him missing the dinner service."

"That's right," I said. "I'm afraid I tarry too often on that account."

Mrs. Cabell observed our charade with obvious delight, though she played her part as written. "Why, it is not yet ten o'clock in the morning!" she said.

Lorrie, searching for some prop that might convey me safely out of doors, fixed on the parcel of food—nut cakes and jam—that either the forgetful servant had forgotten to take up to Dr. Cabell or the ailing professor had sent back untouched.

"Here you are, then," Lorrie said, pressing the package into my arms. "If you are hungry, don't wait."

And so I found myself back on the Lawn bearing exactly what I had brought. I was hungry, so I broke off some of the nut cake. It was dry and tasteless, probably baked several days previously. I did not care. I stood in the colonnade a moment and listened to Mrs. Cabell's laughter behind the front door. Now and then Lorrie's voice rose an octave, bringing her aunt to new hysterics.

I was embarrassed in the most wonderful way. Eventually I turned and set off down the Lawn. The grass was still wet with dew.

# 34

A DANCE WAS HELD that evening at the apartments of a generous professor called Dougal. He was hardly older than most university men, which fact accounted for his participation in various of the social events organized by us. Dougal was a Scot, recently over from Europe, and like most Scotsmen he was involved with the natural sciences. He had a cheerful if homely wife called Maria, who was unusually tall and slender, so that her shoulders stood rigid like a level board about her neck. She had a tongue on her, and we students took more stories from an evening with Maria Dougal as we did in a month of drinking and cards. Professor Dougal cherished his bride, wasting no opportunity to lavish her with embraces even in the company of others.

The Dougals lived in a house just north of the University Grounds. The house was blessed with a large, unpillared, and undivided room at the rear, which at night was cleared of furniture for the purpose of dancing. It was rumored that the Dougals danced alone most nights—that is, the nights when they did not host a gathering—and the image of the willowy Scots waltzing about their home to the sound of a silent orchestra, while never observed by me, made a lasting impression in my mind.

At that time there were few venues for dancing in Charlottesville. The owners of Farmington, an estate west of the University, hosted regular occasions, but they were by and large unwelcoming of University men, except those gentlemen hailing from families in Albemarle County, whose reputations were known to the hosts, and also those men like my roommate who came from families known generally throughout the Commonwealth. As the son of a Lynchburg garment manufacturer, I was invisible to the Farmington set, and thus found myself among the University men seeking a venue for spending a Saturday night. There was among us an informal society—a club without a clubhouse—that organized dances wherever space could be found. When no enclosure beckoned, we laid planks upon the ground and danced under the stars. We danced in church basements, in well- kept barns, and in all manner of private homes. But the Dougals' was the best of these, not for the space itself, which was hardly worthy in its own right, but for the bright and lively manner of the hosts, which spread among the partygoers like a happy contagion.

Miss Lorrie and I arrived a half hour late on account of her tardiness at her preparations. I had arrived at the door of the Cabells' pavilion a few minutes shy of seven o'clock and was told by the maidservant that Miss Lorrie had only just returned home from her afternoon activities.

"Oh?" I said. "Was she gone long?"

"She been down Red Hill way, sayed she been shopping." The maid paused. "'Course, I ain't seen nothing in the carriage, Mis' Muro. Not a thing a- tall . . ."

I always regarded the Cabells' Eunice as a particular gossip, willing to fabricate an item from speculation, if not from pure imagination.

"I shall wait in the parlor," I said. "Tell Miss Lorrie not to rush; she needs proper time to prepare."

"Is y'all going dancing?" Eunice asked.

"We are," I said. "But no matter—I will wait. Will you tell her?"

"Yes sir."

Alone in the parlor, I dwelled on the way I had, over the stretch of a brief acquaintance, altered my daily schedule to accommodate the strange pauses of courtship: the various chores of a lady's personal upkeep, the powderings, ablutions, &c. As well there were the added social obligations of a public courtship: the elaborate greetings and bidding well to the hosts, the coordination of one's cravat with the lady's shoulder wear, the stopping to chat with any member of the other's family when encountered on the street. A good part of the ritual is waiting, I told myself. And yet I harbored all the while a notion that it was unfair I should have to wait, particularly when the cause of the waiting seemed so avoidable.

Lorrie descended at last in her usual velvet gown, accented by a new macramé shawl of bright violet. Her hair was plaited and wrapped into a loose bun, exposing the warm, glowing skin of her neck. I felt a charge of desire. I wished to go to her and kiss her, to feel her chest press against mine in the embrace. Instead, as was proper in a lady's home, I took her hand to my lips and praised her appearance.

"Why, John, that's not true!" she said with false modesty.

"In fact it is, my dear. You are as lovely this evening as I have ever seen you."

"But in my haste I hadn't the time to do any thing special . . ."

"Even in your haste, you are a triumph. My expectations are exceeded once again."

En route to the dance we spoke, as we often did, on common acquaintances, contributing what information we knew that might push along the person's story like the plot of a novel.

"Do you know that fool Knight came to see me this afternoon?" I said.

Lorrie took this news with something like fright: her face blanched and she said, "Oh? What time was that?"

"Just after noon," I said. "He was not well. It seemed that he had gone without sleep for some time. It struck me odd that he should come to see me. We are not close, you know."

"What was his business with you?" Lorrie's voice betrayed a quiver. I wondered if she were afraid of the man. Having seen him in the flesh, in his disgraceful deportment, I reckoned there was much to despise perhaps, but hardly a thing to fear.

"He asked after B.B.," I said. "The poor fellow had looked everywhere: the town house, the library. I ask you—the library? Of all the holes haunted by that old boy, why the library? Would you ever think to seek him there?"

"I don't think I should ever have cause," Miss Lorrie said, turning her eye away from mine as she spoke, "to seek out B.B."

It struck me that I had not ever heard her call my roommate by his chosen name. "Mr. Baucom" was her usual phrase, accompanied usually by a descriptive word to form an epithet such as "your pig-headed *Mr. Baucom*" or "that lout of yours *Mr. Baucom*." I had observed their interactions at least half a dozen times, at various social functions, and at each of these my roommate implored upon her to call him "B.B.," but to my knowledge she had never.

"Well," I said, "I certainly should not have looked in the library. One would sooner find him in a pigsty."

"Is he so vile, John?"

I knew that a defense of even so disreputable a gentleman as our B.B. was hardly uncommon among ladies of charitable disposition. Miss Lorrie had every right to question my unfounded criticisms of the man, as well the carelessness I displayed in casting him among swine. Such criticism was impolite, and inadvisable besides, as the man was ostensibly my chamber mate and unkindnesses traveled quickly from

lip to ear in our short social circuit. Yet I had to register my disapproval of Miss Lorrie's attitude. A few undeserved praises could just
as easily spread and disseminate the wrong impression—namely, that
Miss Lorrie was some how tarnished by dint of association with B.B.
Taking her hand—to soften the effect, I thought, of my statement—I
said, "It concerns me that you should defend him."

Lorrie pursed her mouth. "Is it a defense?"

"Why, it seems so. Perhaps I spoke too candidly about the gentlemen, but my response to your question, in a word, would be yes. He
*is* so vile."

"I mean nothing by it, " Lorrie said, "though I must say that it
concerns *me* that I must provide a steady flow in insults and denigra-
tions regarding *Mr. Baucom* in order to maintain a suitable distance
from him."

"I wish it were otherwise."

"You do not! On the contrary, you relish his foibles, inasmuch
as they improve your own esteem. Do not think I haven't noticed,
John."

"Pardon me?"

"One thing I can say for B.B.—and no amount of shaming will
compel me to rescind this—is that he has no master."

Incredulous, I shouted, "That is ridiculous! Who is my master?"

"I don't know him," she said. "Perhaps you have never mentioned
him. I fear I don't know you well enough."

"Perhaps not," I said, but the remark had opened my gut like a
shiv. It was as if the girl had crept up like Perseus, forcing a hand glass
upon me so that I might turn to stone at the sight of my true self. *Perhaps not.* I could manage nothing more. I doubted her assessment—or
feared it, doubt and fear being like envy and rage in the closeness of
alliance—but I had no desire to argue. "We have arrived," I said.
"Hurry, we are late already." This last I intended as a dig, a reminder

that Miss Lorrie had a good many faults herself, all duly noted by me, but she did not rise to it. Instead she took my arm and allowed me to hand her down from the hired coach.

On the nights of dances, Professor Dougal installed the musicians in a little service room adjacent to the parlor. My senses brightened that evening upon discovering that the music was to be played by the Scotts, a family of free Negroes regarded as the finest string quartet in the region, black or white. As an aside, allow me to refer to these Scotts any person who questions the aptitude of the Negro to play even the most elaborate musical scores. Excepting their dark skin, one might have mistaken them, in their tuxedoes, for a quartet taken from the Philharmonic Society in Richmond. In some feat of economy, the musicians managed to squeeze four music stands alongside their own bodies and instruments in that tiny room. A child also was present, whose duty was to turn the pages as his elders played. I wondered at the ability of these Negroes to secure sheets of contemporary music in spite of the blockade. The tune playing as we entered was utterly fresh to my ears, and quite possibly Viennese. I supposed that as the scores were the musicians' stock in trade, and their practice would be worthless without them, much as my own or Dr. Cabell's would have been without some form of medications, it behooved them to acquire the sheets, and so they did. We had our methods, and I guessed the musicians had theirs.

We gave our coats to the door servants. (The University owned a small number of slaves, most of whom were aged past any real usefulness. These were made available to professors for a rental fee.) A great crowd was assembled already, and there was scarcely room for another couple in the parlor. Determined to dance, in order to put the previous discussion out of our minds, I led Lorrie to a place near the musicians, where we took immediately to waltzing. Our shoulders grazed our neighbors' as we wound our way around the narrow room.

The ceiling was blessedly high in that place, which afforded some relief from the heat of so many moving bodies, but the atmosphere was deathly close. I began at once to perspire.

I should say here that Miss Lorrie was an uncommon dancer—sensitive to the most subtle lead and willing to follow any instruction even if new to her. Some women force a man to lead them around like mules, as if they had not a shred of intuition about where the dance might lead, nor any spring in their steps that might compensate for surprise. Dancing with Lorrie was not this way; rather, it was like dancing with one's shadow, so precise were her steps and so light her carriage. Her gaze she held steady on my face during periods of light movement, and intermittently during quick whirling. A dance with her had the effect of a good conversation, leaving me always with the impression that our spirits drew closer by the experience.

It was precisely my hope that we might compensate for the quarrel this way, but as the first tune wound down it became clear I would be disappointed. Lorrie was strangely leaden in my arms. She trained her eyes upon the floor and declined to applaud at the end of the song, only clasping her gloved hands together as if in prayer. The Scotts next played a waltz I recognized as the "Radetsky March" of the elder Johann Strauss—one of the few tunes, incidentally, that the Lynchburg Cotillion band dared play that was less than fifty years old.

"Shall I take you home, then?" I said. Lorrie had refused my offer of punch and only nodded silently at the many acquaintances who had drifted over to bid us welcome.

"If you wish," she said in monotone.

"My wish is to remain here for at least a respectable duration."

"Very well."

We danced another three tunes, until I could not stand her silence any longer. At a pause, I said, "I believe we have fulfilled our obligation here," ending with a sort of question, "Don't you agree?"

"Very well," she said once more. I left her alone while I retrieved our coats, and when I returned, I saw that she had been crying. This softened me at once, and I abandoned my petulance.

"What is it, dear?" I queried. I knew the answer, of course, and I heard the foolishness of the words as they left my mouth. "Let's cast off this fractiousness. Why are we quarreling anyway? Would you believe that I have forgotten the source of it? Call me dim- witted."

This brought a smile, and she said, "I suppose that should make me a dim- wit too."

"You have forgotten as well?"

Miss Lorrie produced a handkerchief and wiped her cheek. The lilac of the perfumed cloth reached me at once even in the closeness of the dancing room. She nodded assent.

"Well, then. All is forgiven on grounds of amnesia." I meant this to be light, but the comment was unable to hold up the sadness it was meant to carry off. Were we strangers after all?

# 35

I TOOK A HORSE ON December 24 and rode south. My uncle's farm consisted of just under five hundred acres, of which perhaps two-fifths were under cultivation by tenant farmers in tobacco, corn, and wheat. Arriving at the main house, I put the rented horse up wet and picked my way through the backyard on foot.

The women sat around a table in the kitchen, drinking their after-supper tea while the Brightwoods' girl tidied the dishes. I was scarcely two feet in the door when the whole group of them leapt upon me like hounds at a fox.

Oh! Oh! Let me take your coat, John Alan! My, how you have grown, John Alan! Have you met a girl? I can see by that smile— you've met a girl. Dear me, Regina, he has grown a foot! I love this holiday, how I love this holiday . . .

I shan't describe this scene more than a little, for I have no doubt any man away at school has had a similar response from his female kin upon a safe return. When the cluckings of mother and aunt, of sister and cousin, &c., were all through, I inquired after the male half of our family. I had grown chill from the ride, and I was in need of a generous drink. My hope was that the men had taken enough mulled cider by that point to look the other way if I poured. Surely Sam would help me.

Just then the door from the passage swung open and Uncle James walked in. He was a thick, burly man whose muscular embraces had led me, as a boy, to fear our meetings. In stature, he and Aunt Claire were as incongruous as a man and his wife could be. She was a doll made of matchsticks, he a shaved bear. As I grew older, I wondered how Aunt Claire had managed to produce two children, given the certain discomfort of their marital commerce.

Squeezing me in his vise grip, Uncle James bellowed, "Tell me, nephew, how goes the battle for the souls of the ill?" Uncle James viewed all vocations as variations on his own. The farmer grew wheat to feed hungry souls. The carpenter fashioned chairs to accommodate weary souls. The beadle protected virtuous souls from dangerous souls—but the dangerous souls were actually only errant souls, who with proper shepherding from the judge, the bailiff, the jailor, and so on might become virtuous souls after all.

I have heard that some preachers have two manners—one for the pulpit and one for the home. Uncle James had only one. "Level with me," he said, pinning my arms to my sides as if I were a lamb he intended to shear. "I want God's honest truth: is the Almighty alive in Charlottesville? Because we hear stories."

I had not been to services since leaving home, nor had any of the college men I knew. But the Cabells attended church every Sunday, and by Miss Lorrie's account, I could say with reasonable certainty that they were not alone in the pews. "He is with us as ever, sir—in Charlottesville as in Lynchburg."

Uncle James seemed satisfied with this answer and mercifully released his embrace. "That is good to hear," he said. He smiled broadly, and then slowly let it fade. "Well, you've said your greetings.

Join us in the parlor, won't you?"

I followed Uncle James down the passage into a familiar room. An enormous log crackled on the grate. The air was tinged with the cloying scent of Father's pipe smoke.

Sam was at the window seat with a stack of legal papers on his lap. When I appeared, he leapt up—which is to say, he swung himself erect on his crutch and cried, "Cousin! What a happy surprise! Aunt Regina said you were coming tonight, but I hardly believed her. For fear of disappointment, you know."

Sam's eyes, it seemed, had gone blue. I could not recall if they had been brown or if there was now a chilliness in his stare that I had not noticed.

"How are you, Sam?"

He tapped the crutch. "In some ways the same. Much better in others. You've heard about the mill?"

"I have heard all is well."

"Better than ever," he said. "Isn't that so, Uncle John?"

Father stood up, taking care to steady himself on the arm of his chair. He looked drawn, but hardly unhealthy by the standards I was used to. He held out his right hand. With characteristic reserve, he said, "You've done a good turn for your mother, John Alan. Happy Christmas."

"Aye, the mill steams along nicely," Sam continued. "Of course, there is change afoot—but where is there not change afoot these days, eh?"

Father led me to the chair next to his so that he might be seated and not miss the conversation. Uncle James poured a fresh round of cider for everyone—myself included. I drank the mug half down right away, making sure not to sniffle as the alcohol rose to my sinuses.

"As a matter of fact," Sam said, "I was just now explaining my plan to these gentlemen." He held up the sheaf of papers. "It is all written here, in surfeit detail. But gents, I assure you, the detail is beside the point. The essence of the plan is three words."

Uncle James chuckled. "I suppose those are *coats, jackets,* and . . . what? *Coats* again?"

"Actually, the words are *capacity, tenacity,* and *perspicacity.* I say *capacity* because it is plain to see that this business, like all manufacturing concerns, will be more profitable as its scale increases. Do not take my word for it—the boldest experiments in commerce have borne this out. I believe we are well positioned in this regard as well. Uncle John, you took the first step by your wise purchase of extra labor."

Father squinted at this remark—a sure sign, given his modesty, that he was flattered.

"But we can do more! *Tenacity!* We must strive, gentlemen, never to let the target stray from our view. Uncle, I realize that your condition impairs you somewhat, but let me assure you that I will give doubly of myself to compensate. I intend not to leave the premises of the Bedford Woolery until our goal is met!"

"Our goal?" Father inquired.

Sam hoisted the sheaf of papers high in the air, leaning on his crutch for support. "It is all here," he said. "But do not concern yourself too deeply with figures. Those may change. Indeed, that is why we must be *perspicacious.* For if we cannot discern the real workings of our mill, gentlemen—if we cannot see the material for what it is, laborers as they are, and so forth—then we are lost. Here I am reminded of a lesson General Jackson gave his battalions before Manassas. He told us, 'Men, none but the Almighty knows what fate waits yonder. To believe otherwise is the vilest kind of blasphemy.' Well, as you know, the Lord favored us that day. But it may not always be so. That was the general's lesson. And we must take this to heart. He also said that if your battle plan falters, do not attempt to prop it up with shims and such—raze it and start anew! I will bear this in mind as well, as should we all."

Remarkably, Sam did not flinch or falter as he delivered this speech. It issued from him fully formed, like a gospel. Though I could not speak to the efficacy of his methods, I was duly impressed by his mode. It is said that nothing inspires confidence like confidence, and I was won over.

So were the older men.

"Why, Samuel Brightwood, who knew you had such a *head* on you?" Uncle James exclaimed, clapping his son on the back.

My own father murmured, "Well done, well done," as he poured brandy from a dusty green bottle into four thimble glasses.

After the toast, Sam took me aside. "If there is an ounce of fear in your heart, cast it out," he said. "I will do this family proud."

"You have my confidence," I said.

# 36

THE SOUTHERN VICTORY at Fredricksburg in December of 1862 was rather more like a defeat for our hospital. The first transfers from the field arrived Saturday afternoon, and the trains kept coming—on the half hour, day and night, all through the next week. Even before the battle, every one of our beds had been full, but our acceptance of new men was not negotiable.

For several weeks, as long as he could, Dr. Cabell tried to make do with the old regime. Neither he nor any of the other full- time doctors—Professor Davis you know already, but here I include also the contract physicians, the Charlottesville doctors who took shifts at the hospital for wages—none of them slept more than a few hours any night of the week, so great was the demand for their services. As Dr. Cabell's clerk, I saw firsthand the effects of this policy: Bandages went unchanged on flesh wounds, and the stench of pus and necrotic tissue filled the air. Bowel and chest fevers spread between wards for lack of proper quarantining. Men with common colds saw their symptoms progress to pneumonia, as there was no authority monitoring their decline. There were nurses, of course, but most of them had families at home. Many of the white nurses were the sole support for their children while their husbands fought in the field. Even in his most desperate hour, Dr. Cabell would not order these women to work longer shifts than they volunteered. There was an understanding that each person would work as long and as hard as he or she was able. Each member of the staff, whether clerk, janitor, or nurse, was assumed to know his or her own limit better than a supervisor could. Dr. Cabell assumed—as so many in positions of authority during war did, many times incorrectly—that the weight of our cause should be motivation enough. At this writing, I have now seen hundreds of doctors at work, in wartime and not, with the same ethic displayed regardless of outside stimulus; I might conclude that this has more to do with something innate in the doctor's soul, and not the call of God or country.

After six miserable, sleepless weeks, Cabell issued an order that all students in the medical curriculum at the University were henceforth to serve as full doctors. Among the denizens of the Anatomical Theatre, this came as a burst of good news. Even I, who had been working already at the Delevan, and who should have known better than to be carried away by congratulations, rejoiced that I would be able to contribute a greater service at the hospital than the menial note taking I performed for Dr. Cabell. I had learned more from my hospital work than in all the lectures put together. A doctor's work, especially in the hospital, is largely a practical art, full of cutting and stitching and other manual tasks. In addition there is the filling out of specialized paperwork such as the daily ward tally for the Surgeon General, which is both uninteresting and irrelevant to the academician.

I was assigned the northwest ward on the second floor of the Delevan Building. A nurse—the same one, in fact, who had grabbed me off the street that Sunday afternoon to examine the feverish lieutenant—gave me a quick tour, my first as attendant physician. She nodded as we passed a man with a battered Fenimore Cooper adventure open on his chest. "And you'll recall Lieutenant Stone," she said.

She paid him only a second's attention before continuing down the line.

I paused at the foot of the cot. I hardly recognized him. His color had returned, and his beard was shaved close. There was a dimple in the end of the chin that lent him a certain authority. I wondered if he might have been a minister in his civilian life. He had shed his soiled uniform and wore instead a suit of unseasonable light- colored cotton, which, though well used by its previous owner (as all the donated clothes were), was a good fit, and certainly an improvement over the muddied and bloodied blue wool of before.

"I do believe that's everyone," the big nurse said finally. She shifted back and forth on her enormous feet, clearly anxious to take the five minutes' break we allowed the nursing staff every morning—and which they filled with clandestine tobacco smoking and gossip.

"I shall attend to a few things," I said, giving her a nod to acknowledge the break.

"I will be—outside, if you need me, sir."

"Very well," I said, making my best effort to seem, like Dr. Cabell, to float above such things as smoking breaks.

The big nurse gathered her cohort and the group trundled down the stairs together, leaving the ward empty of women for the time. I went to the oak- plank table near the door that functioned as a sort of way station for the nurses, where they kept the bags of lint, the commonest liniments, &c,, to sharpen my pencil. I had intended to make some preliminary notes on the states of the various patients now under my care. As I cranked the sharpening screw, however, I heard my name—"Say! Dr. Muro!"—and I turned around. It was Stone.

I was surprised that he knew my name. He could not have remembered that delirious afternoon. But he must have, for the nurse had not introduced me to the patients that morning, but only walked me through as if I were touring through the zoological park.

"Is there a problem, sir?" I said. It felt queer to ask such a thing, seeing how the lieutenant had marked his place in the Fenimore Cooper with the bandaged stump of his left arm, which was indeed, by common measure, a *problem*, and would most likely continue to be such for the rest of his life. "That is, can I assist you with something? While the nurses are away?"

"Let 'em stay out there. Bah. A filthy habit."

I myself did not abstain completely from smoking, but had never felt the compulsion experienced by so many men toward the near- constant inhalation of tobacco. "We all require some respite," I offered. I had observed that in conversations with patients, Dr. Cabell aligned himself with the nurses and other, lower- ranking hospital functionaries. It was an important gesture, I sensed, if one hoped to maintain proper control over the staff.

But the lieutenant would hear none of my generosities. "It is a shame, Dr. Muro, and one of the most unexpected and distasteful consequences of our war that the ladies' etiquette which we have strived to build up over so many years—both in my region and yours—should be so casually dismissed. Don't you agree?"

"I do," I said. "Certainly I do. But with so much else going on, so many other ills about us, I hardly find time to dwell much on it."

"Good man," the lieutenant said. And here his demeanor changed, like a cloud rolled away from the sun. "That was what I'd hoped you'd say."

"Excuse me, sir?"

"A test," he said. "A little contrivance to discover your sense of these things. I myself couldn't care a wink about the nurses, their tobacco habits and so forth. But there's been some grumbling here, and I was curious where you stood on the matter. I hope you'll forgive my trickery. I was correct in my suspicions; you keep a sane perspective. A 'long view,' as we say in Pennsylvania."

I was angry at the ruse, but flattered as well. Had he indeed been observing me? Had he singled me out among Dr. Cabell's assistants? It suddenly occurred to me that he might recall more from that delirious afternoon than I'd supposed.

"No hard feelings, then?" he said. He put out his hand—his good one, the right—and I took it. "I don't believe we've been properly introduced. I'm Henry Stone."

"John Muro."

"*Dr.* John Muro."

"I'm not quite—I'm not exactly a doctor per se."

The lieutenant smiled. "*Quidquid latine dictum sit, altum videtur,* eh?"

"Pardon?"

"Ah, well. So you've always meant to be a doctor, then."

"Not really," I said. "Or rather, yes, I have. What I mean is, my father did not always want it for me."

"Oh? I would have thought you'd be any man's pride and joy. Does he know how well established you've become here? The accolades from Dr. Cabell and so forth?"

Deeply embarrassed now, I lowered my head. "I have not relayed much to him, no."

"Why not?"

"He has been ill. And also—well, my coming to the University was more a matter of exigency than faith. My mother asked him to send me. Instead of the army, that is. My father is the proprietor of a woolen mill in Lynchburg. Making uniforms. It wouldn't stand for his son to escape conscription any other way."

The Yankee lieutenant, whom I realized just then from the glint of silver at his new- shaven temples to be rather older than I'd thought, sat up from his pillow and plumped it vigorously with his good hand. I did not know why I was revealing myself to him. To a man who was not just a stranger but an enemy! There was a pleasure in it, but of a painful sort—like the needling- out of a splinter.

"I see," he said, relaxing now into the pillow. "But it occurs to me that it's a rather fortuitous compromise, as these things go. You must have some idea what you're missing, what you're avoiding, by being here." He glanced about the ward—at the stinking, humbled soldiers arrayed like dogs on their cots and stiff- back chairs. I had no need even to turn and see them; I knew the view. I took his point.

"To keep such accolades a secret—I doubt I'd have had the humility to do it, Muro."

"Accolades, sir?"

"Yes, accolades! What else would you call it?"

Stone knew nothing, I thought, of the true reasons for my elevation to attendant physician, nor the countless hours Dr. Cabell must have deliberated over his decision before realizing that he had no choice in the matter.

"I meant only to explain why I have not flaunted myself to my family," I said. "There is a difference, when one moves away, between going forth with a *statement* of faith from one's family and going with faith itself."

Stone did not blink. "Not at all," he said. "It is perfectly well and good to confuse the two. Necessary, even."

I shook my head. I wanted to believe him. "You really think so?"

"I changed my trade when I was your age. No—I was older. How old are you anyway, Muro?"

"I'm nearly eighteen."

He didn't flinch at the number—although he should have—and he waved his hand. "I was nearly thirty! I dropped everything—years of study, you know—and took my family to Connecticut. Have you ever been to Connecticut, Muro?"

I had never been outside Virginia, save a trip to my uncle's church meeting in North Carolina when I was ten.

"It's horrible country: stones in every field, pushing up like Jack Straw's bones, new ones every spring."

"You're a farmer?" I said, hardly believing it.

"Oh, heavens, no—I'm in the insurance trade. In Hartford. My uncle offered me a stake in a company he'd formed with another fellow. He'd heard—well, he took pity on me. How's that for the full faith of one's family? A bone. He threw me a bone."

"And you took it?"

"I sell insurance. Life, property, casualty." He snorted. "It is *terribly* exciting."

"What were you—I mean, if you don't mind my asking—what was your previous trade?"

Here, Stone's gleam returned. "You're doing admirable work here, Muro."

"Sir?"

"You should know I think so."

"Thank you, sir."

"I was a doctor. As much a doctor as you are, that is. I took two years at the Jefferson Medical College, and then another at the University of Pennsylvania."

I was taken aback. I never, but *never*, would have suspected the man of medical training. We occasionally treated physicians in our facility—field surgeons and assistant surgeons who had been wounded or who had taken ill along with the men of their regiments—but they had always, in my experience, made it known from the start that they were of our ilk, as it were, and expected special consideration therefore. Moreover, they were constantly undermining Dr. Cabell's course of treatment with supplemental treatments of their own, and in some cases discontinuing Cabell's recommendations or disregarding them outright. Nurses, it should be known, loathe no patient so much as the ill doctor, for in his eyes, they insist, they can do no right.

But this fellow! I went back to my first impression of him, half insane, scraping his infected arm against the rail of the cot. Should I have taken that as the behavior of a knowledgeable man? Of a scientist? There was no question he'd been taught the most progressive techniques—Philadelphia was then, as it is today, the very frontier of medical knowledge in this country. And to have taken instruction at not one but *two* esteemed institutions! Truth be told, I did not know Jefferson College from the University of Pennsylvania. They were the same thing to me, the same unreachable destination. All at once, my longing returned, with the same full rush as before, as if I had never come to Charlottesville and I was still that boy in Lynchburg with the glory dreams of Northern study.

"Ah," Stone said. "You don't believe me, is that it? I don't blame you; I've hardly made a case for my truthfulness. You'll have to take my word for it."

I hadn't even considered that he was putting me on. Now, though, it seemed a distinct possibility. It has always rankled me that there is no licensing body that issues just the kind of proof I might have required of Lieutenant Stone. The American Medical Association, which aspires to be such a clearinghouse, was only a few years in existence then. Even now, in my humble opinion, it has a long way to go.

"I'll say this," Stone offered. "I had my doubts about your prescription of morphine—you remember, don't you, that afternoon?"

I stared, petrified.

"Well, I wouldn't have given it," he said, "not in the present state of affairs. Not to me, that is." He paused and looked me full in the eye to make sure I understood his meaning. "Morphine is not what my training—as much as I remember of it—would have suggested. But what of it?" He raised his bandaged arm. "You saved me, Muro. Whatever your reasons, you were correct."

# 37

AS IT HAPPENED, Miss Lorrie was possessed of stronger will than I assumed. As I gained my footing in the new role at the hospital, scarcely setting foot outside the Delevan except to sleep, she never cast me out of her mind. She even took to carrying out small errands such as delivering to the hospital a sweater her uncle had forgotten in his haste that morning. Never mind that Dr. Cabell kept a second wardrobe in his office—so often was he called upon to spend the night at his desk. Never mind that Dr. Cabell, often as not, was stripped to his shirtsleeves in the surgery and had no use for a woolen garment. I could go on like this, but you see the point. As you might expect, I was charmed.

On one of her "unexpected" visits to the hospital (during which she always managed, somehow, to get lost and wander into my ward), Lorrie had expressed a wish to take a sleigh ride through the hill country south of town. In order to satisfy her (for I had no sleigh of my own) I arranged to borrow from my roommate a fine one- horse sled of Northern manufacture known as a "cutter."

"Ho, Muro!" B.B. bellowed when I arrived that morning. He was clad in a gray woolen sack coat I had not seen before. I was suspicious of how he had acquired the garment, for it was identical to the coats worn by our infantry, and it might even have been sewn in my father's mill. He was exempt from military service on account of the commutation his father had purchased for him from the War Office in Richmond at the outset of fighting. He had volunteered this information to me at our first meeting. I had already assumed it, of course—the planters' sons at the University were uniformly excused from service by one method or another. (Later in the war, in fact, there was a law passed that excluded from conscription any man owning more than twenty slaves. Judging by the contingent he brought to Charlottesville, I guessed B.B.'s family held upwards of a hundred.)

B.B. did his best to speak of his commutation neutrally, but it was clearly a source of guilt for him. Most of the other commuted men would not even speak of their commutations, let alone dwell on the subject the way B.B. did. "I did not ask for it, Muro," he told me. "But, alas, there are no refunds." This he meant as a joke, of course, but one could not help wondering if he would trade in the exemption if he could.

"Look here," he said, "I have not told you an important piece of news."

Had he enlisted? There was simply no chance: he saw the men coming off the trains. Some of them would have killed their own kin for a commutation. It was B.B.'s duty, in a sense, to remain out of the service.

"We are going to have a medieval tournament," he announced.

I did not know what to say to this.

"The fellows and I invented it last night. There will be tilting. And archery. And women, naturally."

He grew very serious. "Listen, Muro, the greatest hindrance to our cause at this point is not a lack of guns and horses—although that is a problem, to be sure. Rather, it is the general hopelessness of our people. Wouldn't you agree? This tournament will go toward fixing that. It will lift the collective spirit. It will give our men the strength they need to drive back the Northern aggressors once and for all!" He paused a moment, then said, "Pageantry, Muro. Nothing stokes the heart quite like it."

I indulged him. "Have you asked the proctor for permission to use the Lawn?"

"We've done better than that," he said. "The tournament will be held—are you ready for this?—at *Monticello.*"

Now that was something. Since Jefferson's death forty years prior, the estate had been owned by a string of absentees, most recently a rich Northern Jew.

B.B. laughed and scratched his beard. "You're flummoxed," he said. "You are asking yourself how old B.B. pulled it off. Well, I'll tell you. A fellow named Wheeler is the groundskeeper up there, and the two of us happen to be acquainted. I can't say how, of course . . ." B.B. was a regular patron of the town's several bordellos, and I did not doubt that he socialized with groundskeepers there.

"I should leave," I said, feigning a glance at my pocket watch.

"Of course," B.B. said. He knew my plan for the cutter, which he acknowledged with a wink. "I would not dream of keeping you."

Lorrie appeared at the bottom wall of the Cabells' garden at half past six, as we'd arranged. She wore a heavy woolen cape, black, about her shoulders, which she must have borrowed from Mrs. Cabell, as I'd not seen it on her previously. I lifted her into the seat, and she arranged her skirts. The cutter was a gentleman's sleigh, with a bench built for one, but we squeezed together so close I had to mind my elbows while driving the horse. B.B. had lent me his best hitch, a stunning bay called Huntsman, who stamped the frozen service road with his left foreleg, anxious to leave the bricked- in town for the freedom of a snowy field.

It was a night well lit by a full moon, and we were alone but for the crows in the trees. The bench was narrow, as I've said, and it brought me closer to Lorrie's side than she allowed under normal circumstances. Her thigh pressed against mine, making a heat bridge between us that resisted, by melting, any snowflakes that had the unlucky lot to fall there. My hands were occupied at the reins; Lorrie's rested on her lap, snug inside a soft black muff. The peak of her woolen hat scarcely reached the height of my chin. A lock of her rich copper- colored hair—gone straighter now in the absence of the summer heat—had escaped the hat and waved fearlessly in the night air. Her mouth was fixed in a smile, so enchanted was she by the ride. The hunchbacked Blue Ridge was indiscernible that night except as a region at the bottom of the sky where no stars shone. Though we chatted amiably about this and that—the gossip of the University, and what we knew of the larger society—we were struck silent more than once when the sudden crest of a hill brought a vision so pure it seemed ill to spoil it with talk of mankind.

The talk that interested Lorrie was always the interpersonal kind—that is, those anecdotes which revealed hidden connections between known personalities. So it should not have surprised me that she supposed she should be connected somehow with my Yankee patient, Lieutenant Stone.

"Let us see," she said. "He would not be of the *Dallas* Stones, would he? No, I suppose not. You say he's from Connecticut . . . do you know where precisely?"

"I believe his people are from Pennsylvania."

She withdrew her right hand from the muff. Feeling the cold nip her skin, she plunged it back in again. "I don't suppose he has a middle name?"

"It is Burton," I said.

"Well there you are! We know many, many Burtons. There are

Heddy Winthrop's cousins the Peter Burtons, in Texarkana. Then there are the Obadiah Burtons, long- standing friends of my family, who do indeed have kin in New England, if I am not mistaken.

"By chance, does this Stone have green eyes and a curved nose like a cardinal's beak?" Braving the cold, she withdrew her hand again and held it to her face to show her meaning.

I indulged her: "He does!"

Lorrie bit her lip in concentration. She was, I suspected, on the verge of a major genealogical discovery when our sleigh came to a sudden halt. The starboard side had dropped at least a foot into the snow, and the horse could not pull it free.

I leapt down and found the issue immediately: the starboard runner had come loose from its moorings and lay free on the snow some yards back.

I cleared a stump of snow with the back of my glove and offered it to Miss Lorrie so that she might sit comfortably while I repaired the runner. She refused, asking only to be helped down so that she could stand nearby and watch me work. She was furious, but not at me. "You borrowed this wreck from Braxton Baucom," she charged.

"What of it?" I said. I failed to see how recognition of this fact would speed the repair work. I left Lorrie sitting on the bench and scoured the snow for protruding logs. I found a length of sufficient girth and wedged it underneath the fallen side of the sleigh. Fortunately, upon examination, I discovered a set of rudimentary tools under the seat.

"You would think," she said, "that a young man of Mr. Baucom's means would take better care of his belongings. Particularly in a time of privation." Miss Lorrie spoke as if she were reading an indictment. "But he does not take care, of course—and that is why we are here."

"He is not such a bad fellow," I said, marveling that the tables had been turned regarding B.B.—now I was his champion and Lorrie his detractor.

"I did not say he was *bad*. Only careless."

"Actually, he cares about a great many things. The war is one. Just today he was telling me about a plan he has conceived to boost the morale of our people."

"I cannot understand why you continue to defend him, John. You owe him nothing for his favors, not even the benefit of the doubt. A horse and sleigh mean nothing to him."

"He did not ask to be born well, Lorrie. And compared with other planters' sons we know here, he is remarkably obliging. He has been very good to me. And I have no doubt that if the time came for it, he would be good to you as well."

At last, the repair was complete, and I helped Miss Lorrie back onto the riding bench.

"We shall be home in an hour's time," I reassured her. The tender lines around her eyes and her delicate nostrils were turned an odd shade of blue. "Perhaps less. We'll see."

"We might have perished, John," she said finally.

# 38

THE LAST MONTHS OF that winter passed quickly, and also not quickly, as winter months do. I warmed the long nights at the hospital with industry, moving quickly into my role as attendant physician and seeing considerable improvement in more than a few recalcitrant cases. Several of the men in my ward showed remarkable progress, and as they were under my care at the time of the improvement, I received what credit there was to enjoy for it.

One poor fellow had lost his lips to frostbite after being left on the field at Fredericksburg overnight. The ambulance corps had found him alive among the frozen dead. An infection of the jaw had already begun by the time he arrived in Charlottesville. Dr. Cabell advised, after an examination that couldn't have taken longer than a minute, that I was to do my best to keep the man's fever down, but that God would do the healing—or not. I took Cabell's dismissal as a sort of personal charge, and as soon as the old doctor moved down the hall to the next ward, I collared a nurse and ordered a strong dose of Dover's powder (we still had in our pharmacy, by miracle, a decent quantity of this mixture, and Dr. Cabell had not forbidden me from using it), to be followed by a strict diet of dried fruit. The boy's name—I remember it as much for the mellifluence of the syllables as for the significance of his case—was Emmanuel Raw. When it got around the ward that he'd been written off by Dr. Cabell, but that the young ward physician had taken him on, the boy Emmanuel Raw became, instantly, a mascot and rallying point among the other men. One ill soldier, a syphilitic quartermaster with a voice like a donkey's bray, began to call out, upon waking every morning, "How there, Raw?" as if resuming a conversation begun the night before. Raw, of course, could not speak—his jaw having enlarged to the size of a cow's tongue, and with the same violet hue. Nevertheless, whoever was awake of the other men chimed in with the quartermaster, offering up encouragements and playful chides: "What d'you say, Raw?" and "Speak it, Raw! Speak it, you Raw dog!" Such commentary invariably cheered the boy, and his eyes often shone with tears.

I don't mean to discredit the encouragements of the common men of the ward, but I do think the contribution of one of Raw's ward mates did more than any other to advance his healing. That person was Lieutenant Stone, whose cot lay two down from Raw's, and who could be heard late into the night whispering advisements, consolations, and admonishments in the gentle tone of a father. I should mention here a fact that older readers will recall, which is that the commonest soldier during the war was not the man of relative age and standing, like Stone, but rather the green country boy. For every Stone there were a dozen Raws, and the atmosphere surrounding any group of soldiers was sure to be given more to the jostling and carelessness observed in a basket of puppies than to the heady consideration of any serious topic. Stone lent the ward a dram of wisdom—not the battlefield variety, for plenty of younger men claimed that—but the simple, useful sense gleaned from years of walking the earth.

One evening—this was in March, when the itch of winter confinement begins to rankle the confined—I was at my desk attending to some paperwork while the majority of the ward dozed. All but the night nurse had gone home for the day, and I was myself looking forward to a rare evening off. I had plans with Miss Lorrie. The ward was silent but for a man mumbling over his Bible, his murmur like the drone of a housefly trapped on the wrong side of a window. Soon, though, another sound floated to me, and I put down my pen.

"That's it . . . a little wider. Almost there . . ." It was Stone. He was propped up, leaning almost directly over Emmanuel Raw. "There you are," he whispered, "just like that . . . Try again."

Silently, I pushed back my chair and stood up, careful to remain hidden in the shadows. I saw that Raw was sitting up on his cot, facing Stone. Both his hands were at his mouth, as if he were a child working to extract a loose tooth. Noises gurgled up from the boy's throat—high- pitched, irregular noises that sounded as though they came at the expense of great pain. His face was flushed from exertion, and the noises grew louder with his frustration.

"Now, now," Stone said, "there's no rush. Remember that. The tongue will move when it's ready."

Unsatisfied with his position leaning over the neighbor, Stone moved to right himself. His legs swung over the side of the cot, pulling with them the thin wool blanket which was his sole bedclothing. The blanket caught on an exposed bolt at the end of the bed frame and ripped audibly. "Blame it," he whispered under his breath.

Stone stooped and fingered the blanket, looking for the tear. As he labored, the boy suddenly broke through whatever impediment had been holding him back and called out, loudly: "Praise Jesus!" His speech was thick, like a drunk's, but there was no mistaking his words. "Praise Jesus Christ!"

Stone turned to find me. I stepped out of the shadow and raced to the boy's bedside, where I was joined by a dozen men, some moving on their own power for the first time since becoming ill. We formed a half- moon around Raw's cot, as silent in awe as the witnesses at Lazarus's rising. Like them, we stole glances at the man who had brought about the miracle. Stone stood by, mouth hanging slack, as amazed as the rest of us—and I wondered if the Son of God hadn't been as surprised at his own power that bright morning in the desert of Bethany.

The boy, for his part, gave a grin as he saw how his speaking had focused the attention of the entire ward upon him—the four Carolinians playing euchre in the far corner (the complete crew, as it happened, of an artillery piece blown to pig iron at Sharpsburg) ceased their gaming for the first and only time in my recollection to witness the occasion—and he tossed off phrases calculated to get the highest rise from the audience.

"My, but I do have a *thirst,*" Raw cracked, his words dulled by the leftover swelling in his mangled lips. "Where might a thirsty man get a drink around here?"

At this the men turned to me. One hollered over, "Ho, Doc—how 'bout a drink for the boy?" Another man—the very quartermaster mentioned above, in fact—extended the request: "How about it, Doctor? A full round in commemoration of the hour!"

"Ah, no," I said. Only Dr. Cabell and Mr. Clarkson, the pharmacist, held keys to the liquor closet.

The quartermaster persisted. "Just a nip, then? To pass around?"

"I'm afraid not," I said, and then, not knowing what else to say, I repeated myself: "I'm afraid I cannot."

By then, however, a flask or canteen of some kind was making its way around the group. Each man tapped his neighbor on the shoulder and then passed the thing, awkwardly, behind his back, regarding me the whole time. I laughed, hoping to make it clear that I would forgive the transgression in light of the circumstances. I even went so far as to raise the canteen to my lips when it came around to me. I did not drink it down, but the gesture was well received by the men. The boy Raw even, who took the flask directly from my hand in plain view now that the ruse of concealment was over, called me out for recognition I seldom enjoyed from the men, and which I suspected had much to do, just then, with my willingness to drink with them.

"A drink to you, Doc Muro," he cried, raising the flask above his head before pressing it to his mouth for a second pull.

His mouth was as repulsive as an ill- healed gash—which, after a fashion, it was. It was grotesque, not yet healed entirely, and still puffy with the vestiges of infection. The ordinary texture of the skin—the ridges and furrows in the lips, for instance—was grown over with smooth gray scar tissue, translucent as wrapping paper wet with grease. I wondered, was there a woman alive who would take him in? I often pondered notions such as this. When the war was over, when these men went home, would they find they were ruined forever? I would revisit the problem countless times as the war pressed on and ruined men continued to pour from my care like the products of an incompetent sculptor. Poor Raw, I thought. He was so young! And so innocent!

But then this poor, innocent boy did something that struck me like a blow to the gut. What happened was this: Raw lowered the flask and wiped his awful lips with the back of his hand. The next man in line, as the bottle was traveling roughly clockwise around the assembly, was Lieutenant Stone. The men beyond Stone were naturally anxious for their turns; they pestered the boy to pass it on. Before he did, however, I took a step forward.

"Mr. Raw," I said, feeling my chest expand with confidence, "I think it's only proper that you take a moment to thank the man whose attentions delivered you." I debated explaining to the men that the mysterious Northerner was in fact a doctor, and that his knowledge in the healing arts most likely exceeded their attendant physician's. I held my peace, though; I was by that point indebted to Stone in my own ways, for guidance both professional and personal, and I did not want to embarrass him unduly. I simply extended my hand, as if directing the ward's collective attention, and said, "Sir?"

Stone dropped his chin to his chest, and the tops of his ears showed pink. He shook his head and raised his good hand to accept, with modesty and admirable poise, the attention of the men. Strangely, though, the moment passed without any kind words from the boy.

"How 'bout it, Raw?" the portly quartermaster cried. "A word of 'preciation for the Yank, come on now."

The boy's eyes darted from one man to the next, all around the room, as if polling their opinions on what he might say.

The men behind Stone grew restless, and one began hooting like a train's whistle, in measured time. "Out with it, Raw!" another hollered. "Speak it, boy! Thank the Yank!" The soldier laughed at the rhyme, which he had not intended, and repeated it several times over to make sure the others appreciated his wit. "Thank the Yank, boy! Thank the Yank!"

Finally Raw raised the flask. The chanting, hooting, and hollering ceased, and the ward was suddenly silent. Slowly, with a shivering hand, the boy brought the canteen under his chin. He dipped his head, and as we watched in amazement, he allowed a line of saliva to spill down over his hideous bottom lip into the open mouth of the flask. He raised his head, smiled, and handed it over to Stone. "Much 'bliged," he said.

The room remained still as the soldiers waited to see what would happen. None had expected the gesture, and not many—this I'd learn later, from eavesdropping on their conversations—knew what to think, whether to applaud or beat the boy senseless.

Stone accepted the flask from the boy's outstretched hand with the same grace he might have employed taking the sacrament at the rail. He bowed his head—the ward was still utterly silent, the clop of horses' hooves audible on the street below—and lifted the spout to his lips. His hand, his good hand, clenched the dented metal in a vise grip, his knuckles white with pressure. He drank, wiped his mouth, and passed it on.

# 39

I'VE SAID THAT I SOLICITED Lieutenant Stone's advice on personal matters, and I'd like to recount one of those instances here. It was a Saturday afternoon in March, that time of year when the weather in Virginia is a roll of the dice from day to day: one week might be as warm as early summer, with forsythia buds notching the canes, and by the weekend the winter will have returned, scattering tiny yellow flowers on the snow. This was one of the warm spells, and the men who could walk were out in the hospital's yard amusing themselves in the sun. Stone could walk, of course, but I specifically requested that he remain, knowing that we might have a few moments' privacy to talk.

I had been troubled for a week by a letter from my father:

> Son,
>
>    I have given you nothing if not the confidence
> to pursue what you desire in life, be it Doctoring or
> some other Profession. However, I do believe that
> the Family works as a kind of Trump Card in these
> matters—that is, in those Times when a man must
> rely on his heart's Sensations to guide him through

*difficult straits. What I mean to say is simple, and here it is: my Fortunes (and by this I mean yours, and Mother's and Parthenia's) have turned ill. The Mill is nearly Failed—the slaves are mostly sold, the supplies of rough textile are all used up without any hope of another shipment, and (this is worst) our very position in the City has been ruined, with our own Neighbors and Friends turning their backs on us for some Reason.*

*Well—I know the Reason. It is your Cousin Sam. Why have I waited so long to tell you this? Your Cousin has made a Disgrace of us all. Naturally, I feel that I cannot blame any one but myself, as it was patent from Sam's first day at the Mill that he was at best ill- suited for this type of work (or I daresay any Work), and that a more forceful proprietor than myself would have ousted the Fool before he had a chance to do any real damage. That would have meant closing the Mill, as I'm sure you realize I was in no health to return to work just then.*

*But, Father, you say, why did you not hire another man? (Forgive me for placing words in your mouth, John Alan, but I see your face before me as I write this, and it seems hardly a stretch to imagine what you must be thinking.) Well, that is a fine sug-gestion, I would answer—except that there is no one left to hire. All the able men are gone away to War or else (like you) gone to employ themselves more directly to the effort than as Foreman of a small Woolen Mill. What would I give for another man like Stokes? Ah—but what wouldn't I?*

He went on to implore my prompt return home, though the entreaty was balanced, as it were, with equal service to the "admirable quality of your Ambition" (that is, my desire to leave Lynchburg) and to my "noble Vocation" (a vocation that you will remember he himself eschewed). Nevertheless, the appeal was, for him, a direct one, and his words tore at me. I imagined that men at college all over the South were that very week reading appeals from their own fathers (or uncles, neighbors, pastors), but was it wrong to believe my predicament unique? Was my work at the hospital not more valuable to the common good than the efforts of a man studying Latin or Greek? In the week since receiving the letter, I had twenty times made up my mind on this question, only to roll over onto the opposite side in bed and find my sense of it changed completely.

"I am yours," Stone said. He lit his pipe and shook out the match. We were alone but for the incorrigible Carolinian euchre quartet, who were so engrossed in their game that we might have yelled our conversation back and forth without being overheard. Stone puffed until the weed burned bright orange, then let the embers settle into the bowl.

"You're a man of business," I said. "Can I ask you about business?"

"That's a broad subject."

"My father owns a mill," I said. "In Lynchburg."

"Lynchburg . . ." He puffed and narrowed his eyes, as if he might conjure the place from memory.

"It's sixty miles southwest of here. On the James River."

I pulled up a chair. The euchre game erupted in cheers. "I've had a letter from home," I said, feeling suddenly young and vulnerable.

"A letter? But the fighting hasn't —you say it is sixty miles southwest?"

"It's not that," I said, sensing that I had rung the alarm louder than intended. "At least as far as I know it's not that. Thank God." I paused. "That is to say, the war is the ultimate cause of all this—Sam being hobbled, you see, and the demands on Father because of the contracts. And Stokes—Stokes wouldn't have left us otherwise. And then there's the extra niggers to consider . . ."

"Whoa, now."

I had been thinking aloud, letting the whole tangled mess of my thoughts come out of me like a cat's hair ball. But what else could I do? I had no means of pulling one strand from the others, stretching it to its full length, and saying, "Ah! There it is!"

I looked at Stone nibbling on the wooden stem of his pipe, and I thought I saw him hesitate a moment. He peered out the window, to the men in the yard under the cloudless March sky. I remember the scene distinctly because a cardinal—a crazed, libidinous cock cardinal, confused no doubt by the warm spell—chose that moment to crash into the pane just over Stone's shoulder.

The bird skittered on the sill a moment and then took wing, vanishing into the afternoon as quickly as he'd appeared. Stone turned to me then, and I understood that I was to tell my story, the complete story, from the beginning. So, I told him about Sam, about the his ride with Stonewall Jackson and his wounding at Manassas. I told him about Parthenia and how I wished Sam had died of his wounds most of all for her sake. I told him about Father's illness, and how I had almost left school, and only stayed because of a girl—a girl whose affections, while earnest at present, could not be counted to remain so. I told him about my father's previous life as a doctor, which must have seemed familiar to him, and which made me realize for the first time that I was speaking these things—all of it, truly—not only to Stone but to Father himself.

Stone knew this, and when he'd heard me out—he did not interrupt even once, but let me spin the whole crooked web start to finish—he gave the advice he knew he must: "Dr. Muro," he said. "Go home."

# Part Three

# 40

I FOUND MYSELF ONCE again at B.B.'s door. Upon hearing my predicament, he bellowed, "Don't take my horse—take the whole team! Take the brougham!" Without waiting for my reply, he summoned the groom. "Bring Mr. Muro the brougham, Aristotle And hitch it for four."

"Yes sir."

I stopped the jacketed Negro. "Actually, a mount would be just as well."

"Just one horse, John? Why, you'll scarcely make the next county with one horse."

"Lynchburg is only sixty miles," I said. "And besides, I thought I'd have Huntsman—that is, if you could think to spare him."

B.B. smiled broadly. I had said the right thing. "Ah, yes. A fine choice. On Huntsman," B.B. confirmed, "you might make the round trip—what is that, a hundred twenty miles?—and that without rest, or very little. Just enough to let him piss, eh?"

The groom laughed obligingly. "Shall I bring Huntsman, sir?"

"Yes, and—" He held out his hand. "Are you leaving now, Muro?"

I nodded.

"Very well," he said and returned to the groom. "Tell May to pack a basket. A sandwich—and what else?"


The flag of the Commonwealth flew above the Lynchburg courthouse, and below it the latest incarnation of the Confederate States' colors. There had been some debate among the states about the proper emblem for the new nation, and for several years each flew its own creation (which in most cases was a variation of the state's own symbol: a palmetto for South Carolina, a lone star for Texas, and so forth). Most towns in Virginia, by virtue of their proximity to Richmond, flew whatever national banner the legislature had endorsed most recently. Thus the flag I witnessed that day beneath the great seal of the Commonwealth was the one—the "Stainless Banner," as it came to be known—that the Senate had ratified only a week before. It featured a miniaturized version, in the upper- left corner, of the star-spangled Southern Cross, with the remaining space an unblemished white linen.

The market square, once the thriving center of the community, lay abandoned but for a woman selling gray eggs from a crate. I nodded to her as I passed, but either she did not see me or did not care to acknowledge my greeting, directing her impenetrable gaze straight forward while a wirehaired terrier made anxious circles around her feet.

My disappointment turned to despair as I moved from the center of town. It was evident that the women of Lynchburg—unlike the professors' wives of Charlottesville—had given up on their plantings, both public and private, so that every inch of road frontage grew over with weeds. Where as a boy I had enjoyed a vantage of well- groomed daisies and summer lilies, I saw now a mess of jimpson and fleabane, mustard and ragweed. I'm aware that much has been made lately of the so- called "natural" principles of landscape, championed by Olmsted and others, but I cannot stress enough how disturbing it was to see an environment fall into neglect that was once so meticulously manicured. Beneath the overgrowth, the features were the same—the town had only grown a vagrant's beard.

I did not pause in front of the house but rode directly to the stable. Heathcliff was there in his little shop, and I was relieved to see a familiar face.

He looked up from his bench and began to smile. "Why, if it ain't little Marse his own self!" He reached for his cane—which I saw had grown feet, three of them, so that the end of it sat on a kind of tripod on the ground. I marveled at the genius of the invention.

"How goes it, Cliff?"

The Negro was all smiles. "Has you growed two, three inches since you went off? Could be 'cause I'm shrinking. Don't you laugh now, it's a actual fact."

"Funny, you seem the same height to me. You got lifts in those shoes?"

This slayed him. "No, no, no," he said. "But I tell you—" He choked on his laughter, and after half a fruitless minute trying to get his wind back, he waved me up to the house. "You go on, now."

I drew water for the horse and hurried off to the house, making a note to ask Cliff later about his magnificent cane. (Regrettably, I never did, and I mourn the omission to this day. Over the years I have put many skilled craftsmen on the task of re- creating that three- pronged foot in a cane for rheumatic sufferers, and none has ever managed it exactly.)

I went in through the kitchen and found Mother stirring a pot on the stove. Peg was out in the privy, her health having decayed precipitously in my absence.

Upon seeing me come through the door, Mother carefully removed the wooden spoon from the pot and rapped it twice against the rim. Only after setting the spoon cleanly on a trivet did she come to me. I did not know how to take her silence. Certainly her hands, pressed firmly into my back, betrayed an enthusiasm for my visit. I returned her embrace with a kiss on the lips—a habit I'd acquired in Charlottesville and not thought to suppress now that I was returned to my former milieu. To my relief, Mother was distracted and did not seem to note any breach of etiquette—or so I thought. As any man who has returned home from a sea voyage can attest, a woman knows from smell alone where a man has been—and with whom. The kiss, in my case, only confirmed her suspicions.

"I figured you must have had a good reason to go back," she said. "After what you saw."

It was a strange greeting. Did I not possess a perfectly good reason to be away? Since when was college the resort of delinquent sons?

"I came as soon as I could," I offered, not just yet willing to pick up her gauntlet, if indeed that was her intention. "With the movements north and all, the rails are tied, and the coachmen are all gone to the service." I stopped then, recognizing upon the globes of her eyes the same glaze I had seen a hundred times as my father talked of work. "You must have heard the news," I went on. "Lee is moving north again." Still no reaction. "This time they say he's apt to win—"

"*Damn* your damned war!"

I had never heard my mother swear.

Her eyes burned with rage. "Do you want to ask about your father?"

"Where is he?"

"To think he lured you back with—what was it, ten lines?" She laughed without mirth, as if she meant just the opposite. "To think he composed himself there, on paper, so that you came running . . ." Her voice changed, and I heard a note of pity. "If he could only apply that skill where it *matters*—" She stopped. "He is upstairs." And then she turned her back on me, but only for a moment, as she whirled back holding a half- drunk bottle of corn whiskey. Corn whiskey!

"Take this," she brayed, holding out the bottle. "You might make friends."

When I did not reach for the bottle, she pulled it back and— believe me, I do not completely believe it even as I am writing this now—she brought it to her lips. I should specify that the bottle was of the ground- glass variety usually employed to hold lye and other noxious chemicals. I had witnessed fellows swilling home- stilled spirits from such vessels on a few occasions, usually in those dark hours just before dawn, as I was walking home from the Delevan. But this was my own mother!

I hastened upstairs and found the door of Father's study ajar, a play of lamplight on the runner in the hall. I knocked lightly and called out, "Sir?" The door fell open. Father was splayed in an armchair, asleep. At my voice, or perhaps only at the change of air in the room (the aged are remarkably tuned to such things), he startled and sat up. At first he said nothing, but only stared at my presence in disbelief. His bloodshot eyes, rheumy as a setter's, wandered back and forth between his son and the door, his son and the door, as if I had not entered that way but merely sprung from the floor like an illusionist.

"You received my note," he said.

"Yes sir. I could not find a coach. So I rode."

Father's brow rose. I had not taken a horse to school, and he must have known that the liveries were all shuddered.

"I borrowed a horse," I said. "From my roommate."

He nodded hesitantly, as if this fact compromised him somehow. "Generous fellow," was all he said.

I said, "There is trouble at the mill?"

"Aye."

"Trouble with Sam?"

"It is."

He did not offer more. I saw that I was going to have to pull the story out of him. But my resolve to be my father's inquisitor was weak at best. I had come, after all, at his beckoning, and I felt that I was due an explanation.

"Is there something the matter with your throat?" I asked finally.

"John Alan—"

"Forgive me, sir, but I cannot fathom why you choose to remain silent, now that you have your wish."

"My wish?"

"That your son stands before you. Is that not what you desired?" I felt the rush of blood to my cheeks, that familiar sense of indignation which masquerades as righteousness in the young. "Because if this is not what you want, I might as well leave. Lord knows there is use for me at the hospital."

"That is your choice," he said, and I became aware that the two of us—grown men both, now—were engaged in a sort of contest of lowliness, to see who might portray himself the more wronged by the other.

"You have no idea of the sacrifices I've made to return here," I said, letting emotion take control of my tongue. "I have real responsibilities. Men live and die on my watch. Do you remember that? Or did your country doctoring never afford any real weight to your work?"

Tears welled in the pits of his eyes, and his mouth pulled tight and quivered as if he might wail. I hated him for it.

"Accept the consequences of your choice!" I said. "All these years you assured us that it was better this way. Well—is it? How goes the mill, Father? How fares the Woolery? Stand up and answer!"

The old man gathered himself and rose to his feet. "You want to know how the mill fares? You shall see for yourself." He sprung up and went to the door, taking his coat from the hook and draping it over his shoulders like a cape. It was an old habit, one borne of midnight knocks on our door from patients' emissaries, urging him to leave at once for this emergency or that. "I will get the surrey," he said. And then, looking me up and down—I was wearing a brass-buttoned waistcoat and a fire red ascot, both B.B.'s—he said, "And put on some *decent clothing,* for the love of God!"

# 41

AS WE DREW WITHIN view of the mill, Father halted the horse and turned to me. "I want to make it clear that I do not approve of what your cousin has done. However, he is family, and that makes our cooperation compulsory. Do you understand?"

I did not. What exactly had he done? When would someone tell me? I had ridden sixty miles, plus another two in this carriage, and I was as ignorant as I'd been in Charlottesville.

Father tapped the reins and the horse lurched forward. We took the final bend in the road, and then I saw the crowd. They were two dozen at least, men and boys mostly, but some women as well, lining both sides of the drive. They held hand- scrawled signs, some stapled to wooden pickets, which they began to wave in our direction as they heard our approach.

"Say nothing," Father instructed, although I was far from doing anything of the sort. "Ignore them as best you can. I shall explain once we're inside." He cracked the whip on Sun Flower's rump and the carriage gathered speed. The gravel roared under the wheels. At twenty yards I began to recognize faces. The postmaster, Tad Keithly, and his two boys were there, as was the county magistrate, Mr. Wade

Hickam. The two men held a banner between them, painted in foot-high letters on a bedsheet: *Emancipation Is Treason.* Beside them stood the pastor of the Presbyterian church, the Reverend Word-ham—a citizen so widely respected that he would have been mayor if not for his collar. Wordham's associates held signs proclaiming all of the usual biblical justifications for slavery. Noah's curse on Ham's son: "Cursed be Canaan! The lowest of slaves will he be to his broth-ers" (Genesis 9:25). And Leviticus 25:44: "You may acquire male and female slaves from the pagan nations that are around you." Even this line from the epistles: "Let as many servants as are under the yoke count their own masters worthy of all honor, that the name of God and his doctrine be not blasphemed" (1 Timothy 6:1).

Our own pastor was there, too. His wife, Dorothea Kibbens, had been my mother's closest friend, and to see her at the gate of our mill, disposed to malice, was like a knife in my side.

The surrey raced past the crowd, and the gate swung in by myste-rious hands. Father did not slow the horse, but charged directly to the rear of the building, where we could neither hear nor see the protes-tors. Two Negroes arrived to hand us down from the carriage, and Father deliberately avoided my eye. He did not speak until we were ensconced in the office above the shop floor.

"Your cousin has freed all the niggers," Father said. He tamped weed into his pipe. The stained wood shook between his fingers. "About a month it's been. He signed the papers without my know-ing. I was abed, mainly. But of course you see how I could never have anticipated such a thing."

I was flabbergasted. Who had the dark people been, then, who had helped us from the carriage? "But—why are *they* here?"

"Where could they go? It is hardly safe for freed Negroes on the street."

I thought I heard a note of sympathy in my father's tone. Though I was no necessary enemy of the Negro, I was disgusted. These people were his property, after all. *Our property.* Their loss would mean, ultimately, my debt. "You allowed this?" I said.

"In a matter of speaking. I hoped my letter would explain it, but I fear I failed on that score. You see, I had no choice. I was abed."

"Abed? You might as well have been dead!"

"Now, John Alan, you mustn't —"

"I mustn't what? Continue to lie? Is that what you want? I might tell you precisely what you wish, that aye, you had no recourse but to trust our cousin. But sir, you and I both know that is decidedly false."

"John Alan!"

"I might tell you that you did the best you could. That God's will be done, and far be it for us to question Him. But again: false."

I pulled my anger back taut as a bowstring, and let out, "You shouldn't have to know what a disappointment you are to me, Father. The mill itself was stupid enough when you had a worthy and sustaining profession already, but to have failed . . . to have turned your neighbors and closest friends against you. Against us! Do you know what has become of Mother?"

He said nothing. Of course he knew.

"It is no wonder! It pains me to see her indisposed, but it is no wonder! And what of Parthenia? Can I admit that I am so terrified to learn her news that I have put off asking all these hours? My own sister, sir, and I cannot bear to hear of her. I ask you, now: was this all your intention?"

Father's pipe gave a blue curl of smoke from where it lay on the desk. The twist lengthened as it rose into the air. I watched for a moment, blood pounding in my temples.

"The only good thing you have—I mean this honestly, sir—the only good thing you have is me."

After this there was the crisp, cold silence such as after a bottle of fine wine shatters on the floor, when all gathered there stand and watch, dumbstruck at the loss.

Finally, a man's voice broke the pause. "And how is that?"

My cousin stood in the door. His eyes blazed with something like zeal, though I could not discern what for.

"Hello, Sam," I said.

"Let's not waste time on pleasantries, John."

"Boys, please," my father said.

"No, no—I want to hear him speak, Uncle."

"Samuel—"

"Why, it's as plain as day, Sam," I said. "You have failed! And now, to turn loose the Negroes . . ."

"I gave you my plan. This is only its logical conclusion."

"I assume you mean *perspicacity* and so forth. I fail to see how that leads us here."

"Jackson said, 'When the plan becomes untenable, cast it away.'"

"He said no such thing!"

"And pray, how would you know? Did you serve with him?"

"Enough of this, Sam," Father said. "John Alan has been busy in his own right."

"Let me finish," Sam barked. He left his mouth parted slightly, as though he might say more. But he only stared at my father. No muscle moved in his body save the patient rise and fall of his breath. I wondered suddenly if the spark I had seen in his eyes was not zeal but *madness*. I had in the course of lectures attributed a whole variety of illnesses to those people I knew best. Parthenia in her pallor and apathy I diagnosed with anemia. I even wrote a letter home on the subject, as I did with all my diagnoses.

But Sam! My mind went over the sequence of presentation: his return from the war, the drinks in the station tavern, the arguments with Father. This was all fairly normal, given his experience at war. The dolor with which he lazed about our house, rising only at mealtimes—now there was something, but again, there was no reason to suspect anything out of the ordinary. It is a predicament any physician sees a hundred times in his career, the masquerading of disease as something benign, for the early symptoms of so many illnesses are indistinguishable from the normal functions of the healthy body. Often, it is the *degree* of the affliction that separates the normal from the pathological, and the measuring of degrees that separates the experienced physician from the novice.

"Come now, Sam," Father said. "Let John Alan have a moment. He must reaccustom himself to this place."

"Why is that, sir? Is he to stay with us? Ten months you have been away, cousin, and it is as if your family never existed. It is simply unfathomable that you are still undecided on the issue of staying or returning to school. When your family has collapsed upon itself like a rotted pumpkin!"

"I have not decided yet what I will do."

"Your father agrees with me. We've discussed this on several occasions. What was it you said, Uncle? That John Alan was the most *selfish* young man you had ever met, or something like that?"

Father bowed his head.

"Oh, come, Uncle. Tell him."

When Father did not answer, Sam went on: "He said he couldn't understand why you hadn't returned the first time he took ill. I rather agree, of course. I can't think of another man who would have done what you have—not even in the army, and there were plenty of scoundrels there."

"Father?" I said. "Did you say these things about me?"

I had a view, his head lowered, of the white fluff atop the old man's head. It was so thin that the pink scalp glowed underneath, as on a newly shorn lamb.

"Father?"

He raised his head and said nothing.

# 42

I REMAINED IN LYNCHBURG another day, just enough to catch up with Parthenia, who had been away in the country with a group of alumnae from Miss Pelham's. My sister, for some reason, had escaped the social excommunication bestowed on Father and Sam. Most likely she was every bit as talked about, but the poor girl hadn't the sense to realize it.

Parthenia and her friends had been on a foraging mission, a "freedom quest," she called it, of begging eggs and hams and other provisions from whatever farmers they could find remaining on the land. What foodstuffs they found were donated to the army—via the Home Guard—along with useful items the girls managed to assemble from abandoned farmsteads: lead pipes for melting into shot, the occasional skein of cotton wool for bandages. They also saved their urine in glass bottles, for distilling into nitre. Of all the sacrifices endured over the course of the war—and everyone had his own, however disconnected from the cause—I admired my sister's most. So pure was her intention, and so repulsive her chores! For girls of Parthenia's ilk, trained as they were to be polite above all, this was an almost unimaginable reorganizing of their most developed sense—that of propriety.

She came to my room first thing upon learning I was home. I was pleased—though I must admit a little surprised—to see that her cheeks had taken on a healthy, ruddy color and that her carriage had lost some of the stiffness that was Miss Pelham's stock in trade. The war effort had done Parthenia well; I assumed it was the result of "freedom quests" and other bouts of physical exercise, which had been all but absent from her previous routine.

"Have you done your hair in a new style?" I remarked when she entered. I had learned from Lorrie that it is better to start a conversation with a compliment than a simple hello—no matter if the conversant is the greengrocer's apprentice or one's own sister. The result with Parthenia was a pleasant surprise, as it always was when I followed Lorrie's social example. Young Parthie, who was at that time just fifteen, patted the back of her head like an old lady at church, as if checking to make sure her combs had not dislodged on the trip.

"Do you like it?"

"I do. You look all grown." I had never complimented my sister, and so my words, though heartfelt, must have seemed suspect—as though I might have followed with, ". . . *for a sow!*" or some other rudeness. But as I say, I was sincere, and in a moment she discerned as much and warmed to me.

"Was your trip safe?" she inquired. "Some of the girls were over the river yesterday and they heard cannon fire."

"Did they?" As a rule, every unknown boom heard in those days— from the felling of a tree to a simple thunderclap—was assumed to be artillery. The burden of proof fell to the doubter. Some say that women were more susceptible to the misperception, but in my experience that was not true. The hearing of men was affected similarly.

"What's more, Lucy Frahley had word from her cousin in Winchester that there were raiders on the street every night for a week." This was another civilian fear: roving bands of cavaliers detached from either army—essentially an armed version of Parthie's "freedom quest." Much lore now surrounds the actual cavalry units who inspired these tales—Stuart's being the most important in a real military sense, and Mosby's perhaps the truest to legend. Lord knows that every private sick with measles in my ward claimed to have fallen off his horse ten paces behind Jeb Stuart—and I may even have treated a legitimate cavalry officer once or twice—but "raiders" I saw none.

"I should ask the same after you," I said. "Peg said you ride without an escort."

"Peg told you that?"

"She hasn't told Mother, if that's what you're worried about."

"Poor Peg," Parthie said. She clutched her cheeks in her palms. "She is in no state to be working. I told Mother as much."

"How long has Mother been *as she is*?"

My sister and I exchanged glances to make sure we were speaking of the same thing. Our mother had never been a drinker of anything stiffer than cream sherry, and I did not know if she hid this development from my sister. The sudden blanching of Parthenia's complexion gave me my answer.

"Not long," she said, speaking just above a whisper. "Perhaps two months."

Two months. I made a calculation in my head. Two months meant that while I was out gallivanting in the fresh snow with Miss Lorrie—simultaneously with that wholly superficial excursion, and only sixty miles south—my mother was taking her first sips.

"Yes, two months, nearly," Lorrie clarified. "It was just after Father got the news about Mr. Stokes."

"The news?"

"Did he not write you? Oh, he was horribly upset. Beyond that, really: we all thought he was hopeless. Mother asked Pastor Kibbens to come, to explain about hopelessness and so forth—about the sin of it—but there was no getting through to him. It was rather frightening. Did he really fail to mention it to you? I find that odd, considering."

"Yes, yes," I hurried, "but what about the news? What was the news from Stokes?"

"There was no news *from* him, John."

And I understood. There was no need for her to elaborate, but of course she did anyway. In those days, the circumstances of a soldier's death were memorized and recited by his family and other intimates as a tribute, an encapsulation of his larger self, as if the force impelling him to charge headlong up a fortified ridge were the same responsible for his handiness in the garden or his uncanny way with hogs.

"He went ill with camp fever. Father received a letter from his commanding officer."

"And that was when Sam . . . Yes, I see it now."

I felt my sister chill at the mention of our cousin. "You've seen Sam?"

"At the mill."

"Do you know he lives there now?"

"So what of you and Sam?" I said, now that the topic was breeched.

"That was a *long* time ago," Parthie cried, sounding every bit the girl I had left the previous June and none of the young woman I discovered on my return. "Besides, he is my cousin. Close blood, you know?"

Though science has in recent years confirmed the dubious merit of cousin marriages, the practice was accepted generally in my youth, and even considered advantageous if done well. One only heard "close blood" mentioned as a spoiler to marriage when there was some other reason to disqualify a union. "Was he not our cousin ten months ago?" I said.

"Psh—"

"Well?" It was my intention to draw out the truth: namely, that cousin Samuel Brightwood had gone mad, and that she had ended their betrothal (or whatever it was) as soon as this fact was made plain. I had not intended to persecute her, but that is precisely what I accomplished.

She lashed out at me: "And what right do you have to judge me, brother, when you have been away without so much as a letter of advice? You might have written your concerns—or better yet, you might have ventured home on your roommate's fancy horse, in your roommate's fancy suit, for—for a Sunday, perhaps? One Sunday! And you *saw* him at Christmas!"

"Parthenia—"

"But no, that would be a step backwards for you. We are beneath you now, is that not the case? All of us, not just Sam. Well, God bless Sam! Never mind that I should consider myself lucky not to have married him. Never mind the poor fool has to live his days with the guilt of driving Father to apathy and Mother to drink. No, let's forget all that—let's drive a needle through Parthie! Yes, *Parthie* is the problem here, silly Pathie, who should have seen it all coming."

Had she ever said this much in one burst? Her tears pooled between her lips and she wiped her mouth on the back of her hand.

"But Sam is an imbecile," I offered.

"Is that your conclusion? Do you believe that all this has come about because our cousin is of unsound mind? Even if that is true, it does not excuse your negligence. Nor your selfishness!"

Her mouth curled into a scowl, which was made all the more frightening by her childlike features: the pink lips pursed like the skin of a dried peach, the little nose creased with wrinkles.

So I had become the focus of my family's displeasure. "But this is about *Sam!*" I protested. "How does this concern me at all?"

"But John Alan—don't you see that is exactly my point?"

# 43

I HADN'T THE PATIENCE to wait for Cliff to prepare my horse for the return trip, so I went to the barn myself. The old Negro's snores wafted from the shop.

Huntsman seemed to have taken well to my parents' barn. When I appeared with his saddle over my shoulder, he nuzzled the slats separating his stall from the next, where old Sun Flower dozed. The mare woke when I unlatched the stall door, and she gave a long and sincere protest as I led Huntsman out. Her whinny seemed to contain more true sentiment than all the words passed between humans over the three days' visit. How discouraging that the same ignorance that confines beasts to lives of burden allows quick bonds between barn mates—and conversely that the sophistication that lifts us above livestock renders us unable, often, to connect with our own kin!

I took Huntsman to the side yard, where I loaded saddlebags with the various supplies I wished to convey back to school: a jar of honey from a neighbor's apiary; a forgotten box of collar studs; an unopened jar of ink from a Christmas long ago. I also took some quick foodstuffs for the road, a half loaf of Peg's white bread, and a hunk of farmer's cheese. Then I went to the well pump to fill my canteen. When I returned, I was startled to find my father standing beside the horse. He stroked the animal's neck.

"So soon?" he said.

I noticed that he held a small leather purse in his hand, and I discerned at once the purpose of this exchange.

"Have you come to wish me well?" I said.

Father shrugged and handed me the money. It was heavier than I expected—full of coin instead of paper notes. I loosened the tether. The purse held at least a dozen silver dollars, and another dozen gold.

"I reckon those are safe from inflation," he said. That word—*inflation*, as in *inflation of the currency*—was on everyone's lips just then at the University, and I was taken aback for a moment to hear it leave my father's mouth. Such talk carried with it a tone of flippancy, as it was one of the commonest topics of both gossips and naysayers, and it seemed also disrespectful, like speaking of battles in terms of strategy instead of cost in blood. Of course, as a businessman, my father had real cause to fear such things as inflation.

I cinched the purse and gave it back. "Keep it," I said. "The bursar is gone off anyway." This was true: the little man who administered the finances of the University had surprised everyone, most of all the faculty, with a sudden decision to enlist in the infantry. A truly diminutive fellow, no more than five feet tall and one hundred pounds, with a mind for figures so sharp it seemed a waste to let him go to war—he surprised the entire University by carrying through with his intention, riding off to join a field unit outside Richmond. A month later some one got a letter: he had been posted at the railroad switch in Orange, figuring the timetables of transport trains. The thought of the little bursar at his desk in Orange, frustrated and boiling over with blood thirst, swept in and out of my mind in an instant, but it made me consider if Mr. Stokes had been handled the same way. Perhaps

Stokes hid his considerable talent at logistical matters from the officers and earned the right to fire a weapon before he fell ill.

"Have you heard from Stokes?" This I said quickly, as if the thought had just crossed my mind.

Father nodded rapidly. "Yes, of course. He is well. A bit daunted, I guess you would say, by the Yankees' ironclads. You know they have a whole fleet of them now? Word is that they're moving down to Norfolk from Massachusetts or whereever they make those infernal engines."

So that's the way it would be. As soon as the window had opened, then, it was shut tight. Father avoided my eyes as he spoke, rubbing the sole of his shoe back and forth over the raw grass of the side yard.

"He's well, though, quite well. Why do you ask?"

"No reason," I said. "It's just that he was . . . he was almost family, I suppose."

"Aye, that he was," Father said, not catching the tense of his comment.

We then discussed the route I was to take back to Charlottesville. As I spoke of the well- known rough spots, the well- signed fords, and easy crossings—all of which I knew and had no reason to review with my father—I fought back tears.

I was successful in this right as far as Tye River, where I stopped to water Huntsman and to fetch the snack from my saddlebag. That is when I found the purse—the second purse, which he'd hidden before our conversation. It was comparable to the first and similarly laden. My will crumbled, and I regretted all my words.

# Part Four

# 44

"DO YOU THINK I'M the selfish type?" I said between lungfuls of
sweet, rich smoke from B.B.'s pipe. He had been sitting, curiously,
on the south steps of the Rotunda when I arrived in Charlottesville. I
say curiously because it was getting on evening and B.B. was usually,
on those days when he deigned to attend lectures at all, long since
gone from the Grounds by that hour. Upon sighting his unmistakable
form at the head of the Lawn, I urged Huntsman to canter the final
yards. B.B. waved, and after tying the horse to the rail before Pavilion
II, I sat down to accept his offer of a smoke.

"My sister accused me of it—selfishness. I have to admit I'm bewil-
dered."

B.B.'s lips popped as he drew air through the bowl. "If you're
selfish," he said at last, "then what am I?" He smiled and passed the
pipe to me, the thick aroma of the tobacco wrapping pleasantly about
our heads. It had stormed recently and the air of moldering leaves rose
from the Lawn, an earthy complement to the smoke. It was the best
and most flavorful weed I had ever tasted, the produce of the Bau-
coms' land in Charles City.

"But honestly, John, no man at this university works as hard as you.

Night after night at the hospital, day after day in the classrooms—is she mad?"

"Is who mad?"

"Your sister—it was your sister who charged you?"

I nodded.

"The fact of the matter is that a bit of selfishness, in your case, might be seen as a positive development. I often wonder how you manage in that place, with the quantity of beds and . . . and *sicknesses*."

In fact, I doubted he ever wondered anything of the sort, but I appreciated the sentiment. His was my thinking as well: how might I be accused of self- indulgence when I hardly had time to attend the body's most basic functions?

However irrefutable, this logic did not dispel the nagging sensation that Parthenia and the others were correct.

"It's true I work more than they know. But what if—I don't know—perhaps I am lacking in some other field. The domestic, perhaps."

"The domestic?" B.B. smiled as his eyes traced the east colonnade.

"I mean with others, outside of work. With women. With Lorrie."

There was a moment's pause, quick as a bird's shadow, in B.B.'s reply.

"You might ask her," he said calmly. As I say, any hesitation on his part was but a finger's snap, followed by perfect composure. "Are you selfish with her?" Here he paused to let the prurient entendre sink in. He smiled. "A woman is a tender thing, John. You know they can break if you're not careful."

"Is that funny?"

"I thought so. At any rate—you treat her well, or at least as well as can be expected, given your schedule."

It was another irrefutable point. And yet the nag persisted. "I'm asking you to erase the hospital from the calculus," I said. "Pretend I'm reading philosophy."

"Ah. That changes things. The world with one more philosopher would be a different place. But it seems fundamental to your character that you would never read philosophy. Me, if I were inclined to read anything, I might read it, but not you. You're much too concerned with making good of yourself."

For all his faults, B.B. had a remarkable self- knowledge, and a kind of modesty I had not encountered before I made his acquaintance. In the years since, I have known several men of means—a few intimately, as they have been patients of mine—but I have never known any to mitigate as successfully as B.B. the repulsive quality of wealth. It is a common trait of such men to make stabs in that direction, but few ever truly succeed. When they do, they are all the more charming.

"I believe you castigate yourself too readily," B.B. said. He produced his tobacco pouch and began to pack another bowl. "Perhaps you'd feel better if you had some honest sins to your name. I doubt you would worry over selfishness if you'd killed a man in cold blood, for instance. Now, I've never done that—not that I'd admit, anyway—but I have plenty to flog myself about, if I choose to."

"Such as what?" I said.

B.B. turned away and struck a match, cupping his hand around the flame out of habit, for there was no breeze on the Lawn that afternoon. He did not answer the question.

After a while, he said, "It looks as though the tournament will go on as planned."

"Good news," I said.

"I think so. Have you thought of riding with us? We could use another man."

"I couldn't ," I said, searching for an excuse. I could not plead lack of a suitable horse, for B.B. would surely furnish me in that respect. "I reckon I'd be more use as medic. Tilting is a dangerous business, you know."

"As you wish. But I doubt there will be cause for field surgery, if that's your meaning. If not in a saddle, I want you dressed to the nines, do you understand? I'm telling everyone—I cannot stress this enough—it is a show, spectators included. The more we participate, the greater the effect on morale."

"Very well. I will raid the armoire."

"That's a fellow."

B.B. passed me the pipe and went to Huntsman, whom he untied and stroked readily about the neck. We had not discussed that he would ride home, but of course it made good sense. We could not have arranged it better, in fact, and I wondered at the coincidence. And so you see that roommates do enjoy a certain telepathy—even those mates who do not actually share a room!

# 45

IT WAS THE WELCOMEST relief to resume my duties at the hospital—and in fact to be back in Charlottesville altogether. I took comfort in my work, and in time spent with Lieutenant Stone, who resembled more and more a father to me, and indeed filled that exact void in my heart. I expect I served a similar purpose for him, as he had been then two years away from his own children (he had three daughters), and I should hardly assume his interest in our friendship was any less a coincidence than mine.

He did give me a brief scare, however, upon my first arrival back to the Delevan. As I entered my ward from the second- floor hall, I was startled to see the cots disordered from their previous formation, with Stone's moved from its location between the two middle windows. There were the men playing cards at the far corner, and in my head I took a hurried roll. Stone was nowhere to be seen. My heart seized at the thought that he might have passed away in my absence, through a relapse of his infection, or God forbid through the ire of one of his ill- tempered neighbors.

Thus I was relieved beyond measure when a moment later Stone's tall and crooked figure appeared at the door. He brightened on seeing me, and ambled in with remarkable agility. I learned that his condition, contrary to my fears, had made a marked improvement in the previous week, his strength being recovered to the point where he no longer required assistance to move about upright, and he had just been in the yard, taking the exercise that he knew he needed in order to keep the infections from manifesting afresh.

"It couldn't have been the air," he said, for it was then the first of July (I mark the day exactly, for reasons the reader shall note in a moment). "But it was not a change in diet, I can swear to that." The military- style cuisine of the hospital kitchen—growing more spartan with each passing month of privation—was the subject of constant grousing by the patients, though not previously by Stone himself. "Ah! I know it now. I've had a new idea, Muro, regarding the war. It is rather simple, actually: new hands. Across the board, your side and mine, politicians and brass."

There was a soldier on the next cot—a Virginian—who had been listening to our conversation. At this last remark of Stone's, he added, "Aye, let's change the guard all around. And we'll start with your bastard Lincoln!"

Stone did not flinch. "I could hardly agree more, sir," he said. "That is my meaning exactly. And I appreciate your offer to assume the duties and responsibilities of the office when Mr. Lincoln is put out to pasture. It is really quite noble of you."

The other grays nearby—they were the man's mates, it happened, having all been laid ill by a certain lady in Baton Rouge—howled with laughter. "There's a wit on that Yank," one of them said. Then, to his brother in arms: "Send me a post- card from Washington City, Pres'dent Schiff!"

The laughter had the effect of a powerful drug on the room, levity of any kind being so rare in that place. Satisfied by the exchange, the soldier went back to the card game, and Stone returned to me.

"So tell me—was it worthwhile?"

"Worthwhile?"

"Your trip."

I gave a facial contortion that I hoped would carry the weight of a thousand words.

Stone laughed. "What in heaven's name is that supposed to mean, Muro? Women raped and land salted? Be clear about it, son. I'm getting 'land raped and women salted . . .' Speak—don't just shake your head like an idiot!"

I have always thought it a sign of a healthy friendship when a man risks insult with a comment such as this, but I have to admit I was taken aback.

"Do you really want to know?" I said.

"Do you intend to tell me?"

"I thought I would, but if you're too busy . . ."

"John, please."

"It was a disaster. A *disaster.*" On repeating the word I felt a sudden and unexpected tightening in my throat. "The mill is gone to sticks, or close to it. Mother drinks. Father cowers. The slaves are . . . even the *servants* are sick." I meant Peg and Cliff, of course; I did not go into the business of Sam and the mill slaves with Stone.

"And that's not the half. My sister had the gall to ask me—well, tell me this: Do you consider me a selfish man? Is it greedy, what I've done? Coming here, to school?"

Buoyed by B.B.'s enthusiastic support for my rightness in the matter, I was not prepared for Stone's reply. Now, years removed, I can say that it did more to change my sense of the world—that is, the order of it, the social and metaphysical rules that govern each of us—than any other dictum, creed, or advice I've heard. Like the battle that was taking shape just then on a Pennsylvania farm, Stone's comment would stand as the point where the past ceased and the present began.

"Not one of us," he said sternly, "who has enjoyed some measure of success in his work, who has taken happiness from it, perhaps, or only the satisfaction of having trod where his feet liked—none is innocent of the crime you're worried over. The fisherman whose catch feeds his village for a week: he left his family when he put out to sea. No matter how loud the band plays on his return, no matter what fame he earns or what gifts he brings from faraway ports, his family may never forgive him the absence. Never. It is illusion that a man can be both provider and comforter at the same time. Rather, he must learn to stomach the lack of one or the other—the deficiency or the crime. For it is a crime; you are right to see it thus. Pride, ambition, egotism, selfishness—these qualities are so ubiquitous in a certain class of men that they might be seen as a mark of expectation rather than disgrace. I saw it on you, Dr. Muro, the instant you appeared in this ward. I'm speaking not of the occasion when you were promoted, but on that first afternoon. I'm sure you remember. I certainly do. You had a choice to make—to treat this feverish, raving soldier, this Yankee soldier, or to demur for lack of know- how. The reprimand from Cabell—yes, I know about that, too—it was nothing compared with the ire you found at home. That is only my suspicion, but I can see on your face that I'm correct. A disaster, you say. Ah, and whose making was that disaster? Why, yours! There is no escaping that, John. But neither is there reason to discount what you've done here. The mark of a grown man, you see, is not the courage to take strange steps but the fortitude to live with their consequences. You'll learn it. And if not, you will die confused and unsatisfied."

I allowed his words to settle. The men on the yard hollered—one of them had a baseball. Eventually I said, "But what about you? You walked away from your vocation."

"I struggle with that decision every minute of every hour, now and always. It's no advice at all to say to you, 'Son, make the proper choices.' That is not my advice at all, and besides that, it's impossible to know what is proper and not at your age. We must persevere, regardless. That is the only choice."

# 46

ASIDE FROM THE ROUTINE triage of new sick and wounded men—routine only because the human soul can grow accustomed to absolutely any horror—there were two results from Gettysburg on our little college town. Both concerned the spirit of the citizens—the *morale,* in B.B.'s parlance—and they tended to run astride each other like thoroughbreds at a race. The first was a perceptible redoubling of the will to crush our enemy, as if nothing shy of victory could make fair payment for what we had suffered already. New flags went up as fast as the ladies' clubs could sew them; old dishes were given patriotic names such as "victory stew" for succotash and "Dixie Porridge" for hominy grits; and new traditions—a distinctly Southern paradox, by the way, for even the newest routines are endowed with a hasty pedigree in Virginia—new traditions rose like mushrooms from the fertile soil of young minds. One of these was the venerable (if brand- new) institution of the "starvation party." At such events, no refreshments or liquor of any kind was served, and a collection was raised for some noble aspect of our cause, such as the relief of families whose fathers and husbands had been killed or had perished from disease. It was always a paltry sum, never amounting to more than $50 or $75 Confederate, which inflation diminished further. The chief attraction of the starvation party was the linkage of sentiment with action, which was something many private citizens felt ashamed of lacking, there being only so much one might do, if one were not enlisted to fight, to help the war effort. Dressing up and attending one of these parties, however, was a definite contribution and could be quantified, as in, "I attended six starvation parties in a fortnight."

The other trend, then, was a general fearfulness among the population. Exhibited only in private, and never spoken about except in whispers, this was the logical complement of the above: that is, both resulted from an acknowledgment of the current period as the most exigent of the war thus far, and the same impulse that begat action also, conversely, led to cowardice. On one hand was resolve; on the other, fear. Like an experiment of chemistry where the requisite substances are always present but no reaction occurs until a certain atmospheric condition is achieved, the town boiled to a frenzy after Gettysburg. And the people who marched their support for Lee, waving red- and-blue flags the length and width of bedsheets, were the same who the following morning lay in bed an extra hour, searching for the courage to go on another day.

No person better exhibited both tendencies than Lorrie Wigfall. By midsummer, our courtship had withered to an afterthought—I was too much distracted with hospital matters, and with school, which continued defiantly through the season. I would not have blamed the girl if she'd written me off like a bad debt. So it came as a surprise when she began to call on me again. This was August 1863. We began to meet for coffee—the "Kentucky" variety, brewed from the pods of a native tree, the actual article having been used up many months prior, with any private sources remaining necessarily clandestine.

She was as lovely as ever, the auburn tresses streaked with honey from the summer sun. I am not overamorous by nature, but in those months when the air thins and the afternoon shadows grow longer, I find that I am given to sentiment. Even now, with so many years passed, I think back on that autumn—as indeed every autumn before or since—with a wistful air, tinged with sadness, as if the shadows themselves, the black fingers on the ground, had been the memories, present in the moment only to insinuate themselves to posterity, and eventually to blot out the actual facts of the past in their bittersweet wash.

I recall one September evening I gathered Lorrie from the Cabells' home just as the sun was coming to eye level in the western sky. As we passed through the portal where the west colonnade ends at the pediments of the Rotunda, where the brick walk leads down several steps to reveal a broad, sloping field—where, at the northwest boundary of the Academical Village one is first exposed to the world outside—there, the burnt orange ball of sunlight caused us to shield our eyes, and that being not enough protection for Miss Lorrie, she buried her face in the crook of my arm. The cicadas in the tall oaks and sycamores churned their mechanical song, and I was frightened at the sudden deprivation of my senses. That instant—blinded, with my ears ringing and this girl clutched to my arm—stretches out forever: I detect the note of manure on the air, as well as a stove fire from one of the hotels. Lorrie's face, her cheek, is cool against my hand, and her breath tickles my skin. I feel each brick under my sole as we make our way down the walk. In that moment I exist in a mythical autumn, the one my sentiments swear to, where life's exigencies are only nuisances, and not great ones, and one moves through the atmosphere by magnetic force to the next great and memorable circumstance. In that place, the mosquitoes and biting flies only kiss the flesh, perhaps leaving there a bit of perfume or honey. This is the place, also, where Lieutenant Stone's brutal compromise is not necessary—here it is possible to please every seeker, including one's own ambitions, and to delight in the challenge. Years later I would hear a man describe a similar effect, which he called the "eternal moment of youth." I expect this is what he meant. But it is not pure youth that I recall. Rather, it is a moment between youth and manhood, a divine interstice, where the benefits of both were present without the accompanying curses. Strike "youth" from the label, then: call it simply "the eternal moment."

With Lorrie on one arm and a picnic basket on the other, I walked up Carr's Hill, a grassy clearing a stone's throw north of the Anatomical Theatre. I had identified this spot early on, as it was visible through the high windows of the lecture hall. My attentions often wandered in that direction when the subject onstage was too arcane, or when the previous night's shift ended too late to secure satisfactory rest.

Now I was realizing a long- standing goal of picnicking there, while also providing a pleasant diversion for Miss Lorrie, who was under stress in her own right. She had joined a women's relief society not unlike the Lynchburg group championed by Parthenia. The chief difference between the two groups, as I saw it, was sophistication. As with the plantings and so many other things, the ladies of Charlottesville seemed far more concerned with outward appearance than their Lynchburg counterparts. The locus of this sensibility was a core group of a dozen or so women associated with the Farmington estate. Any account of Albemarle County during this period is sure to pay significant attention to these women. To the young ladies of the area, these women, who were mostly of the elderly persuasion but included a few young wives given entrance by dint of good birth or good marriage or both—these women were the envy, the very idols, of every girl for miles around. They carried themselves like the old English aristocracy, which was likely what they believed themselves to be, venturing into the public eye only on certain predetermined and highly orchestrated occasions, such as the Governor's Ball in spring (indeed, the governor always made an appearance, as he had every year since the office was held by Jefferson himself). Like English aristocrats, too, the Farmington women cloaked themselves in a vast mythology of historical and genealogical lore. That Jefferson had designed their temple, the main house at Farmington, was beyond questioning—in fact, our third president had lent his hand to a number of private homes in the area, but of these only Farmington wore the association as a badge. Other aspects of the lore—that Mrs. Cartwright, the matriarch of the set, was descended from King George III, for example—were questionable not only on their merits but on their value even if they could be proved. Old King George—the "mad" monarch, the last sovereign ruler of the thirteen American colonies—was hardly as attractive an ancestor as, say, Sir Isaac Newton would have been. But that is my opinion. Certainly King George served just fine to dazzle the minds of society aspirants, and Mrs. Cartwright and her ilk put so much chalk in the myth that they had a pamphlet printed that listed the complete ancestries of each of the leading ladies of the set, with biographical notes to explicate the more obscure historical figures.

The reason I mention these women—for you can see they were not favorites of mine—is that they had lately extended to Miss Lorrie the rarest of entrées: an invitation to join their event- planning body. This move was generally regarded as tantamount to full acceptance into the Farmington set, and thus it was as if Miss Lorrie had been tapped by the fingers of a very powerful and much- admired angel.

"I can't see why they chose me," Lorrie said as we climbed Carr's Hill. "A girl from Texas? I'm flattered, of course, but I don't pretend to understand their motivation."

She handed over the letter she'd received. In flawless calligraphy, on gilt- edged stationery, it began: "In salutation of our dear Miss Wigfall . . ." The envelope had been sealed with real paraffin wax, which was no small thing, that substance being one of the commodities most frequently commandeered from private citizens by quarter-masters and their agents. My mother, for instance, had long since taken to sealing her correspondence with paste.

"But surely you deserve it," I offered. "You have family connections with at least a few of those ladies, don't you?"

"Oh, but that's nonsense; you know those charts are hardly worth the paper they are scrawled on."

"Is that so? I thought you held Mrs. Cartwright to a judge's standard."

"You know what I mean."

It was the first time I'd heard Lorrie doubt the veracity of any genealogical claim. A small landmark, perhaps, for anyone but her.

I spread the blanket over the grass and weighed the four corners with rocks. It was cool in the shade, and the ground was well drained despite the recent heavy storms.

"You should accept them," I said.

"I will. But I must, mustn't I? I mean, what would it say about me if I refused? What would the girls say about me then? Lorrie Wigfall was too proud for the Albemarle Ladies."

"But you are not considering refusal, are you?"

"Of course not! But it is delicious to consider, isn't it?"

"I suppose so."

"*Look at Miss Lorrie—why, her nose is so far in the air, I wonder if she can breathe in such a pose! Oh dear me. Lillian, do you suppose she sleeps that way?*"

Lorrie was enjoying herself at this little charade, and I did not disturb her out of it, even though my mind quickly wandered. Was she a silly girl? Men often dismiss the fairer sex with such characteristics, but I must conclude there was something else at work with Lorrie. For it was not silliness whence stemmed this ritual of impersonation—rather, it was an honest and devoted self- inquisition. I always esteemed in Miss Lorrie this quality, which I consider among the rarest of all human traits. She always wished to know herself, which is more knowledge than most of us can bear.

"Will you send a letter, then?" I asked.

"Oh, no. Mrs. Cartwright—did you not know this?—Mrs. Cartwright has put a gig at my disposal. I had some time explaining it to Auntie. She does not place much by the Cartwrights, you know."

I greatly admired the Cabells for their subtle resistance to the various Albemarle oligarchs. This urge followed chiefly from Dr. Cabell's notion that the professional man ought to exist apart from the gentry. Even in those cases when a physician happens also to be a man of means, Dr. Cabell maintained that he should, at least in public, maintain a clear and discernable distance between himself and his kin. Cabell's reasoning was that if the trade of medicine is ever to be elevated in the public mind above the curse of quackery, the doctor must present himself as a disinterested purveyor of the purest science. "There is no doubt of a mathematician's intentions," he famously told a lecture hall. "And why is that? It is simple: because there is no money in mathematics!

"In our discipline," he said, "the cost of supplies alone is such that no patient should ever expect services rendered gratis. It has been my experience, in fact, that most if not all sufferers are glad to pay. But that is precisely the weakness charlatans have exploited for extreme profit. Thus we cannot rely on the recipients of medical treatment to set the prices thereunto. Rather, we must take it upon ourselves to set reasonable fees, for it is my belief—and that, you will note, of many of the most esteemed practitioners of medicine on this continent and the last—that the only way to insure a decent living for ourselves is through a slow and gradual accumulation of public trust." That speech was the talk of the medical curriculum for many weeks afterward. How can we take such advice, argued the naysayers, from a man paid nearly $6,000 per annum? How they arrived at that figure I will never know, but it was something of a moot point. Whatever Dr. Cabell was paid, it was tendered in Confederate notes, and by the time he was delivering his lectures on ethics—November 1863—his salary would have held more worth if it had been paid in salt.

"The driver waits in the mew every morning and evening behind the pavilion garden. Have you seen him? The dark fellow in the top hat? I must accept. Oh! Can you imagine how delighted he will be?"

"The driver?"

"Yes! Take me to the Cartwrights, please. Yes, yes, miss. Right away, miss. Oh, John—you must come with me. Can you come to Farmington? Say you don't have to work tonight."

"I'm afraid I must."

"Hmm. Shall I speak to Uncle?" She had never yet followed through on this threat—though she tendered it often.

"Tomorrow," I offered. "But . . . as long as you have Mrs. Cartwright's gig, why don't we take a spin this afternoon? Before my shift begins."

She giggled. "You know I can't do that."

I said, "Why not?" and I meant it solely as a rhetorical parry. But as my words hung in the air—as Lorrie shook the crumbs off the blanket and we replaced the utensils in the picnic basket—I realized I was absolutely correct. She had made the grade. She might use the Cartwrights' carriage for any purpose whatsoever.

"I suppose I shall go alone this evening, then. They are quite lovely people, John, and I wish you would give them a chance."

I pictured the two of us at Farmington, being handed down from the gig by a servant in white gloves, the scent of citronella burning somewhere, the ladies of the club waiting in a row along the drive.

*And who is this?* I would kiss their bird- boned, wrinkled hands one by one by one, and answer their overfelt greetings with my own empty words. My mouth went dry.

"I'm sure they are," I said. "But alas, I have to work."

I hid my delight. You see, for all the complaining of medical men, night duty has its privileges.

# 47

ANOTHER NOTEWORTHY occurrence that autumn—that is, besides
the legions of sick men we were forced to receive, men for whom we
had neither beds nor cheer, by the decampment of Lee's army from
the northern region of our state—was the absolute and final drying up
of certain chemical preparations from our pharmacy. Most important
of these was quinine, the chief ingredient in so many remedies for
fever. It is especially indispensable against malaria, which was hardly
rampant in December but loomed sure as spring rain in the mind of
every doctor on our staff.

I mentioned that we had been able to obtain, through sources
known and unknown to Richmond, quantities of several valuable
ingredients. These were generally the trade of smugglers, although in
the early months of the blockade, supplies were discovered in unexpected locations, such as in the back room of a bankrupt export house
or some such place. Those surprises were all used up by year three.

Then Vicksburg fell, and the Yanks had control of the Mississippi.
Dr. Cabell called us into his office to deliver the news. "Gentlemen,"
he said, "from this point hence we shall have a new formulary." The
other student physicians and I exchanged looks. A new formulary?

We had been prepared for the news that there would be no more special deliveries of pressed opium, nor any phials of quicksilver appearing without explanation. But a new formulary? With what materials, we wondered, would this formulary be composed?

The bewhiskered doctor put a small sheet of paper—a broadside, as it was called—into my hand. An identical sheet went to the fellow on my right. "I have only two copies of this at present, so we will have to share. Read it over, and note the indications, some of which may surprise you. I must admit they did me.

"The Surgeon- General has asked that we procure adequate supplies of these items as soon as possible. I have set Mr. Clarkson to it, and he assures me that the most rudimentary preparations you see here—those requiring no distillation beyond simple addition of spirits, in other wise—shall be available by the week's end."

The list was organized in this manner: the name of the preparation in the leftmost column, followed by the Latin and common names of each ingredient and the proportions of each. In the rightmost column was listed the various indications—the illnesses to be addressed with each remedy—and the recommended dose. I scanned the indications first, as Dr. Cabell had instructed, and I was surprised to find among them nearly all of the commonest complaints: there was simple fever, constipation, loose bowels, rheumatic fever, chills, sweating, headache, boils, grippe, pneumonia and other pulmonary complaints, heart palpitation, vertigo—and so on until my eyes grew dry from staring.

But the column that caused me nearly to drop the sheet was the leftmost one—the preparations themselves. Gone were the familiar remedies, the calomel and cantharides, morphia, &c. In their place were the names of plants I had known all my life but never stopped to consider in the context of pharmacy. In fact I winced at the very mention of some, for they ranked among the most noxious and loathsome weeds in the Southern *botanicum*. Take Jamestown, or jimpson, weed. There, in neatly printed letters fresh from a Richmond press, was argued that two drams of the aqueous extract of this vile, thorned intruder of cornfields everywhere, this bane of every farmer from Campbell County, Virginia, to Campbell Springs, Texas, was in fact a powerful diuretic, the equal of our most advanced chemical preparations.

"Repeat as necessary," read the instructions. Indeed, I thought, one might repeat it all he liked, until the patient dropped like a thirsty horse! *Jimpson weed?*

I read on. An infusion of dried fleabane—those are the white daisies, no wider than a penny, that grow in clumps along road-sides—was said to ease rheumatism. The oil pressed from yew leaves lessened fever if given immediately before bed. Rosewood, rose hips, rose water . . . lemon peel, lemon balm, lemon grass . . . Some botanical ingredients that were known to us already for certain purposes were given brave new properties. Sassafras root bark, for instance, which was concocted with syrup to make a refreshing soft drink, suddenly claimed itself a remedy for gout. To think that root beer might have relieved so many! I was flabbergasted. And then, of course, I was suspicious.

"In the interest of preventing a mutiny"—Dr. Cabell cleared his throat—"I should say that I resisted this as long as possible. In the end, however, I concluded that we risk nothing in accepting the recommendations of the Surgeon- General. We have accepted a great many of his recommendations, some of which we have opposed quite strenuously, if you will recall."

This was understatement, and characteristic of Cabell. I could tell from the slowness of his speech, the deliberateness with which he chose every word, that it pained him to cede to his rival once again.

"In fact, gentlemen, I have taken the liberty of testing certain of these recommendations in our practice here, and though it injures my pride to say so, the results are rather favorable."

My astonishment redoubled. It was perfectly reasonable that he should wish to see evidence before extending the order to his staff—but were the claims of this broadside even worth the trouble?

"We must remember that these treatments, however unconventional, must be compared not to the proper formulations we have grown to rely upon, but to the absence of treatment."

Here he wore his teacher's hat, deftly converting our bewilderment into knowledge.

"Though we call ourselves scientists, our foremost duty is not the advancement of science, gentlemen, but the well- being of our patients. Comfort first, science next."

The sheets had been passed around the room and sat now in front of Dr. Cabell. Snatching one off the desk, he raised it above his head. "I should urge every one of you to walk out if you are too proud to use these cures. Does that describe anyone?"

The half dozen of us stood still, silent.

"Very good. One copy will reside with Mr. Clarkson at the dispensary, and the other I will make available here in my office. Please commit it to memory as soon as possible." He smiled, his first hint of amusement at the matter. "I expect that will take all of . . . five minutes? Or ten?"

A few of the fellows chuckled. The tension eased, as if every man present had just loosened his collar.

"One last request, gentlemen. Do not mention the composition of these new remedies to the patients. I know that we have among them some rudimentary knowledge of the medical arts, and more than that in some cases."

He looked at me. "We are to proceed as normal. Do you understand?"

# 48

MISS LORRIE'S ASSOCIATION with the Albemarle Ladies was an immediate triumph, and as I had expected nothing less from her, I was not surprised by it. For a time I was able to avoid contact with the ladies of the club, but as the weeks churned behind us and Lorrie became more and more an integral piece of the relief society's philanthropic machinery, it pressed upon me to make appearances at her side. I found myself measuring very carefully my days off from the hospital, as I knew that any evening spent outside the Delevan was likely to be spent at the Club (for that was how the Ladies called the Farmington estate) or at the residence of one of its members.

I will recount one such evening in order to convey the sense of these gatherings. It was the first week in December, a Wednesday. I was to meet Lorrie at the home of Mrs. Eugenie Wells, a widow living in the Park Street district. Lorrie herself was to be conveyed the two miles or so between the University and Park Street in Mrs. Cartwright's gig, which had become, for all intents and purposes, her own personal transport. The carriage, the horse, and even the driver now resided on the premises of the Cabells' pavilion—the cart and mount in the appropriate outbuildings and the servant in the basement quarters where the Cabells lodged their help. The loan of a carriage was a token of Mrs. Cartwright's esteem, to be sure, but it was also a constant reminder of Lorrie's debt to the Ladies—a distinction I'm sure she noticed, although we never discussed it as such.

I arrived at the Wells home shortly after six, on foot, and before entering the gate I made sure to pause and wipe the sides and soles of my boots. I had procured a rag for that purpose from the hospital laundry. After carefully folding the rag into squares and stashing it in my innermost coat pocket, I smoothed my mustache and paced the last dozen yards to the door. The brass knocker weighed as much as an ancient pistol, and it lodged against the wooden door with a tremendous thud. A Negro maid answered. She was wearing a starched white pinafore over a gray apron. "Evening, sir," she said. "Miz Lorrie is expecting you in the drawin' room."

I followed her down a wood- paneled passage into a wide parlor where women sat on couches and upholstered benches, cooing like pigeons over this and that. Though it was not her domicile, Mrs. Cartwright was installed at the center of the group, with Miss Lorrie attached like a handmaiden at her right arm. When the maid announced my entrance, Lorrie rose at once to greet me. I took her hand and let my lips linger a moment longer than usual on the cool, smooth skin. I had made a policy early in Lorrie's association with the Albemarle Ladies to squeeze as much flattery and hand kissing as possible into my appearances, so to make up in the quality of those appearances what would be lacking (I hoped) in quantity.

"Ah, Dr. Muro!" came a familiar booming voice. "At last! We were beginning to worry after you."

"Good evening, madam," I said, taking up Mrs. Cartwright's fleshy paw. She was a rotund, flanneled creature who smelled always of bergamot. "Once again, a pleasure."

Of all the ladies, Cartwright was the one most responsible for my policy of affection. She rose and fell with my taunts and compliments, with my tender taps and kisses, like a girl. (No one knew her age precisely, but it was commonly assumed to be approaching sixty.) She urged young people to call her Bibbsy, a ridiculous moniker that a favorite niece had applied to her once upon a time. To my knowledge no one in her circle ever took her up on the offer. To refer to such a grand and grandiloquent personage by such a diminutive was unthinkable. I called her Mrs. Cartwright.

She kept hold of my hand after I rose from the greeting. "Come, sit down. I trust you know all present? Mrs. Wells?"

Here the thin, mousy woman stepped forward and extended her hand. We had met once before, at Farmington. Then, as now, she wore an extraordinary quantity of rouge upon her cheeks, doubtless to compensate for an unfortunate slackness of the elastic tissue there. The effect was not a good one, however, and in conjunction with the dark pouches of skin under her eyes, and the bleached cornstarch she used to try to cover that disfigurement, she looked like a clown.

"I thank you, madam, for having us into your home. We are delighted to be here, as I am sure Lorrie has expressed already."

"She has, Doctor," Mrs. Wells said. She had a pleasant voice, clear and sonorous as a wood thrush's. "And I do appreciate your coming. Mrs. Cartwright was just telling us of your plans for the Christmas season at your hospital. Tell us which building is yours, now?"

"It is the Delevan," inserted Lorrie. "And indeed, John has plans afoot to—to bring *good cheer* to the men." She gave a paralyzing glance, and I understood that these plans were to be mine in name only, and that it would be my duty to nod and confirm whatever she proposed.

"There will be garlands, of course, which we intend to hang at least a week before the dinner . . ."

"The dinner!" cried Mrs. Cartwright. "Why, there must be a hundred beds in your hospital, Doctor!"

"I'm afraid the total is much greater than that," I said, taking care to watch Lorrie for any signal. "The entire complex—that is, the Delevan and the adjoining ward buildings and tents—the total is closer to ten times that many."

"Ten times!" said Mrs. Wells. "What is that, now—a thousand? How shall we ever—"

The women seized on the matter like pigeons over a sackful of spilled grain.

Though Mrs. Cartwright flung her hands about the air and made attempts to stand up, it was Lorrie who finally wrestled the session back to order. "My dear ladies," she said. "Please." Her tone was authoritative, firm. I was impressed and—dare I say it?—*aroused*.

"Let me ask you this, ladies: what are we if not a superior group of minds? I have no doubt, none whatsoever, that if Dr. Muro sets us the challenge of raising a meal for twelve hundred"—for indeed she knew the true figure of beds in the facility, which I had intentionally understated—"Tell me, why on earth can't we see it through?"

A woman seated on a high- backed upholstered chair, whose snow white hair matched exactly the bleached lace of the antimacassar that framed it, let out a squawk like an irritated hen: "There is quite a difference, Miss Wigfall, between a meal for twenty and one for—what is it now?—*twelve hundred.*"

"Indeed there is, Mrs. Clemons, and I, for one, am grateful for it. For what sacrifice would it be—and what accomplishment—to put forth the same thing we have done many times before? Did General Jackson complain when the Yankees did not line up in neat groups as his mock opponents had in training? Why, of course not!"

Whence came this rhetorical cyclone? I scarcely knew her! Together with the ladies of the club, I sat and listened as Lorrie—that is, *Miss*

*Wigfall*—laid out a complete plan for the execution of the Christmas meal, no less ambitious or less detailed, surely, than the battle plans of Lee & Co. Clearly she had given the subject considerable fore-thought, and its introduction into the evening's conversation had been anything but coincidence.

"Thus with the employment of your kitchen, Mrs. Randolph, and the spare team from Ginnie's farm at North Garden . . ."

By the time dinner was served at Mrs. Wells's long table, Lorrie had been elevated to the rank of logistical genius in the minds of all present, including me. Her challenge was great, for her legion was a collection of women chosen not for their aptitude at execution but at judgment; not for planning but for questioning plans. Christ himself set forth with a more capable crew, sinners and tax collectors notwith-standing. And yet I had no doubt that she would succeed. There was something in the clearness of her eyes, the unwavering quality of her voice, that inspired confidence.

As the servants cleared away the coffee cups and the tiny plates that had held chess pie, I reached my hand under the table to touch Lorrie's thigh. This she acknowledged with a simple and sincere gaze, a beneficent gaze.

In the gig on the way back to the University, I held her close. She collapsed into me readily, as if the exertion of standing so high had led to a refractory period of weakness. What she required—and I sensed this wordlessly, as if by conveyance through our skins—was a strong hand to hold her, to replenish the strength she had drawn down that evening.

Thus she did not balk when I asked the driver to leave us off, please, not at the Cabells' pavilion but farther down the mew, at the end of the east colonnade. In my room, we sat on the bed, and I poured her a drink. We toasted to her challenge, then to its success-ful completion. To my men, and to her ladies. To Presidents Lincoln and Davis; to the sun and the moon; to her, to me, and to us. Around midnight, lips raw from kissing and brains addled with drink, we walked down the mew to her pavilion. She did not wish to leave my company that night, and neither did I hers. When we parted, eventually, at the gate, Lorrie walked along one side of the serpentine wall, and I walked along the other, each holding an arm up that our fingertips touched at the top. When the wall became too high, her fingers disappeared.

"Good night, Doctor," came the whisper from the other side of the wall.

"Good night," I whispered back.

# 49

IT WAS DECEMBER 22, 1863, the evening of Lorrie's Christmas meal at the Delevan. The staff of doctors was gathered in a surgery on the top floor of the building, joined there by the senior membership of the Albemarle Ladies. The medical equipment in the room had been cleared out and replaced by wooden furniture hauled up by the Ladies' considerable servant corps. The table was set with white linen and polished silver, cut-glass goblets and fine china. The Ladies' appreciation for the physicians of the hospital—a secondary mission, in my mind, to the primary goal of uplifting the morale of the patients—was further evinced by the presence, in a polished oak crate, of a dozen bottles of French claret, a late-fifties vintage, contributed from Mrs. Cartwright's *cave*.

The medical staff—Professors Cabell and Davis and the half dozen or so practicing physicians from the community we employed under contract—were accompanied by their wives or, in the case of Dr. Orianna Moon, husband. We student physicians had been encouraged to bring a companion each as well. Two of the other fellows had girls with them, two did not. I counted myself somewhere in between, for Miss Lorrie, who was of course to be my companion, was at the moment in one of the mess tents—they numbered three—which had been erected to house the warming and distribution of the meal. It was Lorrie's intention, further, that each plate be delivered not by the usual nurse or dietary steward but by a young lady of poise and distinction. These she recruited from the ranks of her young admirers. Since her acceptance into the Farmington elite the throng of girls orbiting Lorrie had grown considerably. As the dinner day approached, no aspect of the plan so vexed her as did these girls. What if they were to faint—or gag? My recounting of daily life at the hospital, the odd characters and intractable cases, had prepared Lorrie for what she was to see, but what of a girl of sixteen fresh from a mansion on Park Street? How would she react if a soldier swiped at her buttocks? If he spit in his food? The attending physicians of each ward had been instructed to inveigh against misbehaviors, with threats of disciplinary action for all infractions. But what of it? Men are men—and soldiers especially.

When the time came to hang the decorations in the wards, the girls, to a one, acted with courage and grace. Sure enough, there was catcalling, and blue words were uttered within earshot of the impressionable young ladies. There was hallucination as well: one man, a crumpled private from the Second Alabama, swore that he saw heaven up a young lady's skirt as she stood atop a ladder hanging boughs. I happened to be standing nearby, and I can attest from personal observation that there was no such sight to be seen; the girl's pantaloons well covered all flesh, right down to her boot tops. "My Lord, I've died," the man cried out. "Today, I died. Praise the Lord Almighty!"

The boughs of fresh balsam, holly, and red cedar improved the surroundings not just by an infusion of color but also by the wonderful aroma they imparted to the wards, which normally smelled of feet, old bandages, and rot. On the evening of the dinner, the girls also lighted sticks of cinnamon and spice. The expense of procuring all these supplies—in money and in labor—was hard to fathom. Several times Miss Lorrie asked me to consult her ledger, to check the figures there, and I was taken aback at the amounts. Owing to my distaste for the Farmington women, I had been skeptical that they would make the sacrifices required to fund the endeavor. In the end, it proved more difficult to find supplies to acquire than funds to acquire them with. Even though the Ladies proffered gold—Mrs. Cartwright insisted that she carried paper notes "only to be reminded of Jeff Davis's handsome face"—even gold could not buy meat that simply did not exist.

It was Lorrie, once again, who found the sources for the meal; she who found the old farmers holding back turkeys and grain; she who disarmed them with benign- seeming banter and then snatched up their stores before they had a chance to refuse. She had acquired a cartload of fowl for the Christmas meal, guinea hens and ducks and what- else, besides a pair of choice gobblers. The latter she ordered reserved for the doctors' table; the white meat lay expertly sliced and awaiting gravy on a giant silver platter at one end of our table. I felt ashamed to be in the presence of so much meat—indeed, I had not seen a turkey properly dressed out in two years. The smell was intoxicating, as they say, and it prevented me from paying attention to the table conversation. The others must have felt the same way; they only succeeded better in keeping up appearances.

"Say, Dr. Moon," began a colleague of mine, a bachelor who had declined to bring a date, "have you seen the jaundiced fellow in First West? I have reason to believe he is healed."

Dr. Moon was a dark, elegant woman in her middle thirties. She had come to Charlottesville with her husband, who had once been an importer of some repute. He had been introduced to the young Orianna, the daughter of Czech merchants, during a trip to New York. The husband's business failed soon after they were married, and together they had returned to his family's estate in Albemarle.

He could be found most evenings in one or another tavern. B.B., in fact, once asked if I knew an Edmund Moon, who claimed his wife was a doctor. I told B.B. I knew the wife, and that she was a fine doctor—among the finest. She was of the grand old school of European medicine, which is conservative to a fault, preferring in all cases the poultice to the knife, the atmospheric cure to the one mixed up and injected. She was therefore the perfect physician for our times, where in the absence of proper chemical indications, a dose of restraint was often not only the wisest choice but the only one. Despite her sex, she was respected widely and was in fact the first outside physician Dr. Cabell had called when the word first came from Richmond that his modest teaching clinic was to become a general hospital. Dr. Moon had served with diligence, without complaint, and deserved the turkey dinner more than any other person present, save Dr. Cabell himself.

On this occasion, however, Dr. Moon—understandably—wished to pretend she was somewhere besides the Charlottesville G.H. She touched a napkin to her lip and said to the student, "I trust your opinion."

The fellow took the rebuke for affirmation of his diagnostic abilities. He looked around the table catching eyes and smiling. Dr. Moon returned to her husband, whom she interrupted just as he lifted a full loaf of bread to his mouth. She scolded him, and he dropped the bread. He looked sheepishly around the table to determine if anyone had seen.

A procession of Lorrie's girls laid out the vegetable dishes. First was a crock of buttered cowpeas, which a very pretty girl in a red- and-white pinafore centered on a trivet *just so,* as if placing the final block on a delicate tower. She hurried out just as the next girl, of raven hair and slightly upturned nose, came into the surgery with two plates of greens balanced precariously on her outstretched arms. A mild blonde followed with potatoes.

The girls set me to thinking about Parthenia, who was likely engaged in Christmas folderol with her own ladies' group. She had not answered any of the three letters I had sent since my visit. Sitting down the previous night to write her again, I stopped when I realized that it would have been the fourth consecutive letter without an answer. Now who was the selfish one?

The table filled with side dishes until it seemed the serving girls would have to leave plates in the guests' laps, or on top of the supply cabinets filled with gauze and bandage clips. There was a parsnip puree, mixed with a dram of beet juice to make it pink, as was then the fashion. There were minted carrots. There was a cabbage salad with onion seeds and some kind of crackling bits sprinkled over it. There were fruit dishes, too. In fact, the girls placed before each guest an individual fruit salad, composed of half a preserved peach doused in sweet mayonnaise, topped with shreds of orange cheese, all atop a bed of tender lettuce.

By the time Lorrie arrived I was into my third plate of food. I say this without compunction only because I was not alone—in fact, a certain gentleman among us (I shall not give a name, but report only that it rhymes with "rabble") was seen to make arrangements so that the platter bearing the meat was stationed just astride his own plate, thus making it easier to shovel helpings unnoticed from one to the other. After Mrs. Cartwright's French claret was drunk up, the girls uncorked a local variety, which at that point in the evening tasted every bit as wonderful.

The diners raised their glasses to salute Miss Lorrie. Dr. Cabell, his concentration blurry no doubt from the chemical properties of turkey, stood up and called for a toast. "To my niece, who continues to surprise me."

"Here, here!" shouted the ladies and gentlemen.

But the good doctor was not finished. "God only knows where

young miss found all this," he said, indicating the spread of ransacked platters. "But God bless her, eh?" He came awkwardly to the playful tone, forcing a laugh that I am sure he meant in sincerity, but which for lack of practice came off as insincere. "I can't decide what I shall tell your mother when she returns for you," he said. "You were a girl when you arrived. But now—"

"Take note, Dr. Muro!" bellowed Mrs. Cartwright, and the table erupted in laughter.

"Aye, Muro," Cabell said. "You have a force of nature here, I'm afraid."

Lorrie blushed at the sidelong compliment, though I could see from the sparkle in her eyes that she was pleased. It was just the reward she'd sought—indeed, more than she'd sought, to be the toast of the medical men *and* the Farmington wives. It was almost too much for her to bear.

"You flatter me, Uncle," she said.

"Bah!"

"Really, I could not have accomplished a thing without the help of so many fine young ladies." And here, as if on cue, the line of girls who had been our servers traipsed in from the hall. Servers no more, they smiled with fresh- powdered cheeks and licked lips. As Lorrie called each girl's name, she came to a place at the head of the table and bowed. The doctors clapped heartily, pausing only to pour wine when their glasses keened low. The ladies of the club—for whom the introduction was intended, with all due respect to the doctors— applauded politely with fingertips.

At last, when the introductions were done and a final glass had been raised to the girls, Miss Lorrie took her seat. I might have imagined it, but I recall a certain heat coming off her that night, as from a stone that has lain under the hot sun all afternoon and gives back its energy throughout the evening hours. It was the radiance of fame,

I suppose, and I was not immune to its allure. She looked magnificent—truly magnificent—even though she had been at work since dawn. Her eyes were shining specks of jet, and they fixed upon her audience like magnets. The dessert arrived—pecan pie, with *crème fraîche* and more peach preserves—and as the guests around us ate, Lorrie blessed me with her attention.

"Has it been well received in here?" she asked eagerly. "I was so worried. I really did wish to be here, but poor Mildred Latchum was laid up with ague . . ."

"It could not have been better," I said, and I meant it. I had not seen such joy in years. It was frightening in its unfamiliarity.

"What a relief. Have you eaten well, my love?"

Ah! Can I say that I was never more in love with her, never in thirty years of marriage, than at that moment? She had woven a sprig of mistletoe into her hair, and the little white berries twinkled like jewels. She was a goddess just then, a provider of many delights: of the table, certainly, and of the eye. "Oh, my," Heathcliff might have said if he'd met her, "my, but she's easy on the eyes." Under the table, I took her hand in mine. She smiled and bowed her head.

The dessert plates were carried away. I had spooned mine, shakily, with my free hand and somehow managed to scoop up every morsel. I should mention that there was no coffee. Lorrie was talented, to be sure, but she was not a miracle worker. It would have taken an act of God to assemble enough coffee for even the weakest brew. The substitutes, such as bee- balm infusion and "Kentucky coffee" pods, either tasted foul or failed to quicken the pulse—or both. Thus, Lorrie decided not to serve a hot beverage at all. Better to let the diners dwell on the high notes, she reasoned, than to leave with the taste of rubbish on their tongues. And so it was: the plates were cleared, and the doctors and their wives, the Farmington chaperones, and the students of medicine went their separate ways. Lorrie, of course, had the matter of striking the temporary kitchens and returning the tableware to its proper owners to attend to. She deposited a kiss upon my brow and excused herself.

"Will I see you?" I said.

"I beg your pardon," she said coyly. "But you would like to see me *how*?"

We had taken of late to amusing ourselves most nights in my room. Unbeknownst to her aunt and uncle, the dainty Miss Lorrie scrambled out the second- story window of the Cabells' pavilion and picked through the gardens to the wall behind my room. There she made a signal, and I emerged—through the window, of course—and pulled her in. We played whist and smoked various pipes of B.B.'s, sometimes in the company of fellows from other Lawn rooms, sometimes alone. I will say this: Lorrie was careful not to let me get the wrong idea about these clandestine meetings. When the air turned too thick—my kisses lingering too long on her lips, my embrace too slow to release—she announced that it was late, and that she had best go home. In fact, it was often past late and into early morning when she left my room, with the chickadees calling *too- hee* and flicking from bough to wall as I lowered her down. She might have used the door at that hour—no one but servants were up and about—but I suspect she would have rather quit coming altogether. Though a poor substitute for carnal satisfaction, the thrill of sneaking around like a thief was attractive to her, and she relished the experience.

"No ways except the usual," I replied.

"We shall see," she said. This was the other cherished bit of the routine—keeping me in the dark, as it were, as to whether she was coming. "I ought to pay the cooks."

"Yes, of course," I said. "And I had better check my ward. Just to make sure all is well after the meal."

"Of course," she said. She smiled, and there was my answer.

Naturally, I stopped at Lieutenant Stone's cot. He was pleased, taking in the scene around him with a beneficent glow. Some of the men had trays remaining next to them; Stone did not, but I took from his demeanor that he had enjoyed the feast very much.

The balsam and cedar scent of the decorations had only hinted at the olfactory transformation precipitated by the meal itself. Where once there had been a wall of stench at the threshold, there was now a gentle puff of roasted meat, of seasoned greens, and of ginger.

"Muro!" Stone called. "There is a rumor floating about that the gentle ladies put on a show for the staff. Dance of the seven veils, I believe it was. Is that right, Schiff?"

"Aye, seven veils." The Alabama private made an obscene gesture with his right hand.

"It's just a rumor," Stone continued, smiling from the side of his mouth so that the young Alabaman might not see.

"I can neither confirm nor deny said rumor," I said. "Though I will say the ladies performed admirably."

"You see! Hoss, I told you. I *told* you!"

"You did, Schiff. That you did."

At that moment a kitchen hand, a Negro I knew, appeared at the foot of Stone's cot. He was carrying a tray of food—not the Christmas feastings, but the usual dietary regimen of the hospital: grain mash, some dried apples, a bit of jerky plumped in boiling water. The tin cup of water shone with grease. At first the boy addressed Stone, but when he saw that the patient's visitor was the doctor of the ward—I was clad in dinner attire—he turned his attentions to me. "Where you like me to leave this, suh? Next to the bed here all right?"

"I don't understand," I said. "This man has already eaten. What is this?"

"I was told, suh—"

"And besides that," I continued, growing more incensed at each beat, "besides that, why on God's earth would you think it advisable to waste a measure of perfectly good ration when you *knew* there was a special meal tonight?"

"Suh?"

"Muro," said Stone. "Leave him. It's not his fault."

"Why, it most certainly is! Did you prepare this meal, boy?"

"Yes suh."

"John. Here—" Stone sat up and took the tray with his good hand, setting it on his lap. The rehydrated jerky smelled like wet leather.

His chore completed, the Negro hustled away. There was an odd silence as I stood alone with my anger, Stone with his meal. He picked up his fork and began to eat right away.

"You're still hungry?" I asked.

"Still?"

"Did you not get your fill already?"

"Ah," said Stone, washing down a lump of mash with a swig from the tin cup. He smiled. "No, this would be my meal. And I'm rather glad the good fellow remembered me."

"But they must have come around. The ladies—who came with the trays?"

"Just one, actually. A lovely girl, with auburn hair and these tremendous eyes . . . She stopped right where you're standing now, Doc, and she said, You understand there's none for you. And I understood. I didn't appreciate it either, what with all the other fellows eating, and—well, you know what I mean."

He paused and looked up. "But, Muro, she was so *handsome* with those sprigs in her hair. My wife . . . well, Sarah used to wear mistletoe around Christmas. So I was angry, sure. But what could I say? She just looked so damned *beautiful* . . ."

# 50

"DO YOU LOVE ME?"

"I don't know."

"Had I known you felt this way, I would have brought him a plate from *our* table."

"That is easy to say now."

"Oh, I mean it. Why won't you believe me?"

It was Friday, Christmas Day 1863. I was seated in the Cabells' parlor, on an armchair upholstered in red paisley. Lorrie knelt before me. She was not minding her voice, and I was sure the help were listening through the wall.

"Why won't you listen to me? You're not even listening to me. I love you, John. From the moment I saw you at the dining hall. You are a decent man, and Uncle speaks the world of you. In all her letters, Mother says I have found a perfect match, and that I ought not to let you get away. But, oh—I fear I have!"

She resumed crying. Her eyes were pink from it already.

"I've not slipped away," I said.

"But you have. And it's my fault. Do you swear there is no way I can prove it to you?"

I put my arm around her. The lambs' wool shawl across her shoulders was warm from her agitation. She had painted her fingernails with a peach- colored enamel—surely for the dinner, although I had not noticed it then. She clutched her hands in her lap.

I felt generous on account of my newfound position of control. "I'm angry with you," I said. "But it will pass. And anyway, you should be congratulating yourself. This morning, on my way to the brick house, you were the first word on Crofton's mouth." (Crofton was another man in the medical curriculum, who had been at the dinner service in the surgery.) "Do you know what he said to me? Not *Merry Christmas, John.* Not even *Good morning.* No, straightaway he said, *Your Lorrie set the town ablaze last night.*"

Lorrie raised her head. "Did he really say that?" Then, remembering her penitence, she said, "I would cancel it all not to have made you cross with me."

I was having trouble believing her supplication. She had scored a coup, no doubt about it; Crofton was not the only man to sing her praises, only the first. In fact, almost every man I encountered that morning and for weeks afterward mentioned the dinner, even those who had not attended.

"I fear you've taken the exception as the rule, John. I am not the sort of person who makes discriminations between groups."

"So you deny what you did?"

"No, I . . . Ugh!" She buried her face in her hands. "Why must this be so difficult? Yes, I scrimped on your friend, but that's all it was! Do you have any idea how many mouths we had to feed? It was loaves and fishes, for powder's sake!"

"But you knew who he was. You knew that he was not some ordinary patient."

"Yes, I knew he was your friend. But if you don't mind my saying so, I find it patently ridiculous that you should call him that."

"What—a friend?"

"Let me ask you, John—if you found yourself on a field of battle, and your Lieutenant Stone had just slaughtered your neighbor, would you hesitate to shoot him dead?"

"That is ridiculous! You might substitute any man for Stone—Dr. Samuel Gross even."

"Who?"

"Any Northern man! Longfellow! Would you shoot him?"

Lorrie was fond of *Hiawatha* and had staged a reading of the poem with friends before her assumption to the Farmington set. "I suppose not," she said. "But Longfellow is not a soldier, and neither am I."

"And I am a doctor. Should that excuse us from the exercise?"

"You're evading me."

"I'm doing no such thing." I stood up and moved toward the door. Hurried footsteps echoed in the passage.

"Don't leave," Lorrie begged. She remained stubbornly on her knees, like a penitent at the altar rail. "I only meant to say that I find your affection for Lieutenant Stone . . . odd. Were I in your position, I would never have made friends with the man."

"You are not in my position."

"I do not mean to belittle you in any way, John. On the contrary: I have delivered only a fraction of the praise you deserve for your work. I don't know if I should tell you this, but I overheard Uncle speaking with Dr. Davis after supper last week and he said that he might consider promoting you to assistant director of the hospital. After the war is done, of course."

This hit like a rum punch—first, the exhilaration of the news followed immediately by the slow, numbing realization that any promise predicated on the successful conclusion of the war was like the tail end of a hyperbolic function in algebra, one whose graph so nearly approximates nil but never actually arrives. It was not blasphemous so much as self- annihilating to think this way, but only an idiot would have laid an honest bet on our side. As we Virginians lay snug abed that winter, watching the snow cover the trees outside and extrapolating that the same snow fell upon the guns and war carriages of Lee's brave army, our next thought plural was of the ever- stoked and unstoppable war machine possessed by the other side: the factories and foundries and ports spread like a team harness to all the healthy cities of the North, to New York and Philadelphia, Boston and Baltimore. We imagined pistons churning toward victory, well- fed and cocksure men at their controls, smiling wide at the taste of it. And we had what? I thought of cousin Sam at my father's desk—or *under it,* curled up in the leg hole, raving.

"He said that, did he? And what was Dr. Davis's response?"

"He said, 'A good man, Muro,' or something like that. I don't recall it exactly."

"This was how many weeks ago?"

"I meant to tell you, of course, but with the planning for the dinner . . ." She waved her hand in dismissal. "I apologize. I should have told you sooner."

"No, no," I said, "it's not the type of thing one speaks aloud. I'm sure your uncle did not intend you to hear." I rose up like a balloon—and thus condescended in reverse proportion. I knew that Lorrie loathed it when I called Dr. Cabell "your uncle." She said it sounded as though I were speaking to a child.

"I suppose there is no way for you to glean more. How would you? Uncle, say, I heard you and Davis speaking . . . Bah. Forget it. You've done well. Thank you."

My mind raced to examine the news in the best possible light. The exigencies of war fell away, and I saw my promotion as the sure and gleaming path before me. (It seems ironic, in retrospect, that I should have reacted by canceling the war from the equation, when the war was the very circumstance responsible for every opportunity I'd enjoyed.)

"John? Are you happy with me again? I must know."

Lorrie rose from her knees and moved to a low sofa, where she gathered her legs to one side and sat down.

"Because if you're not, I don't believe I could go on."

"I said it will pass, and it shall."

She brightened, convinced at last. "Oh, John! Oh, *Dr. Muro!*" She rose and stood before me.

The Book says a wife is a comfort, but then the Book says a great many things that are at odds with what we know.

# 51

ON THE DAY APPOINTED for the tournament, God saw fit to give B.B.
a sky unseasonably clear and calm. Together with a fellow called Plimpton, who lived in the room opposite the Lawn from mine (fifty- one was
his number), Miss Lorrie and I set out for Monticello after breakfast.

Plimpton was joined by one Alice Small, a recent acquaintance.
The two had been introduced at Farmington. It was not clear whether
Lorrie had made the introduction, but she certainly knew the girl.
Miss Alice was rather young, appearing a touch underseasoned to my
physician's eye. The small hands and planate chest suggested a girl
just shy of her time.

Our hired coach stalled often in the mud on the rutted Monticello
road, and we were forced to make small talk with Plimpton and the
girl while the coachman pulled us clear. Plimpton took the opportunity at the first such delay to explain to Miss Alice my tenuous con-
nection to the tournament.

"The man of the hour, Mr. B.B. Baucom, is this very chap's
roommate!" he said, clapping my back with his broad, furred hand.
Plimpton was of the line of Scotch- Celt ancestry, set apart by a profusion of orange hair all over his body.

"We share quarters," I said. "Ostensibly."

I began to explain the actual nature of the arrangement—B.B.'s town house, his infrequent visits to the campus, &c.—until it became clear that Miss Alice had no interest whatsoever in the present course of conversation.

"Will there be swordplay?" she asked.

"I hope so, my dear," Plimpton said. He took the opportunity to move an inch closer to her on the bench. "Do you enjoy swordsmanship?"

"Oh yes, very much," replied Miss Alice. She had a thin, raspy voice, like the mew of a kitten. Her teeth were as short and widespaced as a child's.

Plimpton ventured his hand onto the girl's knee. "Ha- ha!" he said. "I do enjoy a lady with a sense of sport!"

"Psh!" Lorrie snapped. "You enjoy what you enjoy—and I would scarcely call this girl a *lady*!"

"Now, Lorrie," I said, hoping to defuse the argument before Plimpton took it up.

"I see no reason to change the subject, John," Lorrie said. "Harold has given notice of his preferences, and I intend to recognize them."

The coach was drafty on account of the raw spring air leaking through the floorboards, and I pulled up the collar on my coat. "No doubt you have a wealth of insight, dear," I said. "But for courtesy's sake, might your observations go unpublished this once?"

"Let her finish, Muro," Plimpton said, casting his orange paw into the pit of the cab.

"Thank you," Lorrie said. She took in the young Miss Alice with a sidelong glance. "As the only grown woman in present company"— Lorrie was at that time a wizened seventeen years old—"and as a firm believer in the necessity of truth and honesty between the sexes, I should ask Mr. Plimpton if he might state directly and in no uncertain terms his intention regarding Miss Small. For I hardly expect it goes beyond the carnal."

"I shall state nothing of the sort."

"Well then, we must assume the worst!"

Lorrie then conveyed to Miss Alice a conspiratorial glance that made clear to Plimpton and me that the two had been allied the whole time, whether the girl knew it or not.

Miss Alice folded her arms and bunched her thin, rouged lips into a knot.

Thus repudiated, Plimpton lifted himself to the far side of the bench—not quite a foot from Miss Alice but hardly the half inch he'd ventured previously—and directed his gaze out the window. The coach lurched forward as the team succeeded at last in budging the wheels from the mud. I offered a word of nothingness to Plimpton after a while—my suspicion that the wet weather had been dampening all our moods of late—but he declined even to acknowledge me.

At our sides, the women flittered joyous against each other: "Oh, I do not fancy swordplay," Miss Lorrie cooed to her newfound confidante. "It is so brutal, don't you think?"

The girl giggled. "Yes, but that is the fun of it. Have you really never been to the fairgrounds in Richmond? You must, you simply *must!*"

The driver let us off at the top of the mountain. We were among the last guests to arrive, and the lawn in front of the house was already full with spectators. There were perhaps two hundred in all. I recognized several dozen men of the University, along with the usual coterie of young ladies, but there were also many guests I did not know: a contingent of recent widows, for instance, gathered together at the far end of the field—a mass of black crepe dappled with dour white faces.

B.B. or one of his minions had partitioned the front lawn so that guests were kept from a narrow stretch of grass along the center. Along one side of this playing field was a wooden stand, hastily constructed, and raised a yard off the grass. The stand was festooned with ribbon and several lovely flower swags, but it stood empty of spectators.

I did not see my roommate anywhere among the crowd; I guessed that there must also be a staging area some where nearby. And where was Lorrie? I had been so taken by the sight of the gathering that I had not noticed when we'd drifted apart.

I found our companions, Plimpton and Miss Alice, standing along the drive, Plimpton having thawed their silence to the point that the young Alice was smiling and chatting amiably. In three years' time they would be married—Plimpton a well- respected barrister in Richmond, and Miss Alice raising a flock of bright children. Theirs would be a long and fruitful journey. What a pity to dwell on the awkward first steps! I looked past them to the other parties just arriving and saw two ladies in gray wool. Neither was Miss Lorrie.

Then at a distance of twenty yards, I found on a set of lovely shoulders a gray woolen mantle like the one Lorrie wore that day. But before I could see the face of the wearer, a horn blast sounded from the front portico of the house, and the crowd packed tight together, obscuring my view.

The herald—a schoolboy wearing green tights and an odd leather tunic about his waist—stood alone between the two center columns. He lowered the horn from his lips and spread his arms to quiet the crowd. "Knights and ladies of the Piedmont!" he cried. "On behalf of the right and noble competitors gathered here, I welcome you to the first Virginia Tournament of Victory!" At this there was a loud cheer from the assembly, followed by vigorous handclapping. "The order of events this afternoon will be as follows . . ." The boy's voice was not yet broken, but his delivery was as calm and confident as a trained actor's. I marveled at B.B.'s resourcefulness in finding such a polished, if unconventional, master of ceremonies.

"First, the rules," the boy continued. "The competition will be divided into three rounds: the first on horseback, with spear and lance; the next on foot, with sword and shield; and the final with bare fist and brawn!"

The cheers from the crowd grew incrementally with the description of each round, with the last—the bare- knuckles scrap—drawing by far the loudest applause.

The boy paused until the crowd subsided. "Now, ladies and gentlemen, without further delay, I present you with—the teams!" He raised his horn once more to his lips and blew a long fanfare. On cue two lines of horsemen, each a half dozen strong, came forth from opposite sides of the house. The riders continued to the far edge of the lawn before circling back and taking their places in neat rows on the playing field. All the while, the spectators cheered and whooped— some men even tossed their caps in the air, and a few fired pistols. I had not witnessed such exuberance since the secession day.

The men who rode out from the north side of the house wore coats of blue wool, with matching trousers, that I could not but assume were meant to resemble the uniforms of our enemy. In truth, I had never seen a clean Union suit—the only ones I saw were soaked through with mud, if not also with blood. The sight of unblemished blue was thus not familiar to me except in my mind's eye.

The other team, of course, wore the familiar gray wool of our troops. Five of the six in this line featured cavalry epaulets on their shoulders. All had caps of wool felt—"slouch caps," as they were called—and trousers of standard issue.

I recognized two of the riders instantly. B.B. rode at the head of the gray line, and Mr. Knight rode in front of the other. I wondered that Knight must have fallen from B.B.'s graces, for I could not imagine him choosing that side on his own.

The horses were calmed, and our attention returned to the herald. "In the times of our ancestors, the winners of these games were decided simply and finally," he said. "That is, by the death of the vanquished." A few gentlemen chuckled at this. "These being civilized times, we forgo such decisive measures in favor of an alternative: the jury."

Here the boy raised his horn and began to blow the opening strains of "Dixie." On cue, a line of young women drew forth from the crowd and began to ascend the viewing platform. The first girl paused and waved from the top of the steps before continuing to her seat. The next girl did the same, and the next. I wished that Lorrie were near— I wanted to hear her assessment of the girls, for I must admit I had become something of a connoisseur in the months of Lorrie's involvement at Farmington. She had a way of sizing up girls like brood mares at auction.

And then, as if simply by my invoking her name, Lorrie appeared on the platform. The same gray mantle was draped over her shoulders—I wondered that I had not noticed it at once. She waved to the crowd and smiled.

The bugler blew the first call, and the riders broke formation and retreated behind the house, leaving B.B. and Knight on the field. An attendant brought each his lance and shield, and the two drew to opposite corners. B.B. hoisted the lance under his arm and pulled the shield across his chest. Knight was heavier than B.B., but his physique had already begun to decline from its peak condition, as often happens to those men upon whom manhood comes early. (Knight boasted about having first taken the razor to his cheek at age twelve; now, in his eighteenth year, his hairline was already retreating up his scalp!)

The boy presider produced a pistol, and the crowd fell silent as he raised it in the air. I looked to the jury stand to see if I might catch Lorrie's eye before the match began. She was not, as I had hoped, searching frantically for my face but rather attending the blast of the gun.

At the crack, Knight and B.B. spurred their horses. The hush of the spectators grew to a roar as the riders approached the spot of convergence. I saw many women—and also a few men—holding their hands before their eyes. The roar peaked and then fell as the riders passed without striking blows. Their momentum carried them to opposite ends of the course.

I followed the action curiously, unsure if the combat was only a charade or if there was a possibility of real injury.

As B.B. and Knight turned their horses for the second pass, certain men in the crowd yelled encouragements for the man in gray.

Knight, for his part, appeared emboldened by the criticism, goading his horse with the spurs while holding him tight at the reins so that he rose up like an overstoked fire licking the stove door. At the gun, Knight released the animal, and nine hundred pounds of horseflesh raced for the center of the field. B.B. charged as well, but he lacked the steam of his opponent, and it was clear from the difference in their velocities that if this was indeed meant as true combat, then there would be disastrous consequences for my roommate.

The space between the riders narrowed to yards, then just feet. They met with a horrible crunch, like the arm of an oak tree felled in a storm, and B.B. was thrown clear. He crumpled into a mass upon the mud.

The imperturbable Huntsman continued the length of the field, reins dancing along his muscled neck. Knight ran on also, circling his horse only when he noticed the odd silence of the crowd. Thankfully, B.B. showed life, scrambling quickly to his knees and wiping the mud from his face with the back of one hand. There was upon his face a hideous scowl—made all the more appalling by the streaks of red- brown earth that ran like Indian war paint from cheek to chin.

An attendant caught Huntsman's reins and led him off the field. B.B. limped after. The boy retook the portico and signaled an entr'acte with his post horn.

In the pause I turned again to the stand, where Miss Lorrie and the other ladies of the jury conferred with one another, plumed hats bobbing to and fro with animated conversation. I did not see how they could mark the previous match as anything but a victory for Knight.

The next tilt—and the four following it—went off as planned. That is to say they went decisively in favor of the gray riders, and without any hard blows exchanged. The only injury inflicted in any tilt was the dislodging of the opponent's lance—and in one case also the shield. The blood- lusting spectators decried the action as conservative. ("Bit of a tease, eh?" quipped Plimpton.) I paced behind the crowd uneasily, apprehensive of the next meeting of the principals.

Soon enough, B.B. came out alone and knelt before his sword. He wore a leather vest, covered all over with brass studs, and a soft helmet with ear covers. His shield was the same he had used in the tilting—oak wood with iron backing.

Knight emerged a moment later similarly attired. On foot now, the men made their way to the center of the field, where there was marked in brick dust a circle approximately twelve feet in diameter.

"At the sound of the gun," the bugle boy proclaimed, "the contestants will step into the ring. Once inside, neither shall exit until a victor has been declared."

I looked to the jury box. Lorrie sat patiently on the bench, whispering now and then in the ear of her neighbor.

The noise of the crowd was now a deafening cacophony of cheers, shouts, and whistles. Gone was the reticence of the first match: not a soul shielded his eyes as the pugilists entered the ring.

"Stick him, gray! Send him back where he belongs!"

"No mercy, Southerner! Give 'im hell!"

The two men circled each other cautiously. Without their colored coats, and with helmets obscuring their features, it was difficult to tell one from the other. Knight was heavier, as I've said, but through the wild tangle of limbs and bobbing heads, they looked the same. Naturally, the crowd preferred B.B.—our surrogate—but it seemed to me that whoever was judged the winner, the Southern states would lose. It was a ritual of self- annihilation.

"Gore 'im, son! Go ahead!"

These taunts, I should note, came not from B.B.'s brothel mates but from some of the most respectable citizens in attendance. A gentleman in a tailored English greatcoat—probably the richest garment of any in evidence that afternoon—pushed his way to the rope and hollered at the top of his voice, "Show me a pint of blood! Ten dollars for a pint of Yankee blood!" The man drew a wad of green bills from his pocketbook and waved them in the air.

Knight, understandably, took these threats at face value, and he swung hard from the moment he entered the ring. An experienced fencer, B.B. parried the thrusts with skill and precision, but he grew annoyed as five minutes stretched to fifteen, and it became clear that Knight was not following the script. In time his own strokes—at first mannered, almost fey—became quicker and more determined.

Then Knight knocked away B.B.'s shield and backed him against the edge of the ring with a flurry of blows. Knight lacked B.B.'s finesse, but his weapon was hardly a fencing foil, and he used it well. With one blow he dashed B.B.'s saber to the ground, bringing my roommate to his knees.

Real fear gripped B.B. His eyes shone like pools of milk.

On the jury stand, Miss Lorrie was on her feet, fists clenched at her sides. Her brow was crosshatched with worry.

Knight raised his sword and plunged it downward. But B.B. escaped, rolling sideways in the mud. He crawled to his own sword, retrieved it, and returned to his feet. Then, silent and staid, like a hangman at his work, he charged Knight and ran him through.

Knight clutched his gut. His armaments tumbled away. B.B. withdrew the blade, and Knight collapsed in a heap.

B.B. remained still a moment, then dropped his sword and began searching the crowd. "Muro!" he called. "Dr. Muro! Has anyone seen Dr. Muro?"

I stood numb like every one, eyes fixed on the bleeding man. At last B.B. found me and the crowd drew back.

He was frantic. "You must save him!"

The blow had opened a wound below Knight's rib cage, and blood oozed like warm molasses under the studded leather vest. There was no sign of breath. I wished that I had my tools—a phial of salts, anything. At least, the tools would have given the appearance of diligence, which would have helped to cover up the fact that I was powerless. Knight was dead and could not be revived—that much was clear to me right away. Nonetheless, I felt that I must not give up when there were so many people watching. Rising to my knees, I bent over the dead man's chest and beat down with one fist, approximating the rhythm of a functioning heart. From the crowd there was only the sound of rustling fabric—the dresses and coats, the collars and hats, the gabardine and chiffon and starched cotton.

I continued to beat the dead man's chest for several minutes, but the pressure only increased the flow of blood to the wound. The mud around us grew dark with it. Several women began to cry. Only the fact of being watched by five hundred people prevented me from collapsing in the mud beside my patient.

I finally stopped when I felt a hand on my shoulder. It was the gentleman in the English coat. "Let God have him, son," he said. Then, in one graceful, fluid motion, he removed the coat and draped it over the body.

# 52

NEXT MORNING I ROSE while it was still dark outside. There had been a hard frost overnight and the moon glittered on the icy earth as on broken glass. I picked my way down Main Street, where the previous evening's horse tracks had frozen into the mud. As I approached the Delevan I saw a light burning in the basement. This was the kitchen, where the night steward was finishing his rendering and stock boiling before the steward and his crew of cooks arrived.

I went to the second floor and entered my ward without knocking or giving any notice of my arrival. The attending nurse, who had been asleep, started and pretended to mark a place in the novel laying across her lap.

"Is that Dr. Muro?" she cried. Then, catching herself, she lowered her voice to a whisper. "Hello, Doctor. Good morning."

"Nurse."

"Is everything all right, sir? It's rather early for you."

I knew from the earnest tone of her query—no hint of irony, no prodding—that she had not heard the news from the tournament.

"Very well, thank you. Has it been a quiet evening?"

"Oh, yes." She stole a glance at her book.

"Very well." I ended the conversation by proceeding to my desk in the corner. I lit two candles and took up a report I had abandoned midstream two days prior. It was an inventory (so many inventories in those days, without a thing to count!) of the "durable" materials in the ward; that is, not just the cots and so forth but any needle, blade, and tong that might conceivably be reused ad infinitum. It was a dull task, and a pointless one in my judgment, and I abandoned it for staring at the wall.

I thought of what I had seen the day before, the senseless bloodshed, and although the death of one man should not have moved me an inch—had not thousands perished senselessly? And how many in this very ward?—I could not help but feel that some mechanism of the world's logical calculus, the rules that governed right from wrong, for instance, had been finally and unalterably damaged. In those days dueling was not uncommon, although it had declined much in popularity; I asked myself, who died in a mock duel? Even the Romans, who fed men to lions, could not have dreamed it. Had we fallen so far?

I knew that a talk with Stone would help sort my thoughts. I would need to tell him about Knight, anyway. He would hear about it— every man in the hospital would have heard the details by breakfast, to be sure—but I wanted to tell him myself. I stood and walked down the line of cots. The nurse had fallen back asleep, and I lightened my steps as I passed so as not to wake her. At Stone's cot I knelt and prodded his foot. He was usually a light sleeper, and it worried me that my touch did not wake him.

"Eh- oh?" came a voice from the pillow. A man sat up and rubbed his eyes. "Is that you, Doctah?" Sensing opportunity, he reached under the mattress and brought out a tarnished flask. "Much obliged for another pour of that Kentucky 'lixir. My blood—" Here he coughed, raising a fist to his mouth to deflect the spittle. "I was sayin', my blood is so *thick* right now, it's just creeping along in there. Needs a little grease, Doc, if you hear my meaning."

Even in the low light, I saw the telltale spots of measles on the man's face and neck. Now uncovered, he took his coat from the hook on the wall above his head and pulled it across his shoulders. He was an infantryman. A Confederate private.

I stood up and looked this way and that, counting the cots in both directions.

"I know we just met," the man said, "but I sure would 'preciate it. The doc at the last place I was at told me whiskey wasn't the right treatment for what I got. Imagine that, Doctah—whiskey ain't the right treatment! Tell you what, if whiskey ain't the treatment, then I ain't sick!" He laughed, but softly, conscious of the dozing men all around him.

I had the right cot. Quickly, I invented a scenario in which Lieutenant Stone had been taken by a lightning fever while I was at the tournament. Was it possible? Had I been gone so long?

I paced the center aisle, double- checking the order of cots.

There was no mistake.

The nurse saw me worrying and padded over. She had deduced the cause of my frenzy. "You were away, sir," she said. "A paddy wagon came and took some of them."

"A paddy wagon?"

"It was a prisoner exchange. One of ours for one of theirs. You seen the new fella?" She nodded at the man on Stone's cot. He had given up begging for alcohol and was busy fluffing the pillow under his head. "They took all the Yanks in the hospital." She smiled then, and although she was already speaking in a whisper, she cupped her hand to her lips. "Good riddance to 'em, far as I'm concerned. You know what I mean?"

# 53

"YOU'RE TO BE PAID a salary, of course," Dr. Cabell said, "for what that's worth." He had called me into his office to deliver the news of my promotion. He was simultaneously excited for the news and apologetic for what he perceived as its inadequacies.

He apologized for the delay, which he blamed on the bureaucratic morass in Richmond. The position of Assistant Surgeon carried the rank of first lieutenant. I was to be commissioned—not only in a manner of speaking, but duly *commissioned*—and thus the final word from Richmond was slow in coming. At the beginning of the war, the Surgeon-General's office had been strict about preserving the number of full surgeons, assistant surgeons, and the like. The Surgeon-General himself held the rank of colonel, and though he never signed his letters Colonel Moore, or Colonel Dr. Moore, or any such thing, it was clearly important to him that the trust and respect of the Richmond military leadership not be lost by our frivolous awarding of army commissions to any fool with a lancet. I knew all this because it was a common topic among the medical students, who worked nearly the long hours of Dr. Cabell and Davis (full surgeons both, and thus army majors) without the validation of any rank whatsoever. I had never felt as strongly as some of my colleagues about the issue. I knew that my commission was not to be taken lightly, and that it was sure to chafe those others who felt passed over.

"I would have told you earlier, son," Cabell said as I refolded the letter he'd given me. It was dated April 15, 1864. *EFFECTIVE IMMEDI- ATELY*, read a stamp in blue ink across the top margin. A hasty *S. P. Moore, Surgeon General, C.S.A.* was scrawled below the orders.

"Actually," I said, "Lorrie hinted something to this effect. I did not believe her, of course."

"Wise man. A year ago it wouldn't have happened."

"Sir?"

"I don't mean to say you're undeserving. No, you've made leaps this year, to be sure. I only meant that you're not the first man I've recommended for promotion."

"Of course not, sir."

"The reason is Moore. He's slipping, you know." The old doctor nodded and pulled at his side- whiskers. "I suppose the ship is sinking."

He did not seem particularly worried as he levied this assessment. To be fair, I'd heard it many times before, from his mouth and others':

*We'll be living in South New York by spring!*

*There's no more food, not even a peach in Georgia!*

They're drafting men from Canada—and England's next!

"You really think so, sir? More than usual?"

"I fear so, Muro."

The spring campaign had only just begun, but it was shaping up to be the bloody climax everyone feared. Lincoln had moved a new general to the head of his army in Virginia, Ulysses Grant, late of the Tennessee front. There had been the usual bravado in the Richmond papers, which proclaimed him "Little Mac with a Beard" (referring to General McClellan, whose remarkable ineptitude had saved Richmond from annihilation via the Peninsular Campaign two years prior). But there also appeared in the rear pages of the same journals some sober assessments of the new Yank general in chief, including one unsigned editorial that purported to contain the off- the- record warnings of none other than Uncle Robert E. Lee. The word on Grant, the writer claimed, was that he liked to fight.

To us, as hospital staff, such a rumor caused the ears to prick up. More often than not we had no advance warning of battle. The news came in the form of boxcars full of fresh evacuees. Details followed from the men themselves as we pulled them off the train. So, by necessity, we calibrated our readiness on the likeliness of the rumor—and its source.

By all measures, the fighting seemed to be closing in on us. In February, Albemarle County had seen its closest brush with action, when a force of fifteen hundred Union cavalrymen chanced upon a tiny fortification at a bluff known as Rio Hill, four miles northeast of the University. The rebel soldiers on watch scrambled to their artillery and got off a few quick shots. This startled the Yankee commander, who had been on a scouting mission and had not intended to engage. He ordered only enough return fire to cover his retreat, and that was the end of it. The newspaper called it a "skirmish."

Though there was some cheering over turning back such a large enemy detachment, no one at the Delevan held any delusion about what had happened. A force of fifteen hundred cavalrymen could have taken all of Albemarle County, including the town and the University, in a matter of hours. A soldier in my ward who had been a logistics officer before losing his eyesight to shrapnel at Sharpsburg speculated that a single company of well- trained cavalry could hold all the critical sites in the county. That would be something less than two hundred men. The force at Rio Hill had been seven times that.

But perhaps the most enduring legacy of the skirmish was that it marked the first time many of us had heard the words "George Armstrong Custer"—for that was the name of the Yankee commander. Though it is impossible now to imagine George Custer in any role except that of Indian fighter, I assure the reader that he was well known to us for other reasons. The name struck the same fear in the breasts of Southern observers that Stuart's and Mosby's did in our Northern counterparts. Young Custer was daring in raids, and yet uncommonly cool in battle. He was ascending the Union ranks like wildfire, having been brevetted colonel at just twenty- five years of age. And he was everywhere—at Manassas, at Gettysburg, on the Peninsula. Colonel Custer was involved in so many engagements up and down the Blue Ridge that one might have thought him a ghost haunting the region.

Now he was on our flank. In our country.

Dr. Cabell stuffed the Surgeon- General's letter into the top drawer of his desk. "There's something else, John," he said.

"Sir?"

"You mentioned Lorrie a moment ago . . ."

"Yes sir. She's my girl, still. In case you were wondering. I know we haven't always seemed the most agreeable couple."

Dr. Cabell smiled. "Well. Looks can be deceiving, believe me. But John, the reason I mention the girl is that I'm afraid I need to trust you with a piece of news."

"News, sir?"

"Yes, and also a request."

# 54

I HAVE MENTIONED THAT the gardens behind the professors'
homes were separated one from the next by Jefferson's serpentine walls.
These were approximately head high and only a single brick thick, so
that they were forever being knocked asunder whenever a liveryman
backed his cart or some piece of machinery into them for carelessness.
Many of the gardens were also divided internally into upper and lower
halves—the upper being the one most proximate to the pavilion and
thus held as the private sanctuary of the family in residence. The lower
gardens, however, were open to use by all—chiefly students, but also
those members of the faculty not senior enough to warrant residence
on the Lawn, who lived in homes or boardinghouses nearby.

I relate all this by way of explaining that when Miss Lorrie and
I set out a picnic- basket meal within the confines of a garden not
belonging to her uncle's pavilion, we were not trespassing, but only
using the property for its intended purpose. But why, you ask, might
we go to a foreign garden when the Cabells' private one sat vacant
not a hundred yards distant? The answer, of course, was privacy,
which was precious rare in the Academical Village, especially for one
as well connected and as socially diligent as Miss Lorrie. If we were

to sit, for instance, on one of the stone benches ringing the terrace of the Rotunda, we might not converse five minutes without being interrupted by the well- wishing of Lorrie's passing friends and acquaintances.

That is why, when I had something important to say, such as on this particular Saturday afternoon, I insisted on repairing to the peace of Garden IX, that being the garden directly behind the pavilion of that number and as far a distance from the foot commerce of the University as one might travel without leaving the property. I had brought with us a supply of fresh strawberries, the first of the season, furnished to me by a solicitous nurse at the Delevan. As Lorrie spread a blanket on the grass, I began coring the berries with a penknife.

We had been discussing the effect of my promotion upon the attitudes of the hospital staff. Lorrie refused to believe my assertion that the other student doctors were loathe to acknowledge any thing had changed.

"Next time you visit," I said, "watch the nurses." I took a strawberry between my teeth and felt its cloying sweet juice trickling into my mouth. "The nurses have taken it well."

"And the others?"

"Consider Richardson," I said, referring to the fellow who worked in the next ward on the second- floor hall. "You can see the effort on his face when we speak, trying to keep the words from escaping. Would it hurt him too much to say *Congratulations?* Blast it—I'd settle for a jealous insult. Anything but silence."

"Are you sure they know? Richardson might not have heard the news."

"Dr. Cabell made a general announcement at this week's staff meeting."

"Then perhaps it is uncomfortable for him to mention your promotion."

"To be sure. The real question is how long he can keep at it before some circumstance dictates he acknowledge it."

"That he acknowledge what?"

"Why, my rank." I took another berry in my mouth and mashed it only lightly before swallowing it down.

"It is unlike you to be arrogant, John. I don't like it."

"But you must. Haven't I always been too callow for your taste? Haven't you always fancied a cavalier?"

Miss Lorrie turned away, picking at a burr on her skirts.

The afternoon was not unfolding as I'd hoped. There was still time, I knew, to straighten it out, but I felt entitled to the indulgence of reveling in my good fortune, if only for a moment.

"There's talk of another march north," I said. "Never mind that I don't believe the speculation . . ."

"Oh, keep your war!" She turned to me suddenly, and I saw that her face was full of rage. "What do you care if there is a march north, or south, or any direction at all? What is it to *you* if we have another year of this? I'd say the war has been rather good to *you*, Dr. Muro!"

"That's not fair."

"Is it not? Tell me, where were you three years ago? Let me assist your recollection: you were working in a wool mill. And now? It's a wonder you're not more grateful. Really."

"I am grateful. For you, and for other things—"

"Psh! For me among a hundred other things. Do you know how long I've waited for you? You have no idea what goes on around you, do you know that?"

She paused a moment. "I have had *offers*. Several of them. And do you know what? I'm beginning to think I erred in telling those men I was taken."

"You've had what?" I said. Then, as quickly, "From whom?"

"I want to spare you, dear, but understand that a part of me wants to crush you all the same. Do you really want to know?"

"Tell me," I said.

"From your murderous roommate, John! Your very own dear B.B. He brought me roses, and perfumed scarves, and so many other things I can't remember them all. You could take a lesson."

"How long has it been? How long have you two been . . . well, *how long?*"

"Six months? A year? I don't know. Long enough that he felt confident to propose."

"To propose!"

"And I refused him, thank God."

I stood and paced the garden, which seemed small and contrived all of a sudden, with its ridiculous walls. "What did he say? Tell me what he said."

"He said he loved me, and he asked if I would be his wife."

"A planter's wife," I said, "for ever and ever."

"John, I never wanted that."

"I find it hard to believe that you'd prefer me."

"You can believe what you wish."

Beyond the University to the west lay a hill visible from any spot on the Grounds. This was called the Wishing Peak by the students, who asserted that if a man fixed his eyes upon it, and then checked to make sure no one else was looking at it just then, his wish would be granted forthwith by the Great Spirit of the Piedmont or some such deity. I had always thought it rubbish, but I looked this way and that. We were alone. Lorrie's back was to the hill.

I recalled Dr. Cabell's confidences to me after he had revealed my promotion: "My wife's brother—Lorrie's father—is dead," he'd said. "It was a camp fever. Took out the whole regiment from what I understand. We had word from Richmond yesterday. I wanted to tell you before I broke the news to her. In case you were planning any news of your own. Let me ask you, son—have you thought about marriage?"

In the garden, I fingered the ring in my pocket. I'd purchased it with the last of Father's gold coins.

"With her father gone," the old doctor had said, "you should not be put off for a lack of suitable authority. You have my blessing, John. But that much should be clear by now."

I had thanked him, shaken both his hands. "I know it, sir."

"If you have ever considered a proposal, son, this would be a fine time to do it. I know that it would please Mrs. Cabell to know her niece was well looked after."

A fortnight had passed since that conversation, and Dr. Cabell still had not told Lorrie the news. Nor did he mention it again, not once, during the course of any private business at the hospital. Eventually I understood that he was waiting for me.

"Braxton is an overgrown boy," Lorrie pleaded. "You are different. You have your faults, to be sure, and Braxton has his moments of startling maturity. But I choose you. I have deliberated over this so long . . ."

I saw in her anguish that she was telling the truth. Perhaps even understating it. Yes, she had thought long over her choice—but I wondered if the tears in her eyes welled from regret. *A planter's wife*, in Charles City! I would never give her that. Nor, I knew, would I ever proffer perfumed scarves or any of the other frilly things in B.B.'s repertoire. That kind of romance was not in my constitution.

"I know what I want," she said, "or rather, whom. But John—is there something wrong with me? Why won't you have me be your wife?"

I withdrew the ring from my waistcoat and knelt on the grass. The sun warmed my back.

"Miss Wigfall, would you consider—"

She began to laugh. And thick tears grew in her eyes, and she said, "Oh dear . . . Oh my . . . Oh dear . . ." She clutched both my hands to her face. We embraced, and then we sat silent for a moment. Neither of us felt like eating.

When Lorrie spoke again, she said, "I never blamed you for waiting. Everything is so wretched."

"Yes," I said. We were silent again. I thought—and I'm sure Lorrie must have thought this as well—that it was true we had been stalled, but that the true obstacle, above all else, was the war. And the war would end, would it not?

That was the highest point we reached together.

# 55

I TOOK HER BACK TO Pavilion II by a circuitous route, approaching it from the rear so that we passed the stables on the way up the hill.
There was a unfamiliar coach among the usual ones—the broughams
and gigs of the professors and their wives—and a rough- looking soldier stood before it, tapping oats into a feed bag. His uniform was
gray, dusty, and he puffed a rancid weed in his pipe. The coach was
not fancy. On small staffs abreast the driver's seat flew the flag of the
Confederate government and the lone- star banner of Texas.

"Father has come!" Lorrie cried. She raced up the alley and nearly
reached the garden gate before turning back. "And what news we
have to share!" She took me by the hand. "Oh, John, you two will get
along famously. *Famously*, do you hear?"

I followed at her heels through the garden and up the rear steps.
We excused ourselves, brushing rudely past a Negro servant with a
tray of crackers and tea. The girl said nothing, but only held the tray
aloft to avoid a spill.

Lorrie gained the landing and thundered down the first- floor passage. Her boots left burnt orange mud tracks on the wood. Reaching
the parlor, she flung wide the double doors.

There were three figures in the silent room: Dr. Cabell, in his usual wing chair, looking even more somber than usual; Mrs. Cabell, standing behind her husband; and a woman in black velvet dress. She sat in the rocking chair near the hearth.

"Mother—"

We watched as Lorrie took in the meaning of the assemblage. Her delight wilted to understanding, thence to woe. There were no words exchanged between mother and daughter, only the silent probing of their eyes. The rocking chair creaked in the silence. Lorrie collapsed at her mother's feet and laid her head upon the velvet lap.

Dr. Cabell rose and took his wife's hand. They walked to the passage door before Mrs. Cabell stopped him and whispered something in his ear.

He came to me. "John," he said softly, "we ought to leave them alone."

# 56

OVER THE SPRING AND summer of that year we saw our prayers for peace dashed on the fields at Cold Harbor, in the breastworks at Petersburg, and in the flaming cauldron of Atlanta. Our only tactic was the prolongation of the fight, which our commanders seemed willing to sustain indefinitely. Whenever it appeared as if the Yanks had their boots on our throats, we slithered out and made scarce before returning to fight another day.

Another battle, another day. There was a stretch in May and June when our humble depot in Charlottesville felt like a city terminus with the constant arrival of trains from the front. The fighting was north of Richmond then, and east, but Grant held all the counties from Hopewell to Hampton Roads. The sick and wounded were sent west, to wherever beds existed to receive them. The most serious cases could not weather the long ride to Tennessee, so they were left off with us. I attended 175 deaths that summer. That figure, noted with emphasis in my journal, does not include the men who expired outside the wards, in the tents behind the building. These were "holding pens" for new arrivals we simply could not accommodate under permanent roof. The care available in the tents was virtually nonexistent. The medical staff hated even to step inside the tents, because we had no hope to offer the men there. Though we called the tents holding pens, they were not actually purgatory but rather hell. Whenever a cot became available in one of the permanent wards—only by the passing of some other patient—the vacancy was filled not by the longest resident of the tents but by a body fresh off the train, which was already loaded onto a stretcher.

I worked ceaselessly, night and day, pausing only when my open eyes, by fact of fatigue, failed to see. It has since been discovered that temporary blindness is a common consequence of exertion, but I ventured a different hypothesis—that my eyes were begging mercy from exposure. No one should have to see what I saw: men with bits of case shot peppered all over their faces like cloves in a roast; men whose filthy eyes were black with infection and swollen to the size and glaze of billiard balls; men whose last ounce of earthly life was spent trying in vain to form the word *Mother* with lips deadened by tetanus. I read once about a king in ancient China who refused ever to weep for fear of losing the life carried on his tears. I was scared to cry, but there was no life in my tears, only salt. And I could no less afford to lose that.

I managed at least one day's furlough, however: Lorrie and I wed on a Saturday afternoon in August, and I did not report back till Sunday noon.

The wedding was held at Farmington—but there was no white tent and no orchestra. By that time the crimp of privation had reached even Mrs. Cartwright and her kin. Lorrie furnished our humble reception with salt- cured ham (the rotted parts cut away in a back kitchen, unbeknownst to the guests) and a bland farmer's cheese. And that much was hailed as a triumph.

It was a brief affair, befitting the spirit of the time. I am often asked by youngsters curious of the mood of wartime why we did not spend more time in church. (A hungry soul will gorge on what prevails, &c, &c.) I always report the opposite: that in general folks were so galled by the carnage and by the humiliation, too, of seeing our stand exposed as folly that we were in no mood to rise and sing hymns.

The parson of Saint Paul's parish presided over the ceremony, which was attended (on the bride's side) by Mrs. Wigfall, the Cabells, Mrs. Cartwright, and several other ladies of the club. There were also in attendance a detachment of Lorrie's admirers, girls too young to know that although the date and time of the ceremony was not held secret, it was not expected to be a public event. Though I was annoyed at the time, upon reflection I credit the cadre of giggling girls with lending the occasion what little mirth it enjoyed. Lorrie received them graciously, and they fawned over her, making noise about her bouquet and hair dressings.

I must say she was a vision that afternoon. When I answered the parson's query in the affirmative, I had not the slightest reservation: there was no girl more lovely or more poised, and certainly no one more capable in her own right, in Virginia or any other place. She wore a simple white dress, sewn of sateen salvaged from an ill-fitting gown of Mrs. Cartwright's. No one but the donor, the wearer, the seamstress, and I knew this fact, and it was to remain so. Mrs. Cartwright was very clear about this. "Tell no one, John. You think it won't matter, but you are wrong." Since the announcement of our engagement, Mrs. Cartwright had taken to calling me by my Christian name. I had been "Dr. Muro" theretofore, and I suspect the transition caused her at least a pang of regret. She had come to appreciate me, or at least to respect my value to the community—that is, as a professional man—and her use of my title belied, at least in my mind, her tacit blessing of my association with Miss Lorrie. For my part, I had come to understand that she was not a monster, but rather a well-meaning (if misunderstood) force of nature. What I saw in her at first as misguided patriotism (news of fresh defeats arrived with each day's post, but still she refused to admit the possibility even of a truce)

I came to regard as real faith, and by extension an admission of want. With her husband twenty years deceased, without children of her own, she was fundamentally out of balance, and her actions might be construed as attempts to rectify the condition. Her various initiatives—her "causes," be they Confederate partisanship or the promotion of Lorrie Wigfall to the highest tier of social life—were only attempts to fill the void she harbored within her massive corpus. After the wedding, she was generous in helping establish our household, and her many gifts of furniture, linens, &c, I shall never forget.

The parson held out the ring. I slipped it onto Lorrie's trembling hand.

"And do you, Lorrie, promise to obey your husband, come what may?"

"Sir, I do."

We received our guests in the octagonal banquet room of the house. The room was much too large for our meager party, and the voices of congratulation echoed off the cleared floors and tall windows like the cries of cave dwellers. We ate our fill of the ham and cheese, but the slices of cake were scarcely deposited in their boxes before we excused ourselves upstairs.

I had a revelation, then, that perhaps the reason for the storied restlessness of the bridegroom to end the wedding reception as soon as possible was not what I had always thought it to be—an itch to make off and enjoy his wife with the full sanction of God and his neighbors—but only a desire to end an uncomfortable and humiliating ritual. Owing to circumstance, our wedding was understandably more uncomfortable and more humiliating than most. At what wedding reception can you recall the guests noting happily, without irony, that the bread was not stale?

Of course, all analytical notions were thrown away several hours later, in the confines of a guest suite, when we found ourselves alone and unencumbered. I should be clear that the thought of ravishment was never far from my mind during all the preparations for the wedding, and in fact it took great effort many times to get on with the mundane chores of preparation—consulting with the pastor, arranging for flowers to be delivered, &c.—without lingering over the pleasant notion that we would soon be free to do as we pleased in the sanctity of the marriage bed. We had come close so many times—the happy circumstance of my oft- absent roommate saw to that—but as principled young people, we never trespassed upon our license. Now we commenced to make up for lost time. Lorrie proved a ready lover, and we finished the marriage act three times that afternoon. The charitable reader will indulge me for relating these details in the interest of public knowledge—that is, to the end of informing young men and women that the frequency of congress between a newly married man and wife is no cause for shame. Rather, it is the natural impulse of an animal forced so long to abide. Nor should a bridegroom be alarmed if his young wife breaks down in tears soon after. I woke to the sound of Lorrie sobbing and sprang immediately from the bed. She had installed herself on the window seat with an afghan and a small round pillow.

"This is all wrong," she cried, "all of it."

"Do you mean to say that I'm wrong?"

"Yes—and the fact that I should be married at all. I don't deserve this, John. I am a hateful girl."

"Now. You are nothing of the sort."

"I know how you feel about me. You will never forgive me— never—and besides that, you never wanted to be married at all."

"Why, that is rubbish! Of course I wanted to be married."

"I know what happened—I know that Uncle put you up to this."

"He most certainly did not!"

"Oh, quit. Auntie told me."

So there—what could I have said? I could hardly breathe without perjuring myself. It was true, on one hand, that Dr. Cabell had planted the seed in my mind. But what is a seed without tending and care, without water and sun—and had her uncle provided all those things too?

Further, had he shouldered her betrayals? Had he stomached her alliance with the Farmington set? No, this was my doing, this marriage, and mine alone. I was to blame if it proved ill advised, just as I was to credit if it proved a lasting bond. With due respect to God Almighty, I was the master of this union.

"I married you of free will."

"If that's the case," she said plainly, her sobs ceasing for a moment, "then you don't know your own will."

I succeeded, over the next half hour, in talking her down, invoking the joy of the occasion, the weight of our times, and a hundred other things. But these words of hers stayed with me: You don't know your own will. It enraged me to think that I might not know my own heart, but the accusation stung like truth.

Is it wrong to say that a marriage is measured in transgressions? Neither man nor wife marks the everyday good that transpires between them, the happy kisses hello and good- bye, the brief notes left on scrap paper when one or the other has stepped out to fetch the mail. We in the medical profession have no use for the hundreds of thousands of beatings that a healthy heart undertakes before that one which precedes an attack. It seems to me that love, like medicine, is a record of trial, and that when a man is asked to recount his marriage he is likely to begin and end with the trespasses of his wife.

So, in the end—when the moment of doubt was past and we set forth in our traveling costumes for the wedding breakfast, and thence for the briefest of honeymoons (for that was all my schedule would allow, notwithstanding Dr. Cabell's beneficence toward his niece)— in the end it was my faith, not hers, that emerged shaken.

# 57

IN THE PRECEDING ACCOUNT, the reader may have puzzled over the absence of the groom's family at the wedding, Let me summarize thus: they were never told.

Approximately one month prior to the wedding—in the early summer of 1864—I had received by messenger post a sheaf of neatly copied legal papers. Under the masthead of a Danville law firm were laid proposed terms for the liquidation of my family's assets, including (but this is not a complete list) the land, improvements, and durable equipment comprising the Bedford Woolery; Father's stake in a handful of river barges; and all inventory produced by the mill that might be warehoused off- premises awaiting shipment (there was presumed to be some $50,000 of this, which figure I doubted very highly, considering my cousin's abject failure at production). Finally, the suit called for the selling- off of the slaves (approximately one dozen in number) registered either to my family or to the mill.

All monies received from Liquidation shall be used to retire the Debt of $57,771.25 owed to Mr. Archibald Ramsay of Salem, Va.—which Sum is composed of $50,000.00 in unpaid invoices for Broad Cloth & other Textiles delivered in good faith to Mssrs. Muro and Brightwood, 15 August 1861 through 31 March 1864, plus $7,771.25 accumulated Interest as of 30 June 1864. Failure by Mssrs. Muro and Brightwood to surrender the Assets named above shall result in the immediate resurrection of the Civil Action brought 18 January 1864, in Bedford County Court, by Mr. Ramsay against Mssrs. Muro and Brightwood.

The news both surprised and did not surprise me. On one hand, it had been plain from my last visit home that the mill (with my cousin at the helm) was set on a dreadful course, which in time was sure to bankrupt or otherwise annihilate the enterprise. On the other hand, I had no idea of the size of the debts carried by the mill. It appeared that neither Father nor Sam had paid their suppliers in quite a long time—perhaps since the beginning of the war.

Attached to the settlement were several supporting documents, including copies of correspondence addressed to the Danville firm from my cousin. The first began, "Dear Sirs:"

> *I have received your proposed Settlement in this morning's Post, and I wish to advise you of several errors in your appraisal of our Assets: first, there is no store of undelivered Inventory in any Warehouse, anywhere. It has been delivered to the Confederate States Army, as contracted—a fact which should inspire you to greater deeds than the swearing- out of Legal Complaints against your Country Men. Second, you have overestimated the number of our holding in Chattel by at least Ten: we claim possession at this moment of exactly two House Servants, both of whom, owing to advanced Illness, declined our offer of Manumission.*

The next letter from Sam was a reply to the lawyers' discovery that no deliveries such as the ones Sam described had been made to the army from the Bedford Woolery in the period specified.

> *Let me ask you, Sirs, if you believe that the War has*
> *been lost over the absence of a thousand Sack- Coats?*
> *Though certainly I mean no offense to your ancient*
> *Profession, I cannot help but conclude that the Attor-*
> *ney- at- Law is generally narrow of thought—a trait*
> *that places him at great disadvantage at the present*
> *time. What difference might a barge- load of coats have*
> *made at Gettysburg? Even in victory we might err to*
> *credit any factors beside God and perhaps Luck. Last*
> *week at Cold Harbor, for instance: was it the Yan-*
> *kees' new caps which marked them easy targets for our*
> *rifles? I venture it was not.*

The next attachment was a motion filed in the same county court asking that the list of debtors be expanded to include one *John Alan Muro (Junior), presently of Charlottesville, Va.* My first instinct was to fold the page up and take a flame to the whole lot. I could claim ignorance of the matter. Riders were lost all the time to raiders and vandals, were they not? Besides that, what zealous magistrate would bother to pursue a student over the settlement of so large a debt?

As the news settled over me, however, I realized the logic that had led the Danville drapers to me: I would not be a student at medicine much longer. Soon, I would be a full practitioner of such, with presumed enjoyment of the fees commanded by the profession. Debts, I knew, could stand for years, passing from generation to generation like the oaks lining the drive of a great estate. It displayed foresight on the part of the drapers—they would, after all, establish through this motion a claim not just upon me but upon my children. I have never had more than a passing familiarity with the law, but I knew enough to fear it. I vowed to take action—as brisk and ruthless as the situation required—to avoid entanglement.

I knew the cure by instinct: I would have to sever all ties to my father and Sam, immediately and irreversibly, so as to establish myself as an entity apart from my family, thus immune to implication in my father's affairs.

I went at once to my room, where I found my dusty box of stationery. The paucity of leisure hours had precluded correspondence with anyone for some time. In fact, at that time I wrote precious little apart from the official journaling and report making required of me at the hospital. What brief notes I managed to post were most often scrawled on the backs of hospital forms, or on fly sheets torn from medical texts. I am embarrassed now by the forced illiteracy of those years, but what of it? A man has his twilight years for scribbling, but only youth is well suited to strenuous work. Also, had I not saved the writing till now, I shouldn't have had any story to relate!

I composed two letters that evening—one to the lawyer in Danville and one to my father and Sam. I shall reproduce both here, as memory serves.

First, to the lawyer:

> *To: Ronald H. Barker, Esq.,*
> *100 First Street, N.W., Danville*
> *University of Va., 18 June 2005*

*Dear Mr. Barker,*

> *I thank you graciously, sir, for your dispatch of 10 August, as it served as my first notice of the lamentable state of my father's business affairs. It has been three years since I left*

*Lynchburg for the University, and in this interval my contact
with the Bedford Woolery has been nil. If you must know, my
relationship with the entire family has soured considerably.
While I doubt this constitutes a legal argument against the
motion (31 May, Bedford County Court) naming me in the
claims of Mr. Ramsay, I must inform you of it all the same,
and I implore you to suspend the motion in good faith.*

*My current station is Assistant Surgeon at the Charlottes-
ville General Hospital (C.S.A.), pursuant to which I would
be happy to provide you with references.*

*I await your reply.*

> *Yours sincerely,*
> *Lieutenant John A. Muro, C.S.A.*

This was the only time I ever invoked my rank, by mouth or by
pen, in an attempt at influence, and it shames me to recall it. The
word *lieutenant* came slowly to my hand. I sensed that its application
to me insulted and even *defamed* men who wore the stripes not just
when it was convenient, but even when it brought danger. I had never
showed my rank on the field of battle, never said to the enemy, "Shoot
me first—if you have only one bullet left, aim it here."

You shall read in a moment the just reward of my hubris—but
first, the other letter:

> *To: Mssrs. John Muro and Samuel Brightwood,*
> *Bedford Woolery, Lynchburg*

> *University, 18 June 1864*

*Dear Father and Sam,*

*Words cannot express the sadness, nor the disappoint-
ment, that I feel just now. I had a letter today from a lawyer*

in Danville—the collecting- agent of your erstwhile supplier
Mr. Ramsay. As you might expect, I was surprised not at the
notice of the Mill's failure (which I could not help but expect)
but by the news that Mr. Ramsay aims to recover his losses
by my labor as well as yours. I am of half a mind to wish him
well, for I have none of your Loot but the coins you gave me,
and those are long spent on other things.

I am not disposed to be Passive in this matter. I have written the lawyer to say that I have been for some time Estranged
from you, and that furthermore I had no part whatsoever in
the ruination of the Bedford Woolery. I cannot pretend to
know what high Foolishness impelled you, Sam, to despoil
a profitable business, nor what possessed Father to allow it.
Surely Mr. Stokes turns in his grave at what you've done.
You should be ashamed of yourselves.

Where but in this ragged and blood- torn country can we
see the Scripture reversed? A well- born young man leaves
home only to return years later to find his birthright squandered in his absence . . . I ask, which of us is the Prodigal?

You have left me no recourse but to quit you forever. I shall
continue to reside in Charlottesville—into the near future, at
any rate, or as long as the War persists—but I implore you
to consider me dead. These days it is hardly rare for a son to
leave and never to return. In my official duty, I have turned
away the entreaties of a hundred mothers and fathers—ghost-
seekers from Alabama and Texas, North and South Carolina,
&c. Count yourselves now in this number.

If I am owed any recompense at all, perform this final
service for me: tell Mother and Parthenia that I was killed in
the War. There is no reason for either to suffer for knowing
the truth. As I've said, it is a common hardship to lose a man,

*and they will shoulder it, I know, with Grace and Poise.*
*Gentlemen, know that I might have sent this very Lie to*
*you—there are a hundred Soldiers at my disposal who might*
*have penned a false note of Consolation—but I did not. You*
*alone will know my true disposition. That is your burden.*

*With great sadness, then—I die.*
*John Alan*


My hands shook as I sealed the envelope. I thought of what Father might say. Would he try to calm Sam by reassuring him that I did not believe what I'd written? Would Sam punch a wall? I had heard from older doctors—men who had actually practiced during peace—that fractures of the metacarpals were among the most common injuries treated in hospital triage. "Cuckold hand," it was called. But they were as apt to have no reaction at all. There was no predicting the antics of madmen.

There was nothing for me to do but carry on. I tried to live as if I had been deposited on the earth with no family at all. It was not hard; I had lived outside their influence for several years already. It was a matter of pushing their memories out of mind. In a state of distraction and constant fatigue, I managed this nicely.

Lorrie never knew. When the time came to make invitations to the wedding, I asked if I might write those to my family personally. Of course I never did, and I fibbed again when she asked if they had acknowledged their receipt.

"What kind of parents cannot attend a son's wedding? Is it the expense of the trip? Or the risk? You know, I have heard that the road south of Charlottesville has been quite dangerous with raiders and such . . ."

It saddened me to see her struggle with the implausibility of my lies. But I held fast, knowing that I might be exposed if I altered my story.

"In weak moments I can't help thinking their qualm is with me," she said.

"Don't think that," I said. "Believe me: they have no qualm."

"But why, then? I don't understand it. Not even your sister?"

"I'm afraid not." I sighed then and shrugged my shoulders to convey my own exasperation at the perceived slight.

"Well, no matter," I said finally. "Put it from your mind. We are together, and will be together—that is the important thing."

"Yes, you're right. We are fortunate in that way."

But Lorrie refused to surrender the notion that my family's neglect was a reaction to her shortcomings as a bride. I did my best to reassure her to the contrary. The words came easily, because it was all true: no member of my family, in point of fact, had ever expressed any doubt whatsoever on her worthiness.

Several times, to my horror, she came close to guessing the truth. Once we were at church, in the Cabells' pew at Grace Church in Cismont. Since our announcement, I had made every effort to attend services with Lorrie's people. It was my wager (correct, it turned out) that this weekly gesture would do wonders to compensate for the dozen other engagements I was forced to miss each week on account of my schedule. My attendance was noted most of all by Mrs. Cabell, who took it upon herself to thank me each and every time "for the sacrifice of time." For all her outward devotion, Mrs. Cabell had precious little interest in the actual content of the service, and she routinely chattered to the ladies in the adjacent pews over parish gossip. On those occasions when a name in Lorrie's acquaintance came up—given Lorrie's arachnoid social web, this was rather often—the whispered conversation drew close.

"Is it Judith Carr of whom you're speaking, Auntie?" Lorrie said.

"Oh, heavens, no—Judith Carrington, of Castle Hill. You know her sister's child, don't you? Angela Barlow?"

"She's a dear. Of course I know her."

"Psst—Mildred! Did I hear Angela Barlow just now? You know what trouble she's in, don't you? Oh, I do not envy her . . ."

Lorrie raised the hymnal to conceal her lips. "What's this about Angela Barlow?"

"Oh Lorrie. You haven't heard? Her fiancé left her. Left town, in fact, and not for the service."

"No . . ."

"It was a week ago yesterday. I can't believe she didn't tell you."

"She must be devastated."

"Well." The speaker was a lawyer's wife, who, despite her age and considerable heft, insisted on wearing dresses that featured her pendulous breasts like melons in a grocer's display. She caught Mrs. Cabell's attention and rolled her eyes. "I suppose she must be troubled by it, yes."

Lorrie grew impatient with the old women. "What else is there? Tell me. Why, you act as if she deserved it!"

"Heavens no, young lady, I am suggesting nothing like that. I only mean to *underline* the fact that Miss Barlow hardly knew the fellow."

"Now, that's true," Mrs. Cabell said. "I would not recommend any girl marry a man before all his mysteries are revealed."

"Oh Auntie—if that were true, what joy would remain?"

"This is not for joy, dear. This is marriage."

Soon thereafter the congregation rose to sing, and the conversation was drowned in a cacophony of raised voices.

*All people that on earth do dwell,*
*Sing to the Lord with cheerful voice!*

We drove home alone in the gig, the Cabells having remained in the county to dine with friends. It was not until we were crossing Pantops Mountain, at that stretch of road just after the Minor estate whence one can spy the light dome of the University library, that Lorrie confessed to dwelling all afternoon on her aunt's warning. "What if I don't know you, after all?" she said. "You must admit the possibility. I have never met your family—what if they are all a bunch of raving fools?"

"They are not, I assure you."

"What if your father's mill is nothing but a loom in the basement and your sister is just a cat?"

"Lorrie—"

"Who else? Oh, your cousin, what is his name? The one with the leg injury. Suppose he was never injured in the war, as you say he was, but instead met his fate in a duel?"

"You're making fun of me now."

"Well, yes, I am. But you must admit these things are *possible.*"

I shook the reins, and the horse gathered speed. The road descended off the mountain and the pretty spires of Charlottesville disappeared behind a wall of trees. We sat silent as Lorrie waited for me to pick up my end of the conversation. I said nothing.

"You mustn't pout, John," she said finally. "It is unattractive."

# 58

WE TOOK A HOUSE just north of the University in a neighborhood inhabited by young faculty and their wives. It was a short distance to the hospital, which I covered easily on foot, thus freeing us from the necessity of a keeping a horse. Whenever we needed to travel into the country, we simply borrowed conveyance from the Cabells, who were always generous in that regard. Our rented home was clad in red bricks, with white trim and an excellent tin roof. It belonged to the wife of a stable man who had joined the cause early and gotten himself killed at Second Manassas. The rent was a pittance—just enough to keep the widow in beer and porridge, or however else she passed the time at her sister's home in Gordonsville.

It was a long and leafy fall, and it would have been a decent circumstance for two young marrieds but for two detractions. First was the close and continuous presence of Lorrie's mother, who had leapt at Mrs. Cabell's suggestion that she stay on in Charlottesville rather than return to her husband's family in Texas.

The Cabells, however, did not mean that she should stay with them. Rather, she would have to lodge with us, because it turned out that Dr. Cabell—genial, gracious Dr. Cabell—did not appreciate the company of his sister- in- law with anything approaching brotherly love.

"She grates, John," he explained to me over a pipe in his office at the Delevan. We were enjoying a rare break—which he had allowed himself (and me) only because of the unpleasant duty he had to discharge. "I have discussed the matter with Mrs. Cabell, and she supports my decision." He looked up from his pipe and searched me, unsure if my new status might have changed our rapport. "I'm truly sorry, son," he said. "If it were Mrs. Cabell's mother, I would take her. I want you to understand that."

"If you don't mind my asking, sir, what is it that perturbs you in her? So I know what to watch for . . ."

"Ah. I suppose it isn't anything at all. You'll find as you grow older that you need no reason to dislike some people. Maybe you've experienced this already."

"Not to my knowledge, sir."

"You will. It comes to me like hay fever the moment this person walks into a room. I do regret Wigfall's passing—he was a good, decent man—but I confess that I was of two minds when she appeared at our door."

I had never heard such talk from Dr. Cabell. Here was a stolid Christian! I considered if I might have misheard him.

"Are you certain you feel this way, sir?"

"Am I certain? Oh, I'm certain. The way she dangles her chin when you speak straight to her—the way she just sits there and takes your criticisms. I tell you, sometimes I want to take both her shoulders and shake with all my might. I'm sorry, John; I know how this must appear to you. I mean it only as an explanation, not an excuse."

"No matter, sir. I am happy to oblige the family."

I felt sincere in this assertion—it was indeed my obligation to do as the Cabells wished, after all they had done for me, and especially for Lorrie.

Moreover, I felt tremendous guilt at cutting off my own sister, and by this good turn I hoped to make some amends on that score.

Unfortunately, Dr. Cabell was correct in his assessment. Mrs. Wigfall was infuriatingly passive, and by the end of her first month with us, I was ready to shake her myself. She ate almost nothing and made no mess, so there were no tangible reasons to resent her. But her silence nagged. It was like living with a ghost. Upon arriving home from work I routinely laid my stack of papers on a high table in the entry hall. I then went to the bedroom and cleansed my hands and face at the basin. After a while I would return to the entry hall table for my papers but would find them gone—moved to some destination deemed more appropriate by Mrs. Wigfall. It is a small annoyance, perhaps, but I refer the doubter to Dr. Cabell's testimony as proof that the peeve was not mine alone.

She was furthermore an unrepentant eavesdropper. The geometry of our little rented house was such that Mrs. Wigfall's bedroom lay directly above our own. She was rheumatic, and also a bit deaf in one ear. Thus she moved about constantly, bumping into furniture, and other things in an effort to gain better purchase on the conversations below. We were powerless to prevent her from hearing, for the house was not more than seven hundred feet square, and to be honest, in the heat of argument, neither of us cared much who overheard.

The banging- around upstairs signaled which of our conversations she relished most. These were chiefly the arguments—soon, nightly occurrences—on the topic of children. Lorrie had not conceived in five months of marriage—a fact that did not worry me at all. A pregnancy is not a mystical occurrence, but rather a biological feat requiring the precise alignment of many factors. After learning the science behind the endeavor, the conditions necessary in the womb, etc., one marvels that conception ever happens at all!

Of course, Lorrie did not share this point of view, and she concluded right away that my schedule at the hospital was to blame. "If you were present in this home more often," she inveighed, "we might know for sure that the *machinery,* as you say, is sound."

"The machinery is sound!" I countered. "Why don't you believe me? It takes patience, most of all. I've read accounts of women who conceived only after giving up hope, because only then were they able to relax sufficiently."

"I am relaxed, John. Look at me—I'm relaxed." An artery thumped in her temple, and her trembling hand looked as though it might drop her mug of raspberry- leaf tea. No matter how much evidence I presented to the contrary, Lorrie insisted that the consumption of raspberry- leaf tea was a medically necessary prerequisite to conception, that it would "steady" her uterus. When I inquired after her source, she stated proudly that she had read it in a ladies' magazine. Ask any doctor if he minds being asked for medical advice and he will answer on the contrary; most of us feel as though we are not asked enough. A medical education can feel like a burden when one stops to consider the quantity of lies and half- truths circulating on matters of physical health. Had I been a man of any other vocation, I might not have noticed my wife guzzling raspberry- leaf tea, and I certainly would not have asked after her rationale. But as a doctor I could not hold my tongue.

"You might as well sprinkle pine duff into your kettle!" I said. "You are a doctor's wife, for the love of God—it's time to start acting like one."

"You mustn't swear. Suppose I am pregnant after all."

"And what then? Can the fetus hear me?"

"Perhaps."

"Don't be a fool, Lorrie."

"I'm not a fool, and I don't appreciate you calling names. You've grown intolerant, you know. You didn't use to be this way."

"I have always been this way. There is no sense in spreading foolishness such as fetuses speaking English when you know better. You're a bright girl. At least, you were."

"So there it is—you've been tricked. I suppose we should be divorced."

There was a squeak of floorboards upstairs as Mrs. Wigfall adjusted her position. I raised an eyebrow and said, "At least you won't have to live alone."

"Oh, you rotten man. How dare you say that? After what she's been through . . ."

"I only mean to say that you wouldn't be left on your own."

"I understand what you mean. And do you know what? You're right. You've been this way forever. I should have seen it coming when you divorced your family. Isn't that what you did? Either that or you had them killed. Which is it? Perhaps they are the same thing. You have a weak spine, John Muro. And you are a coward. A hundred ways you're a coward."

"A hundred ways?"

"Shall I list them for you?"

"Please."

Our arguments went on like this most nights until one of us caved from fatigue. We would then patch our wounds as best we could and retreat to the bedroom. I would perform the marriage act, and we would fall asleep without further exchange. Sometimes the arguing resumed in the morning, picking up the thread just where we had left it the night before.

"I ought to list a hundred ways," Lorrie would say on waking. "You would recall perhaps five."

"Lorrie—"

"No, you're dull. You are."

"I would never say such a thing about you."

"That is because it would not be true."

I dipped my bread carefully into a saucer of milk. "Very well, then. Give me your list."

"Item number one: Braxton Baucom. You made as though you were surprised when I told you he'd proposed."

"But I was surprised! I had no idea. At least, not of that particular transgression."

"I wonder, John. Would that be my transgression, in your opinion, or his?"

And so went our war. There was no victory to be had in these arguments. Our motivation devolved into the simple desire to injure each other, to quench a momentary lust for revenge, and thence perhaps to earn a moment's peace.

Mrs. Wigfall, for her part, never mentioned our bickering. But the fact of it opened a canyon between us. When she and I spoke, it was usually to ponder idly, in that common, public way, the declining fortunes of the Confederacy. ("Perhaps this month we have peace?" "One can hope," et cetera, et cetera.) We never once touched upon the subject of the confederacy unraveling under our roof.

# 59

SO WHAT OF THE FATE of the Confederate States? Much has been written, with just cause, about the Yankees' savagery in conquest. I can report that the University of Virginia was spared, as were the hospital facilities adjacent. This was due in large part to the diplomacy of the chairman of the faculty, Professor Socrates Maupin.

On the morning of March 23, 1865, Professor Maupin set out from the University with a white bedsheet hoisted on a pole. There had been news from Shenandoah Valley via night rider that Sheridan's army, which had laid waste the whole area from Winchester to Staunton, was moving east. It was said that certain units of Federal cavalry had already crossed the Blue Ridge at Rockfish Gap and were bivouacked at Afton. These were rumored to be the forces of Colonel Custer.

A panic gripped the town. Custer was camped on our side of the Blue Ridge. There was debate about the smartest course of action—that is, the one most likely to preserve life and limb. It was assumed that all property, real and chattel, would be lost. This posed certain issues regarding non- owned property, or property owned by the state. I'm speaking of the University, of course, which was, as you have seen here, not just a venue for lectures but a veritable village in itself. There were families thereCabells, for instance—who faced the possibility of becoming tenants of the state of Maryland or Massachusetts or whatever other political entity claimed the premises. There had been no free claims staked on Virginia land since the days of crown rule. Unlike those territories in central Europe whose sovereign changes with the weather, we were new to surrender, and no one knew just how it would occur.

Socrates Maupin was not going to wait for the answer. He marched his little squad out to the main road so that he was there, waiting, when the first riders appeared on the horizon. He stopped the men and demanded an audience with Colonel Custer. He was told that the colonel was some distance behind, and that he loathed stopping short of his goal for any reason save watering his horse and watering the plants.

Maupin had been prepared for resistance, and he engaged the Yankee cavalrymen in conversation about their homes. A soldier enjoys nothing like talk of home—a fact I would not have suspected Maupin knew. Having spent the better part of three years in the constant company of home- sick soldiers, I knew it, but Socrates Maupin was a chemist. He had, however, visited the Northeast in his student days, which put him in good stead to discuss the particulars of the country his conquerors had left behind. *Ah, Pittsfield! That is in the western portion of Massachusetts, no? I've been through that way— simply stunning. We have no maples here, you know, which dampens the colors in fall . . .*

By a stroke of God he was granted the interview and proceeded to secure the safekeeping of the campus and all its inhabitants. The professor had come equipped with a ring of keys, which he presented to Custer, reportedly to the colonel's heartfelt appreciation. (I trust he had prepared choice bits about Custer's native section of Ohio.)

The full cavalry arrived that evening, and the next morning General Sheridan himself rode through town, en route to his commandeered lodgings on Park Street. As I have mentioned, the common soldiers pitched their tents on Carr's Hill, which is directly opposite the Anatomical Theatre. This cut off the easiest route from our rented house to the University, so in mind of protecting Lorrie and her mother, I moved the household to the Cabells' pavilion.

By the terms of Maupin's surrender, the University remained off limits to the marauding Yankees. Thus the Academical Village became a refuge not just for academics but for respectable citizens of all persuasions. Mrs. Cartwright, for instance, lowered herself to take residence in one of the vacant dormitory rooms on the east colonnade. Lorrie and I took up in the Cabells' basement, the help having vanished at the news of the Federal advance. Mrs. Wigfall shared the Cabells' bed with her sister- in- law; Dr. Cabell slept on the daybed in his study.

There was an air of strange excitement among the refugees. Medically, I attribute this to the phenomenon of a long- standing fear coming suddenly to pass. It is a reaction seen most commonly in soldiers who experience a long delay between enlistment and first action. Often, the experience of the event is indistinguishable from the sufferer's dreams of it. This explains the sensation of dislocation reported by so many of these cases—for they are, in a very real sense, dreaming the event as it occurs.

That is the medical explanation. As a sufferer, I would describe it differently. The morning after Custer's bloodless coup, I stirred in the moldering basement of Pavilion II, my wife dozing beside. I had not slept. The only light in the room came through grates high on the forward wall. Through these I saw boots shuffling back and forth through the slush. The spring thaw was under way. In the Virginia Piedmont this is usually a stepwise affair, with every warm spell undercut by a cold snap of equal and opposite force until at last the weather obeys the calendar and summer begins in earnest. This was one of the warm times, and what snow remained on the ground was rapidly becoming mud. A line of filthy black water ran the height of the basement wall, from the window grate to the cold packed- earth floor. I pulled on my trousers and coat and made off silently up the stairs.

None of the Cabells was awake, nor Mrs. Wigfall. I shut the front door behind me. A man in evening tails passed along the colonnade. "G'morning," he chirped. He was of middle age (perhaps fifty) and bald. I opened my mouth to return the greeting, but no sound came. I watched the man's tails flap about as he hurried down the walk. I followed for twenty yards. There was a tune on the air, and I realized the man was singing to himself. Eager to catch him, I quickened my pace. The rotten snow crunched under my boots. I drew nearer the man—near enough to notice the tune he was singing. It was "Kooka-burra," the children's rhyme, and he sang the words under his breath as he jogged: *Kookaburra sits in the old gum tree- ee. Merry, merry king of the bush is he- ee. Laugh, kookaburra. Laugh, kookaburra, gay your life must be!*

The song, which had been a favorite of mine, struck me now as melancholy. The rising sun shone on the tin roof of a farm shack in the distance. I lost my focus. I slipped just short of the last steps and tumbled onto my back. My skull rapped against the bricks. When I came to, the man was gone.

I sat up. My coat was soaked in filthy slush. As I struggled to shed the sodden garment, I spied the number fifty- two on the door before me. The chase had inadvertently led to my old student room. Not thinking clearly on account of the fall, I ambled over and tried the knob. The door swung open.

The room showed no signs of habitation. I had returned my key to the proctor some nine months before, making clear that I would not be returning, for I was to be married and was taking a house in town with my wife. Old Frock Coat had nodded and noted the fact in his book.

In the dark I made out B.B.'s armoire. He had assured me that he would send a man to cart it off, but that had not transpired. After the tournament he seldom showed his face outside his house. There were rumors that the county authorities were preparing charges against him—or else that the faculty were gathering to expel him—but neither occurred before he was called home. His father was concerned about the Yankees' advance up the Peninsula in the direction of the family's estate in Charles City. As I heard it, B.B. had resisted his father's entreaties as long as he could—that is, until the old man stopped paying his bills. That had been in the fall. Now the Yanks held both sides of the James all the way to Hopewell. I wondered if B.B. had fled—and if so, where?

I hung the wet coat on a peg and opened the armoire. All of the garments had been removed. I suspected the stewards. They had, however, left a couple of thin wool blankets on the top shelf. I wrapped myself in these and stretched out on the bed. The combination of cold, damp, and the blow to my head made me drowsy, and I fell asleep at once. I slept for many dreamless hours. When I woke, the room was light.

And that is when I saw the envelope on the floor.

# 60

**IT LAY SO PLAINLY** before the door that I wondered how I had missed it upon entering. There were other items scattered about— candle stubs, an old newspaper—and at a distance there was nothing about this envelope that suggested that it was anything but litter. The corners were rounded from handling, and the wax seal had been broken. The address was written in a hand I did not recognize.

*To: Dr. John Muro, 52 East Lawn, Univ. of Virginia, Charlottesville*

The envelope bore a Philadelphia postmark. Correspondence in those days was routinely opened by the censors. This letter had likely been read by authorities on both sides of the picket. If nothing else, they had been deliberate: the date on the postmark was nearly three months past.

I unfolded and read:

*My Dear Friend,*

*I sincerely hope that this Letter finds you well. I regret that we were not able to speak before my hasty departure from Virginia, but I am sure you have gathered that the circumstances of my release were fully unexpected.*

*I have been discharged from the Army. The doctors here commend the care provided by you and the others, but they insist that I am unfit for further service on account of my arm. I have found, however, that I am less disadvantaged than the government maintains. I am capable of performing nearly all of the daily tasks of civilian life, including writing, feeding, and personal hygiene, plus some gentle physical labor. Though Sarah was horrified at first by my disfigurement, even she now admits that I am nearly as capable as I was before the injury.*

*It has been a mixed blessing to be reunited with my family. They cling so. I can hardly blame them in this, for I was absent so long, but it leaves me little time for reflection. I grew quite fond of the state of independence I enjoyed in the Hospital. Yes, I was laid up, but I was beholden to no one.*

*Whenever I am afforded a quiet moment, I reflect on my time in Virginia, and especially in your ward. I can say without qualification that you saved my life, John, and for that I owe you an eternal debt of gratitude. Yours is unique talent, and I have no doubt that you will rise to the absolute pinnacle of the medical profession in short time. Know that it was my intention, always, to thank you in the flesh for your dedication to my case. I hope that you will accept this note in the interim.*

I opened the letter to its full length. A small card toppled out of the fold and settled on my desk. It was a postcard depicting a boating scene on a river. The caption read: *THE BLUE SCHUYLKILL—PHILA-DELPHIA, PENN.*

*You will be pleased to know that upon careful consideration of our final Chat—that being when you asked about my residence in Hartford, and the wisdom therein, &c.—I decided shortly after arriving home to move my family back to Philadelphia. Furthermore, I have abandoned the insurance trade and plan to establish a medical practice here. It is my sincere wish that when this deplorable Conflict has run its course you will join me as my Partner. My daughters are excited to meet you, John—I have told them all about your skill in the medical arts, as well as your considerable Charm.*

*I look forward with great anticipation to your reply, though I understand if conditions preclude much time for Correspondence. But—even if the merciful Lord has intervened and ceased our War while this letter is in transit, do not rush your answer: I am sincere in my wish to bring you here, and I would prefer that you give a considered response rather than a hasty Yea or Nay.*

> *With Warmest Regards, I Am,*
> *Your Friend,*
> *Henry Burton Stone*

I sat for a long time with the letter. It was bright in the room, but very cold. My breath rose in a thin cloud before dissolving into the sunlight. Clutching the blankets close, I read it again. The most stunning revelation of all was the assertion that I had inspired Stone to change his course in life. I was flattered, but I had trouble believing it was true. And yet—why would Stone be insincere? He was free to say and do as he pleased. He was a citizen of a conquering power. Why should he be interested in me? This offer to establish a practice in Philadelphia—I wondered, was that sincere as well?

I turned next to the card. In the drawing, a man in a tall hat rowed a lady across the flat water. A group of buildings loomed on the far bank. I imagined that this was the great Medical College, and that the dock in the foreground was the house of the rowing club.

In my scenario, the woman in the skiff was Lieutenant Stone's favorite daughter.

And the man in the hat was . . . me.

From the sun's bright effort through the dormitory window I guessed it was ten o'clock or later. I had left no note, and Lorrie would be worrying after me. I stood and folded the blankets neatly into the abandoned armoire. Outside, there were people on the Lawn—dejected men and women wandering hollow- eyed through the morning. It was the first morning of our occupation—the first day of what is lately termed "the reconstruction."

I stuffed the envelope, letter, and postcard into my jacket pocket. Then, taking a deep breath to calm myself, I started up the colonnade.

# 61

IT WOULD HAVE BEEN naive to assume that the change in venue—
that is, moving into the Cabells' home—would quell the tension
between Lorrie and me. In fact, the relative isolation of the basement
quarters encouraged ever louder and more vituperative arguments.
Our quarrel had been enlarged from the specific topic of children to
the more general question of our suitability for each other as man and
wife, and it seemed increasingly clear that I was not the man Lorrie
needed—or even the one she wanted.

"You should have married B.B. while you had the chance."

"This is not about B.B."

"You lie."

"Oh, but you wish I were lying!"

"I wish you would come clean, Lorrie—if you have a complaint
against me, then say it to my face."

"I have said it and said it again. If you haven't heard you're either
deaf or stupid."

"But not both?"

Occasionally she turned cloying in the middle of a tirade. She would hover over me, so close that I might smell her breath, which she perfumed with mint.

"We shouldn't fight, Dr. Muro." She used my title in anger and in flattery; often I had no idea which she meant.

"I think we should. You have a grievance and I mean to address it."

At this she bore in: "You mean nothing!"

"Lorrie, please—"

She slapped my hand away. "I don't want any more promises. I have no child and no father, and my husband disappears for hours on end."

"You're referring to this morning? I wanted to let you sleep."

"In the niggers' quarters, John? Is that where you wanted to leave me?"

She turned away, took up her novel. I watched her try to read, then shut the book. She took up the lamp, which we had positioned on the little table between our beds so that we might share a single candle, and put it on her lap. She poised above it, cheeks full, and stared at me. A puff, and then it was dark. The smell of burnt wick carried through the room.

# 62

THE HOSPITAL DID NOT close down when the Yankees arrived. On the contrary—when our facility became known through the ranks, we were inundated with new patients. Every morning, it seemed, another sick Yankee presented himself on the steps of the Delevan. We were, of course, obliged to attend him, the conquered having little power to refuse their conquerors.

There were also requests to make calls to the Yankee camps. Due to a shortage of medics in Sheridan's units—a product, I think, of the ease of manufacturing soldiers compared with physicians—many of the common soldiers, and even some officers, had attempted to treat themselves. They were certainly well supplied to do it. In fact, that was my first reaction to the condition in the Yankee camps on Carr's Hill. *What a bounty of chemicals!* One addicted captain held in a single saddlebag more narcotic than had passed though our hospital's pharmacy in two years. It seemed that essential preparations like mercurous chloride and quinine had been issued like hardtack in the Union Army. According to policy, the soldiers were not permitted to share their stores with civilians, but when it became known that doctors such as myself would make calls to camp if paid in drugs, they used the little phials and powder packets as currency.

I recall a private from Vermont who had been the subject of a strange charade. He had come down with a horrible dysentery and accompanying fever just after the army left Harrisonburg. This had been at least a fortnight before I saw him. The other fellows in his unit had been concerned for his health ("He was shootin' his guts out the ass, Doc!" quoth one fellow) but there had been no opportunity to stop and seek the medical attention the poor boy required. So, the others propped him on a horse, took the leads, and marched on. At each night's campsite, the platoon secreted the boy into a tent. In the morning, they propped him up at roll call—I still wonder how he was able to bark his name, but that discrepancy was never addressed in the telling—and he was returned to his horse for the day's ride.

When I arrived at Carr's Hill, the boy was a dried- out pith. He could not focus his eyes, and his forehead burned to the touch. I called for a broth and a strong dose of quinine—both of which were fetched to me in a matter of minutes—and by sundown the boy was on the mend, smiling and even swearing at his mates.

For my services, I took a packet of quinine tablets from each man in the platoon—nearly two dozen in all. Thus laden, I returned to the Delevan a conqueror in my own right. Our hospital had had no steady source of quinine since the blockade went up in '61, with the exception of those infrequent shipments shunted our way by generous "importers." (On a side note—how fascinating were the changes in nomenclature after the war ended? Blockade runners, suddenly, were *importers*, and the traitors who had deserted the cause to flee North during the fighting were now *ambassadors of the New South*.)

I know doctors who take great satisfaction in the way our profession appears to operate independent of the corrupting influence of politics.

For the most part, I join them—but you must understand that our occupation by the Union Army represented much more than a change in political leadership. We had been separated so long from any hint of prosperity that the sight of the Northerners on our streets was like a vision of a foreign race. The brass buttons on their coats shone like gold. Their horses exuded a glow of healthy, well- fed calm that made even our best mounts look like knobby- kneed foals.

When the first Yankee medical officers finally arrived in Charlottesville we had a second revelation: we learned how far behind the pace of medical science we had fallen over the course of four years. The Northern doctors' instruments, procedures, vocabulary, and virtually everything else about their practice was so different from ours that I questioned my entire store of knowledge. Bear in mind that on account of my extensive clinical practice, I was better trained than any student in the medical curriculum at the University of Virginia had ever been—and I daresay better than any ever will be. I mean this humbly, for it is simply the truth. I was forced to practice as a full- fledged physician almost from the minute I arrived at school. I am indebted, in a sense, for the experience, but it is my sincerest hope that there shall never be another such practicum, and that no medical student should ever again have to train in the darkness of political isolation.

A Yankee surgeon by the name of Gilpatrick was placed in charge of the Charlottesville General Hospital the first week in April 1865. Richmond was by that time in the Yankees' possession, and General Lee was on the run. He would surrender just a few days later.

In that last week before the truce, there were rumors of ragged, gray- coated men appearing on doorsteps all over central Virginia. Dr. Orianna Moon, whose people lived in Scottsville, reported that her sister- in- law had seen a plume of smoke rising from a rickety smokehouse on her property that had not been used in twenty- five years. The woman did not go out to the shack—her husband was away, and she did not think it prudent—but the lack of tangible evidence did not deter her from feeding the gossip mill. He was a scout, she swore. Was this not irrefutable proof that the final stand would take place right here in Albemarle County?

Unfazed by the possibility of a reckoning—or perhaps because Union intelligence did not predict any such thing—Dr. Gilpatrick went immediately to work making over our hospital. His first aim was to thin the ranks in the permanent wards. He was aided in this by unseasonably warm temperatures, which allowed noncritical patients (those for instance with chronic conditions such as gout) to be moved into tents in the adjoining fields. This was, of course, our action every summer, or as soon as the warm weather permitted us doing it, but the arrogant Yankee surgeon assumed full credit and trumpeted his accomplishment as if he had just invented the tined fork.

I shall recount one conversation between Gilpatrick and Dr. Cabell, which I heard through the canvas walls of one of these tents, in order to illustrate the general method of this new administration. Bear in mind as you read that Gilpatrick was young enough to be Dr. Cabell's son.

"Very well, sir," Cabell said, "I shall have the staff report at seven tomorrow."

"At seven, you say? Why so late?"

"Is seven late in your country?" (Gilpatrick was attached to an infantry unit from Delaware.)

"No," Gilpatrick said. "You're right. Make it eight."

"Are you sure?"

"Why—what is the matter with you, old man? Do you mean to confuse me?"

I can attest that Dr. Cabell meant nothing of the sort. He knew only that it was no easy task to carry a command to all of the disparate wards in the sprawling hospital complex, and he wanted to be absolutely sure of the content before sending out the message.

"It's no wonder your men fight like cowards," Gilpatrick went on. "I have witnessed a distinct lack of discipline in this facility. Also patent disregard for authority. You should know I will be reporting this to my superiors."

"You may report whatever you wish," Cabell said. He hadn't a hint of combat in his voice—only a desire to end the conversation, which he must have regarded as pointless quibbling, to return to more useful work.

"So you wish to be reported?"

"Not as such. But as I say, you should report as you see fit."

"As I see fit! You know, I ought to dismiss you right now. Insolence is the root problem with your people. That and plumb wrongheadedness. I look around this place and what do I see? In the pharmacy, for instance—bales of little ditch flowers! Is that a joke of some kind? Were your men to sneeze their way to recovery?"

"With all due respect, Dr. Gilpatrick, you don't know the disadvantage—"

"Which you created for yourself! Did the Union Army ask you to secede?"

A long pause ensued in which neither man spoke. On the other side of the tent wall, I sat preparing a plaster for a lacerated scalp. I had not been paying attention to my work, and the mixture began to harden in the mixing bowl. I quickly added water and scraped the sides with the spatula.

Dr. Cabell's voice came through the wall: "I don't see how that is relevant to the suffering here."

Before Gilpatrick could answer, an assistant ran up and announced he was needed somewhere else.

"We shall take this up later," he said to Cabell. There was a hint of relief in his voice, as though he knew there was no logical parry to Dr. Cabell's observation.

The assistant began briefing him on the urgent matter—an orderly in another ward had stolen a joint of lamb from the kitchen, and did Dr. Gilpatrick wish to hear the case himself or have it referred to the divisional authorities? Their voices faded into the night.

I applied the plaster carelessly to the drowsy soldier's forehead and handed the spatula and bowl to the nurse. I felt compelled to speak with Dr. Cabell at once. I had puzzled many nights over the accounting of blood for moral debt. But even supposing secession were the worst kind of sin—which was surely Dr. Gilpatrick's belief—was not the punishment disproportionate to the crime? How many thousands of men must expire? And how did their expiring right the wrong?

Every time I struggled to balance this equation, I came up empty. But now, in Dr. Cabell's formulation, I saw the true sense of it: there was no balance to be had. The puzzle pieces would not fit together, no matter how many ways they were spun around.

Further, I saw that war was not a rational thing, but rather like a fire: unthinking and unfeeling, and heedless of everything but fuel. Once ignited, a conflict such as ours might burn indefinitely—certainly beyond the ability of the combatants to remember their grievances. Thus the real task in battle was not to win but to finish. The sides are joined by a common enemy, and that is the fact of war itself.

# 63

I BEGAN TO CARRY THE letter from Lieutenant Stone with me
at all times, transferring it from one jacket to the next to keep it from
Lorrie and her mother. In spite of myself, I began to consider his
proposition seriously. One afternoon, during the half hour Dr. Gilpatrick allowed the staff for lunch, I walked over to the depot. I asked the
stationmaster if there were any trains heading north.

"How far you hoping to go?"

"Philadelphia," I said.

The stationmaster was gaunt but not ill, the kind of stick- figured
man who would have been thin even in times of plenty. His white hair
was cut straight across the forehead like a boy's.

He chuckled. "Are you, now? Well, I cain't help you there. Off
the record, though—and you didn't hear none of this from me—
there's been transports coming through here every night about dusk
time. Fetching all the loot back, I reckon."

"The loot?"

"You know—all that gold we was hiding. Don't give me that blank
look, son. Ev'body knows what they came here for. Plain as day."

I waited for him to laugh, but he did not.

Gold or no, the Confederate States of America had been wiped off the globe. General Lee had surrendered what remained of the army on April 9, 1865, at Appomattox Court House—less than ten miles from the Brightwood farm. The bloodiest war in our history was done, and there was no question as to the outcome.

I doubted Lincoln took much joy from the victory. Oddly, my first thought after hearing the news from Appomattox was of him. I wondered how he had taken the news. Had he been relieved? Had he been disappointed at the lack of a grand reckoning? When he was murdered a week later, I envied the convenience of his death. He lived long enough to see the satisfactory conclusion of our struggle, but not so long that he had to endure its ugly aftermath. Better to die clutching the knowledge that one's goal was attained. If that goal was peace and the peace lasted just one day, best to die on that day and carry peace to heaven.

The truer picture of the war's gloaming is seen in the mysterious plume of smoke rising from the abandoned shack in Scottsville. I've mentioned that Lee's army dissolved just prior to surrender. Some of them simply went home. But many had no plan, just a notion to lie low for the near term. The sight of strangers "on the skirts of town" was a common report, as indeed it is today. It was not always so! Let me testify to the absence of these men in our communities before the war. These were our tradesmen, our teamsters. Many times I have driven past a tramp and marveled if he were not the spitting image of Mr. Stokes!

"I seen a couple guys hanging off the cars, is why I mention it," the stationmaster said. "Most of them cars is empty on the northbound."

I pushed a twenty- dollar Confederate note across the ledge.

The old man held the bill to the light and smiled. He replaced it on the ledge. "Someday they'll thank us," he said.

# 64

MY ROOM ON THE EAST colonnade remained vacant, and I secreted myself there each day in the hour between the end of my shift and the curfew. Sheridan had pulled out of town only a few days after his arrival, and the citizens who had flocked to the University for protection from the invaders gradually made their way home. Lorrie and I (with Mrs. Wigfall in tow) moved back to our little house north of campus. After the relative opulence of the Cabells' pavilion, the house seemed more cramped than ever, and I cherished the moments I spent away from it.

There was another reason I hid out in the dormitory. After the tip from the stationmaster, I started to compile the items necessary for a flight north. Taking just a little each day, I began stealing from the hospital. All aspects of the Charlottesville Hospital were now buoyed by the infusion of supplies from the Yankees—from chemicals to lint, and everything in between. I do not mean to suggest that the plentitude excused my thievery, only to explain how the sudden availability of such things, the dizziness after feasting, might have led me to err.

I took meal and flour from the hospital mess, certain vital preparations from the pharmacy, and even a pint of pure distilled alcohol.

Some items, such as a pocket- sized pill press, I stole because I had only heard of such things—and now here they were, unwatched and easily accessible!

By the time Lee's truce was a month old, I had turned 52 East Lawn into a storehouse to rival the back room of any country store. The goods were laid out, for the most part, in the shelves and drawers of B.B.'s furniture, though I had also scavenged a few warped barrels, which I filled one pilfered pocketful at a time with flour, meal, and other milled stuffs. I had made no provision for transferring this bounty to the train—especially if my passage therein was to be, shall we say, unofficial—but that did not deter me from continuing to acquire until the room grew crowded from the stockpile. A wedge of cheese I had lifted from Gilpatrick's own dining tent began to molder and stink. By the end of June 1865, I sensed that the time to go was upon me. I knew that if I didn't leave soon, I likely never would.

I had observed the daily passing of the transport trains and committed their schedule to a secret ledger. Consulting this, I chose the 26th of June, a Monday, for my escape. The plan was simple, and I had more than enough time to carry it out: the day before, I would hide a sack of supplies in the woods beyond the tracks. This I would sheathe in oilcloth, in case of rain, or in the event some circumstance prevented me from meeting the schedule. The transport rolled through town at a quarter to six in the evening. It would be an easy trick to leave my ward on an errand—a consulting opinion from Dr. Gilpatrick, perhaps. I would retrieve my bag, get in position, and hop aboard.

As the day approached, I could not help worrying that I had overlooked some fundamental matter, and my plan would fail. Afternoons in the dormitory I packed and unpacked my suitcase, a little carpetbag I had appropriated from the Cabells' attic. I filled the bag with twenty different collections of items. In one iteration I set out a dry peck of flour and another of oats, and an entire box of new starched collars.

In another, I included no food whatsoever save a wrapped chunk of salted ham. In the end I settled on the following: two canteens, a jar of crackers, a candle lamp, candles, matches, and a change of clothes, which I would save until minutes before arriving at Stone's door. I did not have the number of his house, and that worried me a little—as did the fact of jumping aboard a moving train, to be honest—but I cast that fear aside in deference to the monumental task of *leaving*.

By now, surely, the reader has asked himself how a respectable man should ever consider abandoning his wife (and mother- in- law) for such a risky endeavor as this. I counter that the spirit of the time was such that this was not only wholly possible, but even *probable*, for a man lucky enough to have a legitimate opportunity to pursue. I know that there has never been another time in the history of this nation where a section of the population has felt such shame, disgrace, and general dissatisfaction with its lot. I say that life carried on as normal, but that is only to say that life carried on—the circumstances that had become *normal* by the spring of 1865 were hardly desirable, and certainly not supportable for a peacetime life.

The fact remained that aside from supplying our hospitals with drugs and our commissaries with foodstuffs, there was no effort made by the Federal commanders to soften the blow of defeat with goodwill. We were subjects, and no good Union officer was going to forfeit his hard- won chance to play lord. Ironically, for all the talk of "Northern aggression" before the secession vote, Virginia had never been so squarely under the foot of a foreign power as in those months after the surrender.

Worst, we remembered Fort Sumter. There was no doubt who had fired the first shot. And now we were proved arrogant. Our urge, therefore, was not to restore our society to what it had been, but rather to cut ourselves loose from its remains. Our culture now reeked of weakness and defeat. Most of us had no recourse but to weather the assaults on our pride—the Dr. Gilpatricks and so forth—but for the few, there was a choice.

So, the morning of the 26th I woke as usual and dressed for work. I had stashed the carpetbag in the woods the night before, giving Lorrie the excuse that there was a man in my ward whose unusually high fever required that I check his status at least once that night. I was forever using the excuse of needy patients to get away, as I imagine all doctors do. It is our right, after all—the just recompense for the quantity of legitimate calls we are required to make at inconvenient hours.

I recall that the oatmeal was cold that morning. Lorrie's mother had rushed out early to a special gathering of the Ladies' Society at church—this new development, a dawn service, was the latest attempt by the diocese to force structure upon its flailing, drifting congregations. Mrs. Wigfall dutifully subscribed to every new suggestion, from silent retreats to ceremonial tree plantings. Though I did not object to the activities themselves, I resented her devotion.

The house was quiet. Across the table, my unsuspecting wife sat spooning cold mash into her mouth. No matter how many times she used the possibility as ammunition in our arguments, she had not yet conceived a child. Once every four weeks I came home to find her locked in our bedroom, weeping. And each month, it seemed, her disappointment grew more bitter. She lashed out at me first, and when she tired of my face, she turned against the features of her environment. "This horrid place," she cried. "This house, this town! If I'd done the sensible thing and stayed behind in Texas, well, I would have been more successful than I have been with *you*!" Naturally, the blame always circled back to me.

She had been lately in the habit of sending me off to work with a choice insult ringing in my ears—a sort of angry gift to carry through the day. This morning, though, there was nothing. No vitriol, no emotion. She was silent.

"Are you well?" I asked.

"I am."

"Do you have plans for today?"

"Actually, I have not a single thing to do."

This was one of her *oyster* moods—so called by me because of the difficulty of prying open her mouth. It was an act, of course; in fact, the feat of keeping mum probably required more of her than my patience required of me.

"I see. Well, you will have to scare up something. Is Miss Ferguson available?" This was a neighbor who had lately been drilling Lorrie at piano.

"I suppose."

We carried on like this until the dishes were cleared and the time was nigh for me to leave. I might have walked out just like that, but for a thought that occurred to me as I laced my shoes: we might never see each other again. I don't know why it had not occurred to me before, perhaps because I had expected a scene of rampage at our parting, with the house lit and high flames licking the windows, and with great passion felt on both sides. Instead, there was barely a whimper.

"You ought to do something," I said. "In general, I mean. Not just today."

"I ought to say the same to you."

"I work."

"And that absolves you from criticism? Why, if that was all it took to be successful, I would go out and find a job tomorrow."

"Maybe you ought to."

"What on earth do you suggest I *do*, John?"

"Well, you have a knack for organizing, for one—"

"You are just making yourself feel better." She paused, then parted her lips as if to continue before closing them again. Finally, she said, "You are leaving me. Whenever you start listing out my options—my knacks for this and that, if that's what you want to call them—whenever that happens, you are thinking about leaving me."

My face betrayed nothing, though I was seething inside. "How do you know what I am thinking?"

"Oh, John—you have a glass skull!"

"I have no such thing!"

"You do so. Admit it."

There was an odd coy note in her voice—a hint of playfulness. I ignored it. She had squandered my goodwill. If this was the way we should part, I thought, so be it.

"Good- bye," I said.

She followed me to the door. "Kisses to your fever man!"

# 65

THE WORKDAY WENT OFF uneventfully, with Dr. Gilpatrick appearing no less than half a dozen times in my ward to check up. I sensed that he was beginning to appreciate my service. Several times over the last weeks he had raised his brow approvingly at my explanations of treatment—why I had given this patient a poultice but that one only a bottle of hot water, and so on. I considered if what I had mistaken for arrogance was in fact a deep and abiding devotion to the practice of medicine. He demanded perfection from his staff—something Dr. Cabell, for all his accolades, had never been able to achieve. Under Cabell, I had logged as many hours, but I had never applied such discipline to my practice. The goal, Gilpatrick explained, was for the doctors on his staff to be uniformly excellent—"identical in perfection"—that a patient would enjoy the same confidence no matter who treated him that day.

With respect to secession, slavery, and a hundred other controversial subjects, his questioning was constant, but honestly intentioned. Above all, Derwood Gilpatrick was a seeker. He would not be satisfied on a problem until he identified a single, well- defined answer. This meant, of course, that he was often disappointed, particularly on questions of war and moral accountability. For all this, he was an earnest and intrepid scientist, and I admired him much by the end.

But alas, my mind was set on leaving, and my future would be peopled with a hundred Gilpatricks. In the City of Brotherly Love, one could not spit without injuring an esteemed man of science. I imagined that the city streets were like a rarified social club, with gentlemen of all professions rubbing shoulders and exchanging thoughtful bits of wisdom at every opportunity.

The corners of both Stone's letter and the boating- scene card, still with me at all times, had grown worn from handling. The characters in the boat had become my intimates. As I labored in the ward—leaning over bedsides, mixing preparations at the bench—the rower called out words of professional advice: "Easy with the calomel, Muro. Forget the heroic dose, just tap a little . . . That's it, yes. Fine work." I grew to depend on his encouragement, and it gave me peace to know that he would be with me on the journey north.

The lady—she of the tall, flowered hat and unshakable demeanor—was with me as well, though she tended to make herself known after working hours. In particular, she came to me in my private dormitory hours. She was forthright in her admiration: "Ah, John," she would say, "I do love you . . . How strong and skilled are your hands, how agile your mind . . ." Though it shames me to admit it, I would often reply to her with words of my own: "Be patient, dear," I would whisper. "It will be soon, I promise." And she was patient. She heeded everything I said.

And so, with the postcard chattering in my pocket, I left the Delevan. I retrieved my carpetbag from its hiding spot and was halfway to railroad when I began to worry that I needed an extra canteen of water—it was late June in Virginia, and there was no telling if the transport train might lay up at a siding or something like that. Fortunately, I had several spare canteens in the dormitory. But I had to be quick. With the carpetbag tucked under my arm, I hurried along backroads to the south gate of the Lawn.

With classes in summer recess, there were no students lingering about the Grounds. Neither was there any of the familiar bustle of groundskeepers tending house or garden. As I've mentioned, the University owned a small number of slaves, who together with freemen made up the majority of the service staff. Of these, all but the most physically encumbered had vanished with Sheridan's army. I suspect they were disappointed in that pursuit, for the Federal Army had no provision for refugees, nor had the individual soldiers any particular sympathy for the souls they sloughed off the landscape like lint off an old rug.

At any rate, the University was suddenly and conspicuously without help. The Lawn itself was high as a meadow, astir with butterflies and leafhoppers. There was no one left to mow it, nor even any boys to bring goats to pasture.

At the opening of number 52 I set the carpetbag on the doorsill and fished in my pocket for the key. As I leaned in, however, the door gave way and swung open. There was a man sitting at the desk.

"Muro!"

The voice was familiar; the form not at all so. But it was unmistakably B.B.

"You look good," he said.

I wished I could say the same for him. He had let his beard grow long. His hair hung over his ears like a sheepdog's. His clothes, too, were oddly disheveled—odd for him, that is.

"I'm fine," I managed. "You?"

"Same here. Couldn't be better, considering."

There was an awkward pause as we recovered from the surprise, each taking a full view of the other.

At last, he said, "Actually, things are bad."

This turned out to be an understatement. Between slugs from a hip flask, he told of the pillaging of his land by the invading Yankee infantry, the rape of his woman servants, and finally the torching of the family home. His father, driven to insanity by the ordeal, refused to exit his study on the top floor of the mansion and was consequently consumed in the blaze.

"We never spoke again after he bolted himself up. One moment all was well—the army was going to skirt around our property—and the next they were upon us, whooping and firing their guns in the air. It couldn't have been more than a score of them all told—but no commanding officer, or none that I could see. They torched the wheelhouse first. That's what sent Papa upstairs.

"The army had given Papa an assurance that our property would be spared. But that happened before I came home. I knew nothing of the particulars. At any rate, Papa was unreachable. I heard the bolt on his rifle, then he began shooting out the window. He must have picked off one of the soldiers, because all at once the windows on all sides of the house were being shot out. I ran downstairs, but they were already in the parlor, smashing Grandmother's vases and all the rest. Mother and Grandmother were gone already—Papa sent them to stay with our kin in Rocky Mount. I suppose that's something to be glad for."

B.B. took another long pull on the flask. He wiped his mouth on the back of his hand.

"I smelled smoke. So I continued downstairs to the basement, where I ran through the tunnel to the kitchen. It was dark in there, and I hadn't a candle or even a match. I kept crashing into obstacles, folding trays or whatever—I hadn't been down in the kitchen tunnel since I was a boy, you know—but eventually I reached the kitchen. The shutters were drawn over all the windows, which I thought was odd, so I went to the nearest one and swung it open. And do you know what I saw in there? It was all the niggers, scared out of their wits. Maybe fifty of them, huddled together, just row on row of these faces, and none of them said anything, even when they saw it was me. I didn't know what to do. You know I'm no overseer. Christ—I probably know more of Greek comedy than running a farm. And you know how much I studied Greek!"

He laughed weakly. I could see that he was recounting these events for the first time, puzzling over them himself as he went along.

"Anyhow, I just broke for it. I closed the window shutter up just the way the niggers'd had it, and I ran. By now the fire was spread to the whole first floor of the house, and flames were licking up on the second story. Every so often there was another crack from Papa's window. The soldiers were going through all the buildings, filling sacks with whatever they could get their hands on. I saw a fella with a handful of nails, another with a hen under each arm. I was leaning behind the kiln, which I figured was a safe spot. Now that I think about it, though, it wouldn't have surprised me one bit if they'd have tried to haul off some bricks. Think of it, bricks!"

He told me then how he'd ridden off through the woods and set a course west, avoiding major roads as much as possible. He had intended to rest at a cousin's home in Hanover County, but he found it ransacked and vacant. Same for an acquaintance's farm in Goochland, and another in Louisa. At each stop he took what provisions he could find. As he grew nearer Charlottesville he gave up calling on friends, because the disappointment was more than he could bear.

"But to find you here, Muro—whew! I thought I'd never see a friendly face again." Brightening, he said, "I believe congratulations are in order for you, old man! Harriette Willson wrote with your news."

"News?"

"Why, the wedding, of course. Congratulations to you!"

B.B. stood and clapped me on the back. He smelled of sweat and stale whiskey.

"Ah. Thank you."

"She is a catch, Muro, that's for certain. A young lady of the first order. Bully to you, boy."

I paused, unsure how to proceed on the topic. "I know about your proposal," I said.

B.B. was completely surprised. He stammered, "My proposal— well, as you know, I admired her very much—"

"But why *my* girl, B.B.? Out of all the girls in town—hell, in all Virginia—why Lorrie?"

Here he did not hesitate. "There is no one like her in all the world. I'm quite sure of that. I have encountered no woman—not at academy, not in travel, not anywhere—who commands attention as she does. She holds her own as well on the dais above a banquet as in a simple tea with church ladies. Granted, all things have changed since the end of this wretched war, but in the past I have made no secret of my political ambitions. She is a governor's wife, your Lorrie. Does that answer your question?"

I was tempted to ask if manslaughter was a suitable qualification for high office.

"Listen, Muro, if there is anyone who should be hurt by this, it's me. Did she tell you what she said to me? Her reply to the proposal?"

"Not in so many words."

"I recall it exactly. She said, *Though I am flattered, I cannot accept. I intend to marry Dr. John Muro.*"

"She did not."

"She did indeed! And she had some choice words for me, if you really must know, about arrogance, my tactics as a suitor, and so forth. The usual stuff—and not all of it false, to be honest. So I asked her— forgive me—I asked, '*Why John Muro?*'"

"A fair question."

"I'm glad you agree. Well, she took a deep breath and burst forth with a flood of reasons: "*Because he is an excellent student, who Uncle believes will be perhaps the greatest Southern medical doctor of our generation. That's one. Because he is cool under stress, which Auntie says is the best insurance a marriage can have—and which, by God, Braxton, you are not! That's two. Because he is polite and well- liked by my friends. That's three, and not an insignificant one.*"

B.B. paused and sat down. "You may think it odd, Muro, that I recall this verbatim, but let me tell you, each of these reasons was like a dagger in my chest."

I said nothing.

"Do you want to hear the rest?"

"There's more?"

"One more. She said, '*This is the most important reason, Braxton, so listen to me closely: because John Muro loves me.*'"

"I was incensed, as you might imagine. And not because I doubted that you loved her, but rather because she doubted I did! I said, 'Lorrie, dear, I love you every bit as much.' And she said to me, '*You call it love, Braxton. You want to marry me very much. That's a different thing. Sometimes they go together, but not in your case.*'"

"So I said, 'What if Muro doesn't want to marry you? What then? Will you wait around forever?'"

"She said, '*If need be, yes. But he will come around. Just you see.*'"

My shame at that moment is inexpressible in words. Nothing so humbles a man as another's true expression of faith—and none so much as his wife's.

"She loves you, John—I mean truly loves you. I don't think it's immodest to say that most women would have leapt at my proposal. But Lorrie Wigfall—not only did she not leap, she ran away. And you had not even proposed, correct?"

"That is correct."

"Furthermore, she *believes* in you. Her family believes in you. No marriage is ever perfect, but frankly, it's enough to make a man green with envy."

Just then, in the distance, a locomotive's whistle blew three bursts.

"Can I admit that, Muro—that I'm jealous? Sure you've earned it all—God knows I could have cracked a book now and again while I was here—but I can't help thinking there is a benevolent power looking out for you."

He paused and looked down at the floor. For the first time, he noticed the carpetbag.

"Taking a trip, are you?"

The dormitory's windows rattled with the passing train.

I was twenty-one years old.

# Epilogue

**AT THE STATION, LORRIE** and the twins rushed off the train and called a cab, hoping to make the shops on Rittenhouse Square before dark. Ted and I stayed behind to attend the manly business of room letting. It was our first railroad trip as a family, which might have shamed me, considering my daughters were nearly finished with school and our son had been old enough for some years to appreciate a journey from home. Perhaps I should have been embarrassed. None of our children had ever ventured more than a day's ride from the house where I was raised. After the war I had set up what was intended to be a temporary practice in Lynchburg. Twenty years later, I was rooted. I had buried both my parents in the yard of our church, which was a stone's throw from the house I had built for Lorrie and the children. A year or so previously, we had buried Parthenia's first husband there as well.

Over the years, I had gained some attention by my correspondence on clinical matters with colleagues at the medical schools in Chapel Hill and Clemson. I had also on several occasions welcomed students from the teaching hospital in Richmond into my clinic for observation. But this trip represented another level of professional engagement altogether. I was anxious for the hours to pass quickly and mercifully.

As we stood on the platform waiting for the porters to unload our baggage, a man called out to us, "Dr. Muro, is it?" He was young and at first glance appeared closer to my son's age than mine, but when he drew near I saw that he had a peppering of gray at the temples and distinct lines at the corners of his mouth.

"Dr. Stone is detained at the hospital," he said. He took my hand and smiled warmly. "I am Thomas MacKay, sir. Dr. Stone's partner."

"Yes, Dr. MacKay," I said. "Lieutenant—pardon me, *Dr.* Stone—wrote that he had taken on a partner." I paused. "I'm sorry—it will take a while before I straighten out the title."

"Not at all," said MacKay, drawing solemn for a moment. "You must forgive my approaching you directly, sir, but I feel as though I know you already."

I smiled, not sure how to reply. "I'd like you to meet my son, Edward," I said.

MacKay shook Ted's hand with the same brisk affection. "Welcome to Philadelphia, young man. I assume your journey was satisfactory. You are on time—that is a good sign."

"Is it?" I said. "I'm afraid we don't travel very often."

"Which is precisely why we are so lucky to have you. The College of Physicians is thrilled that you were able to make the trip. It is considered quite a coup that Dr. Stone lured you here."

"That's very kind," I said, "but it was the least I could do. I have been meaning to make this trip for a long time."

"Is it just the two of you, then?"

"No, my wife and daughters went ahead—"

"To the dress shops," Ted said, screwing up his face in disapproval.

"Ah. My wife is fond of those herself. Lamentably, we live rather near the shopping district."

The bags arrived, and MacKay directed the porter to his carriage. Ted and I watched as he produced a clip of green bills and peeled off several for the porter.

"So, gents, where were we? Yes, my wife. An expensive habit, but quite worthwhile."

The terminal building opened onto Chestnut Street, and the noise of carriage traffic on that thoroughfare, in tandem with the roar and hiss of locomotives in the railyard, was almost deafening. Pedestrians attempting to cross against the flow of carts and carriages shook their fists at the headstrong drivers. The drivers slapped the reins across the backs of their sweating teams. As we waited for our bags to be loaded onto MacKay's brougham, I saw a door open across the street to divulge an ancient man with a snow white beard holding a bass drum on a lanyard around his neck. The drum was larger than the man, so that if he were to assume the fetal position he might fit inside. He turned left upon reaching the pavement and began to march, beating the drum as he went. I believe not a pair of eyes but mine paid him any notice whatsoever.

None except Ted's, that is. My son's face lit up upon finding himself in such a place. One could almost see the orbits in his brain spinning as he struggled to take stock. He was fifteen years old, and though I knew it would embarrass him for me to do so, I took his hand and drew him in.

"Now then, off we go." MacKay held open the door to the brougham, and we climbed inside. It was a remarkable vehicle, lacquered inside and out with a glowing black enamel. The upholstery was sewn from a rich, handsome red fabric as soft as velvet. I guessed that the carriage might have cost more than I made in a year at my practice in Lynchburg.

Two aspects of the city impressed me right away. One was the palpable energy of the place, a kind of nervous energy, which exuded not just from Dr. MacKay and other ambitious young men, nor only in the strange drum thumper, but in virtually every person I encountered—from the solicitous manager of our hotel to the muttering crone who scattered bread crumbs every morning to the pigeons in Rittenhouse Square. Perhaps it is truism to observe that life is slower in the southern latitudes, but it is true nonetheless. Lacking the mental acuity for conducting business at such a pace, which is by necessity well developed in Northern men, I was unprepared for the change in velocity, and thus was exhausted in short order by the schedule of my appearance.

I was impressed also with the wealth of the professional classes in Philadelphia. It came as a revelation that men such as MacKay should drive about in lacquered broughams when they pressed the same pills and sewed the same wounds as I did. Naturally, men of certain vocations have long argued in favor of more remunerative compensation for labors requiring advanced schooling—not only lawyers, you see, but also those of us in the medical arts and in various new branches of engineering. We have even joined the burgeoning organizations that purport to advance our general interest—the American Medical Association, for instance, of which I am a hopeful, if skeptical, member. But as yet no great wealth has accumulated to Virginia's professional men. Even with the loss of five hundred thousand slaves—appraised by the Federal government at something close to $100 million—the nexus of wealth in Virginia remains (as I suppose it ever will be) in the possession of titled property.

The emergence in Virginia of a professional class to rival the society of landholders is a thing I do not expect to see in my lifetime. However, if our fated friend Braxton Baucom can be taken as an indicator, the veneer of the gentry may indeed be showing cracks.

B.B. remained in Charlottesville throughout the summer of 1865, where I saw him mornings stealing away from the east colonnade, an uninvited guest in the very lodging he had eschewed as a student. In the new year he returned once more to Charles City but discovered that his father's property had been thrown into a type of receivership wherein the military directorate held the title in the absence of the rightful owner. When B.B. appeared and presented himself to the local administrator, he was told that the legal proceedings had gone too far to be reversed. The owner had been presumed dead, and now the entire estate (acreage, ruined house, outbuildings, &c.) were the rightful property of the United States Government.

I do not know whether this was the whole truth of the matter—it was only B.B.'s account, scrawled to me on the verso of a bill of sale from a horse livery. At any rate, he failed on his first attempt to claim the estate. However, he succeeded on another score: he was named delegate to the new state assembly. Having never served in a Confederate uniform—and with the record of his commutation apparently destroyed in the burning of Richmond—he was able to present himself as a nonaggressor, thus gaining entry to the political process. With his name well known in Charles City, he was elected handily. In Richmond, though, he did not get far before his loyalties were called into question. He was observed by certain men who had known him in Charlottesville—including at least one who had attended the infamous tournament at Monticello. A letter was circulated among the more radical members concerning the Charles City delegate's questionable past alliances. Thus before B.B. had cast even his first vote as a legislator, he was indicted on charges of election fraud and misrepresentation of character.

Having no money to retain a satisfactory attorney (his friends in Charles City had gone suddenly amnesiac about their association with his family), young Braxton Baucom III was convicted and sentenced to a stiff term at the state penal farm in Dinwiddie. He wrote me often from there, strangely uncomplaining. It seemed that at last he had the time for the reflection he had needed all along. "I've been a damned fool, Muro," he wrote. "We all have, but me in particular."

Also at Dinwiddie, B.B. found his Lord and Savior, and upon his release he began an itinerant ministry in the far southwestern corner of the Commonwealth. During these years he wrote me sporadically from towns with names like Coalton and Big Stone Gap, always signing his name above verses from Corinthians, Ephesians, and so forth. It was clear that he fancied himself a sort of latter- day Paul, and for all his history of self- aggrandizement, this was actually not far off the mark. He had been brought up in the Episcopal Church, but by the time of his incarceration he was no more Christian than Hindu. He has since amassed a remarkable record of evangelizing. As of this writing, B.B. has either founded or helped to establish over two dozen Baptist churches in the trans- Appalachian region. His fame is spreading quickly. I had a patient not long ago with a case of shingles who was oddly unanxious at my admonishment that the rash might grow more pronounced before it subsided. Such news usually sends patients into a fit of nervousness, if not outright anger at the diagnosis.

"That would be fine by me, Doc," the man said with a conspiratorial grin. He was about forty years old, a laborer, and the years had not been kind to him. The skin hung off the bones of his face as in a man twice his age. "Yes sir, Doctor, I got a backup plan just in case your kind of healin' don't work out. Next week I'm fixing to hear the Word as spoke by the Reverend B. B. Baucom. You hearda Rev. Baucom, Doc?"

"The name sounds familiar," I said.

"Well—he's a close personal friend of Jesus." The man paused, reached his hand under his shirt to scratch at one of the fat red welts on his chest. "You know what? You ought to come along."

"I appreciate the thought," I said, "but I'm afraid I must decline."

"Your loss, Doc."

The brougham bumped along Chestnut Street until we reached a neighborhood of new buildings with wide stone steps smiling down from the doorways. The driver turned onto a side street and pulled to a halt before the grandest home of all. It gleamed from top to bottom, turned out in every detail. The granite blocks had been beveled to resemble a castle wall, and stone turrets rose at the corners. Above the door was a fan- shaped transom of multicolored stained glass.

"I'll have the boy send the bags to the hotel," MacKay said. "Dr. Stone would kill me if I had you wasting time on chores."

Ted and I stepped down from the coach and followed our escort through the gates. MacKay lifted the brass knocker and smiled reassuringly as we waited on the landing. I was still unable to pin down his age. Certainly he was much younger than Stone. Was he my contemporary? The more I dwelt on MacKay, the more convinced I became that he was humoring me.

The front door was answered by the most beautiful young woman I have ever seen. I mean this absolutely: it was as if she had stepped directly from the pages of a ladies' magazine. Her dark hair was arranged in a cascade of ringlets about the shoulders, and her carriage was so effortless that she seemed to glide across the foyer. She smelled of rosewater and jasmine. When she took my hands in greeting, I pulled in closer than usual, just to enjoy her atmosphere.

"You must be Dr. Muro," she said. An elegant smile revealed a row of perfectly straight white teeth. "Father is just home. He will be down shortly. This is just terribly exciting, isn't it?"

I introduced Ted. My poor son, smitten by this woman, could not manage to speak his name. He stared sheepishly at his feet.

"I should say so, dear," said MacKay. He bent in and kissed the woman on the mouth. "Dr. Muro, Ted—I'd like you to meet my wife, Josephine."

"Oh, Dr. Muro," she said, "I cannot tell you what a *pleasure* it is. Father has spoken of you so often. I hope you will forgive me for saying so, sir, but I feel as though I know you already."

"Ha!" said MacKay. He slapped his thigh and leaned up against the doorjamb. "I said the exact same thing. Didn't I, Muro?"

Josephine led us to the spacious front parlor, where she had a tray of tea and small cakes. Her face worried as she poured the tea. "Mrs. Muro did not make the trip?"

"She's shopping," Ted said. He blushed at the sound of his own voice.

"Of course. We will expect them shortly, then." It was not a question, but a statement—Josephine MacKay knew the hours and locations of all the shops, and could doubtless predict down to the minute when my wife and daughters would arrive home from their errands.

Before our tea had cooled, I heard the thump of boots in the foyer, and a moment later, Stone appeared. He had added perhaps forty pounds to his convalescent weight, and his beard was now gray speckled with black, rather than the other way around.

He took hold of my shoulder with his good hand. "My dear, dear Muro . . ." His voice quavered as we embraced. He smelled of pipe smoke and rubbing alcohol. Holding me at arm's length, he took my measure. "How are you? You look fantastic!"

"I am well, sir. And you?"

"Much better that you've arrived. Is this your son?"

I introduced Ted.

"No boys for me," Stone said. "Just these women." He winked at Josephine, who had gone to stand with her husband. "I trust your girls will be with us shortly?"

"Imminently, I'm told."

"Good. I hate to rush, but we must not be late to the lecture. I am, after all, responsible for the talent tonight."

"Perhaps *talent* is too strong a word," I said.

"Or too weak! You really ought to allow yourself to be flattered, Muro, if only just a bit. Your modesty marks you out around here." He gave a conspiratorial wink to the group. "At any rate, we are expecting record attendance tonight. I let the gentlemen know this was a lecture not to be missed." This danced off his tongue with a playful cadence that would have annoyed me, I thought, had I been a junior member of the Philadelphia College of Physicians, thus cajoled into attending a lecture by an obscure Southern physician. Mine was a name not one of them should be expected to know. "By the way, John, I have arranged for the text of your address to be published in the proceedings of the College. Provided that is acceptable to you. Do you have a copy of the manuscript?"

"I have only the working draft," I said. "And it is hardly in any shape to be published, I assure you."

"But wait," he said. He took Ted's arm and raised it up like the umpire of a boxing match. "Here we have an able copyist!" Then he took hold of MacKay's arm and raised it similarly. "And here, an interpreter!"

Ted was thrilled at the attention, but when MacKay saw that his partner was sending him off to play, as it were, with the children, he soured. "Surely the boy can manage his father's script on his own."

Stone rocked on his heels. "Perhaps he can. But would it not behoove you, Dr. MacKay, to become familiar with Dr. Muro's subject before the lecture?"

"Actually, I have read quite extensively on the subject of Southern medicine during the war."

"And you will read some more. You may use my office." Turning to Ted, Stone said, "Dr. MacKay will show you upstairs."

Ted took my satchel and followed MacKay up the wide, curling staircase. When they were gone, Stone took a sip of his tea and for a long while said nothing. The silence was uncomfortable, and I found myself wishing that each grind of a carriage wheel on the road would be Lorrie and the twins. I was unused to flattery, and Stone's effusion had thrown me off guard. I certainly did not require any special treatment. No matter how generously one appraised my contributions to the field of medicine, I did not merit elevation at MacKay's expense. He seemed to be a fine fellow—and surely a skilled physician, to have been chosen by Stone.

"You loathe him," Stone said finally. "I can see it in your eyes."

He turned to a rack of pipes beside the sofa. He selected one for himself and another for me. He packed both from a tin of moist, aromatic weed.

"Who—MacKay?" I said.

Stone struck a match and held it just above the bowl so that the flame was drawn down by the draft. He took a series of puffs, six or eight in rapid succession. The aroma of burnt tobacco filled the parlor. He shook out the match.

"I don't blame you," he said. "In fact, I rather hoped you would."

"I beg your pardon?"

"It flatters me."

I said nothing, busying myself with the pipe.

"You never replied to my invitation, John."

I lit the bowl. When it became clear that I was not going to speak on the matter, at least not right away, he said, "Very well. That answers my first question. I gave the letter a fifty percent chance of reaching you."

*"The Blue Schuylkill,"* I said.

"Yes. I also wagered that you would consider the offer seriously, but that in the final calculation I stood no more than a single chance in a hundred of luring you. I had no doubt that you would agonize.

You were never much of a partisan. But the attraction of one's home is undeniable."

It was plain that he took great relish in recounting his scheme. His eyes glowed like lantern wicks as he gnawed on the stem of the pipe.

"You see, I had to ask. Even if the chance was slim." He removed the pipe from his teeth and grinned. "I have to know—was I close?"

Was he close! Should I have mentioned the months of plotting? The stockpiling? The deception? Should I have told him of the train schedule, and the carpetbag? What about the fact that never in my life had I desired anything more, and that ultimately—"in the final calculation," as he would have it—it was nothing short of divine will that detained me?

"Not as such," I said. My heart pounded in my ears. Sweat prickled on my scalp. "I considered the offer, of course, but I was settled . . ."

"I suppose I might have made the wrong assumptions," he said. He caught my gaze and held it. "But I doubt that very highly."

Just then the doorbell chimed, and Stone rose. I heard a booming "Welcome!" followed by the familiar nervous laughing of my wife and daughters. MacKay and Ted reappeared, as did Josephine, with a fresh tray of tea.

"We were deeply saddened to hear of Mrs. Stone's passing," Lorrie said after the flood of greetings and salutations.

Stone nodded graciously and looked to his daughter. "We appreciate your condolences," he said. Throughout that evening—and in fact for the whole of our visit to Philadelphia—Stone never once betrayed the slightest enmity toward Lorrie. Given his recollection of the calculations surrounding the letter, I had no doubt that he remembered her face from the Christmas dinner at the Delevan. But if he meant to snub her in any way, I did not see it. Afterward, and for many years hence, Lorrie would speak of him as a "perfect gentleman."

Our party had hardly enough time to take two sips of tea before the host implored us to retrieve our hats. "We mustn't be late. You see, I am routinely and tragically tardy—as Dr. MacKay can attest—but tonight I must be prompt. Tonight I have precious cargo!"

When my daughters understood that he meant me, they were tickled. "Really, Father," said Iris, the more loquacious of the two, "you ought to hurry up so Dr. Stone can nail the crate!"

Need I mention that the girls fell in love with Josephine MacKay? For weeks afterward our home would echo with their bickering over who exactly *Josephine* had meant when she implored the girls to write her; or what *Josephine* said about lip rouge and kohl pencils; or what novel *Josephine* swore was her favorite when *she* was fourteen years old, and on and on.

It was not far to the College of Physicians' building on Locust Street, but Stone insisted that we ride in a limousine he had engaged for the occasion. When we pulled in front of the building, I understood from the long line of similar carriages that Stone's insistence was only partially to honor my visit.

We were greeted at the door by a contingent of doctors in dinner attire. I recall only one of this group, and that is because he was none other than Dr. W. W. Keen, whom the reader will recall as the first surgeon on this continent to successfully remove a brain tumor. Dr. Keen was an affable fellow with a sincere appreciation for the fairer sex. When we were introduced by Lieutenant Stone, Keen shook my hand and asked which of the "lovely ladies" (meaning Lorrie and the twins) was my wife. Naturally, Lorrie was thrilled, and she mooned over the bright young doctor.

We passed through a magnificent entry hall laid in marble and hung with wine- colored velvet drapes. In the reception room, a barman mixed our drinks and served punch to the ladies. Iris and Mary Steuart were bored almost at once, and they sat down on a bench and began practicing their proprietary brand of pidgin English, which was one of their favorite pastimes just then. On account of the occasion, Ted was allowed a glass of beer, which he quaffed admirably. Josephine entertained Lorrie with whispered stories about each of the men in the room—the Drunkard, the Popinjay, the Philanderer, &c.—and the two of them appeared fast friends. It pained me to see them side by side, for I could not help but observe the subtle differences in their carriage and countenance. On the one hand there was Lorrie, who had lost the transcendent beauty of her youth, and who in style of dress and grooming looked precisely as if she had spent the last twenty years as a humble doctor's wife in Lynchburg. On the other hand, Josephine MacKay radiated both youth and sophistication, the latter of which raised one's estimation of her age, so that she seemed at once both young and mature. Her style in dress, as I have mentioned, was impeccably modern, yet tasteful. She wore a frock of fine- wale corduroy, which, though not at all ostentatious, drew the eye to the wearer's lovely waist by its intricate garniture.

Our families thus occupied, Stone took me by the arm and led me through a hidden door behind the bar. The passage emptied into a long, high- ceilinged room not unlike the waiting parlor at a rail station, with high triple- hung windows and dark wood paneling on the walls. A haze of smoke hung in the air. There were plenty of tables, and nearly everyone in the room was seated. The majority of the men in the room were of advanced age. I followed my host to the farthest table, where he pulled out two chairs. It took me almost a minute to register the identity of the man to my right, who was leading the conversation.

"What you are stating, sir, is rubbish. Plain and simple."

"But Doctor," inquired the other conversant, who was approximately my age, and therefore well below the median for that room. "Mightn't a less nimble surgeon compensate for a lack of dexterity by applying superior techniques within the limits of his ability?"

The old man peered down his long nose. His brow shaded the eyes so that one was not sure where exactly he was looking when he spoke. "I fail to see the distinction between dexterity and skill."

"I only mean, sir, that if a man were to study the most favored techniques and apply what lessons he could from those—"

"A man ought not get out of bed if he is going to work piecemeal. Does the concertmaster play only those notes which come easily to him? Fah!"

"As you prefer, Dr. Gross," said the younger man. He smiled at the group. "I defer to you, sir."

My heart was still. I looked dumbfounded at Stone, who could hardly control his amusement. Of course he had known all along that Dr. Samuel Gross would be attending my lecture.

"It seems to me a fair inquiry," said Stone, inserting himself into the discussion, "if only for the sake of argument."

But the old doctor was not interested in continuing the argument, no matter how fair the inquiry. He said, "Whom have you brought us this evening, Dr. Stone?"

Stone laid his hand on the back of my chair. "Why, this is tonight's speaker, who has come all the way from Virginia."

Dr. Gross narrowed his eyes. "Dr. Muro, I presume." He did not shake my hand or acknowledge me in any other wise.

"Dr. Muro attended the ward where I was confined during the war."

"Are you coming to us from Charlottesville, then?"

I was stunned that he knew the place. I sputtered, "Actually, sir, my practice is in Lynchburg."

"I don't know Lynchburg."

"Oh, of course not, sir. It is—well, it is not what it used to be. That is, it is not what it *could be,* I suppose . . ."

"Tell me, Doctor," he said, "what is the subject of your lecture this evening? You must know that Dr. Stone has been quite the tout."

The other gentlemen around the table chuckled at this and gently chided Stone.

Stone said, "Dr. Muro will present the experience of the common Southern physician during the war. I believe you'll find it terribly compelling."

"No doubt," said Gross. He nodded to me. "Best of luck, Dr. Morrow." And with that he turned to the fellow on his right and began another conversation.

A half hour and two whiskeys later, I found myself at a massive oak lectern, clearing my throat before a sea of glimmering pates and waxed moustaches. The drinks dulled my nerves not a whit. The only thing that afforded me any comfort whatsoever was the presence, at the foot of the dais, of my wife and three children. Lorrie and I had grown more reliant on each other than I should like to admit—more through shared experience, I see now, than from any inherent compatibility of character. There is comfort, you see, in a wife—both in the fact of having a wife as well as in the woman herself. I should not expect a bachelor reading this to appreciate my meaning. Nor for that matter should any married man who has not shared hardship with his bride understand that it is not the times of bliss that bind, but rather the other kind, and that there is no substitute for the value of trial in a life bond.

I looked up from my notes—I had chosen Ted's neat copy over my own scrawled manuscript, a decision that caused the boy to beam as if I had awarded him the blue ribbon at an exhibition.

"I should wish first to thank Dr. Stone for his most flattering introduction. I assure you he exaggerates my renown."

At Stone's request I had prepared a study of the unorthodox practices devised by Southern doctors during the war. As research, I had interviewed several dozen acquaintances, physicians in Virginia and elsewhere, and found that while there were refrains to be heard in the accounts, no two doctors had met privation the same way. The array of ingenious pharmaceutical preparations alone was subject enough for a dozen lectures. I was allotted only one, but I believe my lecture accomplished the goal of accessibility for the casual listener as well as usefulness to the devoted student. I will not recount the speech verbatim, but instead refer the interested reader to the *Proceedings of the Philadelphia College of Physicians* for August 1883.

In the beat of silence after the close of my preface, I caught a whiff of roses. Iris and Mary Steuart had surprised me with a tiny white boutonniere. They were English roses, tinted pink at the edges of the petals. How odd, I thought, that I should be embarking now on an hour's talk of pokeweed and alum root, and cranes bill and slippery elm and a dozen other noxious weeds—at the same time that my nostrils should be filled with so sweet a fragrance as English roses!

"Whatever may be the final verdict as to the justification of the Southern cause in our late and tragic fight," I read, "there can be no argument over the valor of the Southern man of medicine."

Heads nodded throughout the banquet hall. Dr. Gross, I noticed, was seated at a table approximately halfway back, beside a portly gentleman who had set his hat on the table beside his plate.

"As a matter of background, I should state that one cannot properly convey in words the degree of privation which existed in the Southern states during the war. I shall hope to illuminate just a few of the conditions, and the ready solutions which my colleagues devised to combat them."

I delivered my haymakers first, for example: the fact that in 1863, an ounce of quinine sold for over $100. Such lines garnered the desired reaction from the audience, but I sensed that my presentation lost its appeal soon thereafter. Dr. Gross whispered often to his companion, whose jiggling flesh, rising and falling in silent laughter, told me all I needed to know about my reception in that quarter. A number of gentlemen at the rear of the hall, who had remained standing on account of their late arrival, simply returned to the cocktail lounge after a few minutes of observation.

Of course, there was a contingent of men—generally the younger members, and here I shall hold up young Thomas MacKay as the standard- bearer for the group—who paid rapt attention to my speech. Beside MacKay was a sandy- haired fellow who, like Gross's portly companion, whispered occasionally to his neighbors. His comments produced no laughter, however. Instead each whisper seemed only to draw the men closer to my words, so that by the end of the hour they nodded obediently at the end of each sentence.

Is it ungrateful to say that I resented these young men? Is it wrong that given the choice between Gross's fat friend or MacKay's tow-headed one, I would have preferred an audience composed solely of the former? I had not come to Philadelphia to be the subject of an earnest young man's curiosity. The College of Physicians, I learned, owned an extensive collection of medical oddities—built on the collection of a fellow called Mütter—and I resented the suggestion (or even the *hint*) that I might be considered in that number. And yet, with each paragraph of the lecture I sank deeper into the realm of the absurd:

"Wood anemone was employed as a vesicatory in removing corns from the feet.

"It was discovered by an enterprising practitioner in Georgia that gargle made of sage and honey will cure most cases of sore throat and tonsillitis."

The old men laughed and patted their bellies. *Ha! A wonder they did not surrender sooner!*

The young nodded and whispered: *How very interesting! What ingenuity! What resolve!*

Of course, the truth of my experience—of *our* experience, from

Dr. Cabell to Surgeon- General S. P. Moore—was neither pathetic nor ingenious. Those labels should be reserved for actions in which the subject has some volition. As Confederate doctors, we had no time to consider our course. We pulled the soldiers off the trains, dressed their wounds, heard their confessions. To speak of such things as *pathetic* or *ingenious* is both glib and inaccurate, for it grants us an agency we did not enjoy. Our actions were autonomic, as a knee leaps under the mallet.

And just as a joint cannot be sawn off one body and sewn into another, I could not be torn from Virginia. Only God Almighty can be two places at once.

After the lecture, a dinner of roast duck was served to the hall. My family delighted in the formality of the service—the waiters placed a separate dish before each diner and removed the covers with a flourish. Lorrie beamed as doctors in tailored waistcoats approached our table to profess their admiration for my remarks. They had no idea, they said, that the situation had been so desperate for us! So *primitive!*

Though I am sure the duck was first- rate, I could not eat a bite, and I excused myself after a few uncomfortable moments, ostensibly to use the facilities. Instead, I left the building.

On the front steps, a couple of younger doctors—I recognized their faces from the table of rapt listeners—were having a smoke. The one tipped his hat when he saw me. "Enjoyed your lecture," he said. He turned to his colleague for confirmation. "Very thorough," said the other. I thanked the men with the absolute minimum verbiage required and hurried down the steps. I did not wish to appear impolite, but I had no desire to angle flatteries from these men, or any men. I had never felt so confused in all my life.

I walked several blocks until I found a horsecar with a placard indicating that it was headed west. Though I had only the vaguest sense of the city's geography, I knew the general direction I sought. There was just one sight remaining for me to see in Philadelphia. In fact, it was the truest reason I had made the trip, for the rest of it—the reconnection with Stone; the essay on my experience of the war; even the frocks purchased for my dear daughters—might have been accomplished as easily through the mail. But I had already seen what sense of this landmark could be sent through the mail. I had to make its acquaintance in the flesh.

The horsecar rumbled down the narrow streets of the business district. The squares and churchyards were the only spots of land where the bare earth remained unpaved, and these served as pools of sunlight in the darkening city. It was the longest part of the summer, and I noticed that the sun set noticeably later at this latitude. By my watch it was nearly half past eight when the car stopped at Twenty- fourth Street. I paid the fare and stepped down. I went my way down a stone staircase, scaling the embankment until I reached the walk alongside the river.

And there it was: the Schuylkill. A vein of green water, almost brown, still as glass. It was less than a quarter- mile across. From the buoys on the water and the sight of men hauling rowing boats out on the far shore, I gathered that there had been a type of regatta that afternoon. I followed the path and found more men hauling boats. They were teams, each wearing the colors of its school. The young men traded false blows and teased one another, emboldened by privilege to behave as they pleased.

I found a bench and sat down. The narrow promenade on my side of the river was empty. I watched the opposite shore. When the boys were done stowing their boats, they retreated to a fanciful house perched on piles just over the shore. Lights appeared in the windows. When the breeze carried it, I heard singing and the clinking of glasses.

My gaze returned to the river, and I noticed that one boy remained at the docks. He was smaller than the others and appeared to hop from one pier to the next like a water bug. The boy untied a dinghy and rowed out to the line of buoys in the middle of the river. Working deliberately, he rowed to each buoy, unhooked it from its mooring, and threw it into the boat. When he was finished, he dropped his oars in the water and took two or three good strokes back toward the dock. Then he paused, as if thinking better of rushing back. He pulled up the oars and let the dinghy drift. It was nearly nine o'clock, and the sun was gone behind the university buildings on the West Philadelphia shore. The boy dropped his shoulders. He looked past me, at the city rising up behind.

# Acknowledgments

This book began in 2004 with a summer research grant from the William R. Kenan, Jr., Endowment Fund for the Academical Village in Support of the Education Program at the Unviersity of Virginia. Thanks to Joan Fry, who adminsters that program, and to the staff of the Albert and Shirley Small Special Collections Library, particularly Heather Riser, who steered me toward the good stuff. Thanks also to my friend and faculty advisor Paul Freeman for plot advice and an early read.

I am deeply indebted to the English Department at the University of Virginia, which supported me as an undergraduate and as a graduate student. Thanks especially to Sydney Blair and Lisa Russ Spaar, who make the creative writing program what it is today.

While writing this book, I received support from the Virginia Center for the Creative Arts in Sweet Briar and the Virginia Commission for the Arts. Many thanks to both. Thanks also to Betty Carroll at The College of William & Mary for giving me not one but two honest jobs.

My agent, Jennifer Carlson, changed my life in a matter of months. Her professionalism and business prowess amazed me from the beginning. At Simon & Schuster, Denise Roy is the editor all authors dream about but most never find. I am lucky indeed. Thanks also to

*Acknowledgments*

Victoria Meyer, Tracey Guest, and the rest of the S&S publicity staff for their hard work and expertise.

Thanks to Lindsay Sagnette, a genuine friend who blazed the trail (as far as I'm concerned) between Charlottesville and New York publishing.

I am grateful to my colleagues at San Jose State for taking a vested interest in this project. Thanks especially to Charles McLeod, another trailblazer.

Architects can go entire careers without seeing one of their creations built, but for some reason no one takes you seriously as a writer until you publish a book. Thankfully my family didn't let this bother them. Paul, Diane, and Megan—thank you for indulging me.

I am fortunate to have two incredible grandmas, veteran storytellers both—Mina Rossi and Lillian Taylor, take a bow. Thanks also to Bob and Benjie O'Connell for the generous dowry and moral support. And to Lucy O'Connell and Willie Hoffman for their friendship.

Most of all, thank you to Jessica and Violet. You are the reason I write and the reason I have anything to write about. Thank you for your love, encouragement, and sacrifice. I'm sorry, Violet, that there are no princesses in this book. Maybe in the next one.